PRAISE FOR JANE GREEN

Praise for *Bookends*

"Green gives readers a lovably imperfect protagonist, a heart-to-heart narrative voice, and a bumpy, error-strewn highway to romance. Bottom line: Pluck it off the shelf." — *People*

"A near-perfect romantic wish-fulfillment fantasy . . . only the coldest of hearts will not be warmed." — *Kirkus Reviews*

"Single or spoken for, you'll find a character you can relate to in this page-turner about dating, marriage, parenthood, career goals, jealousy, and, of course, love." — *iVillage*

"Funny, touching, and wise about the importance of friends." — *Woman's Own*

"You'll love this one . . . a bit of candy perfect for the bath, pool, or beach." — *Lexington Express*

"Quick, witty, unputdownable, and perfect beach reading. Don't miss it." — *Mirror* (London)

"A hugely enjoyable novel about love and friendship." — *Express* (London)

"Funny and poignant—you'll devour it in one sitting." — *Cosmopolitan* (London)

For *Mr. Maybe*

"There's no maybe about it: Jane Green's follow-up to *Jemima J* is a righteously hilarious read." — *Glamour*

"A total bonbon . . . Green captures the real pain that women feel as they search to find romantic happiness. Put this one in the winner's circle." — *USA Today*

"Can Libby survive the hideous mustaches, grotty bedsits, and blink-and-you-missed-it sex to find true happiness? You'll have a good laugh finding out." — *New Woman*

"It's as frothy as a cappuccino—you'll want to gulp it down." — *Essentials* magazine (UK)

"Jane Green's third novel about the business of netting a man will go straight to the bestseller lists." — *Marie Claire* (UK)

For *Jemima J*

"[*Jemima J*] conveys with sass and humor both the invisibility of the overweight and the shallow perks that accrue to the thin and beautiful. Green has entertainingly updated the Cinderella story . . . Bottom Line: Sweet and Tasty." — *People*

"Cleverly probes the world of a very smart, very funny, very fat reporter . . . Americans will enjoy this confection and appreciate how Green renders a certain humor-impaired California earnestness about health, happiness, and love." — *USA Today*

"The kind of novel you'll gobble up at a single sitting."

—*Cosmopolitan*

"A brillliantly funny novel about something close to every woman's heart—her stomach."

—*Woman's Own*

"A fun, fast-paced novel about a woman who hates her body and decides to do something about it . . . Skinny or fat, Jemima is always endearing. Green's ability to evoke laughter from a serious subject makes *Jemima J* a charming, worthwhile read."

—Lauren K. Nathan, Associated Press

"Green's Jemima is a charmer."

—*New York Daily News*

"Jane Green proves common ingredients—weight loss problems, dating, and Internet romance—can be used in fresh ways to cook up some delicious comedy."

—*Boston Herald*

"Green writes with acerbic wit about the law of the dating jungle, and its obsession with image. Jolly Jemima deserves to be both slim and happy, and the novel's as comforting as a bacon sandwich."

—*Sunday Express* (UK)

"Light, frothy entertainment."

—*Sunday Mirror* (UK)

Jane Green

Broadway Books
New York

a novel

Babyville

Visit our website at www.broadwaybooks.com

First trade paperback edition published March 2004

BOOK DESIGN BY DEBORAH KERNER / DANCING BEARS DESIGN

The Library of Congress has cataloged the hardcover editon as follows:
Green, Jane, 1968–
Babyville: a novel / Jane Green.
p.   cm.
1. Parenthood—Fiction. 2. Childlessness—Fiction. I. Title.
PR6057.R3443 B3 2003
823'.914—dc21   2002028368

ISBN 0-7679-1224-1

10 9 8 7 6 5 4 3 2 1

For Harrison
and Tabitha

Julia

1

Julia hoists herself around on the bed until her head's at the bottom, then sticks her legs straight up in the air and leans them gently on the headboard.

"You know, you look ridiculous," Mark snorts, walking out of the bedroom to grab some toilet paper from the bathroom, because that is their deal: She will allow the wet spot to be on her side of the bed as long as Mark is the one to clean it up, and she is only allowing it at all because she is thrilled, delighted, amazed that Mark has even agreed to this baby in the first place.

She was thrilled. Nine months ago. Nine months ago when she first broached the subject and told him that she was desperate for a baby, that at thirty-three time was definitely running out; that her mother had problems conceiving her, and it took her two and a half years. That last part was actually a bit of a white lie. Her mother conceived her on her wedding night, but that was the clincher, and Julia finally got her wish.

She watches Mark as he comes back from the bathroom. Tallish, broadish, green-eyed and mousy-haired, he would produce adorable children. They, together, would produce adorable children. They would have Julia's dimples and Mark's eyes. Julia's hair and Mark's physique. Mark's gentleness, calmness, and Julia's tenacity, drive.

They would have so much, if Mark and Julia were able to produce at all.

Nine months.

Ironic, isn't it?

If they had been successful that first time they decided to leave the condoms in the drawer, they'd be having a baby right about now. To be more specific, Julia would be having a baby next Thursday. Thursday the 30th of January.

He or She, or Baby of Mine, as Julia has termed the life that isn't yet growing, would be an Aquarius. Her *Secret Language of Birthdays* book says the following about people born on the 30th of January:

Those commanding personalities born on the 30th of January are born to lead. They have a great talent for guiding, entertaining, teaching, explaining, and in general making their ideas clear to others.

Julia's baby would have shared a birthday with Franklin Delano Roosevelt, Vanessa Redgrave, Gene Hackman, and a whole host of people allegedly famous but not worth repeating.

But Franklin Delano Roosevelt? Well. You can just imagine what Julia's thinking. She lay in bed for hours that first night, eyes wide open, thinking about her son, the future Prime Minister, or her daughter, the next head of the United Nations. Not that she'd planned it, but really, she had thought, is there a better sign in the galaxy?

Baby of Mine would have been lucky enough not to have inherited Mark's Cancerian moodiness or her dodgy Pisces sentimentality. According to Linda Goodman, Aquarian boys and girls can be calm and sweetly docile on the surface, but the north wind can turn them suddenly topsy-turvy.

Expect your February child to have a dream, she says, and hold it fast—until he gets another one. Your little Uranian is, apparently, very special. He's a humanitarian. He loves people. Do you know how rare that is? As society moves into the Aquarian age, his unprejudiced wisdom is leading us. Aquarian boys and girls have been chosen by destiny to fulfill the promises of tomorrow.

All in all, not a bad deal. So rather devastating that Julia's baby chose not to make an appearance.

The first couple of months it was no big deal. It only became a big deal when Sam, Julia's best friend, fell pregnant without even trying. Of course Julia was delighted for her, could not have been happier or more excited, but somehow it raised the stakes, began to put pressure on, and suddenly Julia found this was no longer fun, this was business. For the first time in her life she found herself failing at something.

Julia had always been Golden Girl. Through university, then into her first job on a graduate trainee scheme at London

Daytime Television. Someone somewhere must have been smiling on her, because she was quickly promoted to the better series, and now she's the executive producer of a leading early-evening chat show.

Lunchtimes she finds herself sitting with the President of Entertainment. He digs his fork into her chicken for a taste, in a manner that implies equality and intimacy. And possibly more, although she's not interested. The Head of Drama—much to her continued amazement—calls Julia to bemoan her love life. They sit in the bar after work, as production assistants try to worm their way into their affections by buying them drinks and feeding them office gossip.

Of course Julia has nothing to bemoan. This is what people say about her: I would like to be in her shoes.

She has always had what everyone else has always wanted. From her glossy dark hair—easily her best feature—to her small feet tucked into beaded slippers or sexy pointed slingbacks; from her spotlighted career—she is regularly included in those magazine features on "Ones to Watch"—to her large Victorian house in Hampstead (actually it's Gospel Oak, but given that it's practically on top of the Heath, and that all the estate agents call it Hampstead, Julia is now doing the same thing). And, most of all, Mark.

Julia and Mark met four years ago. He was the company lawyer, had been with the firm for about six months, had become the heartthrob of the office. Julia, to her credit, was blissfully unaware of this, being embroiled in a relationship with one of those dreadful, difficult men who pretend that they love you, but who are actually far too busy with their friends and their lives to give you the time of day.

Perhaps blissfully unaware is not quite true. She was vaguely aware of a new lawyer who had set hearts a-fluttering, and vaguely aware that her fellow female researchers kept dashing upstairs to get something "legalled" that was quite patently legal in her opinion, and even though she knew she had met Mark, had even spoken to him, she didn't think of him as a man.

And then one lunchtime he came and stood by Julia's table, an overflowing plate of spaghetti threatening to tip off his tray, and asked if he could join her. She was Miss Doom and Gloom, having realized that the Dreadful Difficult man was turning out to be too dreadfully difficult, even for her, but within minutes Mark had made her smile. The first time she had smiled for weeks.

Julia never bothered ringing the Dreadful Difficult man to tell him it was over. Then again, he never phoned her either. She is sometimes tempted, four years on, to ring and say the relationship doesn't seem to be working, just for a laugh, but even though the thought makes her smile from time to time, it's not something she would ever actually do.

They were friends for a while, Julia and Mark. She was working all hours, researching a fly-on-the-wall documentary about women having plastic surgery. Mark was, at that point, the junior lawyer. He pretended he was also working late, and would go to her office to persuade her to get a bite to eat after work.

But gorgeous as everyone else seemed to find him, Mark simply wasn't her type. Even now she's not entirely sure he's her type. She tells people she fell in like with him. Because he was kind to her, and treated her well, and because he was such a nice guy. And maybe, just maybe, because she was slightly on the rebound, although the only person she's ever admitted that to is Sam.

And if that were really true, there's no way she'd be with him four years on, is there?

Is there?

They still work together, and everyone still loves him. The researchers, much like policemen, may be getting younger and younger, but they still cluster round in excitement as he passes, or scurry down the corridor to his office, an endless stream of fluffy blonde chicks, desperate to impress. It makes Julia smile. It always did. Thankfully she is not the jealous, or suspicious, type.

They say the ones you have to watch are the quiet ones. That it is always the ones who are least likely to have the affairs that end up having the affairs, and sometimes Julia thinks this will be the case with Mark. But the truth is that she doesn't really care. If Mark had an affair, she's not sure she could even be bothered to deal with it. Maybe she would. Maybe it would be an excuse to end it.

Not that she's unhappy, exactly. But she's not happy either. She just is. For the last couple of years Julia has felt as if she's lived her life floating on a cloud of apathy, and she's really not certain what the problem is. Everyone tells her she's the luckiest girl in the world, and Mark does, did, everything for her, although now when she catches his eye as they sit on the sofa watching television, it shocks her to recognize herself in there; she turns away and blinks, unable to bear the thought that Mark is equally numb, because if that is the case, then what is the point?

A baby is the point, she decided nine months ago, when the numbness threatened to overwhelm her. Because while she may not be entirely happy with Mark; while they may not make each other laugh anymore; while they hardly talk anymore, except to argue, and they don't even manage to do that properly, Mark being the gentle, nonconfrontational creature that he is . . . while she refuses to acknowledge that surely there is, there must be, more to life than this, there are things about Mark that she loves.

She loves the fact that he will make a wonderful husband. A heart-stoppingly amazing father. He is loyal, trustworthy, and faithful. He adores other people's children (even though he always said he wasn't ready for children. Not by a long shot. Not yet), he grew up with three brothers and one sister, and his parents are still married. And happy. They sit on the sofa and cuddle like a couple of teenagers.

"Too Good to be True," Sam stated firmly, after she had first met him, and been well and truly charmed.

"You think?" Julia was blasé, affecting a nonchalance it is easy to have when you are being chased by someone every single one of your colleagues would kill for, and you are not particularly interested.

"Too Good to be True, and In Love with You." That was how Sam said it. As a caption. As a statement that would not, could not, be questioned. A short and simple fact of life.

Julia had shrugged but Sam continued. "Don't let this one go," she warned, and Julia took it to heart. After all, Sam was the expert. Sam had already found Chris, the man she was to marry, so when she told Julia that Mark was a keeper, she took her advice and kept him.

He is a keeper. Sam was right. Julia watches him wash up every night, listens to him whistling as he carries the shopping home, and she knows he deserves better than this. She thinks she might deserve better than this too.

They have found a way of living side by side, without ever really communicating. It had been funny, at the beginning, how different they were. They had laughed and said how lucky they were that opposites really did attract, although even then Julia wasn't so sure.

They told all their friends that the key to their relationship was exactly that they were so different; they thought they would never be bored, each of them having their own interests. Only now can Julia see the chasm that's opened up between them, the chasm that was always there, but, as a hairline crack, was too difficult to see at the beginning.

Mark loves being at home. Julia loves being out. He loves his family, his close friends, and Julia. She loves being surrounded by people, strangers, anyone—the more the merrier. Mark loves puttering around the house and garden, finds true spiritual happiness in Homebase, whereas Julia is at her best in a noisy bar, chattering away over a few Cosmopolitans. Mark would have a panic attack if he ran out of slug pellets. Julia has panic attacks when she can't get reception on her mobile phone.

When they first met he was renting a small flat in Finsbury Park; she owned a tiny, messy terraced house just off Kilburn High Road. Neither of them can quite remember how it happened, but a couple of months after they met Mark had moved in. They don't remember discussing it, just that one day he wasn't there, and the next he was.

And Julia loved it, in the beginning. She'd been on her own

since leaving university, and suddenly there was someone to talk to, someone who would listen if she'd had a particularly good, or bad, day.

Mark quickly assumed the role of housekeeper, chef, organizer. The unopened envelopes piled in the hallway disappeared overnight, and Mark dealt with stuff. Grown-up stuff that Julia had never got around to dealing with herself. He fixed the leaking showerhead, a small annoyance she'd learned to live with. He created a terrace out of a courtyard filled with rubble. He turned her house into a home, and when, after a year, it became too small for both of them, he bought a huge house just up the road in what was then very definitely Gospel Oak.

And now they rattle around together in this big house that is far, far too big for Julia. Julia loved her tiny house, loves small, cozy rooms, has never felt comfortable in this house, never felt right.

Mark, on the other hand, loved it instantly. Because Julia thought she did not really care where she lived, thought if Mark was happy she would be happy, she agreed, even though she now finds she has always been intimidated by the vast rooms, the high ceilings, the floor-to-ceiling bay windows.

They meet in the kitchen, the one place Julia does like, the one room that makes her feel as though she belongs, the only room in the house that bears witness to the occasional times that Mark and Julia laugh together. Talk. Communicate.

Because every now and then they do have a fantastic time. Both of them are still clinging on, hoping that those fantastic times will increase, that they will be able to recapture some of the magic that was there at the beginning.

Which is why Mark agreed to the baby. Julia knew he wasn't keen, wasn't ready, but she has come to believe this baby is their best shot. Of course it's not right to use children as a means of grouting up the cracks in a relationship, but Julia is convinced she'd change if they had a child together. She'd be settled. Happy. They would be a family.

Nine months ago they thought it would be easy. Nine months later they know it's not, and their inability to do something so natural, something that other people find so effortless, seems to be putting yet more distance between them.

They talked about it at first. Tentatively. Nervously. Neither of them wanting to admit that there might be a problem, although at that stage neither genuinely thought there was a problem. They were still having sex spontaneously then. Making love without checking the chart, or taking a temperature, or lying, as Julia is now, with legs raised perpendicular to her chest, to give the sperm the easiest, laziest, route to her — hopefully — welcoming egg.

In the old days they used to lie in bed after each lovemaking session, spontaneously or otherwise, wondering whether they had done it, whether they had created a baby. Friends of Julia said they knew. Sam said she knew. The very moment it happened Sam said she knew, but other people she'd spoken to said it was rubbish, that you don't feel different, that the only reason they ever suspected was because their periods were late.

And Julia has spoken to many other people. Many, many, many, because making a baby has become an obsession, succeeding in making a baby her mission in life. She will gladly speak to friends of friends, distant colleagues, total strangers, in a bid to find out how it is done, how she can make it work.

It is as easy to approach strangers, to quiz them on the most intimate subjects (which, luckily, mothers don't seem to mind, all privacy and intimacy having presumably been removed from their lives at some point on the birthing table), as it is hard to be around people she actually knows who have children.

Stupid. Selfish. Self-obsessed. Julia feels all these things, and yet she knows she cannot handle it. Cannot handle the pain when she sees those precious children, cannot handle the ugly side of herself, the only side that emerges on those occasions.

She has managed to admit to Sam her true feelings: She is jealous and angry about other people's ability to have children. Not strangers; she can happily be around strangers and their children. But friends? Family? There have been times when Julia has been filled with hateful fury. Furious hate. There have been times when she has not been able to speak, so overwhelmed with this anger that she has been scared it will project from her mouth in a stream of invective.

Don't hate Julia for it. She is not a bad person. She's a woman filled with jealousy and resentment, a woman who hates herself for it, but cannot help it.

Hates herself for avoiding situations where she will see people she knows who have children. Avoids family parties because her brother-in-law's sister has a ten-month-old girl called Jessica. She last saw Jessica when Jessica was three months old, and Julia had not yet discovered she might have a problem having a Jessica of her own.

She held Jessica and felt her heart swell with joy, but she can't hold her now. She can't see Jessica's parents, because she so resents them for being able to have her. Time, she prays. It is surely just a question of time before she gets pregnant and she will be able to have a baby of her own.

Once upon a long time ago Julia had an abortion. She hadn't thought about it for years. Recently she finds she thinks about it an awful lot. What she thinks most is that there is nothing wrong with her. She has been pregnant. This is not her fault. And if it's not her fault, then whose fault must it be?

She tries not to dwell on that one, frightened of where it might lead.

And still she stops mothers and asks for their tips, still she tries every old wives' tale in a bid to become pregnant.

The latest is this position, this legs-in-the-air position. This was passed on by a woman in the children's playground. (Yet another place she has been frequenting, eyes filling up with tears as she watches chubby little bodies toddling around, mouths filled with sand from the sandbox while their mothers are too engrossed in chat to notice. Just for the record, Julia thinks as she sits on the bench, she wouldn't be too engrossed. Just for the record, she would be the perfect mother.)

The woman sitting next to her had four children, and this was her tip: legs in the air for five minutes, not a second less. Julia doesn't believe five minutes is long enough for sperm to reach their destination, so she has taken to lying like this for an hour, Mark quietly snoring beside her as she rereads her books on getting pregnant.

Creative Visualization. That's another one. From time to time she lays the book down by her side, closes her eyes, and visualizes those sperm, fighting their way along the fallopian tubes to meet the egg, and sometimes she thinks so hard, she believes she can actually feel it happening.

In fact, is it happening now . . . ? Could that be . . . ? Is it . . . ? Please God, she prays, Let this work. Please God, let me have a baby. Let the More to Life than This be fertilized even as I lie here with my eyes tightly shut.

Just in case you're wondering, Julia hasn't been to see anyone, a fertility expert, anyone like that. God no, she would say. Not yet. On a good day she will tell herself that it's only been nine months, really not that long.

Tonight, as she practices her Creative Visualization with her legs in the air, Julia swears she can feel something happening. Not that she's entirely sure, but this time she thinks they really might have done it.

2

By rights Julia should not be able to see Sam, with Sam's stomach growing, her mind focusing on childbirth, labor, and chocolate ice cream with green olives and prawns. But somehow Julia can cope with Sam, because she loves her, and because, even though she can admit she's jealous, it doesn't seem to overwhelm her as it does with others.

But Sam is only pregnant. She does not yet have the baby Julia so desperately craves, and try though Julia will to be in her life post-baby as much as she is now, she cannot make any promises.

Julia stopped at Pizza Hut on the way. Two large pepperoni pizzas, extra green olives and prawns, to make Sam smile. As expected, Sam sits and picks all the topping off, mixes it in with the ice cream in the freezer, then throws the crust away while Julia makes disgusted faces.

"It could be so much worse," she says, mouth full of the revolting concoction. "Think of all those really disgusting cravings people have. I could be on my hands and knees in the garden shoveling soil into my mouth."

"First of all, what makes you think what you're eating is any better?" Julia ventures. "Anyway, isn't that stuff all an urban myth? I mean, people don't really do that, do they?"

Sam smiles, as she always does. "Yup. And coal. I could have sent you down to the garage for huge bags of coal instead of to Pizza Hut. It's called pica, some kind of iron deficiency. That's the interesting thing. Your body always tells you what it needs when you're pregnant."

"So what exactly is the chocolate ice cream, olive, and prawn thing telling you?"

She shovels a bit more into her mouth. "Probably that I need to put on weight," and with that the pair of them start laughing.

Sam has always been cuddly. She is a mass of blond curls, a tiny waist, and a bottom and thighs that could well have inspired Rubens. But what Julia loves most about Sam is how much Sam loves herself. She has none of the self-doubt we are so used to hearing from women in these times of aspirational skinniness. Sam never asks anyone if she looks fat, or if that skirt is unflattering, or if the heels make her legs look longer.

Sam loves the fact that she's voluptuous, and is loving her pregnancy more than any woman Julia has ever seen. The first thing she did when she discovered she was "with child" was dash out and buy *What to Expect When You're Expecting*. The second was to rip out the chapter about the "Best Odds Diet."

"Bloody Americans," she said, tearing out each page, crumpling it up with relish as she lobbed it into the bin in the corner. "They're all food obsessed. God, this is the one time in your life when you're allowed to eat whatever the hell you want, so bollocks to this. As for putting on no more than twenty-eight pounds, Jesus, I think I put that on in the first twelve weeks."

"So go on, how much have you put on now?" Julia asked.

"No clue. I stopped weighing myself after four weeks. Can't be bothered."

And now Sam is almost entirely round. Rather like a Weeble, she wobbles but she doesn't fall down. And still she looks gorgeous. She is one of those lucky women who don't suffer from spots or lank hair while pregnant. Her skin is smooth and clear, her hair is thick, lustrous, and ever-growing.

"Jesus, don't think I'm lucky," she said a couple of weeks ago, when someone at the hospital, another woman waiting to see the midwife, had commented how gorgeous her hair was, how lucky she was that it grew so quickly. "As quickly as it's growing on my head it's growing everywhere else on my body," Sam had said, rolling her eyes. "I've got a jungle on my legs that only gets waxed when I go to the hospital because I don't want the midwives gossiping, and as for my beard . . ."

Sam's not a natural blonde, and consequently states that were she to be stranded on a desert island for approximately a month, any ship that happened to be passing would simply carry on, unaware that the gorilla waving its arms around under the palm trees was actually Sam.

But no one has ever seen this beard. "Look, look," she says

to Julia, as she often does on a regular basis, craning her neck up and pointing to what looks like nothing.

"I still can't see anything."

"Okay, feel, feel," and she grabs Julia's finger and strokes it under her chin, which is when Julia has to concede that she can feel the slightest, but only the very slightest, beginnings of stubble.

"That's the only thing I hate about pregnancy," Sam sighs. "The bloody hair growth."

"What about piles?" Julia shoots her an evil grin.

"Oh shit. Did I tell you that?" Sam looks embarrassed as Julia nods.

"That doesn't even bother me that much," she says. "I go into Boots and bulk buy Anusol, telling them it's for my husband."

"I don't suppose Chris ever goes in there."

"Only on a Saturday and they've got different staff in on the weekend, so no one asks him how his hemorrhoids are doing."

"Yeah, but Sam, piles are expected during pregnancy, it's not exactly embarrassing."

"Yes, it is. Embarrassing and itchy."

"Okay, okay. Just a little bit of oversharing there, thank you. Tell me about work."

Sam is a graphic designer. You might well buy tins of her soup regularly. It sounds like a glamorous job, but she finds it boring and dull, and not at all creative, not for someone as talented as Sam.

Away from her work she is inspired. Those cushions on the sofa? Sam made them. The beautiful simple blinds with the tiny leaf motifs at the bottom? Sam made them. Those stunning Rothko-esque oils lining the hallway? Right again.

Although she would never admit it, much as Julia wants this baby to heal her relationship with Mark, Sam wanted an excuse to leave her job, and more than that wanted to prove that she would be better at mothering than her own—unavailable—mother.

Sam and Julia had long talked about having babies. Said how fantastic it would be if they had kids the same age, but Sam never expected it to happen so quickly, and Julia, naturally, never expected it to happen so slowly.

There was a third wheel to their gang. Bella. They say threesomes never work, but somehow it always did with them. Maybe it helped that Sam and Julia were friendly first, before Bella came into the equation, but they never had any of the petty jealousies that you so often associate with triangles.

Julia and Sam met first, years ago, at a party. Julia watched Sam turn the music up and start dancing in the middle of the living room, while everyone else stood around chatting, watching her out of the corner of their eyes because they also wanted to dance, but no one else had the nerve.

She saw Julia watching her and went over, grabbed her arm with a smile, and Julia started to dance too. Suddenly Julia didn't care that it was one of those snobby parties where you're not supposed to let your hair down and actually have fun. She didn't care that you were only supposed to stand around sipping wine and making small talk. Sam and Julia, despite having never met before, flung their arms around, gyrated their hips, and bonded over a *Saturday Night Fever*–style pointed-finger movement.

They collapsed on the sofa after about two hours, and once there didn't move for the rest of the night, talking about everything, sharing their lives. Numbers were swapped at the end of the evening, and the next day Sam phoned to suggest going out dancing again. The seeds of friendship were sown.

A couple of years later, Bella joined London Daytime Television. Bella and Julia were both researchers on a news-magazine show, and hit it off almost immediately. I say almost, because the first time Julia saw her she wasn't at all sure. Bella was twenty-four going on thirty. Actually she has always said that thirty-five is her true age, and even when she was sixteen she was mistaken for someone much older.

Bella, in short, intimidated all but the most confident of people, and it was only when they were sent up to Leeds together to interview a couple of people for the show that they bonded.

For a while Julia would see them separately. With Sam she would go clubbing, to trendy bars, wild parties, and Bella was reserved for sophisticated restaurants, chichi dinner parties, even the odd bit of extremely badly played tennis.

Bella and Sam had met. Their paths crossed at Julia's house from time to time, and although they hadn't disliked one another, they hadn't much liked one another either. It was only when Bella met Paul, Sam's then-boyfriend's best friend, and fancied him, that she and Sam started to become friends, but Julia is still the link between the two, the one that binds them all together.

Bella has moved on now. Literally and figuratively. She

was offered a job two years ago in New York: producer of a national morning magazine show, which naturally she couldn't turn down. She was so busy she barely had time to throw a leaving party, and now Julia considers herself blessed if Bella manages to return a voicemail more often than once a month.

On the rare occasions they do catch up, Bella sounds as if she is having a blast. Resolutely single after Paul broke her heart, she has thrown herself into the New York dating scene with wild abandon, astounding her friends back home with the sheer number of men she seems to meet. Most surprising, this, Sam is fond of saying, because she had always thought 90 percent of the single men in Manhattan were gay. Evidently not, according to Bella.

Bella is paying a disgusting amount of money for an apartment roughly the size of a shoebox in a much-sought-after doorman building at 75th and Second. Second Avenue is not quite Fifth, Bella has laughed, but it's still Upper East Side, and in New York address is everything.

Bella has taken to Manhattan like a duck to water. She goes to the gym every morning before work, which Julia and Sam find completely ridiculous, given that the odd sloppy game of tennis Bella used to play was the most she could muster, and even that was only ever an excuse to exchange loud gossip while feeling immensely virtuous.

Bella has always been good at adapting, at adhering to "When in Rome . . . ," and weekly manicures, lunches at Bergdorf's, and navigating her way down Madison Avenue in a pair of lethal skyscraper slingbacks is now second nature to her.

She comes back rarely. Sam and Julia almost failed to

recognize her on her last fleeting visit. They had arranged to meet her in the lobby of the Sanderson, and walked straight past the skinny girl dressed in black, huge Jackie O–style sunglasses obliterating her face.

Most of all Bella adores her work. She is passionate about the show, about the way Americans work, and loves her colleagues to distraction. (Quite literally at one point, given that she was seeing one of the big cheeses at the network for a while, but he was married and that's quite another story. A whole book in itself, in fact.)

We get the show here, if you're lucky enough to have Sky, Cable, or Digital. It's on every day at 2 P.M., so Julia only ever manages to catch it if she's ill or working from home, which she is tending to do rather more often these days, her career taking definite second place to her desire to have a baby.

So Bella. Bella who would like to find the perfect man but does not believe he really exists. Bella who has not the slightest desire to have children. Not yet anyway.

Bella who is genuinely happy. At least that's what she says.

But then again, people say that about Julia, and who knows what goes on behind closed doors?

"Work is as boring as usual," Sam says, hoisting herself up from the sofa with great difficulty to put the empty pizza boxes in the kitchen. Julia considers offering to do it for her, but desists, knowing how insulted Sam gets. "I'm pregnant," she will say, "not a bloody invalid."

23

Of course God forbid no one offers her a seat on the tube in rush hour. "Hello?" she shouts, sticking her stomach out as far as it will go and making sure she catches the eye of some businessman sitting down. "Can't you see I'm eight months pregnant?" They always stand up for her.

Incidentally she isn't eight months pregnant. She's five months. But she could pass for eight. Especially when she sticks her stomach out.

"Can't talk about work," she returns, huffing and puffing from her walk of ten feet. "Just can't wait to leave the bloody place. Chris thinks I'll be going back after four months' maternity leave and I haven't got the heart to tell him he's got another thing coming. But what about you? Any news on the pregnancy front?"

"Too early to tell. Not due for another two weeks."

"I hope you're having sex for Britain, then, because you're at the height of the fertile season."

"Actually we're not. We're trying to have sex every other day, because apparently if you do it every day the sperm get weaker, so it's best to give it a rest, and someone told me Day Thirteen is the important day, which was the day before yesterday, and we did it, so now it's the waiting game again."

"God. Sex. I remember what that was like."

"Sam! You're only five months pregnant. What do you mean, you remember what that was like? You can still have sex, for heaven's sake."

"Julia, not only do I not want to have sex, I can't even stand the bloody smell of him at the moment."

"What?"

Sam sighs. "It's true. He rolls over to face the middle of the bed about thirty times a night and each time he does it I'm awake and I can smell his breath and I want to vomit."

"So what do you do?"

"I hiss at him to roll over and most of the time he just does it automatically without even waking up."

"And if he wakes up?"

"Then he starts shouting at me and I start crying. And as far as I'm concerned right now, actually having sex would be a fate worse than death. Apparently it's a hormonal thing. Chris was dead excited because most of the women we know were like rabbits, but sod's law, I'm the bloody one who gets turned off."

"At least he still wants to have sex with you. Mark says he feels like a machine. He can't stand how sex has become so mechanical, just a means to an end."

"Is he right? Has it?"

Julia thinks back to the day before yesterday. How excited she was because it was Day 13, how she was convinced that tonight would be the night. They ate in front of the television, as they do so often these days, passing the odd comment to one another, but not really talking.

At eleven Julia went up to bed. Mark said he'd come up after the film, at which point Julia gently reminded him that tonight was one of those nights, and could he please come up earlier. He huffed and puffed a bit, but didn't say anything. Just crossed his arms and continued staring at the screen.

Not perhaps the best of starts. It wasn't going to get any better. . . .

25

Once upon a time Julia wore sexy lingerie. She had drawers of lacy scraps of silk, with shoestring straps that slipped off her shoulders. Now she has oversized T-shirts for summer and pajamas for winter. Usually T-shirts that had been sent to one of her researchers, because someone, somewhere, thought that emblazoning an XL T-shirt with a huge logo would be a good selling point. T-shirts that have faded from the numerous washes over the years, that she wouldn't be seen dead in anywhere other than in her own house.

As for the pajamas . . . very definitely not sexy pajamas you might imagine someone like Meg Ryan wearing, nor even someone like Julia. Not the kind of men's pajamas that look cute and cuddly on models curled up by log fires in the pages of the glossy magazines. These men's pajamas are fraying at the edges. The bottom bags down to her knees, and because the elastic lost all its elasticity a long, long time ago, the waist is held together with a safety pin that isn't exactly safe but, amazingly, has never stuck her. They're baggy, colorless, and shapeless, except she doesn't actually care because they're so comfortable and warm.

That night was a pajama night. Julia made an effort to brush her hair and shake it out to sit on her shoulders in the way that Mark always used to love. She sat up in bed reading, intermittently looking at the clock. Even though she had promised herself not to shout at him, after half an hour her frustration became too much: She stormed to the top of the stairs and yelled at him to come up.

Five minutes later Mark came upstairs and stood in the doorway with a thunderous look on his face.

"I was in the middle of watching something that would have been over in fifteen minutes, and you could have been more patient. I'm fed up with everything revolving around you. Whatever you want, whenever you want it . . ." Julia opened her mouth to interrupt but he carried on. "And now I'm not in the mood. I know all about Day Thirteen, but frankly I find it completely implausible, and the last thing I want to do right now is have sex." He spat this last word out as if it were the most distasteful thing in the world.

Julia swallowed her own frustration, something she found almost impossible to do, but after all, it was Day 13, and schedules must be adhered to, egos must be stroked, not to mention anything else.

"I'm sorry," she said meekly, looking up at him from lowered eyelashes as she climbed out of bed and walked toward him. "I was selfish. I wasn't thinking. I'm so sorry." She reached up and kissed his impassive cheek of stone, knowing that there was only one way for this to go in the direction she wanted. She moved her hand down to the zip on his trousers as she lowered herself to her knees.

"Will you forgive me?" she mumbled, mouth full. Then she knew it didn't matter any more.

Ten minutes later she was lying on the bed, legs up in the air, reading a pregnancy book as Mark went to grab the toilet paper in disgust.

He didn't say anything when he came back to the bedroom. Just shook his head sadly as he looked at Julia and climbed into bed. A few minutes later he spoke, and his voice was muted, weary. "Was it ever better than this? Tell me it was better than this. Didn't we use to make love? Didn't it use to take hours? Wasn't it fun before all this baby stuff?" He looked at Julia, as if expecting an answer, but she chose not to reply, so he turned over with a sigh. Within a few minutes all you could hear was the sound of his gentle snoring.

How could she possibly have answered him? There was nothing to say.

Julia looks at Sam and shrugs. "Don't you think the sex always goes at some point?" she says without feeling. "Sure, it was great in the beginning, but doesn't it always wear off after a while? Mark thinks that trying for a baby has made it mechanical and boring, but I'm sure the passion would have gone anyway because it always does. We've been together four years, and you really can't expect your sex life to be fantastic after four years."

"But you're not even married," Sam says, suddenly looking serious. "Are you sure about this baby? Are you even sure about . . . Mark?" She chooses her words carefully, tentatively, for she is voicing things Julia doesn't want to think about, let alone hear. "Julia, all I'm saying is that I don't think it's fair to bring a child into the world if you're not sure you're with the right—"

"Okay, okay." Julia stops her mid-flow. "I'm sorry, Sam, but this just isn't something I can talk about. You know how much I want this child. How can you say these things?"

Julia knows exactly how she can say these things. Sam is only saying all the things Julia thinks when she wakes up in the middle of the night with a pounding heart, almost suffocating with the panic, the need to escape, only bearable because she knows normality will return with daylight. And how can she trust these night fears anyway? How can she trust them when

28

they leave in the morning? If they were real, if she were supposed to be listening to them, then she'd have them all the time, wouldn't she?

Wouldn't she?

"I'm sorry." Sam is contrite. These are difficult words to say. Even to your best friend. "I just worry about you."

"I know," Julia sighs. "I worry about me too."

3

Mark is, as always, the first to wake up. He turns to Julia, still dead to the world, mouth open, hands clenched tightly into fists, pulling the duvet up around her ears, and he leans down to kiss her softly on the cheek. When she is like this, so soft, so innocent, he knows exactly why he loves her, why he is still with her.

He places his feet on the floor, stretches his arms to the ceiling, and yawns before padding quietly out of the room, slowly shutting the door behind him so as not to wake her.

Mark has been working hard. He has been staying in the office late, trying to get everything done, forgoing the gym as there's too much to do. He has stopped eating lunch in the canteen, instead grabbing a sandwich and eating it at his desk, piles of legal papers his lunchtime reading.

He feels tired these days. Always tired, but there's so much to think about, so much to do, that a lie-in is not on the cards. Not that he doesn't want one, but his mind is always racing. Getting off to sleep is fine. Easy, even. But most nights he is awake in the early hours. He lies there, listening to Julia, knowing that she's also awake, but unable to reach out to her, and he thinks about his work, his life.

And he is so used to getting up at 6:45 A.M. for work that even on the weekends he wakes up automatically, at precisely that time, which is ridiculous given that Monday to Friday he needs an alarm clock to wake him. Monday to Friday he stumbles groggily to the bathroom, wishing for more sleep, but Saturday and Sunday he positively bounces out of bed.

Mark goes downstairs and puts the kettle on, placing *The Times* on the kitchen table as he pulls two slices of bread from the plastic wrapper and sticks them in the toaster.

Crash. The noise of the post tumbling through the letterbox and landing on the doormat startles him. He groans as he bends down to pick up the letters, and shuffles through looking for anything interesting as he goes back into the kitchen and tips some fresh coffee into a cafetiere.

Nothing exciting today. Junk mail, junk mail, more junk mail, and bills. That time of year when all the bills come in. He opens the Visa statement and reads through it quickly, stopping to go back and read it again because he can't quite believe what it says.

Now Mark knows that Julia loves cosmetics, toiletries, girly things. He accepts that Julia cannot pass a chemist's without going in, and he knows that, once in, she will happily browse for hours, spending fortunes on pastel-colored bottles of things he's never heard of. She had even once emerged with a selection of velvet scrunchies in assorted colors that she deemed irresistible. When she had short hair.

But he also knows that there are strict rules about the joint account. As independent creatures are wont to do these days, they keep their money separate. Julia has her account, from which she takes money for anything that doesn't involve Mark, and Mark has his. And then there is the joint account, generally used for household bills, restaurants, furniture, food shops, gifts for mutual friends, and holidays. Anything, that is, that involves both of them. Which doesn't include Boots. And, more to the point, how in the hell did she manage to spend nearly two hundred pounds there? What the hell has she been buying?

Julia has been buying pregnancy tests. She tries to resist them, but every month, in that run-up to her period, she gets what she has come to call her ClearBlue craving. Unfortunately one just doesn't supply her with the fix she needs.

She did manage to start off with one test. They always do. Nine months ago she bought one test five days before her period, right at the beginning when they were first trying. She took it round to Sam's amid much giggling.

"I really think it's too early," Sam said.

"But if I'm pregnant, then my body might already be producing the hCG hormone, and if it is, then it might show."

32

"But the packet says you have to wait until the first day of your period, and you haven't even got any of the symptoms."

"I bloody have," Julia said defiantly. "Look at the size of my breasts. They're enormous."

"But your period's due in five days, and they're always enormous before your period," Sam said, grinning.

"And"—Julia paused dramatically—"I've been running to the loo all night. I swear, my bladder's gone crazy."

"You've always had the weakest bladder of anyone I know, but okay, okay. Point taken. Let's do it."

Julia's face lit up. "Great! Can I borrow a glass?"

"What for?"

Julia read the instructions out loud to Sam. "'Place the stick in mid-flow urine, or submerge in the urine.'" She missed the look of horror on Sam's face as she explained that she didn't trust the holding-it-in-the-stream method, just in case she missed.

"You're not bloody using one of my glasses for that!"

In the end they settled for the cap of Chris's deodorant bottle. "For God's sake, never ever tell him. I swear he'd divorce me for this."

"Just rinse it out with bleach when I'm done with it," Julia said, heading for the bathroom.

"I know, I know," Sam shouted back as the door was closing. "What do you think I used for my test?"

The test was negative. So was the one she bought later that day. And the six she bought before her period started. At first it was her secret, but $13.95 is a hell of a lot of money to pay when you need around a dozen of these tests every month, and last month Julia decided that as they were trying for "their" baby, the tests should be "their" expense.

Naturally Mark doesn't know about the boxes of Clear-Blue hidden under the piles of towels. Not that he'd mind them in principle—it's not like your parents discovering packets of the Pill in your bedside drawer when you're sixteen and you know they'd go up the wall—he'd just mind the amount that she's buying, because Mark is nothing if not a pragmatist. He would be horrified at Julia taking the test days before her period is due; at not following the instructions on the packet; at the impatience and extravagance of an addiction that he simply would not comprehend.

Mostly he would not understand because he doesn't understand Julia. The qualities that attracted him in the beginning are the very qualities that are pushing them apart now.

He loved her energy when they met. Loved her laugh, her ambition and unconventionality. He'd noticed her at work, had already made some inquiries before he dared approach her in the canteen, had already decided that somehow he would get to know her, touch her, be with her.

He'd pass her sometimes, in the hallway, talking intensely with one of her friends, and as he approached he'd stare at her, willing her to look up, to notice him, but she never did. Every day there would be a knock on the door from a love-struck researcher with a bad excuse, and he was never interested, because none of them was her.

Mark didn't know how to approach her, what to say, and realized it was sensitive because they worked together. Even though in-house relationships were going on all the time, they were frowned on by management. His own father had always warned him not to dirty his own doorstep. In previous jobs he'd taken this to heart, but he forgot it when he saw Julia.

Even when Julia never seemed to see him.

Mark is one of those men who is good-looking without being arrogant, and it had never served him particularly well. His friends, less good-looking but far more laddish, had always had far greater success with women. The more hearts they broke, the more emotions they trampled on, the more women fell for them. Mark was termed a nice guy, and what can possibly be worse than that? At school he was the girls' best friend because he was good-looking and therefore good to be seen with, but too nice to want to go out with. So nice he was even considered dull.

It was only when he was at university that he came into his own, and even then it took a couple of years. He had been going out with Amanda for over a year, and he ended it because he knew she wasn't right for him, and because he only had a year left to enjoy himself.

Did he enjoy himself. Making his Mark, was how his friends described it with glee, and more than a touch of jealousy. To this day he is famous for his pulling power, with the number of women he is said to have pulled growing, rather like the proverbial fish, bigger and bigger over time. Although the irony was that he never had to try. He had always been Amanda's good-looking boyfriend, and as soon as he was single he became the most sought-after man on campus.

No more Mr. Nice Guy.

Except intrinsically, apart from unwittingly breaking a few

hearts, he was still a nice guy, and still rather shy with women, particularly those he truly fancied. Like Julia. No one could imagine the effort it took to approach her that day in the canteen. By that time he had built her into the perfect woman, placed her on a pedestal so high she was in danger of getting lost in the clouds of his imagination.

Mark loved her vivacity, her easy, expansive, extrovert nature. She was everything he was not, everything he secretly wanted to be. When he was with her, he felt that he really was the best possible person he could be. Mark didn't want to be quiet, studious, introverted, when Julia was around. Being with Julia was like an exhilarating fairground ride, and he knew he wanted this feeling to go on forever.

Forever feels like a long time ago now. Most of the time he is exhausted by Julia. Exhausted and uncomprehending, because their worlds are so very different, and Mark sees that not only can he not escape from who he really is, but that he does not want to. He tried at first. The first year or so. An endless round of parties, of people dropping in, of being surrounded by friends, and friends of friends, and strangers. He enjoyed it for a while, mostly because he assumed it would be dropping off. Nobody can live that kind of life permanently, can they?

Julia could.

Mark realized sometime during their second year together that the constant stream of people through the house did not seem to be abating. That Julia coming home with handfuls of waifs and strays from work and expecting there to be enough food was not going to change.

And Mark knew it wouldn't be fair to expect her to change.

He did, after all, know what he was letting himself in for when he first got together with her, but somehow he thought they'd be able to find middle ground, find a way of making it work.

At the beginning, still flush with passion and excitement, still full of the possibilities of finding that middle road, he had even thought he would propose. He planned a trip to Barbados in January, booked a restaurant overlooking the beach that had been voted one of the top ten romantic restaurants in the world, had even dreamed up his speech.

The unease started a couple of weeks before they left, prompted mostly by an argument about New Year's Eve. They had not been invited to any parties, much to Julia's disgust, and Mark had said that his ideal New Year would be to invite the two, or three, couples to whom they were the closest round for dinner and crack open the champagne at midnight.

Julia was horrified. She wanted to throw a party. A huge bash open to all and sundry, to really see in the New Year with a bang. She wasn't going to give way, so Mark had to, and even as he conceded he was rethinking the prospect of togetherness for the rest of their lives.

But he had already planned Barbados. Already planned the holiday. The proposal. Even the ring. Yet sitting on the terrace, watching Julia's face through the flame of the candle, he knew he couldn't do it. He loved her but he wasn't sure. He loved her, but he wasn't sure that love was enough.

He would wait. Not long, but the ring in his pocket would stay in his pocket, and who knows, maybe next year things would be different, maybe even next month things would be different.

Four years on, nothing is different. Mark and Julia have found a way of living in the same house, sharing the same bed, leading ever more separate lives.

A s he sits at the breakfast table and reads *The Times*, the pile of bills pushed to one side with the offending Visa statement on the top, Mark decides that they are going to have a nice day today, they are going to enjoy themselves.

Today is Adam and Lorna's wedding. They are getting married in Blackheath, a proper white wedding in an old-fashioned church.

Adam and Lorna are Julia's friends. Mark has to make this distinction because so few of their friends cross over. They never have. Julia finds his friends nice but too straight for her, too dull, while Mark has never really understood female friendships, with their gossip and secrets and giggling.

Many's the time he's walked into the kitchen to find Julia sitting at the table deep in conversation with two or three of her girlfriends, mugs of coffee and glasses of wine littering the table, ashtrays overflowing with Silk Cut Extra Low. Their voices are always lowered, they invariably start teasing Mark, which makes him uncomfortable, even though he tries to smile and go along with it. He tends to help himself to whatever it is he needed, before leaving them in peace and disappearing up to his study for the rest of the evening.

"Why can't you make more of an effort with my friends?" Julia asked when she went to bed, much much later that night.

"Why don't your friends make more of an effort with me?" Mark replied in self-defense, although what he meant was, Why can't they understand me? Why don't I understand them?

Mark has retained his friends from school and university, as men tend to do. He speaks to them more than he sees them these days, is adept at catching up with news via e-mail. They meet up from time to time, generally when Julia is away. On the few occasions when Mark tried to bring Julia into the equation it was an unmitigated disaster.

Julia tried to be nice. She tried to like them. But she really had nothing in common with them—less than nothing—and found each meeting more exhausting than the last. Eventually she told Mark she loved him but not his friends: He'd have to see them on his own. Mark pretended to be offended; in truth he was relieved. It was as much a strain on him as it was on Julia.

Now they have their own friends, lead their own lives, but on occasions such as today the two will converge, and the truth is that Mark has always quite liked Adam and Lorna. In fact, with the exception of Sam and Chris, they are probably the people he likes most in Julia's circle. Adam and Lorna have been living in Brighton this last year, he has hardly seen them, but they are coming back to Blackheath, where Lorna was brought up, for the wedding.

Mark likes weddings, has always liked weddings, as indeed has Julia, so perhaps wishing that this will be a nice day is not so unrealistic after all, and to start off the nice day he will bring Julia breakfast in bed.

"Mmmm." Julia slowly props herself up and stretches with a lazy smile as Mark places the tray carefully on the bed. She eyes the tea and toast, dipping a finger into the pot of honey and licking it off, for they have not shared breakfast in such a long time that Mark has forgotten which exactly is her favorite spread. He thinks it's honey, but he doesn't want to be wrong. To be on the safe side he has clustered Marmite, honey, peanut butter, and strawberry jam on one side of the tray. "What have I done to deserve this?"

"Nothing," he says, smiling back, sitting next to her on the bed, and dropping the paper on the pillow. "I just wanted to surprise you. Plus we've got the wedding today and if I'd let you sleep we would have missed it."

"The wedding," Julia sighs. "I can't believe Adam and Lorna are actually getting married. God. I thought they'd just live together forever." She sneaks a sideways peek at Mark. "Rather like us."

"Are you saying you want to get married?" Mark is shocked. It's a subject they haven't brought up for months. Years. Not since the early days. Julia's thoughtful look dissolves into giggles.

"Scared you, didn't I?" she teases. Although Mark won't admit it, his mental sigh of relief is enormous. He hides it by picking up his coffee and taking a sip.

"Seriously, though, I never thought Lorna wanted to get married, but I suppose I never thought she'd last this long with Adam."

"But Adam's a really nice guy."

"Yeah, but let's face it, he's not exactly the most dynamic man in the world. He's practically had a charisma bypass . . ." and she tails off, knowing that she has, in her more vicious moments, said exactly the same thing about Mark. "But he is lovely," she quickly continues, before Mark has a chance to notice, "and I'm sure they'll be very happy together."

"Go on, then."

"Go on what."

"I know what you're thinking. What's your prediction?"

Julia hugs her knees to her chest as she grins at Mark, because at times like this she remembers why she is with him. Although she usually admits it grudgingly, he knows her better than anyone else, knows the way her mind works, knows how to get her attention and keep it.

"Five years."

Mark raises an eyebrow. "That long?"

"Okay, okay. Four years and three months. You?"

"You know I don't indulge in these games."

"I'm guessing you'd give it ten and a half years."

"That sounds about right." Mark laughs, and in that moment of intimacy he leans over and plants a kiss on the side of Julia's neck. She turns to kiss him in return, laying her toast slowly down on the tray.

"Wait," he whispers, pushing her gently away as he lifts the tray from the bed and places it carefully on the floor. Julia inches down in the bed until she's lying down, and Mark lowers himself on top of her, kissing her, smelling her hair, her neck, feeling her skin.

He moves one hand down and unbuttons the top button of her pajamas. "Fuck, I hate these pajamas," he whispers into her ear, and she giggles before moaning as his fingers stroke her nipples to a peak, all the while kissing her.

"Wait," she whispers, pulling back until she can look at him. "It's not . . . you know."

"Not what?" Mark speaks quietly because he knows what she is about to say, and can already feel the mood beginning to break.

"Not, you know . . ." She is embarrassed and she looks away for a second before meeting his eyes again. ". . . the right time."

Mark doesn't say what he would normally say. He doesn't explode. He simply lowers his head to kiss her as his fingers move further down her body. "I know," he whispers as his tongue follows the trail his fingers have left down her stomach, and then neither of them says anything for a very long time.

"Well, that was a lovely surprise," Julia smiles and curls up in the crook of Mark's arm, lazily trailing a hand across his chest. The smile is genuine, she truly had forgotten how wonderful it had once been to make love with Mark. It had always been the glue that held them together, this extraordinary passion they had, right from the start.

The first time they went to bed together it stunned both of them. The electricity was so strong you could almost smell the sizzling in the air. They lay in bed, that first time, breathless, speechless, unable to believe their luck at finding one another, neither having ever experienced anything like that before.

Julia thought it had disappeared. Mark thought maybe he had imagined it in the first place.

He remembers now.

Perhaps that is the problem, Mark thinks, looking at himself in the bathroom mirror and feeling good, really good, for the first time in months. We don't make love anymore. We make babies. And we're failing. We need to make love more, to reestablish the closeness, the warmth, the intimacy that is so lacking.

If we can do that, then maybe we'll be okay. Maybe everything will turn out fine.

4

"Who is that?"

Julia and Mark have been milling
around outside the church, Julia finally
making her way over to the smokers, a small
band of women, as soignee as they come,
apart from the fact that they are all puffing
away furiously, determined to inhale enough
nicotine to see them through the ceremony.

The cigarettes bond these women together, and they close in a tight huddle as
they admire one another's outfits and pass
the lone lighter around, as passers-by—so
dowdy by comparison—smile at the crowd
of wedding-goers, all wanting to share in a
little bit of the hope, the possibility, and of
course, the glamour. Because this wedding is
nothing if not glamorous, each woman out-
doing the last in hat size and high heels.

Julia drops her cigarette and rubs it out with the sole of her strappy Jimmy Choos.

"Great shoes," says a tall red-headed woman standing with the smokers, the woman, in fact, in possession of the lone lighter (Mini-Bic, hot pink).

"Thanks," Julia says, smiling, and offers up a compliment in return. "I love your hat." A moment of awkwardness, and one of them is about to ask how the other knows Adam and Lorna, when Julia hears a shriek.

"Julia! Darling!" She turns round to find Lorna's mother bearing down on her. "You look wonderful!" Mrs. Young launches herself upon Julia, leaning forward attempting to air kiss, holding on to her vast hat. They both laugh as the brims of their hats clash.

"You look amazing." It is what Julia is expected to say, and of course it is true, because despite Julia not keeping up to date with Lorna about her marriage plans, one look at Sandra Young is enough for her to know that this is not Lorna's wedding—it is her mother's.

"Really?" Sandra Young does her eightieth twirl of the day and cocks an eyebrow as Julia repeats it. It is apparent to all that she loves being the center of attention, that her outfit— low-cut, intricately beaded, screaming *designer*—was chosen, consciously or not, to upstage the bride.

Sandra Young twirls round again before spotting more new arrivals. "Uncle Jimmy!" she cries, waving above the crowd, tripping off to perform yet another twirl, as the woman with the hat grins at Julia. "Now that's not a case of the mother trying to upstage the bride," she says.

"But you have to admit she does look fantastic."

"She should do, the amount that dress cost." She looks around to check no one's within earshot, then leans forward conspiratorially. "More than the wedding dress."

"No!" Julia's shocked, because, knowing Lorna, the wedding dress is going to be one-off, designer, and a fortune.

The woman nods her head. "I'm Maeve," she says, smiling. "You're Julia, aren't you?"

Julia nods. "How did you know?"

"I heard Mrs. Young, but I recognized you anyway from Lorna's old photographs."

"How do you know Lorna?" The question was inevitable, and they both smile.

"I live next door to them in Brighton."

"So does she drive you mad borrowing cups of sugar?"

"Borrowing bloody condoms, more like. She and Adam haven't got their contraception sorted out, and being the single woman on the street, I'm the one who's become their secret condom supplier."

Julia laughs, completely unfazed by this woman's honesty. Julia has always had this ability, to make people feel comfortable around her, to make them feel, within minutes, that they have known her forever, and know her well enough to disclose intimate information without a second thought.

"You're single? That surprises me."

"Why? Because someone like me ought to have a boyfriend? Because I'm attractive and successful so if I can't get a man I must be failing at something?" Her tone is trying to be light, but the words are not, and Julia apologizes.

"I just realized what I sounded like," Julia says ruefully. "Like one of my elderly relatives. I used to go to family dos and they'd ask me if I had a boyfriend, and when I said No they'd pat my knee and say things like: Don't worry, you're still young. Or, Mr. Right is out there, you'll find him, you'll see. God, I can't believe I came across like that, I'm so sorry."

"Don't worry about it. It sounds like we have the same family. And I'm sorry for jumping down your throat about it. It's just that I'm single through choice, but nobody seems able to accept that."

"So would you be happy if you were to spend the rest of your life all alone?"

Maeve shrugs and offers Julia another cigarette, which she takes, and there is silence for a while as both light up. "I try not to think too far ahead, to live my life in the present," Maeve says finally, exhaling loudly, "but quite honestly, although I don't exactly relish the idea, it doesn't panic me either. I have a great life. A job that I love, my own home, and I'm not sure I'm prepared to compromise anymore."

"I envy you." The words are out before Julia has a chance to think about what she's saying. And as soon as they are, she stops in shock. She didn't mean to say it. Christ, she didn't even mean to think it, and she falters, not knowing what to say next.

"Nah." Maeve shakes her head. "Different horses for different courses, and you know what? The grass is usually greener. I spent years thinking that maybe my life would be complete if I had a man, but when I did I wished I was single again. And you know, it can get lonely at times, but I think this just suits me better. Oh my God, is this Lorna? I thought they'd hired a white Daimler."

A long black Mercedes limousine pulls up outside the church, and everyone around them starts hurriedly stamping

47

out cigarettes and rushing inside to sit down before the gray-suited chauffeur opens the door.

Julia's about to follow Maeve into the church, but not before catching a glimpse of the dress, because even though she knows marriage probably isn't in the cards for a while, she still finds it difficult to resist the fairy tale.

The door opens, and the collective sigh of relief is audible. It's not the bride. It's a lone woman in a sharp pink suit with a mass of pink and black organza masquerading as a hat, sparkling pearl and gold earrings, and opaque black sunglasses that hide her face almost entirely, with just a slash of pinky-brown lipstick.

She steps out of the car and walks up the steps, and it is only as she passes her that Julia screams.

"*Oh* my God!"

The woman turns round, and lowers her sunglasses to see Julia properly, then grins as she opens her arms.

"Bella!" cries Julia, and flings her arms around her friend, so glamorous now, so New Yawk, that Julia would barely have recognized her. "What the hell are you doing here?"

"Surprising you?" Bella disengages herself and they hold each other at arm's length, examining one another in delight. "And don't you look gawgeous!" They both laugh.

"What the hell's with the car?"

Bella hoots with delight. "Jesus, can you believe it? I'm so used to ordering limos in New York, I didn't even think twice here, and I've spent the whole journey watching people stop in their tracks and try to guess which celeb's inside."

Julia shakes her head but she's smiling. "Only you," she laughs. "Only you."

Bella looks around the crowd, now starting to filter back out of the church again. "So where the hell is Sam?"

"So pregnant she can hardly walk," Julia laughs. "She RSVP'd yes, then decided that her bladder wouldn't be able to survive the ceremony, so I think she's just coming to the meal."

"God, what a complete nightmare. Tell me I'm never going to have children." And then, with a glance at Julia's face, she realizes what she's said.

"I'm sorry, I'm sorry, I'm sorry. You know how I feel about children. But not the children of my friends, so how's it going?"

Julia sighs. Of course she doesn't mind her asking, she'd probably be more offended if she hadn't asked, Bella being one of her familiars, but she wishes she hadn't told quite so many people when they first decided to try for a baby.

Mark kept warning her. Just in case it doesn't happen, he said. Don't tell anyone, he said, but of course she had to tell Sam. And Bella. And Lorna. And all the girls at work. Soon everyone knew, and every time she saw people they'd say: Any luck? With eyebrows raised and hopeful expressions. To be honest she was becoming really rather tired of shaking her head. She wished she'd listened to Mark because every time someone asked, it only served to drive the point home and she felt more of a failure than ever.

But this is Bella, and so she will talk, rather than just smile sadly and shake her head.

"It's a bugger," Julia says. "It's just not happening. Every month I think this might be it, every month my period arrives like bloody clockwork."

"Have you thought about seeing someone?"

"Well, interestingly, I was reading a magazine article last week about a woman who couldn't get pregnant until she went to see a healer. She had one session with this woman and bam. She fell pregnant immediately. I've saved this healer's number and I think I'm going to call her."

"Actually I didn't mean that. I meant a doctor. Fertility expert. Someone who could actually tell you whether there's a problem."

"No. Not yet. And anyway, I don't think Mark could handle it if he found out he was, well, you know . . ."

"Firing blanks?"

"Exactly. Imagine how horrific that must be for a man. God knows the last thing I need is for him to be completely emasculated. But more to the point it hasn't been that long. I don't think either of us is ready for that step yet."

"So you think the problem lies with Mark, then?"

"Put it like this," Julia says. "I've been pregnant, remember?"

"But that was years ago. God, anything could have happened since then. And let's face it, the well-woman clinic isn't exactly a place you visit regularly. When was your last smear, anyway?"

"Don't want to talk about it."

"Okay, okay, sorry. But I know you, and you really should go more often. Plus, if you really think that, that's terrible. You're obviously blaming Mark and you don't have any reason to."

Julia can feel the tears fighting their way up to the corners of her eyes, but she will not cry here. She refuses to cry here.

"Bella, we're at a wedding. I haven't seen you for months and I just can't get into this right now, it's not the time or the place. Tell me about you." She forces a smile and squeezes Bella's hand. "How did you manage to keep this secret and how in the hell do you manage to look so damn gorgeous?"

Lorna always said that she'd be walking down the aisle wearing a grin the size of Brighton Pier, but in the event she looks fantastically demure and truly more beautiful than she has ever appeared in her life.

She tries to stare straight ahead, but she can't quite manage it, and her eyes open wide with delight when she spies Julia and Bella, oohing and aahing at the end of the pew now that they can see her properly.

"Christ." Bella dabs the corners of her eyes. "If I wasn't me, I'd be desperate to get married just to look like that."

"You could always buy a dress just for the hell of it. Save it for a rainy day. And what do you mean, if you weren't you, you'd be desperate? Don't tell me you're antimarriage now as well."

"No, but the married man's been lurking again. Phone calls. Flowers."

"Bella, don't!" Said firmly, and in slightly too loud a whisper. Julia smooths her hair behind her ears and gives an apologetic smile to the middle-aged woman in front who turns round to glare at her menacingly. "Later," she mouths to Bella, and they all shuffle up to sing "Jerusalem."

"What about you?" Bella whispers when the hymn is finished, ignoring the half-turned head of the woman in front.

"Any closer to marriage with the delectable Mark, or is that a no-go area too?"

"Happy as we are." Julia leans in so that Mark, on her other side, doesn't hear. "You know us. Happy as we are."

Mark is slowly starting to relax, copious amounts of wine helping considerably, added to the fact that he is sitting next to Bella, whom he has always found rather scary, but rather attractive at the same time.

Bella is not stupid. She can see that Julia and Mark are not happy, and, although her allegiances are undoubtedly with Julia, will always be with Julia, she sees no reason why Mark shouldn't have some attention paid to him as well.

She has quizzed him about work, showing genuine interest and asking clever, pointed questions, and she has amused him with some anecdotes about the navigation of office politics in America, all the while ensuring his glass is topped up.

Julia is delighted that someone other than she is watching out for Mark, making sure he is okay, and more delighted to be sitting next to Jason, an extremely attractive friend of Adam's who split up with his most recent girlfriend six months ago, is playing the field, and is still under the mistaken impression that weddings are a good hunting ground (these people are in their thirties and really ought to know better).

"I'm Jason," he says, shaking her hand as he sits down next to her. "And I'm on my own today so I'm afraid you might have to look after me."

"I'm Julia." Her eyes light up. For a second she considers introducing Mark, but he's deeply engrossed in conversation with Bella, and anyway, why should she have to explain Mark? They'd never been a MarkandJulia type of couple anyway. "I'm an old friend of Lorna," she continues, angling her body slightly so it faces Jason, and is away from Mark. "What about you? How do you know them?"

They sit and talk for a while, the usual small talk, and Julia can't help but notice that every time he shifts in his seat, be it to place a hand on the table, or uncross his arms, or cross his legs, she echoes it. She must have done it for a while unconsciously, but when Jason rests his chin in his hand, with a start Julia realizes she has just done the same thing. She quickly removes her chin from her hand, and makes a conscious note not to keep copying him. She has read *The Naked Ape*, she knows what echoing body language means.

Suddenly Jason stops, in the middle of an anecdote. "Oh, long and boring story," he says, "and I can't possibly start off making small talk with you, you're far too attractive." Julia feels a blush rise, a thrill that she hasn't felt for years. "Tell me instead . . ." He leans forward conspiratorially, and Julia can't help it, her body moves forward too, until his face is merely inches from hers. He speaks intensely. Carefully. Looks deep into her eyes. "Do you . . ." — he pauses — "or do you not" — pauses again — "think the Clangers should be brought back?"

Such an intimate gesture teamed with such a childlike question, but Jason knows that small talk gets you precisely nowhere, and that nostalgia is a far better emotion with which to pave the way to a woman's heart.

Julia starts laughing. Relieved. A touch disappointed.

"I think they very definitely should be brought back," she laughs.

"And do you or do you not think the Soup-Dragon ought to be seen far more often?"

"Oh my God," Julia's eyes widen in delight. "I haven't thought about the Soup-Dragon for years."

"But I bet you haven't forgotten her conversational prowess."

Julia relaxes back in her chair, thinks for a few seconds, then leans forward again with a few Soup-Dragonish noises.

"Nope," Jason shakes his head. "That doesn't sound like the Soup-Dragon at all."

"Go on, then, you do it."

"Can't. I can, however, do a rather good impression of a Clanger." And with that he says in a singsong voice, "Du du? Du du du du du du. Du. Du du."

"That's rubbish!" Julia starts laughing. "They whistled. Like this." And she purses her lips together and whistles a conversation as the rest of the table stop talking and look at them.

"Clangers!" shouts Maeve, who has been sitting reasonably quietly on the other side of Jason. Evidently the plan was for Maeve and Jason to get together, but Jason's never been one for redheads, and thus far he's left it to Charles, one half of Charles and Claudia, to keep Maeve amused. "See?" Julia turns to Jason triumphantly. "Told you it was a whistle."

"But it wasn't quite a whistle," says Maeve.

"See?" Jason's turn to be triumphant. "Told you it was my du du." He du du's a bit more for the benefit of the table, all of whom agree that it definitely wasn't a du du, was more like a whistle.

"Okay, okay," Bella interrupts with a hand up in the air just as the main course is being placed in front of her. "What about *Hector's House*? That was always my favorite."

"Hector's House!" the whole table chorus in delight, all being roughly the same age, all having grown up with the same television programs.

"What was *Hector's House* about, though?" asks Jason, as everyone starts laughing, convinced that they loved it, despite no one fully remembering it.

"Mr. Benn!" Julia shouts, aware now that this has become a nostalgia free-for-all.

"Now there was someone who really should have come out of the closet years ago." Jason raises his glass in a silent toast to Mr. Benn.

Everyone has something to offer. *Crystal Tipps and Alistair; Mary, Mungo and Midge;* and then the pièce de résistance: *Pipkins.*

"Oh God," groans Julia. "I loved Pipkins. Remember what a snob Octavia was?"

"And what about Hartley Hare?" Nobody has noticed Sam and Chris making their way round the table to their seats, and everyone starts laughing. Hartley Hare. Who has even thought about Hartley Hare for years?

Bella stands up to give Sam a hug, although it's not easy with the ever-growing baby.

"Twins?" Bella cannot resist, and Sam hits her.

"Oh fuck off," she laughs, because she knows that Bella knows how fed up she is with being told she must be carrying an entire rugby team.

"You look exhausted, Chris," Julia says, turning to Sam's husband, who reaches over to kiss her on the cheek, then raises his eyebrows.

"Not bloody surprising, given that Sam is either lumbering out of bed to go to the bloody loo about thirty times a night, and not even trying to keep the noise down in the bathroom, or tossing and turning and making the whole bloody house rock."

He looks terrible. Exhausted, but as he says this he gives Sam's shoulder an affectionate squeeze all the same.

"Why should I be the only one to suffer?" Sam huffs, sitting as close to the table as she can while pulling a giant-sized bottle of Gaviscon out of her bag, thumping it on the table next to her wineglass.

"What the hell is that?" Bella points at the green bottle with a look of horror on her face as Sam undoes the cap and takes a giant swig straight from the bottle.

"Heartburn," Sam explains, sighing with obvious relief as it hits the spot. "Everyone says that if you have terrible heartburn—which I have—then you're having a very hairy baby."

"Is that true?" Mark is fascinated.

"Apparently so, but it wouldn't surprise me. Like mother like daughter." She catches Chris's eye. "Or son, but all I can tell you is at this rate I really am going to be giving birth to a monkey."

Sam and Bella are soon catching up on all their news, and Julia is only slightly pissed off that she is not sitting with them, but then she is sitting next to Jason, who is proving to be the perfect wedding companion, and she is having such a lovely time, feeling so sexy, and flirtatious, and alive, that for a few moments she genuinely wishes she were single.

But she isn't. She is living with Mark, trying for a baby, and this thought sobers her up for a few seconds. Jason sees her pull back and tries a new tack, and soon Julia is laughing again as they try to recall the words to one-hit-wonders from their youth.

"Whatsa matter you, hey," Julia sings. "Why you looka so sad. Whaddya think you do, hey, itsa nicea place, da da da da da, ah shuddupa ya face."

"What exactly does da da da da da mean?" Jason is smiling.

"Probably the same as"—Julia affects his Clanger voice—"du du du du du," and they both laugh. If you didn't know better, you would think they were the perfect couple.

Mark sits back in his chair and watches Julia. He knows she is flirting, but he doesn't mind. He likes to see her have fun—he trusts her—and he likes to watch her like this: animated, sparkling, alive. The Julia he first met four years ago. With a stab of pain he wonders why he can't make her feel like this anymore.

As soon as the meal ends, the bride and groom take to the floor for their dance. "It Had to Be You" comes on, and the men at the table groan at the cheesiness of it, while the women smile even as their eyes well up at this first flush of love and the romanticism of it all.

And then it's back to the seventies for Adam and Lorna, and Mark stands up and pulls Julia to the floor during the Jackson Five's "ABC"; they continue throughout Patti LaBelle's "Lady Marmalade," on through "White Lines" by Grandmaster Flash, finishing with "Night Fever" by the Bee Gees, by which point they're so exhausted they need a water break.

Jason has moved on by the time they get back to the table. He has realized that Julia is with Mark, and is currently busy prowling the other tables, looking for suitable prey. Julia and Mark sit back down and smile at one another.

"I'm having a good time," Julia says, managing to keep the surprise out of her voice.

"I know." Mark touches the end of her nose, an affectionate gesture he hasn't made for many, many months. "So am I."

It is near the end of the evening, and only the hard core remain. Lorna has spent almost the entire time glued to her seat at Top Table, clearly terrified that the moment she leaves her throne she will stop being queen for the day, but now she is able to let her hair down, and she and Adam are intertwined on the dance floor, both gazing into one another's eyes as they sway gently, softly talking and kissing, laughing at the fact they are now man and wife.

Most of the elderly relatives have gone, and a few people stop, on the way out, to turn and watch Adam and Lorna, remembering their own wedding days, thinking how very long ago it all feels now.

As the people file out, the room starts to look frayed round the edges. Several flower arrangements have already disappeared, guests managing somehow to whisk them home unseen, and crisp white damask tablecloths are now shown up as grubby and slightly gray.

Chris and Sam went home hours ago. Sam ran out of Gaviscon, and after three pints of milk and a vanilla yogurt that one of the waiters was kind enough to run out and buy for her, she realized that this was one fight she was not going to win. They left, Sam easing herself up from the chair with trouble, one hand supporting the small of her back as she groaned with effort.

Julia watched her with love. And envy. Bella, now sitting next to her, looks at Julia's face and takes her hand.

"It must be tough for you," she says.

"You can't even imagine." Julia forces a smile, followed by a sigh. "I would give anything, anything, to be in Sam's place right now. I love her, and I'm thrilled for her, but I can't even think that there is a living breathing baby inside her. I can't believe that I haven't got one too." Tears fill her eyes as she finishes this, and a huge sob, fueled by champagne, hangs in the air as Julia runs out of the room, engulfed by disappointment and loss.

Mark stands up to follow her, but the look on his face is one of weariness, and Bella shakes her head and says that she will go; that it's okay; that Julia will be fine. Mark sits back down, grateful for not having to deal with this display of emotion, for not having to deal with the blame, because of course he knows that Julia blames him.

All Mark wants is to be happy. If Julia wants to have a baby, if it will make her happy, Mark wants it too. If Julia wants to see a fertility expert, Mark wants it too. If Julia wants to not have children for the rest of their lives, that will also be fine.

The problem is that Mark has never sat down and thought about what he wants. Perhaps it's time he did.

5

Work hasn't been going too well for Julia recently. She spends more and more time lost in a daydream; her researchers have to fight to get her attention, force her to make a decision.

On Monday her phone rings on her desk, disturbing her latest reverie.

"Julia? Mike here." Mike Jones. Director of Programming. Her mentor.

"Hi, Mike. Everything okay?"

"Julia, I'd like you to come and see me. Have you got a moment now?" In the old days this would have set her pulse racing: Perhaps she was being given an exciting new project. In the very old days, when she was young and inexperienced, and not part of the furniture here, her pulse would have been racing for fear of being sacked.

Today her pulse doesn't even bother to speed up.

She stands up wearily and scrapes her hair back as Johnny, her protégé and right-hand man, looks at her sadly, wondering what happened to the bright, vibrant woman who had employed him and steered him from runner to producer. They used to laugh all the time, she and Johnny, but she is too distracted these days to even crack a smile. He knows about the baby stuff. God, who doesn't. But he doesn't understand why she's letting it get to her so much.

Sometimes he thinks he should tell her about the rumors. Tell her that people are muttering that she's lost it, that it won't be long before she's given the boot, but then again, these are only rumors, and if they're not true he's one messenger who doesn't want to get shot.

That's another thing. She never used to have a temper. Her team used to adore her, they'd go out regularly after work and drink themselves stupid, and Julia was always up for the crack. Now she's far more likely to shout, or belittle, or patronize. The worst thing is that most of the time he can see she has absolutely no clue she's doing it.

Her friends at work have turned against her, and Johnny's only sticking by her because of a shared history, and because he's praying that this is temporary, that one day soon she'll be the old Julia again.

"Off somewhere?" he says, as she starts slowly walking out, a far cry from the dynamo of old, so busy she didn't walk anywhere, she whirled.

"Oh." She turns, blinking her eyes to bring her back to reality. "Just up to see Mike. Shouldn't be long. He probably wants to give me a bollocking about all those complaints." Her last show, *Summer Fling,* sent singles off to the Mediterranean in search of love, but most of the time they ended up with booze and sex, and more than a smattering of bad language. Although the ratings were great, the complaints had gone through the roof.

"I hope you're right," Johnny says, almost under his breath as he turns back to his computer screen.

Julia turns at the door. "What?"

"Oh, nothing. Nothing."

The lift doors open, Julia steps in, deep in thought, and as the door closes she looks up.

"Shit. I thought this was going up," she mutters.

"Julia?"

She struggles for a few seconds to remember the face, then the name, because it is not a face she associates with work. "Oh, hi," she says, placing her. "What are you doing here? It's Maeve, isn't it?"

Maeve nods. "You're never going to believe this, but I've just had a job interview. I was going to call you, actually, when I heard, but then I got so busy preparing for this I never had a chance."

"What a small world. I didn't even know you were in this game. And aren't you living in Brighton?"

Maeve shrugs and smiles as if to say there is a lot Julia doesn't know. "That's the only thing I can't get my head round. London rents. If I get this, I'll have to move back, and the rents have gone crazy since I last lived here."

For a second Julia contemplates inviting her to move in

with them. God knows they have enough space, but she hardly knows this girl, and Mark would go crazy. "You could try the noticeboard," she volunteers eventually, and breathes a sigh of relief as the lift doors open and they are on the ground floor.

"If you get the job and you need anything just call," Julia manages, just before the lift doors close. "Nice to see you again. Good luck."

"Thanks." Maeve smiles a warm smile. "And to you too."

As soon as the doors close, Julia turns and looks at herself in the mirrored wall of the lift. Christ, she looks awful. Her hair's greasy, her eyes are bloodshot, and she could pretty much carry the weekly shopping home in the bags under her eyes. At the beginning of the sleepless nights she tried to disguise it with cleverly applied makeup, but she rarely even does that these days. She sighs as the lift opens out on to the twelfth floor, and walks into Mike's office.

"You look fucking awful." Mike's first words, allowable only because they are friends. And because it is true. "What the fuck is going on?"

Julia smiles. "Lovely to see you too, Mike. And how are you?"

"I'm serious, Julia, you look like shit." Mike shakes his head and sighs, sadness and sympathy combined in his eyes.

Mike Jones is not the sort of man you would expect to work for a major television company, even less to see behind a large beech desk in an executive office, on the executive floor.

He's dressed as he always is (unless of course there's a big meeting with the ITC and Mike has to explain away explicit language or programming, in which case he wears the one suit he has in his wardrobe; the suit's Hugo Boss, except he wears it with Hush Puppies, which kind of destroys the effect), in jeans and T-shirt. Mike would describe himself as a geezer. Others, who didn't know him, might describe him as a thug. Short, crop-haired, stockily built—Julia always used to tease him by saying she was surprised she hadn't spotted him in the latest football violence videos.

His "genuine Larndan accent," penchant for football shirts, and liking for more than a few pints with the boys belie a brilliant creative genius. He is a man who is loved by everyone who's ever worked with him, hated and feared by other television companies.

He didn't go to university ("university of life, mate, university of life. Rest of that stuff's for fuckin' ponces, innit?"), started off at London Daytime as a post boy, and the rest, as they say, is history.

Mike Jones is famous for his mind, his constant use of expletives and his—somewhat inexplicable until you get to know him—ability to pull women. Six years ago, at a Christmas party when Julia was very drunk and still found his power something of an aphrodisiac, they went to bed together. It was never discussed again, but Mike has always had something of a soft spot for her, and he is the only one who is actually willing to talk to her about what is going on.

"So come on, what's it all about? You look like shit, your work's going down the pan, I've got researchers in here every other day complaining about you throwing a tantrum, and I'm wondering why the fuck I still employ you. Would you like to enlighten me?"

Julia has turned as white as a sheet. "Are you serious?" she whispers. "Do my researchers really come in here and complain about me?"

"Never mind about them. I want to know about you. I know you're trying for a baby and I know you're having problems." Julia blanches, but Mike carries on regardless. "I feel for you, I really do, and I can't even begin to imagine the shit you must be going through, but you have to find a way of leaving it behind you when you come to work."

"I thought I had." Julia is on the brink of tears, and Mike's voice softens.

"Look, we think you need some time off."

Her head jerks up. "What?"

"Yeah. Take a few months to get your shit together. Go to a doctor. Go to a health farm. Go on holiday. Fuck, I don't know. Just do whatever you need to do to get back to the old Julia again, and maybe you'll have that bun in the oven by the time you get back."

Julia sits there, stunned. She wants to cry, to shout, to scream, but she knows Mike, and knows it won't do any good. And finally she realizes that he's right. She's exhausted and she feels as bad as she looks.

And suddenly the prospect of a few months off starts to sound really rather nice.

Eventually she looks up at him. "Okay. I think I probably need the time. But what about my new series? What are you going to do about finding someone for *Loved Up*?"

"Just found someone," Mike says triumphantly. "Used to hear about her when she worked at Anglia, but I wouldn't think you'd know her. Lovely girl. Irish. Redhead," and he winks at Julia, who is already aware of his fondness for Gillian Anderson.

"It's Maeve, isn't it?" she sighs.

"I don't fucking believe it," Mike barks. "You know fucking everyone! Maeve's coming in on short notice, and she knows about you, and she's happy to take over. Your team met her briefly—"

"She met the team? Jesus, Mike, I'm not even out the door and you've been sneaking around behind my back. I suppose all my team loved her? I suppose they thought she wouldn't be the type to throw tantrums." This last word is spat out, the smell of betrayal suddenly in the air.

"Julia, relax. No one's done any sneaking. She came in for the first time a couple of weeks ago for another show, and I called her back today because I had *Loved Up* in mind. There was nothing to tell you, and your team hasn't really met her properly. Although Stella met her while you and Johnny were off doing that recce in Swindon."

"No one told me," she says miserably. "They all hate me, don't they?"

"No one told you because no one knew who she was. They probably all thought she was my latest shag."

Julia manages a smile.

"There you go." Mike smiles too. "And no, for your information your researchers don't hate you."

"Thanks, Mike. I feel better now."

"They're fucking terrified of you."

"You wanker." And Julia starts to laugh.

They talk a bit longer, then Mike walks her to the lift, the subject now his beer session of the night before. They stand, listening to the rumble of the lift as it approaches, and Mike turns to face Julia again. "Listen," he says, giving her an awkward kiss on the cheek. "If there's ever anything you need, anything at all, you just call me, okay?"

"Okay," she says, giving him a grateful smile. "Okay."

There's no point in sitting around the office all day. Not now. Not when she's supposed to be working on her new series. Maeve's new series. She doesn't even have the energy to say good-bye properly. She tries to phone Mark when she gets back, not to explain, not on the phone from this open-plan office, but to see whether he'll meet her in the bar so she can tell him, but he's not around. She doesn't bother to leave a message on voicemail. She'll tell him later.

At lunchtime, when everyone's out, Julia goes through her drawers, selecting the few odd things she wants to take home. A quick raid on the stationery cupboard and she's ready.

"Is everything okay?"

Bugger. Johnny's come back into the office just as she's leaving. He looks at her, standing there holding a large cardboard box, incomprehension written all over his face.

Julia stops in her tracks. "I need a break," she says slowly. "I just had a long chat with Mike. We've agreed that I'm going to take a sabbatical."

Johnny doesn't know what to say.

"It's okay, Johnny. I know what everyone's been saying, and I know I've been a bit of a bitch recently, but I do need to, as Mike put it, get my shit together."

Johnny's face is crestfallen as Julia carefully puts the box on the corner of a nearby desk, then comes back to put her arms around him and give him a hug.

"You'll be fine without me," she says into his ear. "Plus you've got a gorgeous redhead taking my place," and when she pulls back she is slightly pissed off to see that Johnny looks the tiniest bit excited at this prospect. His allegiances clearly aren't that strong after all.

The door slams and Julia hears Mark swearing in the hallway. He hates the door slamming behind him, is terrified the wood or doorframe will get damaged, but has no choice when he brings work home and has to negotiate the door with arms full of files.

"Julia?" he shouts from the bottom of the stairs. She walks slowly down to him, toweling her hair dry, stopping a few steps from the bottom as Mark puts his files down, straightening up to look at her.

"Is it true?"

Julia nods.

"Are you okay?"

"I think so. I suppose everyone's already gossiping about it?"

Mark makes a face. "If I believed everything I heard, I'd have come home expecting you to be carried off in a straitjacket by the men in white."

"You are joking." She's horrified.

"Only just. People do seem to think you're in the middle of a nervous breakdown."

"Fuck it, Mark. Why do you have to say things like that? Jesus, you're so bloody insensitive at times."

"Julia, you asked me, for Christ's sake. Why are you having a go at me? God, can't we just have a civilized evening for a change and actually talk about this? All I know is what I've heard in the office and I've been trying to get you all afternoon. Johnny said you left at lunchtime and your bloody mobile's been switched off all day."

Julia is silent. Resentful. She doesn't blame him for anything.

She blames him for everything.

She left the office at lunchtime, took a cab straight home, and then was stuck. Alone, in this huge house that she hates, she wandered from room to room, trying to work out how she felt. Was she relieved? Happy? Angry? Disappointed?

Empty. That was how she felt. That was all she felt. All the time.

Switching on the TV, just to have some background noise, she found herself watching a daytime show about problem children. Hyperactive, disobedient, unruly children, none older than seven, and she wanted to hit the despairing parents. How dare you complain, she thought in fury. How dare you say anything against your children when you are so privileged to even have them in the first place.

She switched off the TV in disgust, grabbed her coat, and stepped outside, bracing herself against the cold January air. Julia hasn't been for a walk for ages. She used to walk a lot, when she was single, and had time.

She walked up to the Heath, running up the concrete steps before she hit the wide open spaces, the children's paddling pool now empty for winter, the running track with a few lone runners. It was good to be outside in the fresh air. Good that her nose was turning red with cold, that she had to bundle her hands down deep in her coat to try and keep them warm.

There was so much to think about, so many thoughts to process, that it was actually easier to think of nothing at all. She walked, and walked, and walked.

A few lone dog walkers had also braved the freezing weather. She did a full circle, then sat down outside a cafe for a while, warming her hands around a mug of steaming coffee, occasionally exchanging the odd word or two about the weather with a passing dog walker.

Just as she was about to leave, a woman turned up with two children. One of them a girl, about three years old, the other a little boy, not more than eighteen months, toddling around the table. The little girl was beautiful. Dark hair, big brown eyes, eyelashes that could have picked you up and carried you away. She was tiny, so tiny and doll-like, with the sweetest smile. Julia couldn't tear her eyes away.

"No, Katie," the mother reprimanded, as Katie crouched down to pick up someone's half-eaten Crunchie. "You mustn't eat that. It's rubbish," and she picked it up gingerly and took it over to the dustbin while the little girl's face was crestfallen. "Here you are, lovely," the mother soothed, reaching into her bag. "Here's your favorite. Yum yum yum. Organic rice cake."

Julia watched them, a smile on her face, which the harassed mother returned, assuming the smile was for her. The little girl took a bite of the rice cake, promptly dropping it on the floor when she saw Julia watching her. She pranced off, turning round so her back was to Julia, then looked over her shoulder coyly, giving Julia a smile.

"Hello." Julia's heart melted as she watched her display. "That's a lovely dress."

The little girl watched Julia, sized her up and down, evidently deciding whether to talk. "It's my party dress," she said eventually. "Can you see my rabbits?" She held up the skirt to show off her embroidered rabbits.

"They're beautiful," Julia said, wanting nothing more than to scoop up this little girl and take her home. "Do they have names?"

The little girl shook her head. "Do you have rabbits?"

"No. But I did when I was a little girl. Like you."

"What were their names?"

"I had a big white fluffy one called Flopsy, and a small brown one called Bugsy."

The little girl bit her lip as she digested this information, then she took a step closer to Julia. "Do you have a little girl like me?"

Julia almost gasped in pain as she shook her head silently.

"Why not?"

"I . . . well . . ." Julia looked up at the sky and tried to blink her tears away. "I'd love a little girl like you and maybe one day . . ."

"Katie!" the mother interrupted, coming over holding the little boy with one hand, her bag under her arm. "Leave the poor woman alone." Taking Katie by the hand, she led her away with an apologetic glance at Julia. "I'm so sorry," she said, pretending not to see the tears, "she drives everyone mad."

"No, no, it's fine . . ." But the woman, seeing Julia's tears, had moved on, and Julia was left alone to grieve for the child she hadn't conceived.

HOW can she explain this to Mark? Mark, who has managed to internalize whatever pain he has been feeling. He doesn't talk about it. Doesn't share it. Figures the best way of getting over it is getting on with it.

Julia is occasionally envious of this. More often than not she is furious about this. If Mark won't share his feelings, then neither will she, but this loss and grief and pain is becoming a burden that's almost too heavy for her to carry, and it is all she can do not to scream at him with fury, using anything as an excuse to vent her rage.

Today, the day that Julia has left her job, has been forced to leave her job, Mark is still standing there, unsure what to say, to do. He feels constantly as if he is treading on eggshells around her. One false move and his whole world will come crashing down. He does feel her pain, does have a sense of her loss, and he wants to reach out to her more than anything. He just doesn't know how to do it. He doesn't know where to start.

And he worries that it might be too late.

"Julia." He reaches out a hand, pleading. "Let's not do this. Not tonight. I want to hear about what happened, not have an argument over nothing—"

"It's not nothing," Julia snaps, but he knows he's winning, and her heart wasn't really in the snap.

"I know, I know," he soothes. "I'm sorry, I didn't mean that. Why don't you finish drying your hair and I'll pour you a glass of wine? How does that sound? And do you want a curry tonight? I could order in? Yes? Julia?"

Julia scuffs the carpet on the stair with her big toe, then shrugs. "Okay," she mutters, sounding astonishingly like a truculent sixteen-year-old. "But I don't want Chicken Korma. I want Chicken Tikka."

"Okay." Mark smiles to himself as he watches her walk back upstairs. It may only be temporary, but his peacekeeping skills have actually worked. In the kitchen he uncorks the wine, pours himself a glass and drinks it down immediately, quickly refilling it in case Julia walks in.

Grabbing the bottle and an extra glass, he takes it through to the living room to build a fire. Not that you're supposed to have log fires in Hampstead, only gas imitations, but everyone Mark knows has a real one. It's not uncommon to bump into the occasional local mate on forays to the Heath late at night in search of logs.

The second glass of wine is gone in seconds. He's not a big drinker, but God knows he needs something to help him through at the moment, something to ease the pain.

If I were a religious man, he thinks, setting the glass down on the table and picking up the phone to place the order, I'd start praying to God right about now.

6

"Oh God, I think I might seriously love him."

"What on earth are you talking about?" Bella's looking at Sam aghast, mostly because Sam looks incredible. Yes, she's six months pregnant. Yes, she's the size of a small whale. But she looks stunning. Sam is—usually—the laziest of all of them when it comes to superficial appearance. The most makeup she'll wear is tinted moisturizer, mascara, and pale-pink lipgloss.

But today Sam wears nearly as much makeup as Bella. Her skin is smooth and slightly tanned, her lips a full glossy pout, and her hair has been blow-dried straight so it bounces gently as she moves. Gone are the dungarees and smock-type dresses she has favored since the beginning of the pregnancy ("I know they're revolting, but they're just so bloody comfortable. You're only allowed to intervene when you find me glancing lovingly at Birkenstocks"). Sam is wearing black bootleg trousers, high-heeled black boots, and a tight orange sweater. She looks amazing.

"You look amazing." Julia's mouth is open.

Sam maneuvers herself into the chair and places a hand over her heart. "I'm serious, girls. I think I'm in love with Mr. Brennan."

"The diabetes bloke?" The midwife had been concerned about the amount of weight Sam had put on, and one of the causes, she explained, could have been gestational diabetes. Sam had now done the glucose tolerance test, and she's fine, but just to be on the safe side she is now seeing the consultant at her checkups. Mr. Brennan.

Mr. Brennan, according to Sam, is not her usual type. He's not very tall, he doesn't have very much hair ("But at least," she justified, "he doesn't plaster it over his scalp"), he is what Sam has described as "definitely cuddly," and has a bedside manner that could charm your socks off.

Sam has taken to waxing her legs and wearing good underwear before every checkup. Evidently that is no longer enough.

"I seriously, seriously have a huge crush on him," she confides, before blushing like a schoolgirl.

"Darling, that's natural," Bella says breezily, beckoning over a waiter for another bottle of sparkling water and a large glass of milk for Sam. "All my friends in New York have huge crushes on their OB/GYNs. Don't worry, you'll get over it."

Sam sits forward urgently. "I think this might be different."

Julia laughs. "Are you trying to say that Chris was a terrible mistake and Mr. Brennan could be The One?"

Sam looks uncomfortable.

"Oh please!" Julia starts to laugh. "You're not seriously trying to say that, are you?"

Sam squirms, then grudgingly admits that last night, the night before her appointment this morning, she had an erotic dream starring Mr. Brennan; that her crush is now major league and she could barely look him in the eye when she turned up there today.

"Details, details." Bella is transfixed. "What kind of erotic dream? What happened?"

"I don't remember how I got there, but I was abroad and I think I started off with Chris and we were in bed together, and suddenly Chris turned into Mr. Brennan and it wasn't so much the sex, but he was so tender and he kept cuddling me and . . . well. That's it, really."

"That's it?" Bella's disappointed.

"No sex?" Julia chimes in, although frankly she too would be more inclined to go for the tenderness at this precise moment in time.

"It was sexual, intimate, without there actually being proper sex, okay? But when I walked into the room today it all came flooding back and I could barely look at him."

"Did he notice?"

"I don't think so."

"And did you have to get your knickers off, then?"

"Bella!" Sam shouts.

"Bella!" shouts Julia.

"Well, did you?"

Sam sits back, fanning an imaginary flush. "Thank God not today. I swear, that really would have been embarrassing.

Having an orgasm during a routine internal examination with your gynecologist. Jesus Christ. Can you imagine?" They all laugh and then Sam's face turns serious. "And the other thing is he told me I looked really nice."

"No!" Julia's turn to be mock-shocked. "Was he flirting with you?"

"No. Definitely not. I wish." She shakes her head, then pauses as she stops to think. "Actually"—she starts to smile, twirling a lock of her hair girlishly as her gaze fixes on to the middle distance—"maybe. Do you think? Could he have been? Oh Christ. I feel like such a teenager. He said that I'd done something different and I just kind of stammered that I'd had my hair done for a party the day before and that really the party hadn't been worth it anyway, which of course was way too much information, but I couldn't stop babbling and I'm sure he knew, and he said it looked nice and now I've spent the last hour analyzing his tone of voice and how he said it and how he looked at me, and whether it means I'm special."

"You're off your trolley," Bella says, not unkindly.

"I know, I know," Sam sighs. "Let's change the subject. But can I just ask one more thing?" She looks both of them in the eye. "Seriously. Do you think he fancies me?"

When Bella was living in London the three of them would regularly meet up for suppers at one another's houses, usually Julia's, as her kitchen was always the most conducive to a girls' night in, plus Julia was the only one who could actually cook at that time, Sam having not yet discovered her culinary skills, and Bella eating primarily in expensive restaurants.

Sam would ring up from her mobile en route, asking, "Anything you need?" and would invariably have to make a stop at Sainsbury's for a packet of pita bread, a tub of Häagen-Dazs, and a couple of packs of Marlboro Lights.

The obligatory bottles of wine would be cooling off in Julia's fridge, and the three of them would chatter nineteen to the dozen as they chopped salads, mixed marinades, poured dips and crisps into bowls.

Food would be eaten around the kitchen table, and depending on their mood they would either sit there into the small hours, talking about their lives, their pasts, their men, their hopes, or gravitate into the living room, sometimes to watch television, sometimes to read the magazines Julia kept in a pile next to the fireplace. Such was the nature of their friendship: easy, natural. As close as family but without the politics.

Now that their lives have moved on, perhaps the one to miss those days most is Julia. Sam is blissfully happy with Chris, and expecting her first child.

Bella has entered another world in New York. She has a new circle of girlfriends who don't go to one another's houses, as they all live in apartments the size of shoeboxes. None of them has seen their kitchen in over a year, they meet up at restaurants and bars, and sit and chew the (metaphorical) fat over Cobb Salads with no cheese, no dressing, and toasted bagels, no butter. Oh, and a serving of cream cheese on the side. Nonfat. Just a schmear. Thanks.

But Julia? Julia tried to blend her life with Mark's, and when it didn't work she let go of her life. Her old life. The friends he hadn't approved of she barely saw anymore, and she hadn't made new ones as—she told herself—she was too busy with him, even though she hardly went out these days.

She told herself she was ready for commitment. For Mark. And a baby. For nine months all her energies had gone into that, and it's only now that the three girls are together again, albeit in a restaurant, that Julia realizes how much she's missed this. Her gang. Her sisters. Her soulmates.

I miss being single. The words enter her consciousness, making her jump with shock. She tries to wash them away with a sip of water, then relaxes slightly. They are only words after all, they don't mean anything. They certainly don't mean she has to make any major life changes.

But it is definitely something to think about, how easily those words slipped into her head, how real they feel, and she knows in an instant it is not the men she misses, or the adventures and excitement of being single, but the freedom.

Trapped, she suddenly realizes. I am trapped in a relationship with a man I like very much, but I would rather be on my own.

Oh God. Did she really just think that?

She shakes her head to dislodge the thought, replacing it instantly with a picture of a cooing, fat little baby. That's better, she tells herself, her pulse still racing from the shock of admitting something she knows deep down to be true, but still won't consciously admit.

Her heart starts to slow down as she brings this picture into focus. A fat little baby lying on a sheepskin rug, gurgling with delight as she holds her toes and smiles up at Julia. I want a baby, she tells herself, adding hurriedly, and Mark. And a family. I will banish all stray thoughts of being single. This is what I'm going to concentrate on from now on.

"*Earth* to Julia, Earth to Julia. Come in, Julia."

Julia shakes her head. "God, I'm so sorry, I was just thinking about the good old days and about how much I miss this."

"Miss what?" Sam is affronted. She and Julia, after all, do still get together, still go out for the occasional lunch if Sam has a meeting near Julia's office and Julia's not snowed under with work.

"The three of us. Together. This is just so nice. It makes me feel . . ."

"What?" Sam prompts gently as Julia shrugs.

"You'll think I'm mad"—she looks at each of them in turn—"but it makes me feel whole."

"You mean you don't feel whole the rest of the time?" Bella glances at Sam as they exchange a brief look of alarm, but Julia doesn't see and Bella is doing a good job of acting nonchalant.

Julia shrugs.

"Do you think," Sam says carefully, "that maybe you're trying for a baby because that might make you feel whole? That maybe you're never going to find it outside of yourself?"

"What do you mean?"

Sam sits back in her chair, for she remembers the Julia of old. She remembers the vibrant Julia, but she also remembers the quieter moments. She remembers the times when Julia phoned her up crying with loneliness, when Julia would disappear for days at a time, isolating at home as she dwelt in self-pity and sadness.

80

Not many people saw this side of Julia. As tough and uncompromising as she could be at work, she was vulnerable and soft in equal measure. And Sam remembers, quite clearly, Julia saying then that she wanted to find her other half.

Sam always said that she believed each of us could be happy with any number of people, but Julia always disagreed. Julia felt that somewhere out there was the man who would make her whole, and even then Sam wanted to tell her she was wrong, she would only ever be disappointed if she led her life waiting for that, but there was never an occasion that warranted it.

"Remember how you used to say you wanted to find your other half?"

Julia nods.

"And remember how I never believed in it? Well, it's just that as long as you're looking to other people to make you complete, you're never going to find happiness."

"But I've been happy," Julia protests. "I was happy with Mark. I am happy with Mark."

"But it's not true happiness," Bella interjects. "I have to agree with Sam. Mark, as lovely as he is, hasn't made you feel complete, and I don't think a baby will either." She carries on, ignoring the pain in Julia's eyes, and covers Julia's hand with her own. "We love you, Julia, but God knows, if there is any possibility that this baby will be a terrible mistake, you just can't go through with it."

There's a long silence and eventually Julia starts to laugh. "What bloody baby?" she says. "At this moment in time I don't think this is something I'm ever going to have to worry about."

Sam is first to leave. As vivacious as she has been, she has got into the habit of mid-afternoon naps, and the other two endured fifteen minutes of her yawning before telling her she had to go.

Julia and Bella stay on. Bella is on holiday, and Julia may as well be. She misses being busy, being needed, but hasn't even thought about the office. Not really.

Johnny calls her from time to time to feed her office gossip, which, although nice, she could take or leave. Maeve is apparently proving to be a popular choice, and the word on the street is that Mike Jones is after her, although she is not an easy catch by all accounts.

The waiter brings yet more cappuccinos, and Bella reaches into her bag. "Listen," she says, drawing out a piece of white paper, "I can't believe that I, of all people, am going to give you this, but what the hell. I know this girl in Manhattan who was trying to get pregnant for about a year and nothing happened. Eventually, she got on the internet to find out about fertility stuff, and found this fertility ritual on some pagan site. . . ."

Julia's heart races as she whispers in amazement and with a touch of fear, "A fertility spell?"

"Kind of. I suppose. But I think you're meant to call it a ritual. The point is, she got pregnant the month after doing it, so I asked her if she could give me the spell, I mean, ritual, and I brought it with me and I wasn't sure whether to give it to you or, hell, whether it's even going to work because as far as I'm concerned it might just as well have been a lucky coincidence. . . ."

"Bella, I love you!" Julia shrieks, grabbing the piece of

paper and flinging her arms around her friend. "I think you may have just changed my life."

They read the ritual together. All the "ingredients" seem accessible. Julia, naturally, wants to do it immediately. Bella had planned on a spot of shopping in the West End, but she too is curious to see this in action, so agrees to be there for moral support.

"You're sure it won't stop the spell, though? I mean, ritual? Me being there?"

"Not if your intentions are the same as mine," says Julia, a huge smile stretching from ear to ear, possibly the first genuine smile to have been seen on her face in months.

"I can do without a baby, thank you very much," Bella says in horror as Julia laughs.

"Silly. As long as you visualize me with a baby and take it seriously, then we'll be fine. Do you think it will still work even though it's not a full moon?"

"Why does it have to be a full moon?"

"Look, it says here 'This ritual is preferably done on a full moon.' "

"If I said no, would you wait until the next full moon?"

"No."

"Well, then. Why did you bother to ask?" And she nudges Julia, who raises her eyebrows but still can't wipe the smile off her face.

They travel home via Covent Garden. Not the most direct route, admittedly, but it is the only place they can think of to

obtain all the ingredients. They find exactly what they're looking for. It's the first time Julia thanks God for all the New Age
shops that she has always deemed so useless. They are not, it
has to be said, usually her style, these sorts of places, and the
smell of incense makes her feel sick, but she is clutching her
shopping list tightly in her hand, and she's unlikely to find any
of the ingredients at Sainsbury's.

Supplies:

> *Two white candles (one for God, one for Goddess. Or,*
> *candles to fit whatever divine forces suit you best)*
> *One purple candle (for meditation)*
> *One green candle (for fertility)*
> *One small drawstring pouch (homemade or store-*
> *bought)*
> *Herbs (poppy, sage, and echinacea root for spell*
> *strengthening, but use anything associated with*
> *fertility)*
> *Pestle and mortar*
> *One rose quartz crystal*
> *One malachite crystal*

This ritual is preferably done on a full moon.

"Begin by setting up ritual space with candles, herbs, pestle
and mortar, and other supplies listed above, then cast the
circle." Julia looks at Bella, both of them now back home,
perching on the sofas in Julia's living room. "What do you
think that means, 'casting the circle'?"

"Probably just place all the candles and herbs and stuff in a circle."

"Maybe. Or do you think it means stand in the middle of the room and draw an imaginary circle around yourself?"

"Dunno. But you could always do both just to be on the safe side."

Both women pick up the coffee table and move it to one side, then solemnly place all the ingredients in a circle in the middle of the living room. They stand back to back in the circle, having changed into white clothes as Julia deemed it a symbol of purity and therefore more likely to get them in the mood, and, who knows, even have a positive influence on the spell. Sorry, ritual.

Except that Julia only has one pair of white trousers, so Bella is standing there in a white sheet draped toga-style across one shoulder.

"Shit." Julia steps out of the circle. "I have to wear a sheet too."

"What?"

"You just look more authentic and you're not even the one this spell is for. Wait here. I'm going to change." She runs upstairs and reappears in an identical sheet a few moments later.

" 'Optional: Carve tunes for fertility on to green candle now,' " Bella reads, squinting slightly as the piece of paper is outside the circle and she has to lean quite far to see it and Julia has decided that the entire room must be lit only by candlelight, so it's really not that easy to see. "What the hell is a tune for fertility?" Bella squints again. "Sorry. Rune."

"Oh," Julia laughs. "Go on, then. You do it."

"What?" Bella's face falls. "What makes you think I know what a rune for fertility is?"

Julia groans. "Can you call your friend and ask her?"

"I haven't got her number here. Look, don't worry, it says it's optional, so presumably it will work without."

Julia's not convinced. Suddenly her eyes light up. "I know, how about carving an erect penis on the candle?"

Bella starts laughing until she realizes that Julia's not joking.

"I'm serious," insists Julia. "You know that huge chalk giant with the massive hard-on?"

Bella looks at her intently. "What. Are. You. Talking. About."

"You do know. The Cerne Abbas Giant. In Dorset. It's that huge outline of a man that is supposed to be a fertility symbol. What could be more fertile than an erect penis?"

"Sperm?" Bella offers, eyebrow raised.

"Bella, given my artistic skills, if I carved sperm into this green candle the higher power would think I was drawing tadpoles and I would end up with a garden full of frogs."

"So what makes you think you'll do better drawing an erect penis?"

"Because I was fifteen once and I still remember how to do it."

The penis is carved, the candle is back in its place, and both women are once again standing back to back in the middle of the circle.

"I can't do this." Bella leaps out and crosses her arms. "I

don't want to get pregnant and what if this thing works? Why don't I stay outside the circle and tell you what to do?"

Julia concedes this point, because really, who knows what will happen, and Bella jumps out to begin the ritual.

"Light the God candle. Say 'I call to the God, Lord, Father, Giver of Life. I ask you to guard this circle and I who are within it and protect me from harm.' "

"Don't you mean 'am'?" whispers Julia.

"What?"

"Don't you mean, 'I who am . . .'? Or is it 'I who is . . .'?"

"That's what it says here. None of them sound right to me. Ssssh. Just do it.

"Now light the Goddess candle. Say, 'I call to the Goddess, Lady, Mother, Giver of Life. I ask you to guard this circle and I who are within it and protect me from harm.' "

Julia recites the words as instructed.

"Now say, 'I call to the forces of nature, Life itself. I ask you to guard this circle and I who are within it and protect me from harm.'

"Light the purple candle," Bella intones solemnly, then quickly shouts, "No! Not the green one. The purple one."

"Bugger," Julia says, almost under her breath. "I can hardly see anything. Can you light some more candles outside the circle?"

"No. Stay in the mood. Sit on the floor now and begin to meditate while saying, 'Cleanse my body, cleanse my spirit, cleanse my mind' for about ten minutes."

Twenty minutes later Julia hisses at Bella, who is now feeling thoroughly relaxed and thinking that Transcendental Meditation probably isn't such a bad idea after all.

"Sorry. Light the green candle. Place the drawstring pouch and crystals in front of the green candle. Take some of one of the herbs, grind it with the pestle and mortar while thinking fertile thoughts."

"What kind of fertile thoughts?" Julia says in a panic.

"I'm coming to that. Visualize being pregnant and holding your new child. When you're done with each herb, place it into the pouch, saying, 'A child will grow inside of me as the God did inside of the Goddess.' "

Julia is now solemn, concentrating on the grinding of marble as she crushes the herbs, thoughts of her baby, her expanding stomach, a tiny gurgling bundle of love filling her mind.

"When all the herbs are in the bag," Bella intones when she sees Julia is ready, "take the two crystals, place them in front of you and imagine a beautiful green light flowing into them, making them glow. When you feel you've done this enough, place them into the bag, again saying, 'A child will grow inside of me as the God did inside of the Goddess.'

"And finally tie the bag tightly and carry it with you at all times, and when 'baby-dancing' place it over your tummy."

Julia stops and looks at Bella in alarm. "Baby-dancing? What on earth is baby-dancing?"

"Probably sensuous dancing with your stomach sticking out. Like this." Bella adopts the most serene expression she can, and belly-dances her way round the circle, holding the sheet carefully so it neither falls down nor trips her up. "Haven't you got any music?"

Minutes later Julia is back inside the circle, losing herself to the rhythms of the Air CD that they both deemed the only vaguely spiritual one in her collection. Her head is thrown back, eyes closed, she is swaying seductively, loving this feeling of freedom, of abandonment, as Bella slinks around the outside of the circle, rotating her arms and hips.

"Ahem." Marks clears his throat and puts his briefcase down just inside the doorway. "I hope you don't mind me asking, but what the fuck is going on here?"

7

"*I don't really care,*" Mark sighs. "I think it's ridiculous, but am I angry about it? No. Do I think it will work? No. Do I think that you might actually be losing your mind?" He glances at Julia and decides to leave that last as a rhetorical question.

Julia sits on the other sofa, sheet still draped around her, the melted candles and herbs now in a pile in the corner of the room, and the coffee table back in place before Mark had the chance to lose it completely.

Bella has slunk off back to her hotel.

"You're the one who keeps saying I needed to do something about it," Julia pouts.

"Yes. I mean going to see a fertility expert. Not dance half naked because of some ridiculous thing you found on the internet."

"How do you know it's ridiculous?"

"Julia. It's ridiculous."

"But Bella knows someone who got pregnant after doing it and she'd had problems for ages."

Mark snorts in disgust.

"What else am I supposed to do?" Julia pleads. "The only reason I haven't gone to see any fertility experts is because I don't want to upset you."

"Upset me? Why the fuck would it upset me?" And slowly it dawns on him. "You really do blame me for this, don't you? You think that I'm the problem. That you would have been pregnant months ago if it weren't for me. Jesus Christ. I don't believe you. What the hell makes you think you're not equally at fault? How do you know the problem isn't yours?"

"Because I've been pregnant," Julia spits. "That's why. Because when I was twenty-two I had an abortion. That's why. So now you know. I don't need to go to any fertility fucking experts because there's nothing wrong with me."

There's a long silence until eventually Mark looks at her with tears in his eyes. "You bitch." It is almost a whisper.

"Oh God, I'm sorry." Julia realizes, too late, she has pushed it too far, and she gets up to go to him, to comfort him, misinterpreting his tears for pain at the realization that he is infertile. She reaches out her arms and he pushes her away.

"You fucking bitch," he says again. "Now I know why our relationship is so shit. Now I know why we hardly speak anymore, other than to argue. You blame me. You think you're perfect and I'm not and you hate me for it, don't you?"

"No . . . ," she falters. "I don't, I didn't want you to know, though. I thought maybe in time it would just happen."

91

"There's only one thing I do know," Mark says, picking up his coat. "You've got some bloody nerve accusing me. So you had an abortion over ten years ago. So what? You're just as likely to have the problem yourself." He puts his coat on as Julia watches him in fear.

"Where are you going?"

"Out." And he turns round and slams the front door behind him.

Oh shit. Oh shit. What has she done? Julia paces nervously around the living room. She phones Sam, desperate to talk, but the answering machine is on, and there seems to be a fault on the line of the mobile phone Bella's rented while she's here.

She pours herself a glass of wine and is astonished to see her hand is trembling. What has she done? What has she done?

Is it too late?

She didn't mean to say those things. Or maybe she did. As scared as she is that this might be it, that she might have thrown away her man, her security, her life of the past four years, she needed to say those things.

A pressure cooker. That's it. She has been a pressure cooker, slowly building up steam but suppressing it, trying not to rock the boat with the force of her anger, her resentments, and now that she has blown the lid off she is terrified. It also feels pretty good.

Good not to have to hide it anymore. Surely she can repair this? Surely Mark will come back later this evening, still hurt, pride wounded, but she will be able to kiss it all better and restore the equilibrium?

She calls Mark. Repeatedly. His mobile is switched off, and she is too edgy to do anything other than sit next to the phone pressing the redial button. Oh God. What has she done? The more time passes, the worse she feels.

The hours stretch out. Eight o'clock. Nine o'clock. Ten o'clock. At eleven she starts to feel a little easier, because where could he have gone other than the pub, and the pub will be closing, he will be home soon.

At eleven-thirty she bursts into tears, this time, finally, reaching Bella at her hotel.

"Where've you been, for Chrissakes?" she blurts out, voice thick with tears.

"Julia? Is that you? What's happened?"

"I think Mark may have left me," and vocalizing it makes it a real possibility. A possible reality. Julia bursts into tears.

"I'll come over," Bella says, but Julia stops her.

"No. No. You don't have to come over." Bella is secretly relieved, given that she is staying in the Metropolitan and is in no mood to shlep back to Gospel Oak today. Once is quite enough, thank you.

Julia tells Bella what happened after Bella left the house, embarrassed at Mark finding them draped in the sheets and baby-dancing.

"Shit," Bella says. "Where do you think he is?"

"I don't know," weeps Julia. "I wish I'd never said anything. I wish this day had never happened."

"You know what I think you need? You need a holiday."

"We're planning on going to Majorca this summer. We

were. Before he left." A fresh round of sobs and Bella waits patiently until there is a gap in the hiccups.

"I don't mean you and Mark. I mean you. Why don't you come back to New York with me? The office phoned just before and I'm needed back. Urgently. They've booked me on a flight tomorrow lunchtime. Bet you there are still seats."

"New York?" Julia's tears are drying up already. "New York?" It's an interesting proposition, and Bella can hear that she is eyeing up the bait. Even though she may not be hungry, she's certainly interested. It's enough of a start.

"You could ring now and book it, and you wouldn't have to spend any money on hotels or anything as you're more than welcome to sleep on my sofa bed, and we'd have the most fantastic time, and God knows you need a holiday and—"

"But what about Mark?"

"What about Mark? You're both unhappy, you've both said terrible things, and the best thing for you both right now is to have some space. Talk to him when he gets home, tell him you're doing this to save your relationship, then come out and have some fun. Jesus, Julia. When was the last time you had any fun?"

"I couldn't. I mean, it sounds great but I couldn't just go. There's too much to do and—"

"What do you have to do?"

Julia sighs. "Okay, it's not that I'm particularly busy, but half my stuff's in the laundry and I haven't got anything to wear and—"

"For God's sake, Julia. New York's the shopping capital of the world. It's cheap and it's easy. Just stick some underwear in a suitcase and come. Anything else you need you can get there."

"I haven't been to New York for years," Julia muses.

"Right. Then you're coming. I'm going to put the phone down now and see if I can get my office to organize your flight. I'll call you back."

Julia is too stunned to do anything, but half an hour later, when Bella calls her back, she goes into overdrive, pushing aside her worries about Mark, and starting to pack.

She's barely thinking, whirling around the huge house, sorting out dark washes from white washes, ironing sweaters, oblivious to the time, to the fact that Mark still isn't home, and, good God, what is that feeling in her stomach?

Not a baby. Not a hope of that when her period has just arrived, but is that . . . could that be . . . butterflies? As she neatly folds sweaters and tucks shoes into her suitcase, Julia is astonished to find she is grinning.

She stops only to put the kettle on and make some coffee, because while her mind is racing, her eyes are starting to close. The coffee manages to do the trick, and finally her suitcase is packed and she collapses on the sofa.

And the key turns in the lock.

Julia turns to look at the clock. It is six-fifteen in the morning. She doesn't say anything as Mark walks into the room, sits on the sofa facing her, unable to meet her eye.

He looks terrible. He looks as though he is either very very drunk, or very very hung over, and Julia assumes he is hung over. His suit is crumpled, tie crooked, and his hair all over the place.

Once upon a time Julia would have demanded to know where he had been, who he had been with, but it has been a long night, and she is too relieved to see him back to put him through an interrogation.

"Are you going?" he whispers finally, and Julia melts, for he has seen the suitcase in the hall and has clearly presumed she is leaving him.

"*No,*" she says, "not exactly. Although sort of." Mark looks up, confused. "I'm sorry for what I said earlier. I'm sorry for everything. I know we haven't been happy recently and I know I haven't been fun, and I really do appreciate how hard this has been for you, this bad luck, and not getting pregnant, and getting obsessed.

"But at this moment in time the only thing I'm absolutely sure of is that I need some space, and I imagine, given your disappearance until"—she checks her watch—"a quarter past six in the morning, you do too. I'm not leaving as in leaving you, but I've decided to go to New York with Bella for a break. I need some time on my own, to think about my life, our life together, and I need to try and, I don't know . . . God, it sounds so stupid to say I need to find myself again, but that's how I feel."

"Are you really that unhappy?" he asks, and Julia thinks for a moment about what to say. She could lie, say that really she was fine, and that it wasn't so bad, and that it was something that would just blow over, but she's fed up with lying.

"Yes," she says. "And you are too. I'm not sure anymore whether that's because of not having a baby, or because of us. Because of what's happened to the relationship, or because of me, but I do know that neither of us is ever going to find out if I just stay here and we carry on in the same old routine."

"I take it you're leaving soon?"

Julia nods.

"Why don't I make some coffee?" she says, and he stands up just as she brushes past him on her way to the kitchen, and in that split second they look at one another, and both reach out and put their arms around one another. Mark squeezes Julia, who squeezes him in return, both clinging on as if for dear life, both shocked at this intensity, both trying to suppress the knowledge that hugs like this mean only one thing.

Good-bye.

Mark insists on driving her to Heathrow, and even though she was planning on taking a cab to Bella's hotel and driving up with her, she knows that they are both fragile, and somehow being together, even after the night they have had, even though this isn't a breakup, it's just a holiday, somehow this semblance of normality is comforting.

There isn't much to say on the way to the airport, clearly not helped by the fact that the lack of sleep all night has now rendered Julia almost incoherent with exhaustion.

"I used to do this all the time," she yawns. "Why do I feel like I've been hit with a sledgehammer now?"

"That's what happens when you reach thirty-three," Mark says, who doesn't feel quite as bad, but thankfully still hasn't had to explain his absence.

"I remember going clubbing," Julia reminisces. "We wouldn't leave the house until midnight, and we wouldn't come back home until at least ten the next morning, and more often than not I wouldn't even bother going to bed that day. I used to be fine."

"And you managed to stay awake all night dancing without the help of any, er, illegal substances?"

"Ah yes." She smiles at her selective memory. "I suppose that might have helped."

Mark turns the radio on to fill the silence, as Julia stares out the window and remembers the last time she was in New York. She hasn't thought about this in years, and as the memories drift back she finds herself smiling.

She was twenty-three. God. Almost ten years. Where does it go? Working on a documentary about female private investigators mostly catching out adulterous husbands. She had never been to America before, and Mike sent her out there with another researcher called Caroline.

She'd been to W. H. Smith's weeks before, and the pages of her *Rough Guide to New York* were already bent and creased long before she even stepped off the airplane at JFK. She'd marked all the places she wanted to go, the bars she wanted to visit, the museums she was desperate to see.

It was late November. As soon as they arrived they were blinded by a hard, bright sun, and whipped in the face by an icy wind. Julia hugged her overcoat around her as Caroline shivered and moaned that Bloomingdale's would be their very first stop for thermal underwear.

Everything seemed so exciting, and they hadn't even left the airport. The cabs really were bright yellow, and the drivers as rude as they always were in the films. The driving was terrible. Mustafa (for that was his name) took great delight in slamming his foot on the accelerator, zooming up to within a foot of the car in front, then slamming on the brake.

Caroline and Julia sat in the back, fighting carsickness, praying the journey would soon be over, both of them far too British and polite to complain.

The skyline swept before them as they crossed the Triborough Bridge, taking their breath away and sending shivers of anticipation down their spines.

Rumbling down Lexington through Harlem, neither girl said a word, noses pressed to the glass as they examined fire escapes, gangs of kids sitting on steps, people everywhere.

"I can't believe we're here," Caroline said, grinning, looking at Julia for only a split second so as not to miss anything. "I feel like we're going to see Cagney and Lacey any second."

Down through the nineties, the eighties, continuing downtown and watching the neighborhood change. And then into Gramercy, where they had booked themselves into the Gramercy Park.

"I think I could fall in love in New York." Caroline flopped back on the bed and sighed dreamily. "I've never seen so many gorgeous men in all my life."

"Never mind the men. I think I could fall in love with New York. This place is amazing."

The work was hard. They weren't filming, not yet, just doing the recce and ensuring they had found the right subjects. Most of their days were spent on the phone, or shadowing private investigators to have a real taste of what the job involved.

The first Saturday they walked to Central Park, hired skates, and stumbled their way around Wolman Rink. A carriage ride round the park was a necessity, as was a hot chocolate in the lobby of the Plaza Hotel.

Over the course of the following week they managed the Empire State Building, the Guggenheim, the Museum of Modern Art, and the Statue of Liberty.

Evenings they went downtown. Wandered around SoHo, sitting on benches in Greene Street and Prince Street, people-watching before going into bars and reveling in the warmth, the friendliness of it all.

Or down to the Village, to bohemian coffeehouses where they'd sip cappuccinos late into the night, start talking to neighboring tables, ending up in bars, clubs, with people they'd never met before but who felt like lifelong friends.

They went to the cinema as often as they could, just so they could go back home and nonchalantly claim to have seen everything already. "Oh, *The Silence of the Lambs*? Haven't you seen it? God, I saw it months ago. You mean it isn't even out for another four months? It's worth the wait. Terrifying."

They managed to fit in *City Slickers, Fried Green Tomatoes, Thelma and Louise, Madonna: Truth or Dare* and, obviously, *The Silence of the Lambs*.

Of course the pair of them had flings. Not sex, not Julia at any rate, the recent HIV and AIDS adverts still positively ringing in her ears, under the misapprehension that she was safe in

England and very much in danger in America, but she had delicious snogs with broad-shouldered hunks with thick necks and thicker wallets.

Julia was overwhelmed by Manhattan, and she'd only seen a tiny slice of it. She'd stayed there for two weeks as a tourist, had done all the touristy things, and had had the time of her life. And now she was going back to stay with Bella! In an apartment! On the Upper East Side! Here was her chance to sample New York as a native, and you know what? She couldn't wait.

Why the hell didn't I come back before now? she thought, a wide smile on her face as they pulled into the short-stay car park at Heathrow. Why the hell have I waited so long?

8

Julia opens her eyes and fumbles for her watch. It's eerily quiet in Bella's living room, and she's not surprised to see it's 3:02 A.M. Eight o'clock in England. Exactly the time she would normally be getting up.

Four hours' sleep is definitely not enough for her, and she snuggles back down under the covers to try to go back to sleep. Forty minutes later, forty minutes of her mind whirling with the excitement of where she is, she throws back the covers and pads into the tiny kitchen.

Bella wasn't joking when she said she lived in a shoebox. Her apartment is basically two tiny rooms, with an open-plan kitchen at one end of the living room and an L-shaped bedroom, the missing chunk having become a tiny bathroom.

"But look at the view," Bella had said, leading Julia to the window last night. "Isn't it extraordinary?" Julia agreed, looking down over Manhattan from the thirty-fifth floor, not fully understanding the currency of having a view in Manhattan. "I know people who've taken leases on apartments half the size of this one for twice the price," Bella said. "They just had a great view."

Julia opens Bella's cupboard doors, looking for something to eat, some coffee to make, and is astonished by the sparseness of the shelves. There is, quite simply, nothing there. And Julia is used to Mark keeping the kitchen fully stocked, prepared for any eventuality.

Moroccan chicken with pine nuts and cracked cardamom pods? You'll find the pine kernels in the second cupboard on the right, the cardamom pods with the rest of the spices in the larder. The pestle and mortar is on the counter next to the toaster.

Homemade sushi? Nishiki rice in the larder (underneath the saffron, cumin, and coriander seeds), nori in the third cupboard on the right, crabsticks in the freezer, and wasabi in the door of the fridge. Bamboo mat lurking somewhere in the bottom drawer, and always, always, avocados in the vegetable drawer.

Not only does Bella not appear to know what a pestle and mortar is, she doesn't appear to have even the basics. No tinned tomatoes just in case. No five-year-old jar of mixed herbs. No cereal. Eventually Julia finds a stray tin of tuna that expired four months ago, and behind the tuna—thank God—a tin of coffee.

But no kettle.

By this time Julia is becoming desperate, and finds a saucepan that she fills with water and puts on the stove. She finds a cup, no saucer, lurking under the sink, and almost starts to cry when she realizes the coffee isn't instant.

Starting all over again and looking in every cupboard again, she sees that this is a no-win situation, and perhaps she will manage to fish most of the coffee grains out of the cup before she drinks it. She has, after all, found a teaspoon.

The coffee is revolting. Gray (the milk in the fridge was definitely suspect, but by that time Julia didn't really care), with black coffee grounds floating up to the surface, in any other circumstances it would be undrinkable. She drinks it through a grimace and walks over to the huge picture window, smiling as she pinpoints the Chrysler Building, the Empire State.

God. The memories.

She considers making the bed and curling up on the sofa to watch television, but instead climbs back under the covers with her revolting cup of coffee, and switches the volume down low to channel surf.

"What are you doing?" Bella stumbles blearily into the living room, a short lilac kimono wrapped around her, and Julia smiles at how immaculate she looks, even at four in the morning.

"Can't sleep. Too excited. Did I wake you? I'm so sorry, did I make too much noise?"

"Nah. Don't worry, it's not your fault. I think they made these walls out of paper." She yawns and stretches, then stops still. "Julia, what the fuck are you drinking?"

"Coffee."

Bella steps cautiously toward the coffee cup, leans her head down and sniffs. "That's not coffee. That's dog pee."

"I know." Julia looks miserably at her now lukewarm cup. "It tastes as disgusting as it looks."

"Darling, it can't possibly taste as disgusting as it looks or there's no way in hell you'd be drinking it. Why didn't you use the percolator, for God's sake? I've even got filters."

"I haven't even heard the word 'percolator' since nineteen seventy-six," laughs Julia, feeling rather stupid as Bella points out a large percolator complete with glass coffee jug sitting slap bang in the middle of her kitchen worktop.

"What did you think that was, then?" Bella shakes her head as she reaches for the filters and starts filling a jug with water. "Chopped liver?"

Julia laughs. "Sorry. But more to the point, what the hell do you eat when you're home? Your kitchen cupboards are disgraceful. Mark would have a heart attack."

"Despite liking Mark very much, he can basically go screw himself." Bella turns on the machine and leans against the counter. "And as for food, nobody in this city eats at home."

"What, never?"

"Never. Look." She reaches down and opens the oven door to reveal what looks suspiciously like a stack of sweaters. "The perfect place for cashmere," she laughs, as Julia shakes her head in amazement.

"So the only thing you ever have at home is coffee?"

Bella shakes her head. "Basically, and usually I don't even have that. I grab a skinny latte from the Starbucks on Second on my way to work every morning. I haven't used this bloody thing for years."

"Great." Julia picks up the tin. "Then I suppose it should be no surprise that this expired last February?"

"What do you care?" Bella swishes Julia's cup under the tap to prepare it for the new coffee. "You were willing to drink it, grains, sour milk, and all. This, my darling"—she hands Julia a full cup of steaming coffee—"is going to feel like you've died and gone to coffee heaven. Right. I'm off to bed."

"Don't go to bed," Julia pleads, but Bella shakes her head as she disappears into her bedroom.

"Early to bed, early to rise, gives a girl energy and skinny thighs. See you in the morning." She blows Julia a kiss and she's gone.

"*What* the hell?" Julia squeezes open her eyes to see Bella bouncing round the living room in purple bootleg exercise pants and a black crop-top, noisily opening all the blinds.

"Rise and shine, rise and shine. Remember what I said about skinny thighs? You and I, my darling, are off to the gym."

"You must be joking," Julia groans, turning her face into the pillow to block out the shafts of sunlight now streaming through the room. "Jesus. What time is it?"

"Six-thirty. Just the right time for an hour's workout."

"Six-thirty? I only went back to sleep half an hour ago."

"Why? What have you been doing?"

"Watching TV."

"Find anything interesting?"

"Yeah. The E! channel. I watched a fascinating program about a child star I've never heard of, and his descent into drink and drugs."

"Gary Carlucci?"

"How did you know?"

"He's done every talk show in town."

"Including yours?"

"Naturally."

"Anyway. I'm exhausted and the only place I'm going right now is back to bed." Julia pulls the pillow over her head and rolls over to face the window. "Have a good time. See you later."

"Nope. Absolutely not." Bella rips the bedclothes off Julia and physically pushes her until Julia has no choice but to climb out of bed. "When in New York act like a New Yorker. And anyway, you need to do some exercise."

"Oh, thanks a lot."

"Not because you're getting fat, but because you need to release some of those endorphins to make you feel better. I swear on my life that if you honestly feel terrible after you go, I won't make you go again."

"You swear it's just this once?"

"Only if you feel terrible." Bella looks at her watch. "Shit! We have ten minutes. I've left gym clothes and my spare sneakers in the bedroom for you. I'll be in the bathroom."

Ten minutes later Bella emerges with a full face of artfully applied makeup. She looks stunning. Head up, she looks as if she's off to a premiere; head down, she's either stuck in a fashion time-warp of 1982 or she's off to the gym.

"Bella! I can't believe you've put on makeup for the gym."

"Darling, you ought to do the same. I'm telling you, it's a real scene."

"No way." Julia scrapes her hair back into her old black scrunchie. "I'd feel ridiculous. Are you ready?"

107

The pair of them walk out the door and wait thirty seconds for the lift, which then takes eleven minutes and twenty-four seconds to make it back down to ground, as it stops to collect more gym-bound bodies on almost every floor.

"How do you stand it?" Julia says through gritted teeth, ready to kill the next time the lift stops.

Bella shrugs. "This is New York. The price you pay for the thirty-fifth floor."

"Show-off," growls a tiny and skinny old woman with a helmet hairdo and a miniature dachshund tucked under her arm. And then she smiles, as does Julia.

"Could be worse," Bella says to the woman. "We could have said the penthouse."

"Coffee?" Julia says hopefully, bundling her coat around her as they head down Third to the gym.

"Coffee before a workout? Are you mad?" Bella ushers her along, and finally they come to the gym.

And Bella is astonished.

Amazed.

It's barely seven o'clock in the morning and this joint is positively humming. Everywhere she looks there are people lining up for the machines, all chatting to one another noisily, pumping, and puffing, and toning up their already perfect bodies.

Not that Julia's ever seriously gone to a gym in London, but she's certainly joined a few over the years. Never before has she experienced a buzz in the sleepy gyms at home. In London people have whispered to one another, not daring to speak to their fellow exercisers, and certainly not striking up raucous conversations while waiting in line.

Here Sisqo is blaring out of the speakers, and Julia suddenly feels an energy she hasn't felt in months. Years. She positively bounces behind Bella and queues for the StairMaster, itching to get on and get moving.

"Hey, Bella, how are ya?" Tall, dark, and definitely dangerous walks up and plants a kiss on Bella's cheek.

"Great, Joe. You?"

"Can't complain."

"This is my friend Julia from London."

Joe takes Julia's hand and flashes her a perfect smile. "Good to meet you. Have a good workout, ladies," and he's gone.

"Phwoargh," Julia sighs. "He was delicious."

"Been there, done that," Bella groans. "And trust me, he's not."

"Really? What's wrong with him?"

"On paper he's divine. Handsome, charming, fantabulous job on Wall Street, but darling, he has the personality of a wall."

"Of a what?"

"He's just completely blank. Still. Plenty more fish in the sea, all you have to do is throw out some bait." At which point she sticks her hip out and pouts at a sweaty man walking past.

"Great thighs," he says, and Bella turns back to Julia with a smile. "See?"

One workout and two skinny lattes later, Bella and Julia stride up Fifth on their way to Bella's work.

"You know, I really had forgotten how much New York energizes you." Julia takes deep breaths as they power-walk alongside Central Park. "I feel alive again. God, I'd forgotten what it was like to feel this alive."

"Great, isn't it?" Bella laughs. "That's why I'd never go home."

"You're really out here for good?"

"Look at my life. I love it. I love the independence and the buzz that New York gives me. I love that I'm never lonely here, that I can get pretty much whatever I want twenty-four hours a day. I couldn't go back to London. Not now."

Julia sighs. "Last week I would have said you were crazy, that London has so much to offer, but somehow I don't think it will be long before I come around to your way of thinking."

Bella stops and raises an eyebrow. "One day and you've already decided to stay?"

"I didn't say that. Just that I understand why you're staying."

"You know what you really need? You need to start dating."

Shock crosses Julia's face. "Bella, Mark and . . . I. We're not over, you know. This is just a break. And I couldn't . . . I wouldn't be able to . . . it's just not right. Not fair to him."

"I didn't say have an affair. I mean just let men take you out for dinner and treat you nicely. When was the last time you were treated like a princess?"

"Years."

"Exactly. I'm not saying you have to do anything with them, I'm just saying go out and have a good time."

"Maybe you're right."

"I'm always right," Bella laughs. "And speaking of Mark, are you planning on speaking to him or just playing phone tag with your answer phone when you know he'll be out?"

"I left that message, but right now I think we need serious space from one another, and that means not talking for now. I want to leave my life behind while I'm here, not think about any of that depressing stuff."

"Okay. Point taken." Bella sweeps a perfectly manicured finger across her mouth. "Zip the lip. No more talk of home. So what are your plans for today?" They stop outside the TV studios and stamp their feet to keep them warm as they say good-bye.

"I thought I might do a bit of window shopping."

"Window shopping? You're in New York. You have to spend, spend, spend!"

Julia looks Bella up and down, and shakes her head while laughing. She takes in Bella's Ferragamo shoes, her Prada coat, her J.P. Tod bag. "If I could spend, trust me, I would, but today I'm just going to check out the shops."

"So how about lunch? The restaurant in Saks, Fiftieth and Fifth, eighth floor, twelve P.M. Have a good morning." They kiss good-bye and Julia sticks her hands deep in the pockets of her coat and walks off, and it doesn't occur to her until five blocks away that she hasn't stopped smiling.

"I don't believe it." Bella starts to laugh as Julia stumbles over to the table laden down with so many shopping bags she can hardly move. "I see you've had a successful morning window shopping."

Julia collapses on a chair, bags strewn all over the floor, and makes a pained expression. "I tried, I really did, but it started with these fantastically flattering trousers in Banana Republic and it all went downhill from there."

"I don't believe you." Bella tries to count the number of bags. "And did you buy the whole of Saks or just the fourth floor?"

"I couldn't help it. This place is unbelievable. Everywhere I turned there were racks of clothes on sale, and I didn't even realize until I bought two jackets that there's a further thirty percent off today."

"So of course you then had to go back and start looking all over again?"

"Of course! What do you think I am? A man?"

They both laugh.

"Wait till you see what I got!" Julia starts pulling clothes out of bags and holding them up. A Gucci coat reduced from $1,000 to $150, an Armani jacket a mere snip (or at least that's how Julia justified it) at $195, a DKNY shirt for $59.99.

"Bargains, the lot of them. I don't suppose we need to add it all up, do we?" Bella says.

"Absolutely not. What I can't add won't hurt me." And she sits back in her chair with a grin as the waiter puts a wire basket of bread and crackers on the table, and fills their glasses with iced water.

"To us." Bella raises her glass.

"To us." Julia takes a sip and shakes her head. "Bella, I can't believe how different I feel being here."

"New York does that to people. I told you."

"No, it's not just that. God, I didn't want to talk about Mark, but this is the first time I've really been away from him and . . ." She stops, looks at the table mat, and takes a deep breath.

"Are you okay?"

"Yes, it's just that saying this will make it a reality, which is pretty scary. You know how you can think something and as long as it stays in your head it's fine because you can pretend it's not really there, and sometimes it goes away, but then as soon as you say it out loud it becomes real and you can never take it back?"

"I know," Bella says gently. "Just for the record, whatever it is you're about to say, you don't have to say it if it makes you feel in any way uncomfortable. If you don't want it to be real, maybe you should think twice before saying it."

"No, it's not terrible. I'm not saying it's over or anything. But Bella, I've been feeling so trapped." The pain in her eyes is clear, and Bella reaches over and takes her hand. "I've just felt so numb for months, and not being able to get pregnant, and . . ." She stops. "God! I haven't even thought about the pregnancy since I got here. Can you believe that?"

"Why is that so strange? You've been here less than twenty-four hours."

"But Bella, I've been obsessed with getting pregnant for months. It's all I think about. I lie in bed fantasizing about my baby, and I wake up blaming Mark, and spend the rest of the day feeling alternately gooey and angry whenever I pass babies or baby shops."

"Not a great thing to be feeling, considering there's the

most enormous baby boom in New York right now and every second person you pass is a foot high and sitting up in a buggy."

"Exactly! That's the point. I must have been aware of it, even today, walking around, but I didn't think about it in terms of how it affected me!" Her voice is excited, rushed. "Bella, I feel like the black cloud that's been following me around for months has finally gone."

"I think," Bella says seriously, "that black cloud is called depression. I personally would have suggested Prozac, but if retail therapy did the trick, then so be it."

"I'm not on a shopping high," Julia warns.

"Right. Sure." Bella sweeps her eyes over the bags at Julia's feet. "But seriously, I do think you need the space to clear your head. That whole me, me, me thing is so typical. Isolating and being angry with the world because you can't control it isn't exactly abnormal when you're suffering from depression."

"How come you know so much about it?"

"I'm a daytime television producer. I know very little about an awful lot, what's the expression? Jack of all trades, master of none? That's me. Don't question it. It's my job."

"Bella, I love you."

"I know, darling. I'm your fairy godmother. And I love you too, and more to the point I'm extremely glad you're feeling better because tonight, Cinderella, you shall go to the ball."

It isn't a ball. It's a private party in a large bar in SoHo. Julia manages to fight off her jet lag, and they arrive at 11:10 P.M.,

Bella resplendent in a red chiffon and feather number, and Julia in a more orthodox but still beautiful black dress and little beaded cardigan.

They push through the crowds of people to the bar, and within ten minutes they have each had two drinks apiece, bought for them by different men.

Julia shouts to be heard above the crowd, laughs and flirts all evening. She gives her—or rather Bella's—number to three men, and has the time of her life.

This evening she:

Drinks seven apple martinis. Or possibly eight. She loses count around six.

Is chatted up by five men, and is fairly certain of admiring glances from at least three more.

Hits the dance floor with wild abandon and lets her hair down in a way she hasn't done for years, and, what's more, knows she looks pretty damn good while doing so (although, again, that could be the apple martinis).

Passes Sarah Jessica Parker while walking through the room, and actually touches her arm to get past.

Meets Sarah Jessica Parker later in the loo, although it isn't actually Sarah Jessica Parker, just someone who looks very like her, but nevertheless the SJP-lookalike comes straight up to Julia and gushes, "I love your sweater, it's beautiful, where did you get it?" (Julia considers saying Whistles, but figures it wouldn't mean anything, so with an apologetic expression she simply says London.)

At 2:25 A.M. Bella drags a protesting Julia to the door, only managing to get her out by promising her they'll go to another party the next night, "Although," Bella mutters, shoving Julia into the back of a cab, "God knows if I'll be up for anything now."

"Sorry," Julia mumbles happily, eyes closing with exhaustion as she leans her head back, the jet lag finally catching up with her, "but didn't you have the most amazing evening of your life?" With a smile she's asleep.

"Not, clearly, as amazing as yours," Bella says, smiling, as she leans forward and gives the driver her address.

9

"Hello, may I speak with Julia please?"

"Who may I tell her is calling?" Bella adopts her most formal British tone.

"This is Jack Roth."

"And will she know what it's in connection with?"

"Yes."

"Just one minute." Bella covers the mouthpiece and looks over to Julia sitting on the sofa. "It's someone called Jack Roth," she mouths. "Who he?"

Julia shrugs and holds her hand out for the phone. "Hello?"

"Is this Julia?"

"Yes."

"This is Jack. Jack Roth."

"Yes?"

"Jack whom you met the other night at

the Hudson? In the bar? You gave me your number and said to call you as soon as I got back from Argentina."

"How very presumptuous of me. And have you just got back from Argentina?" Julia hasn't a clue who he is, but is nonetheless rather enjoying this conversation.

"I've just stepped off the plane at JFK and I'm about to jump in a cab."

"What? No limo picking you up? I'm not impressed."

"Neither am I," he laughs. "Someone somewhere's going to lose their job over this."

"I hope you're joking."

"I know all the British think the Americans have had a sense of humor failure, but yes, I was joking. So have you worn the Armani jacket yet?"

Julia's floored. God. Who is this man and, more to the point, what else did she tell him? "Um. No, actually." Her enjoyment is starting to disappear, the memory loss rendering her somewhat out of control.

"The Prada coat?"

"Yes, actually. I wore that one today."

"Shame I couldn't see it on you. Maybe you'll wear it when you have dinner with me."

Julia pauses. She wouldn't have made a date for dinner with this man, not when the situation is still so unresolved with Mark. Would she?

"Am I having dinner with you?"

"Oh yes. Absolutely. You swore on your dog's life you'd have dinner with me when I got back from my trip."

"I don't have a dog."

"Maybe it was your brother's. I don't remember the details."

"I don't have a brother, which is rather lucky because I imagine his life would be in some danger by now." Julia laughs, as Bella jiggles next to her on the sofa, desperate to find out what's going on.

"So are you free tomorrow night?"

"I don't know. Hang on, I'll ask my social secretary." Julia covers the mouthpiece as Bella reaches over and bangs the hold button down. "Am I free tomorrow night?" she asks Bella innocently.

"Never mind that. Who's Jack Roth and why are you flirting with him?"

"I'm not really flirting, am I?" Julia tries to look horrified but fails miserably. "Bella, I have absolutely no idea who he is," she says impatiently. "If you remember correctly, I was completely shitfaced at that party, and I know I gave my number out, but God knows to whom. However, he sounds nice and he wants to take me out for dinner, and you were the one who said I needed to date."

"You're right. You're right. But find out a bit about him, for God's sake."

"Bella, I'll meet him at the restaurant. It'll be a public place. I won't go back to his apartment or do anything stupid. Relax. I'm not going to start asking him a billion questions on the phone."

"I told you, when in New York—"

"But I'm not a pushy New Yorker looking for a husband. That's the last thing on my mind. I quite like the idea of having a Magical Mystery Evening."

"Okay, okay. But can I come too and lurk invisibly at the bar just so I can check you're not with a madman?"

"Maybe. But only if you swear not to come over or make it obvious."

"I swear." Bella presses the hold button again and Julia puts the phone to her ear.

"Hello?"

"Hello? Did you go on vacation?"

"I'm so sorry, my social secretary had lots of questions."

"Ah. Tell her I work for Goldman's, I'm in Emerging Markets, hence my traveling to Latin America, I'm six-three with dark hair and brown eyes, which of course you'll remember, and I live on the Upper West Side. Will that satisfy her?"

Julia laughs and mouths to Bella, "Goldman Sachs." Bella nods approvingly.

"So how about tomorrow night?" he continues.

"Bugger. I forgot to ask her. Hang on." Julia confers briefly with Bella, rules out tomorrow night due to dinner with some of Bella's friends, and goes back to Jack to agree on next Thursday night.

Julia tells him she'll meet him at the restaurant and takes down the address for Orsay. She's about to ask how will she recognize him when she remembers this isn't a blind date, not as far as he's concerned, and she decides to turn up slightly late to make sure he's sitting at the table.

"Well?" Bella says urgently as soon as Julia puts down the phone. "Orsay indeed? Goldman Sachs indeed? I'd say your bait must have been pretty tempting."

"Yeah. I actually offered him a lifetime's blow jobs with a free subscription to *Esquire*. What man could refuse?"

"Evidently not this one."

"Bella, I haven't a bloody clue who he is. Is this completely mad?"

"Nope. Probably the sanest thing you've ever done. Getting out and having some fun."

The great thing about staying with someone who lives in New York rather than in a hotel, Julia muses a couple of days later, is that you have a chance to feel what it's really like to live in the city, rather than be a tourist.

Even her gait is different in New York. In London she takes her time, looks around her as she walks, whereas here she strides briskly, eyes fixed on the middle distance, looking as if she knows exactly where she's going and what she wants. A native New Yorker in the making.

She was completely delighted yesterday when two different sets of tourists stopped her in midtown and asked her the way to, first, Rockefeller Center and, second, F.A.O. Schwartz. Delighted and embarrassed, for the minute she opened her mouth she proved herself as alien as they.

Already she has developed something of a routine. Every morning she joins Bella for her workout, before walking her to the office. On the way back she goes a few blocks up to the Pick-a-Bagel on 77th and Lexington, grabbing a cinnamon raisin bagel and a large hazelnut coffee, taking it back to the apartment to eat while flicking between the final parts of the morning shows on CBS and NBC. Later she watches Bella's show on BCA, and late morning she'll leave the apartment for the rest of the day.

Sometimes she walks through Central Park. Sometimes she'll hit the museums. She's revisited her old haunts in SoHo, and found a few new ones. She's ogled her way down Madison Avenue, and bought, in stages, all the stock she can lay her hands on in the Gap.

She has no qualms about eating on her own, and if she isn't meeting Bella for lunch she'll have scrambled eggs and crispy bacon at EJ's, fresh sushi at the Atlantic Grill, a giant burger at Hamburger Heaven.

She has already understood why New Yorkers are always out. So much to see, so much to do, it's always a disappointment to go back home to the apartment late afternoon.

So far she and Bella have spent only one night at home. Julia insisted on Chinese takeaway. She had a vague memory of Cliff in *Dallas* always eating Chinese food out of a small cardboard carton, and remembers salivating at the time, and thinking how much more delicious Chinese food must be when eaten that way.

The food duly arrived in said cartons, and wasn't even a quarter as delicious as it had looked. Nevertheless she and Bella finished everything while watching reruns of *Seinfeld*.

Thursday afternoon Julia walks in after spending a few hours trying to spot the polar bears in Central Park Zoo, and runs to get the phone that's ringing as soon as she walks through the door.

She picks up, unwinding her scarf and pulling off her woollen hat, relieved to finally be in the warmth.

"Hi, darling, it's me. How was your day?"

Julia smiles at Bella sounding like the dutiful wife. "Cold. I went to the zoo."

"Great." Julia can hear Bella isn't in the mood for a chat. "Listen, I've got a proposition for you. How would you like to have a job?"

"What do you mean, a job?"

"I mean we're running a new item on the show called 'Baby Showers,' which will take a week to film. The bloody thing starts filming on Monday and Lisa, the producer, is in hospital with suspected malaria."

"God. Poor girl. So what's 'Baby Showers'?" Julia puts on a deep, and rather sardonic, American accent.

"For the last few months we've been doing stuff on parties. Every week we change it so we've had bachelorette parties, sweet sixteens, bar mitzvahs, pre-prom nights, that kind of thing. Think cheesy and American. And now it's baby showers, which is basically when everyone you know comes to your house when you're pregnant bearing gifts for the baby.

"We look at clever things to make as party favors, oops, I mean going-home presents, recipe ideas, themes, that kind of thing. We'll film it next week to air in two weeks' time, so we're now completely stuffed unless you say yes."

"So you want me to produce it?"

"Julia, I badly want you to produce it, but I was so frightened to ask you because I didn't want to remind you about the baby stuff, but we're totally up shit creek and if you could handle it you'd be doing me the most massive favor. It's all set up, we just need someone to oversee the whole thing."

"Don't I need an interview or anything? Doesn't anyone senior want to meet me? And won't I need a green card or something to work here?"

"You don't need an interview because it's a freelance position, and the responsibility comes down to me. All you'll have to do is send in a CV as a formality, but frankly they're all running round in a panic like headless bloody chickens, and they'll be delighted for someone as experienced as you to do it. As for a green card, normally of course you would, but BCA's a global company, so I'm pretty sure I can persuade the British office to pay you. Given this is such short notice, I don't think anyone's going to question us taking on a British producer. The fact is you're here and you're available. Look, if you want it, bash out a CV on my computer at home, e-mail it to me and I'll run it under their noses, but basically it's yours. If you want it."

"Okay."

"Okay what? Okay you want it?"

Julia takes a deep breath. It's only one week, she tells herself. The whole thing for next week is already set up, and all she has to do is go along and smooth ruffled feathers and make sure everything goes according to plan. All the hard stuff has been done, and God knows she's hardly an amateur. How different can America be, anyway?

"I'll do it," she says finally.

"Yessss!" hisses Bella. "My laptop's under the bed. Do the CV now and send it over by the end of the day. You'll need to come in with me tomorrow, is that okay?"

"Oh, I don't know," Julia says, the calmness in her voice

hiding the excitement just starting to bubble up from her stomach. "I'll have to check my diary."

"Oh ha, bloody ha. I'll see you later. Hang on. Tonight's the night, isn't it?"

"Night for what?"

"Jack Roth."

"Oh yes. God, thanks for reminding me. I'd almost forgotten."

"Is that why you went out and bought a shimmery pink dress from Scoop! yesterday?"

"Bugger. I can't get anything past you."

"Damn right. I've got the most gorgeous Manolos that would look fantastic with it. They're in the wardrobe in my bedroom on the far left. Keep digging and you'll find them eventually."

"Bella, you're wonderful."

"Aren't I? I'll see you later, my darling, and I promise to remain incognito at Orsay."

"Are you at least going to meet someone there?"

"Of course. I'm meeting Russell Crowe for a date. I wish. Which reminds me, just as added bait, next Thursday you're going to be filming the celeb vox pops."

"Let me guess, I'm going out to film the Carol Vorderman and Anthea Turner of America?"

"You could say that. Although in this case you'll be filming Elle Macpherson and Uma Thurman."

"*Elle Macpherson!* Wow!" Julia's awestruck. "Uma Thurman!"

125

"I know! Elle and Uma! Maybe you and Elle will hit it off and she'll be our new best friend. Or Uma. I'm not particularly fussy."

"Elle Macpherson. Uma Thurman. Wow."

"Okay. I can see I'm not going to get any sense out of you now. I should have told you tomorrow. Forget Elle and Uma and think of Jack. I want you to start getting ready now. Understood?"

"Have you met my new best friends Elle and Uma?"

Bella laughs. "You're incorrigible. See you later."

Julia is so excited about meeting Elle Macpherson and Uma Thurman she barely thinks about her impending date with Jack. She moons around the apartment like a teenager with a serious crush, all professionalism having long since hot-footed it out the door.

Imagine, Julia thinks, hitting it off with Elle and Uma. Elle liking Julia so much she'd invite her over for dinner with a few friends. Just the usual gang, Cindy and Rande, Brad and Jennifer, maybe Ben Affleck for her. Julia envisages walking into restaurants with Uma at her side, everyone stopping to stare as Julia pretends to feel pissed off at the attention.

Oh, for God's sake, Julia, get a grip. She shakes her head but still can't resist tapping out a merry little dance on her way to retrieve Bella's laptop from under the bed. This was the last thing she expected, after all. A few days' break in New York has turned into nearly two weeks, and now she even has work. Will she ever go home?

Because of course there is Mark to consider, and with a

start Julia realizes she hasn't thought about him for days. She's been far too busy, she tells herself, checking her watch and ringing the machine at home, knowing he'll be at work on a Thursday, but not wanting to talk to him.

"Hi. It's me. Just checking in to say everything's fine. I'm having a great time and guess what? I've been offered some work so I'm off to film with Elle Macpherson and Uma Thurman next Thursday." She tries to sound blasé but fails. "Still not sure when I'll be home," she continues, "but I'll probably be here at least another few weeks. Hope everything's fine, and I'll talk to you soon. Bye." She puts the phone down and sits staring at it for a while, thinking about Mark, their house in London, the life she flew away from, and she knows she's not missing it.

She has barely thought about it.

Until now. Now she sits thinking about her struggle to get pregnant. About the countless nights she lay with her legs in the air, or filled Mark's pockets with juniper berries, or—and she starts to laugh at the memory of this—performed some ridiculous fertility ritual.

What would happen, she wonders, if she thought of a baby now, because she hasn't thought of babies, or pregnancy, since she's been here. She conjures up a picture in her mind of a gurgling baby, the picture that used to reduce her to furious tears, and she finds that she doesn't feel much at all.

No anger. No pain. No fear. Somehow she knows that having to film babies and baby parties for a week is a final sign from God. He's proving to her that she's okay now. That there are more important things in life than getting pregnant, and that in any case pregnancy wouldn't have been enough to cement her relationship with Mark. Even as she accepts this she knows that there are bigger questions she'll have to answer soon.

Questions about Mark. Her relationship. Her things. Questions about roots. London. Work. But she can't think about that right now.

After all, she has a date to attend to.

At twenty past eight Julia and Bella make their approach to Orsay.

"So the plan is you go in first, then five minutes later I'll come in and go straight to the bar," Bella gabbles as they wait round the corner. "After twenty minutes I'll meet you in the loo, and take my mobile so if he's horrible I can call you up and tell you it's an emergency and you have to leave."

"Okay, okay. I'm going in."

Bella turns Julia until they're face to face, grasps her shoulders and looks at her with the most serious expression she can muster. "You're going to be fine," she says in a crappy American accent. "Just relax," she adds somberly. "And good luck."

Julia laughs. Leans over and kisses her cheek. "Thanks. See you in the loo."

Bella gives her a thumbs-up and Julia goes in.

The restaurant is packed. Every table full, all the women immaculately groomed and glamorous, the men wealthy and powerful. A crowd of people wait just inside the door for their tables, and the bar is already three deep in beautiful people.

Julia pushes her way through the people at the door and finds a maître d'.

"Excuse me? I'm meeting Jack Roth?"

He checks the book, then nods. "Certainly. If you'd like to follow me." He leads the way through the restaurant as Julia tries not to feel self-conscious, even though every woman in there looks her up and down. Thank God for this dress, she thinks, so perfect for a restaurant such as this.

Her heart beats a little faster as she sees a lone man sitting at a table. He is facing away from the restaurant, the chair opposite him empty, and the maître d' leads her over, then leaves her to hover awkwardly.

The man turns to see her and his face breaks into a big smile. Julia smiles in return, partly out of relief, for he certainly doesn't look like the madman Bella suspected, and partly because she is astounded she could have forgotten someone like him.

"Julia." He stands and takes her hand, leading her to her chair, and she is delighted he isn't so presumptuous as to kiss her on their first date.

"Jack." She sits down, smiling. "How lovely to see you again."

"You had absolutely no idea who I was, did you?" He smiles and shakes his head at her while talking, and for a second she is embarrassed. She thinks of protesting and then she laughs.

"You're right. I had absolutely no idea."

"I knew you were drunk. I kept telling you that you wouldn't remember me when I called and you kept swearing that you were stone-cold sober and would never forget some-one like me."

"I always say I'm stone-cold sober when I'm rip-roaring drunk. But I have to concede I'm rather surprised I did forget someone like you after all. Are you really six-foot-three?"

"Do I look short sitting down?"

"Not short, just not too tall."

Jack pushes back his chair and stands up slowly as their fellow diners turn to stare. Julia makes a point of looking him up and down with slow approval, and he sits down with a grin.

"I take it I have your approval?"

"Oh yes. I'd say your workouts are definitely doing you good."

"So you do remember something of our chat that night?"

"Er, no. It was a lucky guess. Something about your wash-board stomach tells me you take your gym seriously."

"If that was a compliment, thank you. And seeing as we're exchanging compliments . . ."

"Are we?" Julia's trying very hard to wipe the grin off her face, but she can't quite manage it. She's not helped by the fact that she's just glimpsed Bella, who's walked all the way round the restaurant to see his face, and who is now, unbeknown to Jack, clutching her heart and mock-swooning to the amuse-ment of the people at the table she's swooning next to.

"We were. I have to say that you look beautiful."

Julia blushes. "Thank you. Different to how you remember me, then?"

"Fishing for compliments won't necessarily guarantee you

more," he says, raising an eyebrow. "Oh, all right, then. I remembered you as being pretty and fun and sparkly. I didn't remember you as being quite so beautiful or elegant as you look tonight."

Julia frowns at him, then reaches over and taps him on the forehead.

"If this isn't too personal a question, what the hell are you doing?" he says it with a smile.

"Just checking to see if you're real."

"The only part of me that's wooden is the pencil in my diary."

"I bet you say that to all the girls."

Thirty-four minutes later Julia tears her gaze away from Jack's to see Bella gesticulating furiously.

"Oh shit," she mutters.

"You don't like my amusing anecdotes?" Jack's tone is wry.

"I'm sorry. Will you excuse me?"

"As long as you come back."

"I'm just going to the loo."

"The what?"

"The ladies' room. Restroom. Bathroom. Whatever you call it."

"Powder room," he says as she stands up. "Happy powdering."

"He's gorgeous," Bella erupts as soon as Julia walks in. "I've been waiting for you for bloody ages. How's it going?"

Julia's still smiling. She glances in the mirror and is pleasantly surprised to see how she's glowing, how she hasn't glowed in years. "He's lovely," she says, smiling, turning back to Bella. "He's clever, funny, interesting, and interested in me."

"What more could a girl ask for?"

"I know," Julia sighs, reality starting to hit. "Can you believe I already have a boyfriend?"

"Julia, now's not the time to think about Mark. Mark's your past, and who knows," Bella says, affecting a dreamy tone, "Jack could be your future."

"Oh, don't be ridiculous," Julia snorts, turning to Bella with hope in her eyes. "You think?"

"*I love* this weather," Julia says, clutching her coat tightly around her as she and Jack walk up Third Avenue. "Cold and crisp."

"Unlike rainy old London."

"Tell me about it."

"Tell me about it."

Julia turns to face him. "About what?"

He shrugs. "Whatever you like. Oh, I don't know. You could tell me where you see yourself in five years' time. You could tell me why you don't seem to be in any hurry to go back to London. You could tell me whether or not I could kiss you."

Julia doesn't even notice his face moving closer and closer. She thinks she may have misheard him, but before she has a chance to ask him to repeat the question, because of course if she did hear him correctly then she'd have to say No because she does, after all, have a boyfriend, before she has a chance to say anything, his lips are on hers.

And when he finally lets her go the only thing she can do is sigh contentedly and smile.

10

"*Would you just stop wailing* about it for a second?" Bella says and gets up to grab another wad of toilet paper from the bathroom. "If you hang on a minute I'll go and see if there's a hair shirt hanging in my wardrobe."

"But I feel so guilty," Julia wails a bit more. "I can't believe I did that to Mark. I can't believe I've been unfaithful."

"Darling." Bella sits down next to her, hands her the toilet paper, and when Julia has finished sniffling into it again, Bella takes her hands firmly. "First of all, you haven't been unfaithful, it was only a kiss, for heaven's sake, not full-blown sex. More to the point, I think now is the time for you to realize that Mark and you are not, how shall I put this . . . meant to be?"

Julia looks up at her and sniffs.

"The pair of you have been ridiculously unhappy for years, and that whole baby obsession was because you were so unfulfilled you needed another focus and you thought a baby would somehow make everything okay again, but the fact is you and Mark are completely incompatible."

Julia gasps. "I can't believe you just said that."

"I know." Bella looks shocked. "Neither can I. But Julia, you are the only one who hasn't been able to see how different you both are and how unhappy you've both become."

"But that's just a temporary phase."

"A three-year temporary phase?"

"It hasn't been that long . . . has it?"

Bella nods. "Perhaps I shouldn't say this but since you've been here I've seen the old Julia again, and I've missed her so much. We all have. You were always the life and soul of the party, always happy, always smiling, but since you've been living with Mark you've been so unhappy.

"And I don't think Mark's a bad person. Really I don't. But you rattle around in that ridiculously huge house of his, and I know you're not at home there, and you don't seem to have anything in common. All those times I phone and you say you're staying in watching television, and you never used to stay in, God, your flat was just the base for your answering machine and a place to lay your head, and not even that very often in those days."

Julia smiles fondly at the memories and then shrugs. "I was young then," she says. "We all were. Life is very different now. We have responsibilities . . ."

"That's rubbish," Bella says firmly. "Look at me. I'm out every night, I have my own apartment, great friends, a string of men to call on should I feel in the mood for sex. I'm thirty-three years old and I still party with the best of them, and you know what? I love my life. There is absolutely nothing in my life I would change."

"So you'd be happy to be on your own for the rest of your life?" Julia's fascinated.

"Once upon a time I would have said the thought of spending the rest of my life on my own was terrifying, but you know what? Now I'm not so sure. I don't have to compromise for anyone, I don't have to stop doing what I want to do because my partner doesn't feel like it. And I know I've been accused of being selfish, but so what? I am absolutely happy with my life exactly as it is right now. Can you say the same thing?"

"I'm happy right now," Julia says firmly, reluctant to face the truth, but Bella pushes.

"Right now you are. You're in New York and living the life of a single woman. But are you happy living with Mark in London? Are you happy in that house? Is a baby really what you want? Is Mark really what you want?"

Julia doesn't say anything.

"Okay. Put it like this. If you weren't able to have a baby at all, would you still want to stay with Mark for the rest of your life?"

Julia still doesn't say anything, but after a few seconds she shakes her head sadly, still too frightened to say it out loud, to admit it to Bella, to make it real.

"Julia, I know you thought you wanted marriage and babies, but have you ever stopped to think that maybe you're not ready for that? Maybe you made a decision and felt that you had to stick with it, even though your life had moved in a completely different direction."

Julia looks at Bella, pain in her eyes, and her voice emerges in a whisper. "But I'm so scared of being on my own."

"Oh, Julia." Bella puts an arm around her and squeezes her. "I know it must be scary when you've been with someone for years, but look at how alive you've felt since being here, look at how happy you've been. That's what your life could be like again. It's not so bad, is it? Is it?" She nudges Julia until she gets a smile. "See? You could be my new partner in crime. You've already committed your first offense with Jack."

"Jack," Julia moans. "What am I going to do about Jack?"

"What do you want to do about Jack?"

Julia shrugs.

"Tell me again how you left it?"

"He asked if he could see me again and I said he should call me."

"Well, then. No point worrying about something that hasn't even happened yet. Let's cross that bridge when we come to it, but one question . . . Do you want to see him again?"

Julia hesitates, then nods with a faint grin as she reluctantly admits, "That kiss did send a shiver down to my toes."

"That's as good a reason as any. So when he calls you'll say yes."

"You make it sound so simple."

"It is simple," Bella is exasperated. "It's what being single is all about. In the meantime it's now one o'clock in the morning and you're supposed to be coming to the office with me tomorrow, so both of us need to get some beauty sleep." She leans over and kisses Julia on the cheek. "I'm glad you had such a special evening. Sleep well and see you in the morning."

"Do we have to go to the gym?" Julia moans, just as Bella's shutting her bedroom door.

"Of course we have to go to the gym," Bella shouts back from behind the closed door. "It's our new religion, for heaven's sake."

"Congratulations, my darling!" Bella lifts her champagne flute in a toast. "Welcome to BCA!"

"This just feels so ridiculous," Julia says. "I can't believe I came out here for a spot of rest, relaxation, and shopping, and now I'm working."

"This, remember, is the land of opportunity," Bella laughs. "Not to mention the land of reinvention. You can be anyone you want to be, why do you think I love it so much?"

"But you haven't reinvented yourself."

"Julia, everyone at work thinks I'm Lady Bella Redford."

Julia starts to giggle. "Tell me you're joking."

"Of course I'm not joking. If I'd known how helpful a title was in opening doors I'd have invented one years ago."

"I can't believe you."

"Why not? You could be one too."

"I think I'll just stick to being your lady-in-waiting."

"I didn't really think anyone would take it seriously," Bella lowers her voice and leans forward confidentially. "I was having a row with one of the other producers and she said 'Bella!' in this really nasally condescending way, and without even thinking I shot back, 'That's Lady Bella to you,' and the next thing I knew the whole bloody office was calling me 'Lady Bella.' I had to spend the next two weeks graciously telling everyone that it wasn't quite the done thing to address me as 'Lady Bella,' and that I only used it for formal functions, and calling me 'Bella' would be fine."

"You really are outrageous," Julia laughs.

"I know. Just pray no one lands their grubby paws on a copy of *Debrett's*. So how did you find today? What did you think of the office, and, more importantly, what did you think of everyone in the office? I've been dying to do the postmortem with you all day."

"God, where do I start?" Julia smiles and wearily lays her head back against the sofa. It's been a long day, and she's tired, and she never thought it would feel this good to be back in an office again.

They had arrived at BCA that morning when the live show had just started. Outside the building were streams of black limousines with tinted windows and uniformed drivers. Clusters of young interns stood around with walkie-talkies, barking instructions to unseen colleagues, managing to switch on the charm when a new limo drew up and out stepped an important guest for the show.

Bella seemed to know everyone they passed along the corridors. They walked through large open-plan offices as people stopped to smile, wave, or shout a quick hello. Every now and then Bella would actually stop and introduce Julia, who was welcomed warmly, before they moved on.

And on to the other side of the building, where they stepped into a lift and took it to the twentieth floor.

"This is where all the boring stuff gets done," Bella confessed, stepping out of the lift as she chucked her coffee carton into a bin. "The studios are on the first floor, so I'll take you down there soon to get a feel for that." She checked her watch. "There's a video tape slot at eleven, so we can go down then and you'll meet Carrie and Bill."

Julia nods, following Bella mutely as she tries to take it all in. Bella has arranged an empty office in which Julia can watch all the videos of the previous party strands during the morning, but first she takes her in to meet Rob Friedman, the producer of the show.

He's charming, affable, and frighteningly young. He shakes Julia's hand warmly and welcomes her to the team, and tells her he's very impressed with her resume and that she should come see him if there's anything she needs. Anything at all.

"Is that it?" Julia whispers as she and Bella leave his office thirty seconds later. "Doesn't he want to talk to me anymore? Find out who I am, whether I'm good enough?"

"Darling, I wouldn't have recommended you if you weren't good enough. I told you there was nothing to worry about."

Bella settles Julia into the office, and by ten to eleven, when she returns to take her to the studios, Julia's watched what feels like a hundred videos. She yawns, stretches, and turns to Bella with a shake of her head. "If my career ever dies, I'd make a killing as a party organizer thanks to all this bloody stuff you've made me watch."

"But you have an idea of what we're doing?"

Julia laughs. "Of course. It's easy as pie. I just need to see the schedule for next week and meet the team. But if I ever have to look at another piece of sushi I think I might have to scream."

By the end of the afternoon she's met the team, read through the schedules, reconfirmed the time and the guest list with the woman who's holding the first baby shower at which they're filming, and spoken to all of the various experts who'll be giving opinions.

She's exhausted and exhilarated. She's fueled herself with strong black coffee all day and is delighted that she can work at this pace without feeling stressed.

At eight-thirty that evening she and Julia are sitting in the bar at the end of the block, drinking champagne.

And with a start Julia understands why working here feels so very different from the work she was doing at home. It's not the job. It's not even New York.

It's simply that the passion has come back.

The passion for work and the passion for life. She's rediscovered her zest for living, and it feels "fanfuckingtastic," she tells Bella.

"And how about passion for Jack?" Bella teases.

Julia mimics Bella's voice perfectly. "Darling, we'll cross that bridge when we come to it."

Monday, Tuesday, and Wednesday fly by. Julia's so busy she barely has time to think. On Monday they filmed a baby shower in a pretty house in New Rochelle. Heavily pregnant Jodie could barely contain her excitement at being on BCA,

141

even when Julia's team of experts moved in and rearranged every piece of furniture in her house.

"Jodie, honey," said Sally, the interior designer, who was proving you could create a stylish and comfortable atmosphere in even the smallest of homes, "your walls just aren't working for me. You mind if we quickly paint them?" Jodie shrugged and nodded as Sally's two painters appeared and laid down dust sheets. Within an hour the entire room was painted, and Sally was right, it was transformed.

Julia had never known anything in television to happen so calmly and efficiently. At three in the afternoon all Jodie's friends arrived, bearing gifts, and the filming was a breeze.

On Tuesday they moved to Riverdale to discuss recipes with George the chef, who was full of clever ideas: pink and blue heart-shaped cookies; nutritious spring rolls folded over to look like a blanket in a crib; pacifiers made of two Life Savers—stuck together with a jelly bean in the middle and a ribbon attached.

Wednesday they filmed at a smart penthouse apartment on 68th and Park. The wife was married to a wealthy banker, and, despite her apparent joy at the impending arrival of their first baby, Julia had the distinct impression that she never saw her husband. All the money in the world—they clearly had a significant chunk of it—couldn't alleviate a deep unhappiness. This was only confirmed when her friends arrived, all of them stick-thin with tiny bellies, immaculately groomed and dressed in exquisite clothes, terrified of putting on any excess weight in case their husbands might find them unattractive and leave them for a younger, thinner model.

Thursday was Elle and Uma, both of whom were professional and charming, neither of whom were, Julia realized, destined to become her best friends, but nonetheless it was an enormous thrill to be leaning against the windowsill in Elle Macpherson's apartment, watching her play with her little boy as she talked about her own baby shower.

Friday was the final day of filming. Out in Great Neck, Long Island, it was a thirty-five-year-old woman who had published a book of her friends' tips, given to her at her own baby shower, and then collected at subsequent baby showers. Her baby, Alicia, was now eighteen months old. Julia fell in love at first sight.

Alicia followed Julia around during filming, toddling awkwardly over to her, holding out her arms and demanding cuddles. If Julia sat down, Alicia would put her little arms around Julia's legs and lean her head on her thigh, sucking her thumb as she watched all the mayhem in her mother's house.

She was divine. Julia picked her up and cuddled her and covered her with kisses as she squealed and giggled.

"I can't believe how much she's taken to you." Jackie — Alicia's mother — smiled fondly as Julia played with her daughter. "You said you didn't have children, but you look like you're really ready."

Julia put Alicia down gently on the floor and smiled at Jackie. "You know what? I thought I was really ready too. I tried for nearly a year to get pregnant with my partner, but it didn't happen."

"Oh, I'm so sorry." Jackie is mortified.

"Don't be. I'm not. I thought at the time that the only thing that mattered to me was having a baby, but now I know it wasn't the right time. And it wasn't the right man."

Jackie nods. "Your husband?"

"No. My long-term boyfriend."

"I take it you're no longer together?"

"Not really. I came to New York just to get some space, but I've realized it's not working anymore. I know he knows it too, we just have to sit down and say the words out loud to one another."

"That's tough." Jackie nods thoughtfully. "But you know, you can't underestimate the importance of a strong relationship when you have children. I know too many people who've tried to use a child to steady a rocky relationship, and all it does is throw it off balance completely."

"Did you have a strong relationship with your husband?"

"Thank God, yes, or we wouldn't have survived it. Nobody can really make you understand what the first year is like when you have a child. They tell you but you just can't understand until you go through it. The sleepless nights, the feeling of being trapped, the loss of self. I hated my husband for the first year. I resented him not understanding what I did. He'd go to work every day and then come back and just want to read the paper, and I'd be furious, because I'd been with the baby all day and up most of the night, and I knew he could never be as exhausted as me.

"I was way too tired to have sex, and we spent a year bickering and being nasty to one another. I'd lie in bed every night thinking, There's always divorce."

"It sounds horrific."

"It was. But you know what? Almost every new mother I know goes through the same thing. They all had a horrific first year, and none of them was prepared. All I can tell you is we nearly split up, and we have a strong relationship. There's no way we would have made it had we had basic problems in our marriage in the first place."

"So what happened?"

"Amazingly we had a turning point toward the end of the first year. I guess it helped that Alicia started sleeping through the night. We both started to catch up on sleep, and we found the time to sit down and talk to one another. We were so busy trying to convince the other one how we were having the harder time, we'd stopped listening to one another."

"And now?"

"Now I love my husband again. I remember why I married him, and I wouldn't change it for the world."

Julia sits in silence for a few seconds, digesting what Jackie has just said. Eventually she looks up. "Your daughter is the most divine baby I think I've ever met, and seeing her makes my heart ache, but I also know that you're right. It's not enough for me to be ready to have a baby. My life has to be working and I have to be with the right man. And the truth is I'm not even sure I'm ready."

"Right." Jackie nods. "You're suffering from Grandparent Syndrome."

"Grandparent Syndrome?"

"Uh-huh. You picture a baby and you think of the closeness and the cuteness and how wonderful it would be, but you don't think of the fact that you can't just hand them back at the end of the day. That's it. Hello baby, bye bye life."

"You're right," Julia laughs. "I've definitely been suffering Grandparent Syndrome, but, having heard you, I now never want a child."

Jackie's face falls. "Please tell me you're joking."

"Don't worry," Julia laughs as Alicia toddles over and holds her arms out to her. "I'm joking."

It's a typical New York day. Cold and bright, just getting ready for spring. Julia scuffs her boots along the path and digs deep in her pockets as she walks through the park to the Boathouse.

"I'm not supposed to see you again," she says as she approaches Jack, who is casually leaning against a tree by the entrance.

"You had that bad a time at Orsay?" He raises an eyebrow, unfazed by her direct approach, for he has, after all, been trying to reach her for nearly two weeks, and is delighted she's here at all.

He has left countless messages, both at home and at work, and finally resorted to turning up at her building this morning and refusing to leave unless she came down and talked to him.

She wouldn't come down—hung over and looking dreadful—but agreed to meet him later in the afternoon in Central Park. She has—thanks to the good old British cure of a fry-up (actually not very British at all, as there was probably more fat to be found in Julia's teeth than on her plate at the restaurant this morning)—recovered from her hangover, and has pulled her hair back into a sleek ponytail, eyes shaded from the sun by a large pair of tortoiseshell sunglasses.

Julia sighs deeply. She still feels guilty about Mark. She shouldn't even be thinking about other men, not until things are resolved with him, but she has tried to avoid Jack, and really it's not her fault he's been so persistent.

It doesn't help that he's turned up looking all tall and sparkly-eyed and sexy. Oh no. It doesn't help at all.

"I had a wonderful time at Orsay."

"But of course I knew that," Jack says. "That's why you've returned all my calls." Julia starts to apologize but Jack stops her. "Come on. Let's get a table." They walk through the restaurant and outside to the riverbank. A few brave souls are dotted around, but it's far too cold for the Boathouse to be busy, and Jack leads the way to a table halfway between the bar and the edge of the river.

"I'll just go and get drinks," he says, without asking Julia what she wants, and a couple of minutes later comes back from the bar with two steaming mugs of spiced wine.

"Here." He hands her a mug and she gratefully wraps her hands around it. "This will keep out the cold." They sit awhile, sipping slowly, and eventually Jack speaks. "If you had such a wonderful time at Orsay, why have you made it so hard to see you again, and more to the point, why are you not supposed to see me again?"

"I have . . ." Julia looks at him, then looks away, knowing she has to tell the truth but not sure how to say it. ". . . I have an unresolved situation."

"Ah." Jack nods slowly. "I have to say I did have a feeling it might be something like that. You're married, aren't you?"

"God, no!" The vehemence in her voice startles him.

"So what is it, then?"

And out comes the whole story.

Two hours later Julia tails off. She's told him about her life before Mark; about then moving in with him and knowing that her life would now be mapped out: marriage, babies, although not necessarily in that order. She's told him about her increasing unhappiness; about Mark and her growing so far apart it wouldn't be possible for them to find their way back. She's talked about her obsession with children; about needing a baby to repair her relationship; and she has talked about coming to New York and finding herself again. About knowing that it really is over with Mark, but not knowing how to tell him.

And now she sits back and looks at him, waiting for his response, because even though she hardly knows him, even though this is only the third time she's met him, he is someone she'd like to get to know better.

Although having just poured her heart out, she feels this is unlikely.

Jack doesn't say anything for a while. He looks out at the lake for a few minutes, then turns to her.

"So what about New York? Are you staying?"

Julia nods. "For a while. I've been in the edit suite for the last week and the editor's now seen some of the stuff we shot and he's happy. They've offered me more work, on a freelance basis, but I figure it won't do my CV any harm to have worked for BCA. And I know this sounds nuts, but I'm happy here. Maybe just because it's the place where I've rediscovered who I am, but whatever the reason I feel very settled. Comfortable. A two-bedroom apartment's come up in Bella's building, and we're going to take it. So, yes." She shrugs. "For the moment I'm staying."

"I would imagine, from everything you've told me, that a relationship is the very last thing on your mind right now, but I would also guess that you could do with a friend."

Julia suppresses a sharp pang of disappointment and covers it with a nod. "Friends. That sounds perfect."

"Good," Jack says, grinning, as he holds out his hand to shake on it. "Friends." Julia puts her hand in his and they shake firmly, smiling at one another.

And they keep holding on to one another's hands. Their smiles fade as Julia's heart beats a little faster.

"Seeing as we're friends," Jack says quietly, moving his head closer as he cups her chin in his hand and draws her head closer, "do you think it's okay if we do this?" He kisses her softly on the lips. Once. Twice. Three times. Pulling back slightly to check this is okay, he sees her eyes remain closed, her head inclined, and he smiles as he moves forward and kisses her again.

"Oh yes," sighs Julia, when they finally break apart, as she smiles from ear to ear. "I'd say that's exactly what friendship is all about."

Maeve

11

Funny, isn't it, how life turns out. Just as I was
beginning to seriously stagnate in Brighton
(and yes, I do know how trendy it is, and
yes, I have seen Zoe and Norman walking
around town from time to time, and no, I'm
not mad to have got thoroughly bored with
how small it is and how everyone knows
everyone else's business), along comes an offer from Mike Jones.

Bored with Brighton. Bored with work.
Bored with men. Most of the time I feel like
I've worked my way through all the available men in Brighton. And some of the unavailable. Occasionally the men fall for me,
but I have to get myself out pretty damn
quick, because I'm far too caught up in work
to give a relationship a chance.

Although there are times when someone

will brush the hair out of my eyes so tenderly it will make me want to cry, and I'll want to drop the act and curl up into their arms, feel safe, and warm, and rescued. But then I remember: I don't do relationships.

Once upon a time I did. Back when I dropped out of college I fully expected a strong man to whisk me off on his white charger, to a palace where I could live out my days in loved-up luxury, never having to work again. This sounds ridiculous now, I'm almost embarrassed to admit it, but I was so convinced that that was how my life would turn out, I didn't even bother to get a proper job.

Can you believe that?

God. Just awful. I was stagnating as a shop assistant in a sweater shop in a back street in Hove, praying for my prince to arrive, spending hours mindlessly folding sweaters and day-dreaming about the great love of my life.

But then, much as Born Again Christians find Jesus, I found work. The sweater shop went under (no surprise, given they only had about ten customers the entire year I worked there), and I was left high and dry, with no sign of Prince Charming. I joined a temp agency and they sent me off to work for a local radio station. Ten months filing, making teas and coffees, showing guests from the green room (a cramped airless cubbyhole with an L-shaped filthy sofa that I swear was just huge bits of foam that were covered in fabric, a scratched glass coffee table with a few outdated copies of *Billboard* magazine, and an ashtray that was permanently overflowing) to the studio. Very very occasionally we'd get someone famous and exciting, but most of the time it was struggling bands who were on a university tour, or some town dignitary involved in a local dispute.

After ten months I was taken under the wing of one of the producers. Robert. It helped that I was sleeping with him, and even though I had grown very tired of him after a month, I carried on because, really, one had to think of the career.

Frankly, I've always said the old methods are best, and what's older, or better, than the casting couch? I proceeded quickly from all-round dogsbody to assistant producer on Robert's afternoon show. A few months later Robert left to join another, rival radio station, on the understanding that I would go too, continue as his assistant, and continue our desktop fucking sessions. I bade him farewell—the plan being I would leave a month later, just so no one would suspect—and ran straight down the corridor to the boss's office.

I don't think anyone was surprised that Robert's shoes were a perfect fit, and although Robert was understandably pissed off, I heard that it wasn't long before he found another nubile young dogsbody to train.

Making the jump from radio to television was easy. Admittedly I had to start almost at the bottom again, but by that time I had a few years and a few schemes on my fellow researchers, and again, it didn't take long. That time I didn't even have to sleep with anybody.

Although I probably would have done. The boss at the TV station will have to remain nameless, but he was extremely attractive, extremely funny, and extremely married. Just my type, except for the marriage bit of course. Maybe you're surprised. I know some of my friends are. They think I'm "prime mistress material," particularly given my aversion to any kind of emotional attachment.

But I lived through that with my mum. Lived through the pain of a divorce, and I really don't think I could do that to another woman. Of course I have had the odd fling with an Unavailable, I'd be lying if I painted myself as an angel, but, generally, the flings I had, I didn't know anything about a wife. I'd only find out later, and by that time I would have moved on anyway.

I'm not a marriage-wrecker, you see. I never wanted anything from the men I slept with who belonged to someone else, and I'd never be stupid enough to fall for someone and daydream about him leaving his sad and dowdy wife for glamorous old me.

I am neither that stupid nor that self-deluded. I only appear glamorous because of my red hair, and even that isn't, ahem, entirely natural, although that's not something I make a habit of telling people, and my great-grandmother did come from Cork so I can just about get away with it. I've even been known to adopt an Irish accent from time to time, despite having grown up in West Sussex, but I only do that if there's no one Irish around because it isn't very good and I'd be caught out pretty damn quickly.

But it's amazing how fast you can proceed up the career ladder if your hair is "rich russet red" and almost reaches your waist; if you adopt a uniform of tight trouser suits and killer stilettos; if you forgo the friendship of your equals in the office and concentrate on the people with true power.

Oh but how I missed those friendships with equals. I knew exactly what was said about me. I was a ball-breaker. I was a tough, uncompromising bitch. I was only interested in myself. Of course most of that was true. But no one ever said I could be thoughtful. No one said I was straight and honest. No one talked about the love I have for my friends and family. In fairness perhaps they never saw that side. Perhaps I was too busy furthering my career to concentrate on showing off my better aspects.

I learned very quickly that being nice didn't do it. Being nice won friends, but didn't influence anybody. I craved the influence far more than the friends, but there were times I thought I wanted the friends: when I'd walk into the office and silence would descend as if we were in a Wild West saloon; when everyone would go to the local pizza place for someone's birthday and I wouldn't be invited; when no one offered any help or assistance if, say, one of my guests dropped out at the last minute.

I told myself the benefits were worth it. While they were eating pizza, I was in a local upscale wine bar with the heads of the department. While they were getting pissed on beer and cheap white wine at a party in someone's flat, I was mingling with other television people in beautiful country houses, sipping champagne and making amusing small talk.

It's not what you know, it's who you know, my mother used to say, and nowhere is this more true, I discovered, than in the media.

Every job I ever had, every program I'd ever worked on, every promotion I'd ever been given was, directly or indirectly, as a result of mixing with the higher powers.

And that includes Mike Jones, Director of Programming for London Daytime Television, because I'd reached about as far as I was going to reach at Anglia, and I'd set my sights on something higher.

London Daytime Television.

I know all about Mike Jones, of course. Who doesn't, for Chrissakes? I've spent years listening to tales of Mike Jones's legendary drinking sessions, his womanizing, so I have to say it was something of a shock to hear him on the phone. Not an assistant, not some flunkie. Mike Jones himself.

"We need a producer," he'd said, "last minute. Urgent as fuck. Can you come tomorrow?" As if there were anything to think about.

I contemplated one of my signature trouser suits, and then decided on more of a floaty number. Less of the power-dressing, more of the flirtatious. Less Cindy Crawford, more Pamela Anderson.

But with a hint of seriousness, naturally. I wore a camel knee-length skirt with a lace hem, a pale pink cardigan over a Wonderbra that did a wonderful job of creating a cleavage I don't really have, and the obligatory killer stilettos. In caramel, of course. Shimmery tights, as it was far too cold to go naked-legged, and my delicious red winter coat with a huge fringed collar. I was ready.

I could see immediately what everyone was talking about when they talked about Mike Jones. His power definitely makes him attractive, and I noted him giving me a slow, cool once-over when I walked in.

We talked for a while about the job. He told me the situation, that the producer in question was about to take a sabbatical and was trying for a baby, and that they were looking to fill her shoes.

There was no question about whether I could do it. Standing on my head with my eyes closed.

"We haven't actually discussed the sabbatical with the producer yet," he said, clearly uncomfortable. "In fact, I'd be much happier if everything we discussed in this office is kept strictly between us."

"Of course," I said, nodding. "And what if she, um, decides not to take a sabbatical?"

He was being indiscreet. He knew it. But the television industry thrives on gossip, and he couldn't resist. "I love this girl," he said. "I've worked with her for years and I think she's talented as hell, but she's lost the plot. She's having the sabbatical whether she likes it or not, because she's one of the best people we've got and I can't afford to lose her permanently. But," he continued quickly, "this series is a year. If we like you and you want to stay, we'll move you on and the sky's the fucking limit here as far as I'm concerned."

Now this really was music to my ears.

"So tell me about you," he said suddenly, leaning forward, holding eye contact far longer than most, so long, in fact, I broke a cardinal rule and broke his eye contact first. Something I never do.

"I started working in radio," I said, telling him about my quick progression to producer of my own show, but, obviously, omitting Robert.

"Nah," he said after a few minutes. "Tell me about you. What makes Maeve tick. I need to know if you'll fit in with the team." He looked at my expression and started laughing. "Fuck, I can't believe I just said that. What makes Maeve tick," he mimicked as we both laughed, the ice now broken. "What a wanker."

"I'm glad you said that," I ventured boldly, buying time, because I hate being put on the spot like that. I never know what to say.

"Seriously, though," he said, grinning. "What, for example, is your favorite film?"

I smiled back and relaxed for the first time. "*The Great Escape*," I shot back.

"Interesting choice." He raised an eyebrow. "More of a bloke's film, I would have thought, unless it's because of Steve McQueen."

"Steve McQueen is a factor, but I'm more of a Brando kind of gal. The early days of course."

"Of course." He smiled, enjoying the conversation. "Not George Clooney, then?"

"Oh, please." I grimaced in disgust at the obviousness. "So what's your favorite film?" I took a chance.

"*Sleepless in Seattle*," he said, very seriously, as my mouth dropped open and hit the floor. "Oh, all right, then." He was enjoying my reaction. "I lied. My all-time favorite film is *Easy Rider*."

"Good choice. I take it you have a motorbike?" He nodded. "Let me guess. I'd say Harley but that doesn't seem quite you."

"So what does seem like me?"

"I'd guess at a Norton, even though you're probably more of an Indian man, but I can't see you paying the money."

The phone started to ring and Mike stood up, extending a hand. "Maeve," he said, "you're undoubtedly a girl after my own heart." He picked up the receiver as he shook my hand. "Thank you for coming in to see us. I'll be in touch by Friday at the latest, but I would say be quietly confident." Quietly confident? I was more than quietly confident. When the conversation turns personal and, better yet, becomes fun in a job interview, you know you're in. No question.

On the way out I bumped into Julia, Lorna's friend, whom I'd met at the wedding. I'd liked her then, thought she was the sort of person I could be friends with, but Jesus, she looked so terrible now I barely recognized her. We had a brief insincere conversation in which I told her I was going to call her (which, actually, I would have done, except I completely forgot she even worked there, but that doesn't sound too good), but she was so spaced out she barely registered what I was saying.

It was only as I reached the tube that I was hit by the realization that it might be Julia whom I'm replacing. There, after all, was a woman who appeared to have very definitely lost the plot.

I must phone Lorna when I get home, I thought.

I move down to London a week before I'm due to start. My contract with London Daytime Television is such that I can afford substantially more than I have been paying in Brighton, which is rather lucky, considering that the rent for my house in Brighton would enable me to live in a pea-sized hovel in London.

I end up with a flat in Belsize Park. It belongs to a single woman, Fay, about my age, who is traveling for a year; I met her through a friend of a friend. Her home could not be more perfect: A tiny bedroom is more than compensated for by a vast living room with twelve-foot ceilings and a bay window that opens on to a flat roof just big enough for a table and two chairs.

Her furniture is also perfect for me: Conran-style minimalism via a touch of Habitat and a large dose of IKEA. (Cubed bookshelves: IKEA. Television stand: IKEA. Dining table: Habitat.) Everything is shades of nothing, with white walls and those wooden floors that property developers seem to adore, even though they're actually just plastic.

The rooms are filled with clothes, boxes, and suitcases. Fay tells me she thought she had found someone to rent it, another friend of a friend, but was let down at the last minute. She is leaving in three days and has been in something of a panic. She apologizes for the mess, for the clothes and the cases, but I can see past that. I can see that it is, thanks to the ceilings and windows, an impressive flat. It could very well be home for a successful television producer living in London.

"I won't bother telling you I'll give you a call after I've seen all the applicants," says Fay, as we both drain our coffee cups and place them carefully on the coffee table (Heal's). "I like you. I can see you here, and I'd trust you, so if you want the flat for a year, it's yours."

"I'll take it," I say, smiling, and three days later I am in, with a week to unpack, settle myself, and explore Belsize Park.

Lorna gave me Julia's number. "She's so nice," she said. "You must call her." But I couldn't bring myself to, as by that time I knew I was her replacement, and I wouldn't have known what to say. As hard and ambitious as I am, confrontation is not my style. And anyway, I was here to work. Not to socialize.

162

One week and I love it. I have started work, met the team, checked schedules, cleared budgets, briefed researchers, lunched liquidly, and already feel part of the furniture.

"I can't believe you've only been here a week," says Johnny, once Julia's right-hand man, until I started to work on him. I believe I am making some headway, as his phone calls to her are noticeably fewer (I know he's calling her when he speaks very quietly into the mouthpiece, bows his head, and takes quick furtive glances around the office to ensure no one is listening as he passes on gossip).

I have been invited to sit with various big cheeses in the canteen for lunch, or in the bar after work, and I have accepted as many times as I have declined, because age has—finally—taught me that it is not always wise to ignore your peers. Or indeed your team.

I have been firm but fair with my team. While I'm as friendly as I can be, I have also ensured that they are aware of the boundaries. And respect them. I am happy to socialize with them, to be friends with them outside of the office, but when we are in the office I need them to know that I am not their mate. I have little time for mistakes but will reward good behavior, as these years in the business have taught me that this is the best way to get the best out of people.

In fact Friday night, as a thank you for being so welcoming to me, for making my first week so enjoyable (political? me?), I am taking my team out after work. I suggested dinner and, being young, fun, and full of the joys of the weekend, we have decided to drink copious amounts of alcohol before hitting one of those American-style-baby-back-ribs types of places in Covent Garden.

Don't ever accuse me of not knowing the way to a young person's heart.

This is, incidentally, one of the advantages of working for London Daytime Television. The social life that comes as part of the package is enormous. Every night this week I have ended up in the bar at work, talking for hours, before going out for dinner with at least two colleagues.

Exhausted as I now am, the advantages are numerous. I'm starting to feel very comfortable here, I'm getting to know my colleagues, my face is being seen by all the right people, and I am definitely being seen to be committed. Plus it's a damn sight better than going home to an empty flat and drinking a glass of wine on the sofa alone.

Tonight it's Nat, Niccy, Stella, Dan, and Ted. Johnny wasn't feeling too hot and left early today, and I am thankful for that, because, much as I like him, I find it easier to relax when he's not around. And don't ask me why everyone's names are shortened. I have no clue, but it seems to be prevalent. I would, however, shoot anyone who called me May.

We are starting our evening with a few rounds in the company bar, sitting at two tables pushed together, wrapped in cigarette smoke and laughter.

"Tony Nolan," Niccy is groaning. "Oh God. Do I have to?"

"Yeah!" the others chorus, all leaning in.

"I can't believe I'm going to say this. Tony Nolan?" Stella pauses before giving her verdict, and even I lean forward because Tony Nolan I have met. He is the News Director. Perfectly nice, but with the worst set of teeth you've ever seen in your life. Alternately gray and yellow, they are crooked, overcrowding his mouth, emitting a slightly sour odor that forces you either to back away or offer him chewing gum. Except that he doesn't like chewing gum.

The others lean forward in anticipation as Stella sips her beer before looking up. "Shag!"

"No way!" Dan and Ted almost spit their beer out, and a discussion ensues about Tony Nolan's teeth and how could she. We are playing Shag or Die, which doesn't seem to have any rules, and isn't particularly revealing other than the way people voice their opinions.

"Mark Simpson?" Ted then asks, looking at each of the girls as I listen, unable to join in, because most of the candidates are employees of the company, many of whom I haven't even heard of, let alone met.

"Nat?"

"Phwooargh. Shag."

"Niccy?"

"Shag him senseless."

"Stella?"

"Yes, please. I'd shag him for my country."

"Who's Mark Simpson?" I'm laughing at the ludicrousness of this game, but slightly intrigued at the number of shags Mark Simpson could be getting should he so desire.

"Mark. You know. The lawyer." My face is still blank as Stella rolls her eyes. "You were supposed to have a meeting with him yesterday but you rearranged for next week?"

Ah yes. Now I remember. "Of course," I laugh. "I've had to learn so many names this week, and put so many faces to them,

I couldn't remember. So what's so special about this Mark Simpson?"

"He's just gorgeous," Nat sighs.

"Drop-dead delicious," Niccy groans.

"He is gorgeous"—Stella lights a cigarette—"but that's not what makes him so attractive. He's got this little-boy-lost vulnerability that lawyers aren't supposed to have. No one thinks he's very happy in his relationship. God, it's not exactly a surprise when you think what's been happening there, and I suppose we all suffer from rescue syndrome. You just want to kiss him and make it all better."

"Mmm," Nat chuckles. "Kiss him all over."

"Christ, you're pathetic," Ted says with disdain. And, unless I'm very much mistaken, envy.

"So who's his partner?"

"You didn't know?" Ted looks at me in surprise. "It's Julia."

I think back to Adam and Lorna's wedding. Of course I remember Mark, only I hadn't known this was the same person, and I certainly wouldn't have expected him to be this heart-throb. Handsome? Yes. Nice guy? Yes. Sexual fantasy material? Most definitely not.

Shag or Die? Ah. Well, that's a different kettle of fish altogether.

12

"*Have your ears been burning?*" Stella has an eyebrow raised, a flirtatious look on her face as she looks over my shoulder. I turn to see none other than Mark Simpson standing there. The Mark Simpson. That Mark Simpson. Looking rather different from when I last saw him at the wedding.

This Mark Simpson looks thunderous. Dangerous. Extremely pissed off. He looks, in other words, like a challenge, a rather sexy challenge, and as soon as I see his face I can feel myself rising to it.

No. Stop it. He might be exuding sex appeal as if it's going out of fashion, but this man has been with Julia for years. Whether they're happy or not is none of my business, but I do know it's certainly not an excuse.

And even if I were to go for it, a man

like him isn't the type to be unfaithful. Not that I'd be his type. Julia's got that pretty-girl-next-door thing going on. Even when she looks like shit she's still the type that men want to protect, and me? No one could call me the girl-next- door type.

"Can I join you?" Mark pulls a chair from the neighboring table and drags it in between Johnny and me. He turns to me. "Mark Simpson. Nice to meet you."

I smile as I shake his hand. "Actually we've met before."

"I thought your face looked familiar. Where?"

"Adam and Lorna's wedding. I contributed to the Clangers discussion." I wait for him to smile, but his face is blank, clearly focusing on other things. "Um . . . are you okay?"

He looks at me then. Sees me. "I'm sorry," he says, and immediately I see that this man is really unhappy about something. It may be his relationship, I don't know. I've never been a big believer in office gossip, in that much as I like keeping up to date on things and hearing what people are talking about, I've learned to take it with a healthy pinch of salt.

Rumors become distorted and very quickly turn into facts, and although people had said, even tonight, that Mark was unhappy, I had to judge it for myself.

And now I am judging it for myself. This man is unhappy.

He shrugs. "Just a, well. A home thing. Domestic." And he sighs and, what on earth is going on, what on earth am I feeling? Is this . . . could it be, compassion? For a stranger? How ridiculous.

"Do you want to come out to dinner with us?" I say, because compassion is not a feeling I'm used to, and I'd far rather move this on to safer territory. "We're going to Chuck's Great

American Rib 'n' Beef Extravaganza. I hear it's as good as the Ivy these days."

To my great relief he laughs, and his entire face changes. God. This man really is far more attractive than I remember.

"I'll only come if I'm allowed to have an onion loaf all to myself."

"You can have a whole onion loaf and a whole portion of garlic bread to yourself if you really want."

"Now that's an offer I can't resist."

I look up and see Stella watching us, and I can see that she really does have a crush on him, but I didn't ask him to join us because I'm interested in him, and I certainly didn't ask him to sit next to me. Besides, I'm hardly flirting, I'm just inviting an unhappy colleague out with my team. My Good Samaritan act of the week.

A *huge* basement restaurant, Chuck's Great American Rib 'n' Beef Extravaganza is dark, noisy, and packed with parties such as ours: colleagues letting off steam after a hard week; drinking, dancing on the tiny dance floor in the middle of the room, and, presumably, as is the way with people who work closely together, getting up to rather more.

We contemplate fighting our way through the throngs of people to the bar, but a quick recce confirms that this simple procedure would force us through dozens of men, eyes as watchful as hawks, pretending to talk to mates, but all the while using a sip of their bottled beers as an excuse to scout the room, and the women in it. Standing close to the entrance, flanked by Stella, Nic and Nat, Mark next to me and the boys a step behind, I can see that we, the girls, are already being stripped by dozens of pairs of eyes, and although chatting people up goes along with this Friday night ritual of letting off steam, I am not sure I want to be part of it. Not when I am with my team. And Mark.

We are shown to a table at the back by an excessively cheerful waitress who has a good line in overfamiliarity, but this is what you find in restaurants such as these. I grit my teeth because I am constantly bemoaning the lack of service in this country, and this, although a little too much for my liking, is surely better than a sour-faced girl who does you a favor by deigning to serve you. From the sublime to the ridiculous. Ah well. Never mind.

I stand at the table with the others, all of them wondering where to sit, all of the girls wanting to sit next to Mark, but none, it seems, quite as much as Stella, who pushes her way next to him. I, incidentally, am on his other side, but not from maneuver so much as convenience: we walked to the table together, and this seems the easiest thing.

"And what can I get you to drink?" Shelley, the waitress, is back with her beaming smile.

"Tequila!" chorus Nat and Nic, giggling together, both already more than a little tipsy from our sojourn to the bar.

"Good choice!" the waitress says, and before I can order a gin and tonic, she's gone. I turn to see Mark looking at me with what surely resembles a smile on his face.

"She's going to bring back a bottle of tequila and . . ." he counts the heads, ". . . seven shot glasses. You know that, don't you?" I shrug. "So are you up for it?" he continues, eyebrow raised as he looks at me confrontationally.

"Up for . . . what exactly?" I purr. Stop it, Maeve! Take that flirtatious tone out of your voice immediately.

Mark looks surprised. Shit. He hadn't been flirting. I fucked up. I must be cool. Businesslike. I do not get involved with men I work with anymore, and I certainly do not get involved with men who belong to other people.

"What were you thinking?" he says slowly, and now I am confused, because I can't work out from his tone whether he's flirting, or whether he has no idea of the inference behind my words.

"Nothing," I say succinctly, before leaning toward him and murmuring quietly in his ear. "Just wondering whether you and I, given our responsible positions, ought to be getting drunk with the team."

Mark laughs as Shelley arrives with, sure enough, a bottle of tequila, a plate of limes, and a bowl of salt. Mark pours his tequila and knocks it back, no lemon or salt required. "You know what I think?" He wipes his mouth and pours another. "I think that after the day I've had I deserve to get drunk. In fact I deserve to get royally pissed." He then pours another glass and this time pushes it over to me. "And I also think that you need to let your hair down and have some fun," and he looks deep into my eyes and I pick up that glass and throw it down my throat as quickly as I can.

Stella is watching us. I can feel her eyes burning every time I look away, and I try to position my body so I can't actually see her face when I am talking to Mark, but it is hard.

I am trying desperately not to flirt with Mark, to treat him as a distant work colleague, but there seems to be an intimacy between us, and I could swear it's not my imagination, nor because we are having a heated discussion about the Royal Family, and Mark and I are the only pro-royalists round the table.

Actually, pro might be pushing it. But I'm certainly not anti as all my interns appear to be, accusing them of being paid far too much money and of being outdated with no role in society other than as figures of fun.

"But you can't possibly hate the Queen Mum," Mark says, at one point. "She's just a sweet old lady."

"Do we detect a hint of sentimentality beneath that tough lawyer veneer?" Nat leans forward with a smile that, thanks to the amount of booze, is very definitely more of a leer.

"Beneath this tough lawyer veneer beats a heart of gold," Mark says, smiling.

"I bet you say that to all the girls." Nat's flirting, and I feel a flash of irritation which I quickly suppress. I am very aware of Mark sitting next to me. His arm accidentally brushes mine, and my arm suddenly feels heavy, immobile, and I want to move it but somehow I can't. All I can do is sit and feel the light blond hairs on his arm brush my skin, and try to look away because the sensation is all-consuming, and if I look at our arms touching, I'm not sure I'll be able to make it through this evening. It will be too overwhelming.

By the way, this feeling is not new to me. Love? You must be joking. This feeling—my heightened senses, the fact that I am aware of every movement he makes, every tap of the finger, every blink of the eye — is lust. Good old unadulterated lust. God, I love this feeling. And I had forgotten exactly how good it felt.

But I do not mess with married men. I do not mess with married men. I do not mess with married men.

But he's not married . . . does that count?

Could I get away with it? He is, after all, unhappy, and I don't, after all, have any illusions about happy ever afters, so is it worth the risk?

I tune out of the conversation, putting my lust to one side as I consider the risk. I have been working at London Daytime Television for one week. So far I am very happy here. Could see myself working here for a very long time. Hell, as far as I'm concerned, I can picture the workmen taking down the plaque on the door that says "Mike Jones" and replacing it with one that says "Maeve Robertson."

I could climb the ladder to the heavens here. And Mark is the lawyer. Not just on the legal team, the head of the legal team. As I said. The lawyer. Someone I am bound to come into regular contact with, but even though I know I could handle it, could he?

He is also living with, and trying for a baby with, Julia, who seems to be extremely popular and well respected. Christ, I like her myself. Hmmmm. I look at his arm: strong, tanned, just the right amount of sun-bleached hair. Sexy.

Not tonight, Josephine.

I raise an arm and signal for Shelley, ordering a large bottle of sparkling mineral water.

"I see you're pinning your hair back up," Mark says with a

wry smile. "Clearly my powers of persuasion aren't as good as I thought."

I shrug. "Another time they might have worked, but I'm still new. I still need to impress."

"You don't think you've impressed already?"

"I don't know. What do you think?" Oh God. Insecurity. Never a good thing to show a man you're insecure, because men, basically, just don't do insecurity.

"I'm impressed." He doesn't look at me as he says this, and I sigh, because I could so easily be drawn into this man's web, but I won't. I can't.

"And I'm leaving." I give him a smile that I hope conveys my regret.

"That's a good idea," he says, scraping his chair back. "I ought to get home too."

"Where do you live?" We're standing on the corner of St. Martin's Lane, my coat huddled around me, both desperately searching for cabs. Needless to say, the only ones we see are already taken, and, rather like a mirage in the desert, I keep thinking I see an orange light driving toward me. But I am wrong.

"Belsize Park. You?"

"Gospel Oak. Just up the road! We'll share a cab." It's a statement, not a question. Then silence.

"Should we walk up there? It looks more promising." Mark gestures up another street, as a taxi, probably taken, disappears round the far corner. I take it as a good sign and nod, as the two of us walk off side by side. The lust has, thank God, very definitely cooled since leaving the restaurant. I'm cold and I'm tired, and all I can think about right now is curling up in the back of a lovely heated cab, and going home to bed.

I pull the coat tighter and look down at the pavement, tottering along, wishing I had worn more comfortable shoes, when I'm aware that Mark has stopped. I stop too. I look at him, barely registering the look of sheer longing in his eyes, when—and I swear to you I still don't know exactly how this happened—I find myself locked in his arms, kissing him as if my life depended on it.

I wish I could describe it better: the passion, the lust, the fire. What I can tell you is that I feel as if I'm melting into him, clinging on to him for my sanity, both of us drowning in this incredible intensity.

We pull apart, eventually, and look at each other, eyes wide with shock.

"I'm sorry," he says, and I'm about to reassure him, to say "Don't be," when he kisses me again, and this time, when we break apart, he pulls me into an alleyway.

Let me say this: I am not the sort of girl who has sex in alleyways. I have never been turned on by the thrill of being caught, or being seen, or in fact being anywhere other than an extremely comfortable bedroom. Or living room. I am a creature of comfort, and like to plan things accordingly. I have seduced many men, and I have done it with silkily smooth legs achieved with an Epilady (disgustingly painful but worthwhile), with black stockings and garter belts (so cliché, but effective nonetheless), and with champagne and flattery (guaranteed to get me just about anywhere I want to go).

What I have never done is what I am doing now. Pressed

up against a brick wall in a dark alleyway lit by a single, dull streetlamp at one end. The other end. Mark's mouth is all over me. My face, my neck, my collarbone. Rough, wet kisses that leave me gasping, eyes glazed over as I slide my hands under his jacket, pull his shirt out of his trousers, desperately pull it up until I can feel his hot skin under the palms of my hands.

He tears my shirt open, and I gasp as he moves his lips down my breast, moving my bra cup down until the white mounds of my flesh pour over the top, pulling my nipples into hard peaks with his mouth, his magical mouth, as I close my eyes and groan with pleasure.

I reach down and stroke his cock through his trousers, feeling the hardness, feeling, already, as if I cannot hold on much longer, and then he is inside me, thrusting deep inside me, breathing heavily into the side of my neck, holding one leg up by his waist as I cling to his back and move with him, moaning with lust.

He doesn't look at me afterward. We walk out of the alleyway and I watch the people passing, wondering whether they saw, whether anyone saw. We walk side by side, careful not to touch, all thoughts of a cab long-forgotten, and when we reach the end of the road I turn to Mark to try to say something, anything to break this silence, and when I look at him he starts to cry.

"Oh, Mark, what is it?" Surely the fast, furious fuck of a few minutes ago happened to someone else. I feel like a stranger again, and put an arm round his shoulders awkwardly to comfort him.

"I'm sorry," he blurts out. "Oh fuck. I'm so sorry. I didn't mean to . . . Christ." And neither of us knows what to say.

But I know one thing. I can't send this man home like this.

"I swear on my life that I'm not making a pass at you," I say gently, feeling as if this whole situation is completely unreal, "and I understand that you might feel very awkward about this, but I think you need to talk to someone. Why don't you come back to my flat, just to talk? I'll make you some coffee and then you can go home."

BY the time we walk through my front door, I'm really not sure whether anything actually happened. I look out of the cab window on the way home (it did take forever, but we finally got one) and wonder whether I fell asleep at the table and dreamed that I had the most passionate fuck of my life, with Mark, in a seedy alleyway on the way home. Wonder seriously whether it was only wishful thinking.

I make coffee and we sit on the sofa, a yard between us, neither wanting to be the first to speak, neither knowing quite why we are here.

"This is ridiculous," Mark says. "First of all I don't know you, other than, um . . ." He has the good grace to blush, and I realize that it wasn't a dream after all. We definitely fucked or he wouldn't be blushing. He continues: ". . . and you work for the same bloody company and I can't believe what happened tonight, and now I can't believe I'm even here, and—"

"Mark." I stop him, laying a hand gently on his arm. "I know this sounds bizarre but sometimes it's far easier to talk to strangers than it is to talk to people you know. I am renowned for many things, but what I am really famous for, other than my spectacular ability in bed" (I only threw that in to lighten things, and although it could have been entirely inappropriate it works and Mark does manage a small, sad smile) "is my discretion. This may be none of my business, but you don't seem happy, and you seem to be a man who is shouldering an extremely heavy burden. You don't have to explain anything to me, but, and I'm not saying this because I want a repeat performance, but I would like to help, and I'm saying that because I think you're a nice guy and you seem like you could do with a friend."

I stop to breathe.

"I don't know where to start," he says, before laughing bitterly. "If I started with the events of tonight you probably wouldn't believe me."

"Go on. What happened tonight?"

He tells me he went home and found his girlfriend and one of her friends dressed in white sheets and dancing round some sort of occult circle, almost in a trance as the flames of the candles scattered round the room tried to lick the bottom of the sheets.

"It was actually quite beautiful," he says, "but we ended up having a huge row because the whole premise of it was completely ridiculous. She's desperate to have a baby, has been for ages, and we can't get pregnant, and instead of actually doing something practical about it, going to see someone, she's doing these ridiculous things like making me carry juniper berries in my wallet because it's supposed to increase a man's potency,

178

and dancing round these stupid bloody candles with penises on them."

I can't help it. I start laughing. "What?"

"What?"

"What do you mean, candles with penises on them?" I don't even want to begin to describe the picture that flashes into my head.

"I don't know," he says, shrugging. "There was a big candle with an erect penis carved into it."

"Okay." A thought occurs to me. "Do you carry juniper berries, then?"

Mark reaches into his inside pocket, opens his wallet and pours a dozen juniper berries on to the coffee table with a sigh. We both pick one up and examine it.

"It sounds like she's scared," I offer finally.

"Of course she's scared. I'm scared too. But being scared isn't going to make her pregnant. She has to be more practical."

"I understand that, Mark, but it must be the worst feeling in the world to not be able to get pregnant. I'd be lying if I said I understood it, because children are really not on my agenda, but I'm sure that infertility would compromise your very womanhood."

"But what about me?" Mark says, and as he turns to look at me the pain in his eyes is frightening. "She said it was my fault. That she'd been pregnant and therefore I had to be firing blanks."

"Jesus." I let out a long whistle. "Did she actually say that?"

"Basically."

"That's tough, Mark." We sit in silence for a while. "Can I ask you something else?" He looks at me, and I'm not even sure I ought to be asking what I'm about to ask, but I can't not ask him, it's too urgent. "Do you actually want children?"

"Yes. Of course. I love children. I've always wanted children."

"Okay, let me put it another way. Do you actually want children with Julia?"

It's a loaded question and Mark catches his breath. "What are you asking?"

"I'm asking whether you're happy with her. Happy enough to spend the rest of your life with her. To wake up next to her every morning, for her to be the one you kiss every night before you roll over to sleep.

"I'm asking you, Mark, whether, should you actually get what you're looking for, you want Julia to be the mother of your children. Your partner for the rest of your life. That's what I'm asking. That's all."

There's a very long silence while Mark drops his head into his hands. At first I think he's crying, but after a while he looks up at me and his eyes are dry. "Once upon a time I would have said Yes. Definitely. But now I'm not sure of anything anymore."

13

I love my mum. I mean, I really, really love my mum. She's my best friend in the whole world and I've never understood how my friends can have so many problems with their mothers, because isn't it the most important relationship a girl should have?

Maybe it's because my parents divorced, because my mum and I only had each other, but throughout my teenage years, when my friends would turn up huffing and puffing about how much they hated their mothers and how stupid their parents were and would it be okay if they came and lived at our house, I thought my mum was fantastic.

She truly was the big sister I never had. It helped that she looked just like me, and that she didn't look very old, but then again she actually wasn't very old, as she had me when she was twenty, so when I was a teenager she was, Christ, she was pretty much the age I am now.

God, that's spooky. I could have a twelve-year-old daughter. I see women like that all the time. Women my age with that constantly harassed and tired look on their faces, pushing buggies, explaining things to toddlers, accompanied by pissed-off twelve-year-olds desperate to grow up and get away.

Children have never been part of my scheme of things. Should I spot a Mothercare looming on the particular street on which I'm walking, I will make sure I avert my eyes. So-called cute adverts featuring babies and their bottoms have never done it for me, it's just a cynical manipulation of emotions, and luckily I was born without the baby gene.

I'm not interested in babies, and I'm not interested in talking about babies. I could say they're not a part of my life, but unfortunately they have affected my life, as every time a friend rings me up to tell me excitedly she's pregnant, I'm expected to jump up and down with joy, when in fact my heart plummets to the floor.

And another one crossed off the Christmas card list, for I know exactly what will happen. The more sensitive friends will still see me when pregnant, and will manage to carry on a normal conversation. We will talk about work, friends, life, and men, although not necessarily in that order. I might ask how they are feeling, and they will say fine, and we will leave it at that. The less sensitive will sit there all evening and presume I am desperate to hear about their scans. They will presume I am fascinated by tales of their morning sickness, by amusing anecdotes they have built around their swollen feet to make their tales more palatable. They will bang on and on about pregnancy and babies, and nursery decoration, and I will be mentally checking off the minutes, and wondering how soon I can leave without seeming rude.

Although by that stage I'm not even sure I care.

However sensitive the friend, the final outcome is always the same. You send the obligatory card and flowers when the baby is born, and are then expected to pay a visit. You sit there, bored to tears as they cuddle a screaming infant, and try to look interested as you listen to them recounting their birth story for the hundredth time that week.

You go home filled with sadness, because however close you are, you know that's another friend you won't be seeing anymore. You won't have anything in common anymore, since you are not interested in babies, and they are no longer interested in life.

I shudder even thinking about it.

My amateur psychologist friends (the ones without babies) claim that I'm protecting myself from being hurt. I associate commitment, children, with my parents, and my parents with the pain I felt when my father left. They say I don't want to get married or have children because I'm scared.

I say it's because I have more important things to do.

And it's not as if I had a horrible upbringing, terrible parenting, and don't want to inflict that on any children of mine. Sure, the first year was tough. My mother was, to put it mildly, devastated. I'd bring her cups of tea when she was crying, and curl up next to her on the sofa, stroking her hair because that was what she used to do to me when I was upset, and I didn't know what else to do.

Eventually she cried less and less, and soon there was a

series of friends passing in and out the door, none of whom was permanent, but all of whom helped to keep a smile on her face most of the time.

"Not 'uncles,'" she'd say to me, when I questioned why friends of mine were allowed to call their mum's friends "uncle," and why her friends were just Bob. Or Michael. Or Richard. I understand now, of course. She didn't want to be married. She didn't want commitment. Been there, done that, she'd laugh merrily. She wanted fun. She wanted to feel beautiful, and she wanted to be treated well. Naturally there was sex involved, but it was far more about the attention. And when she felt their attention waning, she'd move on.

So "uncles" implied a familiarity and a permanence that she neither wanted nor needed. A familiarity and a permanence that were never going to occur, even though some of them were really very nice. I remember being particularly fond of Bob. He clearly thought the way to my mother's heart was through her daughter, and, thanks to Bob, my Girl's World had more makeup than any of my friends'. Not only that, my makeup was real makeup and could be used on us as well.

The older I grew, the closer my mother and I became. Some said it was unhealthy, that there ought to be boundaries between a parent and a child, but I loved the fact that I could call her Viv and she didn't mind; that she'd borrow my ra-ra skirts and I'd borrow her jodhpurs; that when I decided to go on the pill at fifteen (not because I was actually doing anything but because I was hopeful), the person who accompanied me to the family planning clinic was my mother.

I loved the fact that after our respective dates had gone

home, be it that night or the morning after, we would sit together on the sofa and recount every detail, giggle together, drink vodka and tonics when we were happy, and eat giant-sized Cadbury Dairy Milk bars when we were sad.

She lives in Lewes now. Still single. There are times when I think she ought to settle down. Not because she's unhappy, but because the older you get, the harder it is on your own, and because I think she deserves someone to take care of her. But she has her friends, her dog, and now her bridge, and she says that's all she needs in life. Oh, and me of course, which is why she's coming to see me this weekend.

"So come on, cagey." Viv's had the guided tour of the Belsize Park flat (which took all of five minutes), and has whisked me up to town to do some shopping. We hopped on the bus at Swiss Cottage and are heading up Wellington Road toward Selfridges, also known, to my mother at least, as Mecca.

"Come on what?"

"I've seen the flat, I've seen how well London suits you, I've heard all about your work, but I haven't heard a murmur about your love life."

"What love life?" I mutter darkly, because that's the one area that hasn't been going too smoothly. In fact, since that one episode in the alleyway with Mark, there's been nothing. And really, I can't count that. Yes, I found him incredibly sexy that night, but it was a true one-night stand if ever there was one, and not something either of us will be repeating.

"Didn't you mention something about a man at work? The,

what was it . . . accountant? No! The lawyer. Didn't you have a bit of a fling with the lawyer at work? What happened to him? He sounded pretty nice."

Bugger. I forgot I had spoken to her the next day, and had told her all about it.

"Nothing's going on," I sigh, looking out the window. "Lovely guy, but he's got a girlfriend and he's at work so it would be complicated even if he didn't, and he probably isn't for me anyway."

"Funny isn't it." She turns to me. "I always thought if I moved to London I'd definitely find a man. I thought the streets were paved with men. I suppose, though, wherever you go, your life is still your life and you're still you. But I always thought things would be different in London. More glamorous. More exciting."

"What do you mean, you thought you'd find a man? You never wanted a man, remember?"

She smiles. "Ah, is that what I said? I suppose I never found a man who matched my requirements."

"What do you mean?"

She shrugs. "The more time I spent on my own, just you and me together, the more expectations I had. It wasn't enough that someone should be loving, or loyal, or good to you. I thought that he also had to be handsome and funny and clever and creative, and in those days I thought money was important too."

"But those things are important," I say, confused.

"They can be, but they're not crucial. I had relationships with wonderful men, but I expected too much from them, and always moved on thinking I'd find the perfect man out there.

186

Someone with whom I would fall passionately in love, who was my soulmate. My other half."

"You might still find him."

"I think I found him many times," she says sadly. "Except I wasn't prepared to compromise. Do you remember Bob?" I nod. "I see him sometimes at the Bridge Club. Lovely man. He was a lovely, lovely man, but do you know what? I thought he wasn't good enough for me because he was a builder. He loved you, he treated me like a queen, and we had fun together, but I was young, and arrogant, and I threw away a chance of real happiness."

"Is he married now?"

"Oh yes. He married Hilary Stewart." I draw a blank. "Remember Josephine Stewart? You were at school with her? A few years after Rodney died, Bob and Hilary started courting. And I hear they're very happy."

"Jesus." It comes out in a whistle, because Josie Stewart was the richest girl in the class. They lived in a huge white detached house and she was driven to school in a dark green Rolls-Royce. Jesus.

"So Hilary didn't have quite the same expectations, then?"

"Easier when you're not used to being on your own."

"I can't believe you're saying all this. I always thought you were on your own because you wanted to be, because you were happiest on your own."

"I'd be lying if I said I was unhappy. I had you, and we built a lovely life together, but would I have been happier with a man in our lives?" She shrugs sadly. "I suppose I'll never know."

"But you're my role model." I feel confused and I'm not

altogether sure why. "You're the reason I give as to why I don't want to get married. I tell everyone about you, and about how you didn't need anyone, and about being happy as long as you have a support structure of friends and family around you."

There's a pause before my mother answers. "Maeve, love," she says, "do you have a good social life here in London? Do you have friends? Are you happy? I'm not saying you have to have a man to be happy, but I know how lonely life can be on your own, and I worry about you when I'm not living round the corner. I know how self-sufficient you are, and I know you think you're fine without a man, but don't do what I did. Don't sacrifice a wonderful man because of your principles, whatever they are."

"Pfff," I snort. "Chance would be a fine thing. London, as you can see"—I gesture outside to Baker Street—"is most definitely not paved with eligible men. Not even when you work in television."

I love that my mother doesn't even bother looking at Jaeger. We head straight up to the second floor at Selfridges, via the loo because I'm bursting, and hit the funkier, younger stuff. Within minutes I've got a tight green cardigan to try on, a hot pink stretchy top, and a pair of navy straight-legged narrow trousers. My mother's holding a black lace shirt that should be far too young for her but will definitely look fantastic, and a tight black skirt.

We share a changing room, and decide to take it in turns to try on, as it really isn't big enough for the both of us, but it's much more fun doing everything in pairs, so she perches on a stool while I try on the tops.

"Well, that's weird," I say, because the cardigan, my normal size 8, is gaping in between each button, showing large expanses of white flesh.

"Have you put on some weight?"

"I didn't think so, although . . ." As I think about it, I realize that my clothes have definitely been feeling tighter. Just the other day, after lunch, I actually had to unbutton the waistband of my trousers to get comfortable. And strange only because my weight has barely fluctuated since I was a teenager. I'm a size 8, no more, no less.

Except clearly I am not. Anymore.

I try the trousers on and turn to look at my mother in confusion, because these aren't even meeting. Not even close enough to shout hello.

"They must be the wrong size. They must have labeled them wrongly." I swivel to see the label, which is tucked inside at the back.

"Bugger. They are an 8. What do you think, Viv? Have I put on weight?" I feel a panic that I've never felt before, because I've never put on weight, never had to think about it, and this is an entirely new problem for me.

"Well, you are looking a tiny bit bigger. But tiny. Hardly noticeable."

We both look at the clothes and look at my body. "Your boobs are rather large, though," Viv says, peering closely. "You're not by any chance premenstrual, are you?"

I start to laugh. "That's why I love you, Mum." I give her a hug, the buttons now almost popping off the cardigan. "I completely forgot about my bloody period." I lean down and pull my diary out of my bag, and flick through as I am so completely crap about remembering my periods, I have to write down a large PD—Period Due—on the due date, except most of the time I even forget to do that.

"Shit."

"What's the matter?"

"I must have forgotten again." I flick back to the last period I wrote down, which was six weeks ago. Which would mean I'm due in two weeks' time. No, that can't be right.

"No, that can't be right." I flick back and try to work it out again.

"So when are you due?"

"I don't know." I hand the diary to my mother. "You work it out. Look, my period was on the twelfth of February, so I would have had another on the ninth of March, which means it's due on the third of April, so why have I got all the PMS symptoms now?"

Viv looks at the diary, then looks into space as she checks off her fingers, then back at the diary. "You did have a period on the ninth of March?" she says slowly.

"Of course I had a period. Didn't I?" I suddenly realize what she's saying and I sit down on the stool with a thump. "Didn't I? Oh fuck. Viv. I don't know. I can't remember whether I had a period or not."

"Look, if you remember what you did around then, you might remember whether you had a period or not, okay?"

"Okay." I nod my head, trying to ignore the fact that my heart is now thumping like a mad person's.

"On the ninth of March you had a meeting with Mike Jones at three P.M." She looks at me expectantly but I shake my head. I have a million meetings with Mike Jones and they're all indistinguishable. "You had a drink with someone called Johnny in the evening."

"Oh, I remember that!" We went to a bar in Gabriel's Wharf. "But I don't remember having my period."

"On the tenth you were in an edit suite."

"Nope."

"Evening you had a meeting with Stella?"

"Nope." It's all blank. And I don't remember if I was having a period.

"I think, my darling," my mother says, gritting her teeth, and unable to hide the pained expression, "that after this we ought to go and get a pregnancy test."

My heart threatens to jump right out of my mouth.

We don't say very much on the way back. Viv's being incredibly sweet and sympathetic, and keeps rubbing my arm and looking at me with this huge concern. At home she sends me off to the bathroom while she bustles around the kitchen making tea and talking nineteen to the dozen about rubbish to try to retain a sense of normality. I, meanwhile, feel as if I have woken up in the middle of a particularly surreal dream. Not nightmare, because nothing has happened yet, but I feel as if I am an observer, as if this is happening to someone other than me, and I am only vaguely curious at the outcome, to see what this person, who looks like me, sounds like me, and talks like me, will do.

191

I have locked the bathroom door and tipped the test out of the Boots bag, and I note that my hands are shaking, but even then I note it only with vague interest. I have never done a pregnancy test before. I have never needed to. And although I am shaking, I also know as an absolute certainty that I will not be pregnant. How could I possibly fall pregnant on the one time, the first time, that I actually allowed myself to get carried away in the heat of the moment and didn't use a condom?

Plus of course there is Mark, because did he not say that Julia hates him because he is infertile? Did he not sit on my sofa, after the unfortunate event that I no longer wish to think about, and say that his relationship is shit because Julia blames him? That they have been trying for months and she has been pregnant and the problem is definitely, undoubtedly, his.

I pull the package out of the box and look at it for a while, then I pull out all the notes and instructions and read them from cover to cover. Not that I'm putting it off or anything. Because I am not pregnant.

"With the tip pointing downward, hold the absorbent sampler . . ."

"Maeve? Are you okay? Do you need me?" Viv's standing outside the door.

"It's okay, Mum." Funny how I revert back to calling her "Mum" at times of need. Not that I need her, but it really is comforting to know that she's here right now. Just in case.

In case of what?

Because there's just no way I'm pregnant. No way. No fucking way.

Eventually I feel the urge to pee again, which isn't surprising because I have been running back and forth to the loo amazingly often these days, but then that could well be because of the water I'm drinking. The *Daily Mail* Detox Diet said at least two liters a day, so I've been swigging it back like there's no tomorrow, and spending half the day sitting on the loo.

I take a deep breath, unwrap the test, and undo my trousers.

It's showtime.

Viv looks at my smiling face and immediately breaks into a huge smile. "Oh, thank God," she laughs, walking over to put her arms round me and give me a hug. "For one long horrible hour there I really thought you were pregnant."

I let her go, the smile never leaving my face, and I hold up the test to show her. Two windows. Two thick blue lines. Viv looks at me in confusion. "This does mean it's negative? Doesn't it?"

And that's when I start to cry.

14

shock.

Complete and utter shock.

This is not supposed to happen. This is not in my game plan. I don't want children. I never wanted children, and the thought that there is something growing inside of me makes me feel ill.

But maybe there's not. Maybe it's a mistake. If there are false negatives, and God knows there are, then surely there are false positives as well?

Viv goes out to buy another test, and I know, I can see in her eyes that she is as shocked as I am, and that the only way for her to stay calm is to keep busy. She first makes me a cup of tea, then insists on doing all the washing up, and practically leaps at the opportunity of going out to the chemist's when I mention the false positive stuff.

Except I've got a horrible feeling there is no such thing as a false positive. I know that I've read somewhere that the hormone that turns the test blue is only present in your body when you are pregnant, and that there is absolutely no way the test can turn blue without it.

Nevertheless Viv comes back with one pregnancy test and one bag of Maltesers (always my favorite when young), and—even more worrying—as soon as I see the Maltesers I'm far more concerned with eating the Maltesers than with doing another pregnancy test, and I really don't do chocolate anymore.

"Maeve, love," Viv says, shooting me a concerned glance as I stuff the Maltesers in my mouth. "I think you probably ought to do another test."

And so I trundle off into the bathroom and emerge a few minutes later with a shrug. "Yup." I collapse onto the sofa. "Still pregnant."

"Maeve, we need to talk about this. We need to talk about what you're going to do."

"I don't want to talk about it," and I realize I don't. I just want the whole thing to go away, I want to pretend it never happened.

"It's not going to go away," Viv says gently, squeezing my hand. "You're pregnant, and now we have to decide what the next step is."

"What do you mean what the next step is? There's only one thing to do, for God's sake." My voice is hard, and I see Viv flinch, but really. As if I have a choice.

"Mum," I sit down next to her and watch her brace herself. "I love you, and I know that you'll support me whatever my decision is, but I also know how much you love children and how much you want a grandchild." I shudder. "Now isn't the right time," I say, as gently as I can. Her eyes well up and I feel like such a bitch, but I have to make her understand. "I'm not ready to be a mother. I'm not you. I know you brought me up by yourself, and I know that even when it felt like the hardest thing in the world you wouldn't have changed it, but we're very different people. I have my career, Mum, and that's the most important thing to me, and I don't want a baby. A baby would ruin everything."

The tears brim over Viv's eyes and trickle down her cheeks, and I put my arms around her to comfort her, and all I can think is that this is so weird. Here I am, comforting my mother, when I'm the one who's pregnant. I'm the one who will be having an abortion.

Viv looks up at me eventually. "Oh Maeve," she sighs. "I do love you, and you're right, I'll always be there for you, but you can't just make a snap decision like this. This isn't just about you anymore. Love, you have a new life growing inside of you, a baby, my grandchild. . . ." And she starts crying again.

"It's not a baby." My voice is harsh. Harsher than I thought, and I stand up and walk to the window, where I watch the cars for a while, wondering how everyone else's life can carry on as if nothing terrible has happened, when mine has just been turned upside down.

Although really, it's only an abortion, for God's sake. Practically everyone I know has had an abortion at one time or another. To be honest it's a bloody miracle that it's never happened to me before now. And everybody else gets over it. It's no big deal.

"It's no big deal," I say, my back still turned to Viv, my gaze now fixed on the lit-up window of a flat over the road. Thanks to the huge Georgian sash windows, I can see clearly into their living room, and of course the irony is that I am looking at a young couple, both lying on the floor playing adoringly with a baby who's attempting to crawl. I watch the baby, on hands and knees swaying from side to side before belly-flopping to the floor as his parents lean down and cover him with kisses.

And I feel absolutely nothing.

The mother looks up and sees me watching, and I pull the shutters across so I can no longer see.

And I feel absolutely nothing.

"It's not a baby, Mum." I walk back to the sofa and sit down, wondering why I don't feel sick. Wondering why I don't feel anything except tired and a bit numb. "It's a . . . nothing. It's nothing. It's not a baby, it's not my child, and it's not your grandchild. You have to stop thinking like that or I won't be able to get through this."

I hear Viv pulling herself together, and eventually she sniffs and says she understands.

We pretend to have a normal evening. We make supper and eat it in front of the television, feet resting on the coffee table as we tuck into pasta primavera. We don't say anything about the pregnancy for the rest of the evening, and every time an ad comes on that features a baby, Viv or I quickly flick the remote control to another channel. It's exhausting, but it's what we need to do. Pretend it's not happening.

"What about the father?" I pause halfway into my toast and look up to see Viv framed in the doorway, eyes still blurry with sleep.

Viv always likes a lie-in on a Sunday, so when I woke up this morning I tiptoed past her, fast asleep on the sofa bed, and snuck into the kitchen to make tea and toast. And another slice of toast. And then another. Christ, I'm hungry.

"What about the father?"

"Are you going to tell him?"

"I don't know. I hadn't thought, but no. I don't suppose he needs to know."

Viv sighs as she comes in, makes herself some coffee, then perches on the stool on the other side of the breakfast bar in my teeny tiny kitchen.

"Maeve"—I steel myself because I can tell from her tone that I'm not about to like what she's going to say—"I'm not going to tell you anything trite like he has a right to know, or you owe it to him or anything like that, because I don't believe that's necessarily true, particularly given that it was a brief fling."

I sigh with relief.

"But," she continues, "this man, what was his name again?"

"Mark."

"Mark. Didn't you tell me he thought he was infertile? Didn't you say that he was desperately unhappy in his relationship because his girlfriend blamed him for not being able to get pregnant?"

"How on earth do you remember that?" I'm amazed and somewhat horrified. I understand the point she's making, and I also know she's right. How could I possibly deny him this knowledge? Not that I want him to be involved in any way, size, shape, or form, but how can I let this man carry on thinking he's firing blanks when he's quite patently not?

"I lay in bed for hours last night," Viv says. "I couldn't sleep and I wanted to wake you up and ask you about him, but you needed to sleep. You know what I'm going to say, don't you?"

"Yes."

"He has a right to know that he's capable of having children. That's all. If you don't want him to do anything else, fair enough, but you can't let that poor man carry on thinking he's the one at fault with his girlfriend. He is still with his girlfriend, isn't he?" Viv's voice is suddenly hopeful, and I start to feel incredibly tearful. Christ. This isn't like me at all.

Oh Mum. She is so transparent. I can see that she's trying her best, but I know what she's thinking. She's praying and hoping that Mark and Julia will have split up, and that Mark will somehow persuade me to change my mind, and that the three of us, baby, Mark, and I, will live happily ever after.

I could give her false hope, because rumor has it that Julia has indeed flown the coop, as it were, and is currently having a high old time in New York, but who knows whether it's true. And until yesterday afternoon I will admit I had entertained the odd fantasy of getting it together again with Mark. After all, it was the most astonishingly sexy quickie I think I've ever had. But it's just a fantasy. A relationship is the last thing I need.

But I have seen Mark in the bar a few times. And the canteen. We've exchanged polite, curt nods, although a couple of times we've held one another's eyes for slightly longer than was altogether necessary, and I have to say I felt a small charge pass through me.

But Mark really isn't the type for a few quick fucks. I know, already, that Mark is a long-termer. He's husband material. A keeper. And that's not what I want. I've been involved with men like Mark before. You go in thinking you both want exactly the same thing. The sex is great, and it's great fun.

Then before you know it they're offering to cook you dinner, then they take it for granted that every time you see them you'll be staying the night, and act hurt and wounded as they sit in bed and watch you pull on your underwear at one o'clock in the morning. But you know it's really over when you find yourself pushing a trolley together in Sainsbury's on a Saturday morning. That's what men like Mark crave. That togetherness. That coziness. That coupledom that is pure anathema to me.

Yeuch.

I don't think so.

So I'd heard the rumors about Julia leaving, and I'd decided that it was none of my business and that I wouldn't pursue it anyway. Not my type. Nat, Niccy, and Stella are, of course, delighted. Many's the time I've walked in on a shared fantasy involving Mark Simpson.

I've got a feeling Stella knows something happened that night. She's my kind of woman, Stella. Cool and clever. If I wasn't so confident in my capabilities as a producer, Stella is exactly the sort of woman who would be a threat. And she's a woman. Nat and Niccy, though bright and determined, are still little girls. But Stella has been around the block a few times. You can tell.

Rather like myself.

Nat and Niccy teased me the week after the evening at Chuck's Great American Rib 'n' Beef Extravaganza, but I laughed it off and pulled it off.

Stella didn't say anything until one night in the bar. The night that Mark and I exchanged glances for rather more than a split second. I had been in the middle of talking to Johnny and Stella, and I had caught Mark's eye over Stella's shoulder, and had faltered in the middle of what I was saying. Had stopped still, unsure of where I was, who I was with, or what I was saying. I shook my head, said, "What was I saying?" and Johnny laughed and reminded me that I had been telling them about the latest ratings war. I caught myself and carried on talking, but Stella swiveled her head slowly to see what, or who, had caught me off guard, and when she turned back to me, I knew she knew.

She didn't say anything until later that evening. Quite a few drinks later. Although that's the thing with Stella. You think she's drinking, but at the end of the evening she always seems to be sober. She always seems to remember everything.

In other words she does exactly the same as me.

We were both leaning over the bar when she smiled at me. "So," she drawled, eyebrow raised. "Mark Simpson, eh?"

"Mark Simpson what?" I was calm.

"Shag or Die? You never said." She knows, I thought. Fuck. She knows, she knows, she knows.

"Hmm." I pretended to think, before affecting what I hoped was a natural smile. "I think I'd have to say shag."

"Funny. Now why does that not surprise me?" And instead of coming up with a quick, clever answer, I stood there flummoxed, and she smiled, raised her glass in a silent toast, and walked away, leaving me feeling ever so slightly humiliated.

But I liked Stella. Like her. She reminds me of me, and even though I know she knows, I also know she wouldn't indulge in idle gossip about it. Or at least I hope I know. She doesn't seem the type. Too cool. And although she joins Nat and Niccy in the elaborate fantasies involving Mark, I know she's backed off now, and that she's only doing it to bond with the girls.

And now I see Stella watching me when Mark's around, watching him to see if there's anything else she ought to know, I am so careful not to give anything away. It was one fuck, I feel like saying to her. One night. It won't be repeated. He's. Not. My. Type. And that, my friends, is why I won't be giving my mother false hope. Because I am not ready to settle down.

"I don't know what's happening with his girlfriend," I say to Viv, my tone of voice gentle. "But Mum, you know how hard I've worked to get where I am. You know me better than anyone, and my career comes first. It always has done. I know it's hard for you to accept, but marriage and babies and all of that just isn't for me.

"Maybe one day," I add to soften the blow. "But I know I'm doing the right thing for now."

Viv manages a smile and then wraps her arms around me tightly. "I love you, darling," she says. "And I'll always support you, whatever your decision."

"I know, Viv. And I love you too."

I know I ought to have called a clinic, or a doctor, or something, but part of me hopes that this will just go away by itself. I'm sure I read somewhere that a ridiculous proportion of women miscarry without ever knowing they were even pregnant, and every time I go to the loo I pray that I'm going to see blood, that nature will somehow intervene.

And I'm only, what? Six weeks? I've still got time. Masses of time. Plus I'm feeling completely fine. Just a little tired but thank Christ not a hint of morning sickness. That I really couldn't cope with.

"Where the fuck have you been?" We're having our regular Monday morning team meeting, and Johnny is late. Fifteen minutes late. He has strolled in fifteen fucking minutes late, carrying a cappuccino as if he hasn't a care in the world, and hasn't even got the good sense to apologize.

His face falls, and I really don't know why I'm so angry but all of a sudden I'm furious with him. How dare he be so late. How dare he walk in so breezily when the rest of us had the courtesy to be on time.

"I will not stand for this," I say, my voice getting louder and louder, and I know I'm starting to shout, which is ridiculous but I can't contain this anger. "Who the fuck do you think you are? Do you think you're better than the rest of us? You're different and it's okay for you to miss the meeting?"

"I'm rea—really sorry," he stammers, crestfallen. "The tube was cance—" but I'm on a roll and quite frankly I don't care about his stupid excuses.

"Everyone else managed to make it here on time, and I will not have members of my team treating me with disrespect."

I burst into tears.

What the hell is going on? What the hell is wrong with me? I run out of the room, sobbing like a child, embarrassed as hell, and crash through the door of the ladies', collapsing on the loo and crying uncontrollably into my hands.

"Maeve?" There's a gentle knocking on the door and I know Stella's concerned, but I can't stop crying. I sound like a child, and I want to stop because this is my biggest nightmare come true. I have lost it in front of my staff; I have humiliated myself in front of my staff, and now I can't stop crying.

And worst of all, I don't even know what I'm crying about.

"Maeve? Are you okay?" I hear more footsteps through my sobs and can just about make out Nat's voice asking Stella what's wrong. "Go back to the office," Stella says, and the fact that Nat does makes me feel a bit better. There's something in Stella's voice that is unbelievably reassuring, and after a while my sobbing becomes hiccuping, and after a while the hiccuping slows down until I'm almost normal. I pull some toilet paper off the roll and dry my eyes, then open the cubicle door to see Stella standing there with a concerned expression in her eyes.

"Everything okay?" I say with a smile, and I turn and walk out the door. I feel absolutely fine.

"*I fucking* knew it," Ted's saying as I walk back into the room, only remembering to wipe the mascara from under my eyes just in time. "She's turning into Julia. I swear, it's that bloody chair. All the women who sit in it start off sussed and sexy, and that chair turns them into mad bitches from hell."

"Johnny," I say, as Ted jumps, then starts shuffling some papers guiltily on his desk. "Can I have a word in private?"

Johnny follows me out the door, both our footsteps echoing in the silence that has suddenly descended on the room, and he follows me mutely to the drinks machine where I put in some coins and punch in the buttons for two cups of tea.

And it's only when I turn to look at him that I realize how upset he is, and I feel terrible.

"I'm so sorry." I hand him a cup of tea, but he still can't look at me. "Johnny, look at me." Reluctantly he raises his eyes, and I continue, shocked at the hurt. "My behavior in there was appalling. I don't know what to say. It had absolutely nothing to do with you but I took it out on you because you were an easy target. There is no excuse for the way I spoke to you, and I promise you it won't happen again." I can see I'm getting through.

"Johnny, there's stuff going on in my personal life. Not stuff I can talk about, but it's a difficult time for me. I should never have brought it into the office, and I should never have taken it out on you. Can you forgive me?"

Johnny smiles a very small smile and nods.

"Okay. Let's get back. Oh, and by the way, can you ask Ted to find out whoever supplies the furniture in this place and get them to change my chair immediately?" With this Johnny gives me a proper smile.

Now all I have to do is apologize to everyone else.

I stop off at the chemist's on the way home again tonight. Every night I make sure I find a different chemist, just so they don't think I'm completely mad. Every night I get home and go straight to the bathroom with a pregnancy test, praying that the blue lines will have disappeared. They haven't.

Viv phones me every day. She phones to see how I am, and when I tell her what happened today, because I am still in shock about my behavior, Viv tells me that her pregnancy with me was exactly the same.

"I didn't have a minute's sickness," she says fondly, "but my hormones were all over the place. I cried at absolutely everything and the anger? I had a positively rageful three months. If I wasn't shouting, I was crying. You're just like me," she says, and then she stops, because she remembers that I am not just like her.

I am not going to have a baby. I am going to have an abortion.

Just as soon as I get around to making the appointment.

15

From sex kitten to blimp in five easy minutes.

I'm enormous. How can I possibly be this enormous when I'm just, what, eight weeks, nine weeks pregnant? Okay, okay, maybe it's down to the sudden irresistible urge I've had for chocolate. Maltesers, Crunchies, Double Deckers. You name it, I've sent Johnny down to the vending machine to get it.

And the reason for yesterday's minor tantrum? The machine was out of Bountys. Who would have thought a bar of coconut covered with milk chocolate would elicit a flood of tears? Certainly not me. Not before yesterday. But if I can't eat exactly what I want to eat, my hormones go haywire, and I know Ted's comments about the Mad Bitch from Hell chair have been repeated amid much mirth.

Oh fuck it.

Viv keeps calling to see if I'm okay. And last week a parcel arrived with a year's supply of Pregnacare vitamin supplements.

"Why did you send this to the office?" I hissed down the phone to her.

"I knew you wouldn't be at home to take it in," Viv said. Then, after a pause, "Maeve, love. I know you're going to have an, a you know . . ." She can't actually say the word. ". . . but you should be taking folic acid anyway. Not just for the ba . . . I mean that you need to be taking extra vitamins and minerals to keep yourself healthy."

"I'm fine."

"They'll help with the hormones," Viv said, at which point I tore off the seal and downed three with a swig of cold cappuccino.

Ah yes. Cappuccino. I have read that coffee doubles your chance of miscarriage within the first three months of pregnancy, and have subsequently been drinking extra-strong cappuccinos from the moment I arrive at work until the moment I leave. The only unfortunate side effect thus far is that I'm spending most of my time at work sitting on a toilet seat, which isn't hugely constructive.

I came back from my thirteenth toilet break this morning (it was 10:34 A.M.) to find Mike Jones loitering outside my office door, pretending to be having an intimate chat with Stella but undoubtedly waiting for me.

"Hi, Mike." I flash him my most flirtatious smile, but evidently my killer smile only works with a killer suit and killer high heels. A huge baggy jumper from the Men's Department of M & S combined with size-eighteen drawstring trousers isn't exactly the sexiest look in the world, I have to concede. (Although my boobs are now fantastic . . .)

He looks uncomfortable, but comes into my office and sits down, gesturing for me to do the same. "Um, everything all right?"

"Yes. Great. Everything all right with you?"

He nods distractedly, then lets out a big sigh, finally meeting my eye. "Maeve, I feel like this is déjà vu. I can't believe this is happening again but I've got to ask you what the fuck is going on."

"What the fuck is going on?" I'm smiling, keeping the tone light, but my heart's pounding, because please God, let me not have jeopardized the one job I've wanted all my life.

"The word on the floor is that you're — "

"Turning into the Mad Bitch from Hell?" I cock an eyebrow and note his surprise. He thought I hadn't heard it.

"Turning into Julia?" I continue, chancing a grin, which is — thankfully — returned, together with an embarrassed shrug.

"Thank fuck for that. I thought you'd start screaming at me too." He looks down warily at the chair on which he's sitting. The chair behind my desk. My chair.

"Yes," I say, nodding wearily. "That is the Mad Bitch from Hell chair, and no, I don't think it will affect you as (a) you're a bloke and (b) — "

"I'm already a mad bastard?" He's enjoying this.

"Well." I shrug. "That is the word on the floor."

"Come on, then, Maeve. What's it all about? All I keep hearing is that you're throwing these tantrums and everyone's scared shitless of you. I had to give Julia a break because I couldn't have all her staff feeling that way, and now you've morphed into her and I want to know why."

I sit up straight and look him in the eye, wait until I have his full attention.

"I'm pregnant."

"You what." The shock on his face is a picture, and I can see exactly what's going through his mind. First, fuck, why did I give the job to some stupid woman who's got herself up the duff in five minutes? Second, who the fuck am I going to get in to replace her, and third, hang on. She's single. Who the fuck is the father?

"Joke," I say weakly, wishing I hadn't said anything, wishing I hadn't felt the need to put him to the test. His sigh of relief is audible.

"Fuck. I thought I was going to have a heart attack." As Mike recovers from the shock, I think quickly. What the hell am I supposed to say? How the hell am I supposed to explain myself? Family problems? He'd want to know what. Mike Jones is not the sort of man to be satisfied with a vague explanation. "You don't like it?" he'd say. "Well, fuck off, then."

"I'll tell you the truth if you won't tell anyone," I say, and he leans forward, his attention immediately caught. "I've been having a few problems."

Mike's eyes are full of sympathy.

"It's actually gynecological, one of my ovaries has a fibroid on it the size of a golfball, and my hormone levels are . . ." I don't have to say any more. Mike has already stood up and is holding a hand up to silence me.

210

"It's all right, Maeve," he says, and my explanation has had exactly the desired effect. It's female, it's gynecological, and therefore he doesn't want to hear any more about it. "I completely understand. Do you need any time off? Is there anything we can do?"

"I'm fine," I say, grinning on the inside. "I may need a couple of days but I'll give you good warning. They'll probably want to do a laparoscopy to investigate the—"

"Fine, fine." He's already halfway out the door. "Just take whatever you need." And with that he disappears back up to the safety of his office.

It's Nat's birthday and we're all off to lunch to celebrate. I tell the others I'll be along in a little while, tell them I just have some stuff to do in the office first, and I sit at my desk for a few minutes, bracing myself before I pick up the phone.

"Viv, it's me."

"How are you, love?"

"Nervous. I'm going to phone the clinic now. I just wanted to talk to you first."

"Do you think that maybe you're not doing the right thing?" Again there's hope in her voice.

"No, Viv. I am doing the right thing. It's just so scary, having to actually do this. Look, I'm fine. Sorry. I'd better go now, just to get it over and done with."

"Good luck," Viv says, but her voice is flat. "You'll be fine. I'll come with you."

"I know, Viv," I say. "I love you."

"I love you too."

211

"*Well* Woman Clinic. Hello?"

"Oh hello. I wonder whether I could make an appointment to come and see you?"

"Of course. Is it a smear?"

My voice drops. I can't help it. Admitting it to someone else feels so shameful. "No. An abortion."

"Of course. Can I ask how many weeks pregnant you are?"

"I think eight weeks. Maybe nine."

"That's fine. You'll need to come in and have a consultation first. How about this Friday? At three P.M.?"

I quickly shuffle through my diary. "Yes, that's fine."

"Do you know where we are?"

"Yes." My finger traces the address in the Yellow Pages. Station Road.

"And if I can just take your details."

I give them to her, feeling as if I'm making an appointment with the dentist, because this seems so ordinary, and I put the phone down, swivel my chair round and smile the first proper smile I've smiled all day.

Until I see Stella.

We just look at one another for a while.

"I'm so sorry." She looks at the floor. "I came back to get my mobile and I walked in on your conversation and I tried not to listen but . . ."

I don't know what to say. I feel a bit shaky, so I keep sitting down, and I just look at Stella, who eventually looks at me.

"I suppose that explains the Mad Bitch from Hell?" She attempts a grin, and suddenly I want to tell her everything. I want to be able to confide in someone other than Viv, and something about Stella just tells me I can trust her.

"Don't tell anyone?" I whisper. "Please. Swear you won't tell anyone."

"Oh God, of course I swear. I swear on my life. But are you okay? How do you feel?"

I hesitate for a second, but I need to talk about this, I have to talk about this. "Other than mad, and bitchy, I'm fine. Oh, and angry, and tearful. And generally as if I'm completely losing the plot. But other than that I'm fine. Can't you tell?"

We both laugh.

"Have you ever had an abortion?" I venture, and Stella nods.

"It was a long time ago. I was at university and we were stupid and I had to have an abortion. I came back to London and had it done in the holidays."

"How was it?"

"It was a long time ago, and I think when you're young you don't process things in the same way. I was eighteen. A child. It probably bothers me more now than it did then." She stops, thinking she's said the wrong thing.

"I'd rather you tell me the truth," I say to reassure her. "You don't have to censor yourself."

"It's difficult. I do think about it now. A lot. But I know that there was absolutely no way I was ready to have a child at eighteen. I guess you're not ready either."

"No. I'm not ready for a child. I don't want a child. Never have. I want a career. Independence. Freedom. I don't want to be trapped by a baby. Plus of course there is the fact that I don't actually have a partner so it's not even as if I'd have any support, emotional, financial, or otherwise."

"It's Mark Simpson's, isn't it?" Stella says simply, after I drift into silence, and I know I should be surprised, but I'm really not. I nod.

"Are you shocked?" I ask, because she certainly doesn't look it.

"No. I knew something had happened that night. The chemistry between the two of you was so strong I could almost touch it."

"Oh shit. Do you think anyone else noticed?"

"No, I don't. I like watching people, but the others were too interested in chatting him up, or chatting to one another, to sense anything. And then one night in the bar I saw you look at him . . ."

"Shag or Die," I say, smiling ruefully.

"Shag indeed." She smiles back and leans forward confidentially. "I'm sorry but I have to ask. Was it—?"

"Fucking amazing." I'm smiling, which is extraordinary really, given the circumstances, but it feels so good to be able to talk about it.

"Shit." She stamps her foot petulantly, then rolls her eyes. "I knew it. So. Are you going to tell him?"

"I think so. Not because I want him to be involved, not at all, but, well. I heard the rumors—"

"That he was firing blanks?"

"Well, yeah. And clearly he's not."

"You definitely need to tell him."

"I know. But I haven't even spoken to him since that night. How would I say it? How do I tell him?"

"What about, 'Babe, your boys can swim'?"

I start to laugh.

"Seriously," Stella says, "why don't you arrange to meet him for lunch? Call him now."

"Now? Christ. I don't want to actually talk to him."

"That's the point. I just passed him in the lobby, leaving for lunch. Call and make an appointment with his secretary. She'll put a lunch in his diary."

"Excellent idea." I pick up the phone, and after a brief chat with Sheila in the Legal Department scribble in a Thursday lunch.

"God," I laugh. "Can you imagine his face when he comes back this afternoon and sees he's having lunch with me on Thursday?"

"He'll probably think you need another shag."

"Yup, because he'd really want to shag me looking like this." I gesture to my jumper and tentlike trousers.

Stella's face suddenly becomes serious. "Maeve, you still look gorgeous. More voluptuous than usual, but that's no bad thing. And anyway, they always say that men prefer women with a bit of meat on them."

"I have to say I do think my new boobs are fantastic."

"There you are, then." Stella gestures at her own flat chest. "There's a bonus if ever there was one."

"Stella, thank you." It's an effort not to throw my arms around her and hug her.

"What for?"

"For making me feel fantastic. I feel like a weight's been lifted off my shoulders."

"Any time. And if you want me to come with you, that's fine too."

"Thanks. My mum said she'd come, but if I need you I'll call you."

"Come on." Stella looks at her watch. "If we're quick we'll still get to the canteen in time for coffee."

I'm nervous about lunch. I'm nervous about what to say, and even though Stella has coached me through the appropriate words, she can't coach me through Mark's reaction, and what to do if he doesn't see my point of view.

I get to the restaurant first. Ten minutes early so I can try to relax as much as possible before he arrives. Under normal circumstances I'd order a drink, but one of the side effects of my pregnancy appears to be a serious aversion to both alcohol and cigarette smoke, so I make do with a glass of sparkling mineral water.

It's not quite the same.

And then I see Mark walk through the door and seconds later he is at the table, confusion and wariness etched on his face.

"How are you?" he says, taking a seat, and of course it is awkward, for these are the first words we have spoken to one another since that night.

"Fine. You?"

"Fine."

And we grind to a halt.

216

A waiter arrives with menus and we are both inordinately interested in the choices therein, neither of us looking up until the waiter finally leaves with our orders.

"So. How's life?"

"Fine. Yours?"

"It's okay."

"I hear Julia's on holiday."

"Yup. New York."

"God, I love New York." Jesus, I'm really struggling here.

"Yup. Me too." And we both run dry. "Maeve?" I look up quickly. "Why are we having lunch together?"

I put down my glass of water, because this is ridiculous. Any thoughts I had of us having a nice lunch, with me casually throwing in the fact that I'm pregnant over coffee, have now disappeared. I have no choice. It's now or never.

"Because I'm pregnant."

"Congratulations."

"Is that it?"

"Well, I'm not sure what else I should be saying."

"Neither am I, Mark, but some kind of emotion would be nice. Look, I'm not expecting you to take responsibility and I certainly don't want you to pay, but I just thought you ought to know, because you told me that night that you were infertile and—"

"What?" Mark whispers, as pale as a sheet.

"What do you mean, 'What'?"

Mark shakes his head, clearly in shock. "What are you talking about?"

"I'm. Pregnant." I enunciate as clearly as I can. "And. You're. The. Father."

His eyes widen, his mouth opens and—Christ, I feel guilty about this—an expression of pure joy crosses his face. But only for a second.

He's back to looking wary. "Are you sure?"

"Mark, I haven't slept with anyone else in months. I'm sure."

And then, before I even know what's happening, he's jumped up, come around the table and put his arms around me.

"Oh my God," he whispers, putting his hand on my stomach as I start to feel sick for the very first time in my pregnancy. "Oh my God. That's my child. Growing in there is my child."

And with those words his eyes well up, tears of joy threatening to roll down his cheeks as he blinks them back.

How on earth am I supposed to do this?

Gently I disentangle his arms from around my stomach, and as he goes to sit down again, his whole face beaming, I don't know how I can do this to a man who is so patently, so obviously, good.

But do this I must.

"How long have you known?" Mark cannot wipe the smile off his face. "Why didn't you tell me before?"

"I'm nine weeks pregnant," I say, "and I'm telling you because you have a right to know you're not infertile. But." I falter but I keep going. "Mark, I'm not ready to have a baby."

A pause.

"What are you saying?"

"I'm saying that I can't have this baby. That it wouldn't have been fair to hide it from you, but that you need to know I'm planning an abortion." He visibly flinches but I carry on. "I have a consultation tomorrow with a clinic, but I imagine the operation will be done within the next couple of weeks. I'd feel happier having it done before the twelve-week mark, at any rate."

Mark is silent.

"Mark? Mark? Come on, Mark. Think about it. You and I hardly know each other, and it's not fair to bring a child into this world without two loving parents. This isn't right."

"We could be together," Mark says quickly. "I know we hardly know each other, but we could try. I know enough about you to know that I like you, that maybe we'd be in with a chance."

"And what about Julia?"

"You're going to think I'm just saying this because of the baby"—already I'm uncomfortable with him referring to "the baby"—"but Julia leaving has been the best thing that's ever happened to me. I feel as if the cloud that's been following me round has gone. And it's not Julia's fault, it's both of us, together. We weren't happy, and we weren't right for each other, not anymore. Probably not ever."

He sighs sadly, lost in memories for a while, then he continues. "We'd grown so far apart we couldn't find a way back, but neither of us was willing to accept it."

"Does Julia know that it's over?"

"I imagine so. She's called me a couple of times, either leaving a message when I'm out, or ringing as she's rushing out to meet someone, do something. She sounded so much lighter. Happier. Like the Julia of old." Mark looks at me. "But that's got nothing to do with us. We could try."

"Mark." My voice is gentle as I reach out and take his hand, squeezing it to impress the point, to make him understand. "I don't want a child. I don't like babies. Stores like Mothercare make me break out in hives and the thought of having a screaming infant in my house is enough to make my blood run cold. I can't do this. I'm a career woman, not a mother. I'm just not the type."

"But this is my child too," Mark says. "I've waited for this child for years."

"And now you need to wait some more, to have a child with someone else."

"You don't understand. My child is here. Our child. You're carrying our child. You can't just take the decision to destroy it because I may or may not create another child with someone else."

"But it's my body." I'm starting to get stressed, emotional, and I can already feel tears of frustration welling up. "It's my body and I'm not ready to give it up. Nor am I ready to deal with the responsibility of a child."

"What if I take on the responsibility? What if I have the child, raise the child? You could carry on doing whatever you're doing. Christ, you could even be back at work a couple of weeks afterward."

I'm so tired I haven't got the energy to argue with him anymore, and Mark sees the chink in my armor and dives in.

"Look, all I'm saying is think about it. At the very least cancel the appointment tomorrow to give us both a bit more time. Even a week. A couple of weeks. Let's take a bit of time so that when we make a final decision we know it's the right one. You wouldn't want to spend the rest of your life regretting your decision to have an abortion, when you didn't give yourself a chance to consider the other options."

"I'm too tired to argue with you," I sigh as our food arrives. "I'll cancel the appointment tomorrow, but I don't want to wait longer than a week. I just want my life to be back to normal again."

Mark lifts his wineglass and shoots me a grin, and in his grin there is delight. Excitement, anticipation, and delight.

"Am I allowed to make a toast?" he says tentatively.

"Not if you're going to toast the baby," I shoot back defensively.

"No. To us."

"To us," I echo warily, clinking his glass gently.

Mark is charming, funny, and protective. He treats me rather like an invalid throughout the lunch, and although, under normal circumstances, this would be enough to make me walk out in fury, right now, given my fragile state, this is exactly what I need.

And Viv would love him. Love him.

Jesus Christ. What the hell have I got myself into.

16

How did this happen? It is three weeks since my first lunch with Mark, three weeks since I told him I was not prepared to wait longer than a week to have an abortion, and at an absolute push I would wait until the twelfth week, but that by week twelve I would be babyless.

And here I am. Twelve weeks pregnant. My resolve is weakening.

How did this happen?

I'll tell you how this happened.

Friday afternoon, the day after I had told Mark the news, I was sitting at my desk, finalizing the schedules of *Loved Up*. The office was quiet as it so often is on a Friday afternoon, my researchers conjuring up recces and interviews, disappearing with a cheery wave at 3 P.M. I know they're all heading off to the pub, but I have learned to be lenient in order to be popular, and God knows I need every ounce of popularity now.

I finished the schedules and tipped my chair back, closing my eyes for a few minutes because this tiredness sweeps over me in waves, and although all I can think of is sleep, I know that a few minutes of resting my eyes will enable me to make it through the rest of the day.

And no more sojourns to the company bar for me. The only thing that seems to float my boat after work these days is a large bowl of pasta, a chunky bar of chocolate, a hot bath, and bed. Last night I dragged the television into the doorway of the bedroom, and what a complete pleasure it was to climb into bed at ten past eight and snuggle up under the duvet to the dulcet tones of Jackie Corkhill.

So Friday afternoon there I was, in my office, eyes closed, and indulging in a fantasy involving Cookies 'n' Cream ice cream and an electric blanket, when my reverie was interrupted by a knock on my already open door. I opened my eyes to see Mark standing there with a bag from Books Etc.

"Hi." He hovered awkwardly until I smiled and gestured to the chair, and he shut the door for privacy before sitting down.

"Hi yourself." I was surprised at how pleased I was to see him. I found there was, is, something immensely calm and reassuring about his presence. Although I would never have said that the night of Chuck's Great American Rib 'n' Beef Extravaganza. Calm and reassuring were not the words I would have used to describe him that night. The night of conception.

Christ. I hadn't thought of that. Imagine if I did have a

baby. Imagine them asking where they were conceived and having to explain that no, it wasn't in the Cipriani in Venice, or the George V in Paris. It was in a dirty, seedy alleyway in Soho, and it lasted all of five minutes. A fantastic five minutes, but five minutes nevertheless.

All the more reason not to have this baby.

"I just wondered how you were feeling." Mark laid the bag on the desk, and I eyed it curiously. "Although now I think you might actually be a bit pissed off." He frowned, seeing me looking suspiciously at the bag. "In fact I think I've done something really stupid and maybe I should take the books back and leave right now." He moved to take the bag but I grabbed it and pulled out two books.

The Pregnancy Question and Answer Book and *What Does My Baby Look Like Today?*

Oh.

"Shit. I'm sorry," Mark said warily. "I thought that since we haven't made a decision, just in case you do decide to keep the baby you might want to know some stuff."

"Like what kind of stuff?"

"Like the kind of stuff you shouldn't be eating."

"Such as?" I don't even know why I bothered to ask.

"Sushi. Unpasteurized meat and cheese. Liver . . ."

"I see you've become quite the expert."

"I knew I shouldn't have done it," he sighed. "I'll take them back."

"No. Wait. I want to show you something." I flicked through *What Does My Baby Look Like Today?*, and found exactly what I was looking for. A picture of a baby at nine weeks. A blob. A nothing. "That"—I turned the book around and pushed it over the desk to Mark—"is what the baby looks like."

It didn't have the desired effect. Mark shook his head. "Incredible," he said in awe, while I sighed and wondered how he could think a shapeless blob that resembles nothing very much could be incredible.

"Would you look at the books?" he said finally. "Just the early stuff about keeping yourself healthy. Just in case."

"Okay." I nodded, knowing I'd drop them in the nearest dustbin outside the tube. "Sure. I can do that."

"So what are you up to this weekend?" His tone was too fake-casual for my liking.

"A party tonight. The pub tomorrow afternoon with friends, then a club in the evening. I think Sunday I'll take it easy and stay at home with a few beers."

He looked horrified. "You are joking?"

"Of course I'm bloody joking. I'm exhausted. My idea of a good night right now involves a bottle of bubble bath and bed by 10 P.M." I didn't tell him it was actually bed by 8 P.M. I didn't want to sound too sad.

"Do you, um. Well, I thought maybe we could go out or something? I could take you for dinner tomorrow night."

Oh, for fuck's sake.

"Oh, for fuck's sake."

"What's wrong?"

"Mark, you don't have to patronize me by pretending to be interested in me because I'm carrying your child, and nor do you have to waste your time trying to be nice to me in the hope that you'll bring me round to your way of thinking. I don't want a relationship and I don't want a baby. And going out for dinner with you isn't going to bloody well change that. Do you understand?"

"Sure." He stood up, his face hard. "I understand perfectly well." And without saying another word he turned and left the office, leaving me feeling like shit. Once again.

That afternoon Sam the post boy dropped off the internal mail.

"Feels like a big one," he said with a cheeky grin, dropping a large, heavy envelope onto my desk.

I opened it up to find two bottles of Crabtree and Evelyn bubble bath with a note attached: "Maeve. I wasn't trying to patronize you. Enjoy your bath. (Not too hot and no gin . . .) Mark."

Good. No "Love." That I don't think I could have handled.

"You know people will start to talk," I said to Mark two weeks after that, when I agreed to meet him for a drink in the bar at lunchtime. (Mark: half a lager. Me: Highland Spring.)

Mark laughed. "They'll be saying we're having an affair."

"Better that than we're having a baby."

He looked up sharply. "Are we? Are you ready to talk about it yet?"

"Not yet. But soon. We can talk about it soon," and I stopped as Mark reached over and pulled something out of my hair. Just a piece of lint, but it unnerved me, this gesture that was too intimate for work colleagues, and I suddenly realized quite what a bizarre situation this was.

There I was, sitting with a man I barely knew, but who I had fucked, albeit briefly. I have no clue who he is. I know neither his likes nor his dislikes. I don't know if he's lazy or sporty or confident or shy.

Yet I am carrying his child.

I have always prided myself on being a good judge of character, and I would have said that Mark is your average nice guy, with nicer-than-average looks, for I know that he is really rather handsome, even though his looks have no effect on me.

I would have guessed that he lives in a large house (for I know what these lawyers earn), and that he loves art and books, and collects something, perhaps original newspaper cartoons, perhaps maps, but that everything in his life is ordered, tidy, beautifully presented.

I would have assumed that he went to a minor public school, and that while there he learned a musical instrument. Possibly violin. And that he went on to Bristol, or Durham, and that his first major buy after graduating was a classic sports car: a Triumph Stag or an MGB.

"Why are you smiling at me like that? Now people really will start to talk." Mark's voice broke my train of thought, and I realized I was gazing at him with a half-smile on my face, trying to figure out who he was.

"Sorry. I just, I was just thinking what a ridiculous situation this is. That I'm pregnant with your child but I know nothing about you."

"Tell you what," he said, smiling, "I'm not patronizing

you, but why don't you come over on Sunday? Come to my house and spend the day. Find out"—and he injected a Scooby-style spookiness into his voice that made me laugh—"who I really am."

"Okay," I said, surprising myself. "I will."

"Okay." Mark finished the last of his lager. "Good."

That night, as I walked into my flat, the phone was ringing. "How are you, love?" It was Viv.

"I'm fine. How are you?"

"Never mind about me. Have you made a decision yet?"

"Viv, I told you that I'd tell you as soon as I'd decided. We'd decided. Don't push me. Please." But I was nearly twelve weeks, that deadline was looming, and yet all I could do was procrastinate. Why hadn't I just done it? Because I didn't want to think about it, that's why. Much less talk about it. To Viv or anyone else. I was still hoping it would all go away.

"I'm not pushing you. I just wanted to check you were okay. I thought maybe you'd like to come up and spend the day here on Sunday."

"I can't. I'm busy."

"Busy? You? On a Sunday? Really?"

Her tone was so incredulous I started to laugh. "If I tell you where I'm going, promise you won't get too excited."

She caught her breath. "If you tell me you're going to interview Alan Bates, I may well have to kill myself."

"Viv! I'm going to Mark's house. For lunch."

She caught her breath again and this time I knew it was for real. "Mark as in the Father, Mark?"

"No, Viv. Mark as in the man who got me pregnant." The Father personalized it. I couldn't think of him as the Father, and I certainly didn't want Viv thinking of him as the Father; I didn't want to cause Viv any more pain than I absolutely had to.

"That's what I meant." She took a few breaths, trying to calm down, but I could hear in her voice that she was smiling. I could hear her hope, her expectations. "How lovely," she said, attempting a brisk tone. "Can he cook, then?" By which she meant, will he be a good husband?

"I have no idea," I said. "But I assume he won't be serving crisps and sandwiches."

"Nothing wrong with crisps and sandwiches," Viv said quickly. "A man who can cook is a bonus, not a necessity."

"A man, period, is unnecessary," I said firmly. "He's just trying to get me to keep the baby."

"Do you think you might?"

"Viv! How many times do I have to tell you? I haven't made up my mind." We said good-bye and I gazed into space for a few minutes, because two weeks ago I had made up my mind. Two weeks ago I was going to have an abortion and carry on with my life as if this had never happened. And now I didn't know.

When did a doubt creep in? How could I possibly think that I have any alternative? Why had I not been able to reschedule an appointment at the abortion clinic?

What am I thinking?

Sunday is one of those fantastic cold, crisp days when the sun is shining brightly out of an ice-blue sky, and you look out your window and know that spring is very nearly here and you can't remember what was so depressing about winter after all.

Stella keeps asking me how I feel. Stella who has become frighteningly close in a frighteningly short space of time.

She was here yesterday afternoon. Just popping in on her way back from a shopping trip in the West End, just checking that I was okay. She brought with her half the contents of the M & S food department, and ended up staying most of the evening.

We dipped into dips and exchanged our stories. Shared our secrets. Laughed over linguine and bonded over banana-toffee pie.

"I miss this," Stella said wistfully as we both scraped our fingers around our bowls, ensuring that not a scrap of banana or toffee would be left.

"What? Staying in on a Saturday night, eating like a pig, and feeling like a beached whale?"

"Well, yes, clearly I miss that too." We both laughed. "But I'm talking about this kind of female friendship. I miss the ease of girlfriends. I miss the comfort of being able to come over to someone's house, like this, and not having to worry about what you look like or what you talk about. I'm not saying you're my best friend—"

"Careful," I warned, but I was smiling, because I felt exactly the same way. "Stalker alert."

"Now you're definitely not my best friend. Stalker indeed," she huffed. "But I miss having a best friend. Do you know what I mean?"

"My best friend was always my mum."

"God, you're joking. I hate my mum. We can hardly bear to stay in the same room together."

"My mum's great. She really is my best friend. And I suppose my only real friend who's a woman. Close friend, that is, because I've got female friends," I said quickly, knowing that it wasn't really true, "but I haven't got a confidante, not here in London, and I hadn't realized until tonight how much I'd missed it too."

"It's good to be a woman," Stella laughed, raising her glass. "To the Sisterhood."

"To the Sisterhood. And to friendship."

I went to bed with a smile on my face, enveloped in warmth and intimacy, feeling that being pregnant might not be the worst thing ever to have happened to me. Feeling that, in fact, my life really wasn't so bad after all.

And now today, the sun is shining and I'm feeling good, looking forward to doing something different, even if I'm not sure about spending the day with Mark. What if we have nothing in common? What if we have nothing to talk about?

So what! I admonish myself. I'm not checking him out to see if he is suitable partner material. I'm just trying to get to know him a little before he and I make the most important decision of my life.

That's all.

"Did you find it okay?" Mark opened the door and I started to laugh because he was wearing an apron—he was actually

wearing an apron!—but he refused to take it off and I rather liked the fact that he wasn't embarrassed by such a ridiculous item of clothing, even if it was a masculine navy and black stripe.

"Your house is lovely," I said, pretending not to have noticed that it's probably one of the biggest houses I'd ever been into. Pretending not to be impressed by the large square entrance hall and steps down into a bright, airy kitchen. Pretending that I, too, lived in a house much like this one. Only smaller. Much, much, much smaller.

"Drink?" he said, pouring what looked suspiciously like carrot juice into a glass.

"That looks disgusting. I think I'll pass." I sniffed it gingerly.

"It's not disgusting. It's delicious. And it matches your hair. It's a homemade mango and banana smoothie. Delicious and nutritious. Try it."

I tried it. It was delicious (and nutritious). "Mmm. Something smells completely amazing." I eyed the various saucepans on the stove and noted that the smell was definitely coming from the oven. "Who'd have thought the London Daytime lawyer would be a cook."

"There's only one thing I enjoy more than a bloody good litigation, and that's slaving over a hot stove. Here, sit down." He pulled a chair out from the kitchen table and I sat, grateful for his kindness.

"See how solicitous I am?" He took my coat and left the room to hang it up.

"Not bad for a solicitor," I grinned, as he offered me a choice of snacks.

"What? No nuts?" I couldn't help it. I'd peeked into the

books he'd bought me, and I knew that pregnant women who binge on nuts often end up giving birth to children with severe peanut allergies. And I knew he'd know this too.

"Er, haven't got any, I'm afraid. You're not, um, craving nuts, are you?" Mark looked so worried, he was so transparent, that I started to laugh.

"Relax." I slurped my smoothie. "I haven't had a single peanut in at least three months."

His sigh of relief was audible.

I stood up and wandered into the living room, looking at the few photos dotted around, examining his bookshelves, idly picking up CDs and putting them back, when I realized that, were it not for the fact that I knew Julia had left only a few weeks ago, I would have thought that Mark had never shared this house with anyone. There wasn't a single sign of a woman living there. Nothing.

The photos were all of people I didn't know. None, incidentally, of Julia. The books were mostly legal tomes, or biographies, or nonfiction stuff that I would assume was typically male, and there seemed to be nothing that would belong to a woman.

"How come there isn't anything of Julia's around?" I asked, wondering whether it was still too painful for him, whether he had already had a chance to remove everything.

Mark came into the living room and topped up my smoothie. "I know this sounds completely weird but last week I was thinking exactly the same thing. And then I realized that there never was. She never felt at home here. She always felt the house was mine. That it was too big for her. And I never noticed that she never had anything here, any stuff."

233

"So why did you buy it?"

"I loved it here. Still do, and I suppose I was selfish. I knew Julia loved her small house, loved small, cozy rooms, but I thought she'd get used to it. I thought that it was inevitable she'd fall in love with it. But now I know she always felt overwhelmed by the size.

"Can you believe I didn't even realize until she'd gone that there was nothing of hers around? That's how selfish I was."

"I don't think that sounds selfish. I think it just sounds as if you were two very different people."

"So tell me something else I didn't know." He smiles sadly.

"Maybe I shouldn't ask this, and if it's none of my business that's fine, but what's going to happen when she comes back from New York?"

"She's not coming back."

"What?"

"She called two days ago. She's been offered a job with BCA, and she's going to take it."

"Jesus. Has she told anyone at work?"

"No, so do you mind not saying anything?"

"No! Not at all." I looked at him closely, "So how do you feel?"

"Sad at the loss of our relationship, but relieved at the same time. I think more than anything else I feel an enormous sense of relief. I'm sure what I'll miss most is being in a relationship, but even that's ridiculous because we barely spent any time together. Anyway, enough about me." I could see he was growing uncomfortable talking about it. "Are you hungry? I think it should be just about ready."

We went into the kitchen and sat down to carrot and coriander soup, with hot, crusty French bread.

I slurped it up, starving, then sat back, eagerly awaiting the main course.

"This is so delicious," I moaned, three mouthfuls into roast lamb with crispy roast potatoes and homemade mint sauce. "I haven't eaten like this since I lived at home."

"That's what Julia used to say when we first met. But then I think she got bored."

"Bored with roasts? Is she mad?"

"Bored with living with someone who loves being at home."

"Oh please. Home is the best possible place to be."

"Now you're surprising me." Mark raised an eyebrow in disbelief. "You're a party girl. A career woman. Home life isn't your thing, surely."

"It's precisely because I work so hard that home is so important to me. The last thing I want to do after work is go out and live it up. But ssshhh," I whispered, "don't let my secret out. Meanwhile," I continued, "I love being at home, by myself, being totally selfish and not having to compromise for anybody. Whereas you, on the other hand, are a completely different kettle of fish."

"What do you mean?"

"Someday, Mark, you'll make someone a wonderful wife."

"Only if ironing isn't written into the marriage contract."

"Oh, so you mean there is something you're not good at?"

"I didn't say I wasn't good at it. I, naturally, am God's gift to ironing," he said, grinning, "but it's the one thing I can't stand, the one thing I pay someone else to do."

"Together with a cleaner, a gardener, and God knows how many others it takes to help you look after this palace."

"A cleaner, yes. I'll grant you Lizzy, who comes in twice a week, but gardener? Absolutely not. See these fingers?" He extended his hands and they were really very nice. Big hands. Strong hands. Oooh. Imagine what those hands could do (for I had forgotten what those hands had already done). A shiver ran through me. No, Maeve. This was the very last thing I needed.

I nodded, still staring at his fingers.

"Alan Titchmarsh has nothing on these fingers. My fingers are so green they're practically in bud."

I started to laugh.

After lunch I collapsed onto the fabulously squishy sofa in the living room, while Mark tried to froth some milk for my decaf cappuccino.

And then I woke up.

The lights were dim. It was dark outside, and for a moment I was completely disoriented. And then I saw Mark, sitting on the sofa opposite me, reading the *Sunday Times*. A fire was crackling and I sat up quickly, embarrassed by having fallen asleep, horrified at the rudeness, at the thought of having dribbled all over his cushions in my unconscious state. Or worse.

Mark glanced over the top of his paper at me and smiled.

"Hello, Sleepy. Or should I say Grumpy?"

I was in no mood to smile back. I know what my hair looks

like after I've fallen asleep on a sofa. "Tea?" he said, and I nodded gratefully, watching him as he walked out of the room and wondering idly why on earth a man like him hadn't been snapped up years ago.

Not that I was interested. I didn't feel anything more that afternoon than I did that morning. I'd had a lovely day, and he was everything I thought he was (except he didn't learn violin at school, it was the clarinet, and his first car was neither an MGB nor a Triumph Stag but an E-type Jaguar); however, I wasn't interested in him in that way.

But the one thing I did have to concede, as I fought off the tiredness driving home later that evening, was that it had been lovely being looked after all day. I hadn't ever been looked after before. Only by Viv, and I wasn't sure that really counted.

Oh and one other thing. I agreed to go for a scan.

Just to be on the safe side.

17

I'm still not altogether sure why I agreed to have the scan. I was tired, it had been a long day, and I felt so comfortable, so nurtured, I didn't want to spoil it all by having an argument.

And I really could see that Mark would be a wonderful father.

Which helped.

I suppose I'd never thought of the reality of the situation before; had only thought I'd be saddled with a child I didn't want; that I'd turn into a stressed-out single mother who tried desperately to juggle her child with a career and a string of unsuitable boyfriends.

But after that day at Mark's, after seeing what he was like, where he lived, how he lived, I could see that I wouldn't be on my own, and more than that I could see that it wouldn't have been fair to deprive him of what he so desperately wanted.

We could share a child, I started to think on the way home. Maybe Mark would have the child during the week and I'd have it on the weekends. A picture of a little girl, looking just like me, forced itself into my head. A little girl wearing those cute little OshKosh dungarees (for no child of mine would be made to wear frilly pink dresses), a little girl so sweet and good that everyone would stop to smile at us, marvel at how I, the head of London Daytime Television (if you're going to have a fantasy there's no point in being half-assed about it), managed to bring up such a beautiful well-behaved child as well.

She'd be the perfect accessory.

We'd go to the park wearing big boots and woollen hats, and handsome single men would find us irresistible. We might even have to get a dog. And maybe a holiday home on the coast somewhere. Not too far, maybe near Viv, but we could play on the beaches and spend our evenings reading Dr. Seuss in front of the fire.

I could teach her everything I know, watch her grow into a little person with her own thoughts, own opinions, and I could stand back proudly as she grew into a beautiful woman.

Hmmm. A little me is really rather enticing.

So when Mark gently suggested it might be a good idea to see a doctor and book a scan, I agreed.

What harm can it do?

Although it doesn't mean I've made a decision.

It doesn't mean I'm definitely keeping the baby.

Not definitely.

"*Can* you see the leg move?"

I'm lying on a table, craning my head around to see the screen, while the sonographer presses down on my stomach, keeping her eyes on the screen, stopping only to note measurements.

Mark's sitting next to me, holding my hand, which in other circumstances I might find off, but in these is enormously reassuring. We're both staring at the screen, and I don't know what the sonographer's talking about because I can't see anything at all other than a greenish tunnel, and suddenly my heart flips over and Mark and I gasp, squeezing each other's hands tightly.

"Oh my God!" we whisper in unison. "Did you see that?" And suddenly the screen becomes clear. There is a tiny leg kicking up in the air, and we follow the leg up as we start to define the shape of a baby. My baby. Our baby. A living being inside of me.

Oh my good God.

I turn quickly to Mark, who has tears in his eyes and a huge smile on his face, and we grin wordlessly at one another before turning quickly back to the screen so we don't miss anything.

"Can you see the spine?" She presses down to the left and points at the screen and I nod, a lump suddenly in my throat.

"Whoops, the baby's on the move," the sonographer laughs, and I watch in awe as an arm stretches out and the baby arches its back.

I start to laugh. And cry.

"Don't worry," she says, handing me a tissue from a box at her side. "First-time parents often find it a bit overwhelming. It's incredible, isn't it? That's your baby!" She smiles indulgently at us. "Everything seems to be fine. See that flickering there?"

A tiny flickering, barely noticeable.

"That's the baby's heartbeat. Nice and strong. You're thirteen weeks and four days? Five days?"

I nod. Thirteen weeks and five days exactly.

"The measurements are incredibly precise at this stage," she says, "so the due date is . . ." She turns to check but Mark and I get there first.

"The thirty-first of October."

"Spooky," she says, grinning, and I don't laugh, because it is at exactly this point that I know there's no going back. No way. No how. My life, from this moment forward, is irrevocably changed.

She carries on for a while, and I try to follow the shape of the baby, but every time the screen changes all I can see are indistinct markings, and after a while I stop looking and turn to Mark.

"You okay?" he whispers, giving my hand a squeeze.

I nod. "You?"

"I think this is the greatest day of my life," he says, smiling.

I smile back.

I don't need to tell him I feel exactly the same way.

Mark drives me home and goes into the kitchen to heat up a can of Heinz tomato soup for me (can that really be called a legitimate craving?), while I head for the wardrobe and pull out the plastic bag from Books Etc.

Page 36 of *What Does My Baby Look Like Today?* tells me exactly what I wanted to know.

Welcome to the second trimester! If you've had morning sickness, it should be starting to subside, and miscarriage is less of a risk.

You should see your doctor and discuss what precautionary measures you should follow to avoid infection by salmonella, listeria, etc., and what tests you'll need to take, for example, toxoplasmosis.

What's Going On with My Baby?

The vocal cords are developing, and the voice box has formed. Your baby's intestines are now coiled and contained inside the abdomen, while the liver secretes bile and the pancreas secretes insulin. And now the really exciting stuff starts! Those little fingers and toes are no longer webbed and the nail beds have begun to develop.

"What are you doing?" Mark comes in and places a mug of soup on the bedside table, then sits next to me on the bed to look at the book. We sit in silence for a while, and eventually Mark touches my arm.

"Can we talk about this now?" he says gently. I nod. "How are you feeling?"

"Scared."

"Does that mean . . ." He pauses. "You're going to . . ." He looks up at me, eyes filled with hope. ". . . Have this baby?"

"Of course I'm going to have this baby. It's a baby! There's a baby growing inside of me, for God's sake, and I've seen it! Mark!" I look at him and catch my breath as the full realization hits me in the face. "We're going to have a baby!"

"I know," he laughs, putting his arms around me and enveloping me in a hug so tight I practically lose my breath. "Isn't it fucking amazing!"

Mark stays for supper. I wish I could tell you I provide him with a similar gastronomic experience to his Sunday lunch, but in the event we order in a curry from the Indian restaurant in the village. I do, however, manage to supply the mango chutney.

We talk for a long, long time. At least it feels like a long, long time, but when I eventually say goodnight and climb into bed, thoroughly exhausted, I manage to catch sight of the clock just before I fall asleep, and it's 9:22.

What did we talk about? We talked about our child. About our values. About children of friends, and what we like and dislike about their upbringing, how we would do things differently with our own.

We didn't talk about the logistics. How two people will jointly raise a child when they are not together, but really, that's no big deal. Look at the divorce statistics in this country, for heaven's sake. Isn't it one in three? Or maybe even higher. It's just as normal for children to grow up in one-parent families, and at least our child won't be subjected to any bitterness or acrimony between its parents, because we were never together in the first place. Well. Barely.

Mark can fulfill his dream of being a father and I can carry on with my career just as I was before.

"The only thing is," I said, when we'd exhausted our dreams, "how the hell are we supposed to tell everyone at work?"

"Ah yes. That had crossed my mind." Mark sighed.

"I told Mike Jones I was pregnant just to see his reaction and he practically had heart failure in front of me."

"What?" Mark was horrified. "You told him?"

"Don't worry. He thought I was joking. I just wanted to test him, and the result wasn't what I wanted to hear."

"So don't tell anyone."

"Oh, be serious. You think that somehow they won't notice?"

He shrugged. "You don't have to tell anyone yet. You're not showing, and we can work out the best way to tell people in a few weeks."

"So you're okay about them knowing it's your baby?" I was flabbergasted.

"I want the whole bloody world to know it's my baby! Especially when everyone knew Julia and I were trying and presumed it was my fault when nothing happened. I don't just want to tell them, I want to commission a television series about it."

"Good idea," I mused. "But not great. Surely a whole series is just a touch over the top? How about a short thirty-second ad to go out just after *Coronation Street* for a week? That's much more low-key."

244

He smiled, but his attention was elsewhere and I knew what he was thinking.

"Mark? What's the matter? It's Julia, isn't it?"

He smiled sadly. "I've been so excited I haven't even thought about Julia in all this. And I suppose if it isn't me, then it must be her, but even if there's nothing wrong at all, how in the hell is she going to take this?"

"Mark, if no one else is going to know for a while, then Julia doesn't need to know either. But when we do start telling people, make sure you tell her first. I can't imagine anything worse than Julia hearing this from someone else."

"I know," he said, nodding, still thinking about her pain. "I know I'll have to tell her myself."

I am a woman obsessed.

I am also a woman who is slowly losing her mind.

I have gone from pretending this baby never existed to longing for my belly to show, longing to be able to tell people that no, I'm not just fat, I'm actually pregnant.

I'm still being careful at work, careful to wear big, baggy clothes to disguise my ever-growing stomach, but I'm so desperate to talk about it, for people to know, I'm accosting strangers in order to share my good news.

"Excuse me? Do you have this sweater in a large because I'm nearly four months pregnant and nothing's going to be fitting me soon?"

"Hello? You don't know me, but my name's Maeve Robertson and I'm a friend of Stella Lord. She recommended I call you because the central heating's not working properly and I'm four months pregnant and for some reason I'm getting really cold so do you think you could send a plumber around today?"

"I'll have avocado, crabsticks, and coronation chicken on granary please. I know it sounds really strange but I'm four and a half months pregnant and I'm desperately craving coronation chicken but it could be worse, ha ha. At least I'm not craving anything weird like soil. Do you have any kids yourself?"

"You look like you're just about fully cooked! How many weeks are you? Thirty-six? You poor thing. Is this your first? I'm only twenty-two weeks and I'm completely shattered so I can't imagine how you must be feeling."

I've resisted the urge to buy maternity clothes for ages, but now I can't resist it anymore. I did actually drive up to Formes at sixteen weeks. I walked in, looked around, and wondered why everyone in there was super-skinny and the sales assistants had to give them cushions to shove under their sweaters to simulate pregnancy.

"Are any of these women actually pregnant?" I whispered to one of the younger shop assistants.

"Oh yes," she whispered back. "I think a lot of our ladies like to come in very early on. Wearing maternity clothes is often the first real sign of pregnancy and they can't wait to show it off."

I turned and saw exactly what she meant, as a woman with model proportions idly flicked through the racks, wearing an empire-line smock that clearly had more space underneath it than Tower Bridge.

"Would you like to try anything on?" the assistant said, reaching behind the till. "We have cushions if you like."

"I'm fine," I said with a condescending smile as I headed toward the door, but I spent the journey home kicking myself. Me and my bloody pride. I was dying to try everything on.

Everyone I reveal my pregnancy to is so kind, which makes it bizarre not to be able to reveal it at work, where everyone treats me as they always did. At work I'm still the same old Maeve Robertson. Only fatter. And more forgetful.

I can't tell which is worrying me more: the fact that my memory has gone absent without leave or that my waist has disappeared.

Of course no one would tell me I've put on weight, and I don't think anyone's guessed yet, but I'm definitely aware that, walking through a crowded canteen at one o'clock, I don't get anything like the admiring glances I did before.

"Do you swear I don't look enormous?" I whisper to Stella, as a floor manager on the breakfast show walks past and smiles at me, all hint of flirtation very much gone.

I want her to say I don't look fat, I look pregnant. I want her to validate me. I want her to give me permission to tell everyone.

"I swear you just look voluptuous and gorgeous."

"So you can't see my bump?" I stick my stomach out, longing for her to say she can see my bump.

"That's no baby," she laughs. "That's just a brie and onion baguette and a double-decker." I laugh too. Even though it isn't the right answer.

"Are you sure I don't look enormous?" I say to Mark, lying on his sofa after we've watched the video of Lord Winston's

The Human Body, marveling at the footage of a baby when it's still inside the mother.

It's a Sunday. We spend Sundays together now, Mark and I, and occasionally a couple of evenings during the week as well. But Sundays are a regular routine: I drive over to his house, he cooks a delicious meal, and I lounge about all day doing absolutely fuck all while he runs around like a headless chicken making sure the mother of his child is happy.

It's sheer and utter bliss.

"Do you want a Bounty?" he asks, midway through the afternoon.

"Mmm," I groan luxuriously from the comfort of my cushions.

"Right." He flings on his jacket. "I'm just popping out to the garage. Anything else you need?"

"I wouldn't mind some coronation chicken."

"You're still hungry after the roast beef?" Aghast.

"Not hungry. Just, you know. A bit peckish."

"We've got chicken and mayonnaise. I'll see if I can get some curry powder."

"Great. Thanks." I've already switched my focus back to the television set, usually a video Mark will have got out for the afternoon, and thankfully we both share the same cheesy taste in old films. *It's a Wonderful Life; Harvey; Some Like It Hot; Gone With the Wind.* Many's the Sunday we've lost ourselves in a fantasy world of an age gone by. The last couple of weeks I've stayed the night.

Don't be ridiculous.

In the guest room of course.

And that is the most extraordinary thing. Aside from the fact that I am carrying his child, I cannot believe that Mark and I ever had sex. In fact, even though I am carrying his child there are times when I think that perhaps it was an immaculate conception and that I simply dreamed that whole night in Soho.

I even had to ask Stella, just to be on the safe side. Was I actually there?

Mark has become my best friend. He is the first person I turn to when I want to share my news, or have a night out, or just have a laugh. He's always there for me; always steady, reliable, secure. He makes me feel safe, and comforted, and loved. And I mean that in a platonic sense.

Because he's the last person in the world I could ever fancy.

I know I fancied him that night. I have a vague memory of the sex being fantastic, but I still can't quite believe that that was Mark. Mark. The same Mark that's sitting opposite me draining a can of Coke and emitting indecently loud burps every few seconds.

"You're revolting." I'm smiling.

"God, I know." He makes a face. "Lawyers are such pigs, aren't they?"

"Not all lawyers. Just you."

Mark burps particularly loudly and grins. "You could have chosen any man to be the father of your baby, but you chose me."

"Trust me," I say. "If I had to make my choice all over again, it would be a very different story."

But of course it wouldn't be, because, while I don't fancy him in the slightest, he has become, other than Viv, my most favorite person in the whole world, and I cannot think of a better person to be raising my child with. I love the idea that my child will be half mine and half Mark's. To be honest I can't think of a better combination. Other than me and Steve McQueen of course. And that, clearly, is not in the cards.

"You know what you are?" I say, later that afternoon, as Mark sits on the floor tinkering with some Victorian lamps we picked up at a garage sale this morning. (A 6 A.M. start. I wouldn't recommend it.) "You're the brother I never had."

Mark makes a face. "Now that really is sick. Disgusting. You're accusing me of incest."

"Don't be ridiculous. I mean just in terms of us. Our relationship. I don't think I've ever felt so comfortable with anyone other than my family. That's what I meant. You know you're my best friend." I'm not sure quite what's come over me, because spontaneous outbursts of affection are really not my style, but I don't think I ever really knew how important it was to have someone before.

And I don't mean an "other half." I just mean someone to share things with. Someone like a best friend. Or a brother. Someone like Mark.

Mark stops tinkering and smiles at me. "That's the nicest thing you've ever said to me."

"Shit," I mumble, opening *Marie Claire* and pretending to be immediately engrossed in the film reviews, the embarrassment of having been so open starting to hit. "I didn't mean it."

"Yes, you did. And thank you. That's lovely to hear, and just for the record I feel exactly the same about you."

250

"I'm the brother you never had?"

"No. You're the pain in the arse little sister I never wanted. Ouch." I hit him over the head with the rolled-up *Marie Claire*. And then he sits back and looks at me thoughtfully. "Seriously, Maeve. You've really changed since you became pregnant."

I snort. "Because you knew me so well before."

"I didn't have to. I only had to look at you to see how hard you were. You're much softer. More vulnerable. If you pushed me I might say you're a much nicer person."

"Uh-oh." I make a face, turning back to the magazine and flicking. "I'm not sure that's such a good thing. No one's frightened of me at work anymore."

And although the fact that I don't seem to wield the same power at work bothers me ever so slightly, secretly I like what Mark has just said. I like the way he makes me feel.

Secretly I'm very, very pleased.

18

The secret's out.

Admittedly at six months it's pretty
bloody difficult to hide a pregnancy, and
now everyone says that they'd suspected for
ages but didn't want to say anything in case
I'd just put on weight.

Although all the mothers said they
knew.

"Yeah, yeah," said Mike Jones wearily
when I went up to his office to tell him. This
time for real. "So tell me something else I
didn't know."

"How did you know?" He was the first
person I'd told, but I was still shocked.

"You've been shouting at people and
bursting into tears for no apparent reason.
Half the time you walk around looking as if
you're in a dream world, and you're eating

like a pig but the only place you're putting on weight is your stomach and your . . ." He grins and shrugs. "I'd have to be a fucking idiot not to realize, especially when you'd already told me."

"So my joke didn't fool you?"

"Nothing gets by me. So now there are two major questions, the first being what are you going to do?"

"As in, am I going to stay?"

He nods.

"Mike, I love this job. I love everything about London Daytime Television, and I still remember everything you said at my interview about the sky being the limit. I never wanted to get pregnant. I never wanted to have a baby, but, now I am, I think it's going to be fine. I'm not mother-material, though, and the last thing on earth I want is to leave my job." Mike nods approvingly. I carry on. "I have a fantastic support system and of course I'll need to take three months' maternity leave, but that's it. You have my word that I'll be back here to pick up exactly where I left off."

"Temper tantrums and tears?"

"Um, no. That's just hormonal hell. You'll have the old Maeve back after the baby, and I'll make sure *Loved Up* gets six million."

"Six million? That's impressive. Are you sure?"

"Yes. I'm sure."

"That still leaves me with the problem of what to do when you're away for three months."

"You haven't got a problem. Stella Lord. She's your answer."

He looks at me, interested.

"Stella works harder than anyone else, she's brighter than anyone else, and she's more ambitious than anyone else. It's about time she was given a chance to prove herself."

"And you're not threatened? What if she's so good that we don't want you back?"

"Luckily I'm not that insecure."

If only that were true.

But Stella is the only person I trust to take over while I'm away. She's the only person who will ensure we get those ratings. I could get six million viewers with Stella in the hot seat. I could trust that she would make the same decisions as me.

"I think you've got a point. Ask Stella to come up and see me this afternoon. I'll see how she feels about it."

"She'll be over the moon."

"I'm sure. So, now it's time for the second question." Uh-oh. I know what's coming. "A little bird tells me that rumors have been flying about you and Mark Simpson. Who's the father?"

"Could I tell you to fuck off and that it's none of your business?"

"No. I'd fire you."

"Okay. Mark Simpson is the father."

His mouth falls open. "Fuck me. You're joking!" There is genuine shock on his face.

"What? You already said the rumors had been flying. Don't look so surprised."

"I was joking. I was joking about the rumors. I've just seen you having a drink in the bar with him a couple of times. Fuck." He shakes his head in disbelief. "I wouldn't have thought he'd be your type."

I don't bother telling him Mark's not my type. That we've come to an arrangement. It's too complicated to explain, and frankly it's just easier for people at work to assume we're together for now. We can always tell them we've split up later.

"Why wouldn't he be my type?" I am slightly curious, despite myself.

"He's not exactly Mr. Outgoing, is he?"

"You're only saying that because the two of you are completely different. Doesn't mean he's a bad person."

"Nah, nah, don't get me wrong. I don't think he's a bad person. I think he's a good bloke, but I wouldn't have thought he was interesting enough for you."

"You mean you think he's dull?"

Mike has the good grace to look guilty. "Not dull, but not a challenge. I thought you'd like difficult men. Challenging. Jack-the-lads."

Rather like you, I think. "Actually," I say defiantly, "that's exactly what I love about him. He's the most stable person I've ever met. He gives me a security that I've never had before, and I know exactly where I stand with him. He has integrity. He phones exactly when he says he's going to phone, and does exactly what he says he's going to do. There are no games, and I've never been happier in my life."

Mike looks as shocked as I feel.

Christ.

Where did all that come from?

"*I couldn't* resist. I know I'm naughty, I know I shouldn't, but I just couldn't resist." Viv's trying to look apologetic as she heaves a huge plastic bag into the living room, but she can't wipe the smile off her face, her excitement at being a grandmother.

"Viv!" I try to admonish, but my heart isn't in it. I've been dying to buy things for the baby, but Mark won't let me. He's suddenly decided he's superstitious, and has stated firmly that neither of us can buy anything for the baby or the nursery until I'm in my eighth month.

It's been such a struggle to walk past Baby Gap and their gorgeous tiny sleepsuits. Such a struggle not to pop up to the fifth floor at John Lewis and spend an hour or so looking at cots and blankets.

So when Viv guiltily pulls out a tiny little pair of green dungarees with a matching jacket, I swoon with excitement, and when she pulls out a yellow-and-white striped sleepsuit, I almost pass out with joy.

"Aren't they gorgeous?" she exclaims with delight. "Aren't they the most beautiful things you've ever seen?"

"Aren't they tiny?" I whisper, rubbing my stomach as baby protests by delivering a swift kick under my ribs.

"Is she kicking?" Viv stops still as I jump and keep rubbing, trying to calm the baby. Not that it's painful, but the shock always takes my breath away.

"It's not necessarily a she," I say, although I'm sure it is. I'm absolutely convinced that this baby will be a girl. "And yes, she's kicking."

"Can I feel?" Viv says in awe, and she moves over to sit next to me, placing her hand on my stomach. "Ah!" she gasps, as baby kicks, and we both start smiling broadly.

"Don't cry," I warn, as tears fill Viv's eyes.

"I can't help it," she laughs even as the tears trickle down her cheeks. "It's just so amazing. This gift of life."

"It's more bloody amazing that you felt anything. Every time Mark's around and baby starts kicking, as soon as Mark puts his hand on my stomach, baby stops."

"How is Mark?" my mother asks fondly, asking about the favored son-in-law, despite never having met him. I know it's strange, but I can't really see the point in them meeting, not yet. He's not my boyfriend, and I'm not looking for her approval, and besides I see Viv so rarely myself, that when I do I like to keep her all to myself.

"He's fine."

"You're seeing a lot of him, aren't you?"

"Yes. I suppose I am."

"Are you . . . have you . . . well. What I'm trying to say is has anything happened?"

"Viv! I've told you. It's not like that."

"But you make him sound so wonderful. And your eyes light up when you talk about him."

"You know what? If I were the type to settle down, Mark would be everything I'd look for. If I wanted a partner, a husband, Mark is exactly the man I'd choose. But Viv, you know me. You know I'm allergic to commitment. I don't want a husband. I want a career."

"The only thing I do know is that you're beginning to sound like a broken record."

"What?" I bark. If she weren't my mother, I'd tell her to fuck off.

"I'm sorry, love. It's just that you've been saying that for-ever, even though your life has drastically changed. I could un-derstand you saying that if you were still living the single girl's life with no responsibilities, but Maeve, you're having a baby. Your life will never be the same again, and your priorities will have to change."

"Viv, a child doesn't have to change things. I'm going back to work after three months and Mark and I will raise the baby together. There are childminders or nurseries while we're at work. It's not like your day. Everyone does it now. It's far more normal for mothers to work than to stay at home. My life isn't going to change as much as you think."

Viv doesn't say anything for a while, just smooths out the tiny outfits with a "You just wait and I'll tell you I told you so" expression on her face.

"Okay," she says finally, meaning, "We'll see."

"Okay," I say finally. "So don't keep asking me about Mark in the hope that we're going to get it together and live happily ever after because I'm very happy on my own and I don't want to settle down. Okay?"

"Okay."

"Okay."

I don't even sound convincing to myself.

I make Viv a cup of tea as a peace offering, because I don't want to have a row with her when I see her so rarely and love her so much.

"Show me what else you bought," I chatter excitedly, drag-ging the bag over toward me as Viv's face, reluctantly, starts to brighten. "Oh! These are the smallest socks I've ever seen!"

"What about you, Mum? How's your life." Peace is now

fully restored. "I feel that these days all we talk about is me and the baby. I don't know anything about you anymore. What have you been doing? Any hot dates recently?"

"I thought grandmothers like me aren't supposed to have hot dates." She's smiling and I know I've been forgiven.

"Don't be ridiculous. God, if I look even half as good as you when I'm your age I'll be a very happy woman. Actually"—I peer at her closely—"you are looking pretty fantastic. Have you done something?"

"Something like what?" Now she looks coy.

"Viv, you haven't had plastic surgery or anything like that?"

"Maeve! Don't be ridiculous! Where would I find the money for something like that? Not that I wouldn't mind having some of that collagen in my crow's-feet."

"Crow's-feet? There's barely anything there. Anyway, they give your face character. And as for money, who knows, maybe you've got some wealthy sugar daddy." I nudge her and she laughs. And blushes.

"Viv?" I'm shocked, because clearly there is something she's not telling me, and that's so unlike Viv, and I'm shocked because I suddenly realize how self-obsessed I have become since being pregnant. I haven't asked Viv anything about herself. Nothing.

But I can make amends now.

"Viv? Tell me why you're blushing."

She sighs. And smiles. "Actually, I have been seeing someone lovely."

"That's great!" I hug her. "No wonder you're looking so fantastic. It must be all the sex. So come on, who is he?"

"That's the problem," she says, looking up at me, her face now serious. "I'm not quite sure how to tell you this so I'll just come out with it." She takes a deep breath. "It's your father."

I don't say anything. I can't say anything. My mouth falls open and I just sit there feeling as if I've been winded. Does that sound over-the-top? Well, I'm sorry, but I feel as if I have just been hit with a large sledgehammer.

"Maeve? Say something. Please." My mother is pleading.

I start to shake my head.

"How can? How? Why . . .?" I don't know what else to say, I only know that my world feels as if it has been turned upside down. Not because my father is a bad person. Not because my father is completely incompatible with my mother. Not because I don't understand why they've got back together after all these years apart.

But because I don't actually know who he is.

Well, I know who he is in that I'd probably recognize him if I passed him on the street, because I used to study photographs of him for hours, trying to etch his face onto my heart.

I know his handwriting from the birthday cards and checks he'd send on my birthday. I'd probably even recognize his voice from the rare occasions when he used to phone.

But that was years ago. I haven't heard from him for nearly ten years. It just became too much of an effort. I kept trying to have a relationship, and he never seemed to be available. In the end I stopped trying.

So did he.

People sometimes ask me about my parents and I speak as

if I only have a mother, and luckily no one pushes the point, too embarrassed to stray into territory that may involve death.

Viv sighs and runs her fingers through her hair. "Maeve, there's so much you don't know, so much I never told you. I don't even know where to begin."

"I can't believe you kept this from me," I manage to splutter.

"I didn't know how to tell you," she says sadly.

"So how long has this been going on?"

"About six months. Give or take."

"How could you not have told me?"

She sighs again. "I was frightened. I didn't know what you'd say. And I didn't know whether it was serious."

"Is it?"

She nods.

"Viv, how could you? He abandoned us! He left you a single mother and had pretty much nothing to do with me, with us, ever since. How can you forgive him?"

"Maeve, it's been a long, long time. Your father was the great love of my life, but he wasn't ready to settle down. I gave him an ultimatum when I fell pregnant with you, and he accepted because he loved me and didn't want to lose me, but he wasn't ready for the responsibility of a wife and child.

"He wasn't ever a bad person," she continues. "And although I was devastated, a part of me understood. It was the seventies. All of us living outside London had a delayed reaction to the free love and sex of the sixties. It didn't hit us until about 1972," she laughs.

"You know his biggest regret is you. All he talks about is

you. He's sat through all the home movies I ever took of you as a child about a thousand times. He's gone through every photo album. He wants to see you. To apologize. To explain."

"How do you know he's not going to do the same thing again?" I say bitterly.

"Because he's fifty-six and he still loves me," she says simply, with a smile. "And because it's never felt right with anyone the way it did with Michael. The way it still feels now."

"Are you going to marry him?" I ask suddenly.

She smiles. "He hasn't proposed. But we've talked about it. Maeve, are you okay?" She takes my hands in hers. "You need to know that I love him, Maeve. I've always loved him, and he's changed. We both have, but there's still something so strong between us."

"What? Describe it?"

"He was always dangerous," she giggles. "We always had the best times when we were together, and I always felt he understood me better than anyone. I understood him too, even the danger, even though it made me nervous in those days. Rightly, I discovered. But now he's mellowed. He's steady. Stable. That element of danger has gone and he's become my rock. My best friend."

"And you'd be ready to compromise again? To live with someone? To make concessions to their way of life?"

She shrugs. "My way of life isn't so good on my own. I've had a wonderful time bringing you up, and meeting different men, but I've also had that life for nearly thirty years. It's too long. I'm tired of doing everything on my own. I want someone else to deal with things. I want someone who can stand up to people who try to rip me off. I want someone to ring the bank when they've cocked up my statement again. I just want someone to share it all with. Can you understand that?"

I nod. Surprised.

I can.

The doorbell rings.

"Are you expecting anyone?" Viv puts down her glass of wine and goes to the door to answer the intercom, pressing the buzzer a few moments after she's asked who it is.

We're lolling about, trying to muster up the energy to go out for supper, because there's less than no food in the house (the midwife would kill me if she saw my ketones today), and neither of us is in the mood for takeaway.

"Quick, quick," Viv hisses, slipping her shoes on and digging her lip gloss out of her bag. "Put some makeup on. Do your hair."

"What? What are you talking about?" It's a Friday evening and I've taken the day off work to spend with Viv, and to be honest I'm extremely happy with a makeup-free face and scraped-back hair. "Who on earth is it?"

"It's Mark," she says, with delight, and anticipation. "Come on," she whispers, "you don't want him to see you like that," and Mark knocks on the door.

Viv shoots me a look of alarm as I slide over to the door in my fluffy Garfield slippers, and I grin at her as I open the door because Mark has seen me in pretty much every state imaginable, except . . . ah. Sorry. I repeat. Every state imaginable. And he doesn't care.

"It's only Mark," I say, grinning evilly at Viv, leaning up

and kissing Mark on the cheek. "What a lovely surprise. Can it be coincidence that I happened to mention on the phone today that Viv was down for the weekend?"

"Ah," Mark says. "Funny you should say that, but I was beginning to think you were keeping me away from your mother for a reason. Hello." He grins at her and shakes her hand. "I'm Mark. And I would say you're far too young to be Maeve's mother but that would sound terribly cheesy so I won't, even though it's true."

Viv simpers. I make a vomiting noise. All three of us go to Pizza Express.

"*He's* wonderful!" I swear, if I didn't know better I would say my mother was floating on cloud nine. I, on the other hand, am floating on cloud seven or eight, thrilled, delighted, amazed, that my mother and Mark hit it off so well.

"Hurry up." I wash my hands and wait for Viv to reapply her lip gloss, snatching it out of her hand when she's done and giving my own lips a quick slick.

"Changed your mind, have you?" Viv gives me a knowing smile, digging out a mascara and handing it over.

"There's no harm in trying to make a bit of an effort," I say defensively. "Come on, Mark will think we've fallen in the toilet."

"But he's such a good man," Viv sighs, as we walk back up the stairs into the restaurant. "He's so warm, and solid, and lovely. And he clearly adores you."

"And I adore him," I say sternly, threading my way through

the tables, which is not easy, given my belly. "And we're best friends and that's it. Okay?"

Viv just smiles to herself.

"Viv? Okay? Okay?"

"The lady," she whispers under her breath as she approaches the table and pulls out her chair, tilting her head and speaking just loudly enough for me to hear, which I know was her intention, "doth protest too much, methinks." Flashing a smile at Mark, who didn't hear a thing, or if he did, didn't know what she was talking about, she picks up a menu. "Dessert, anyone?"

The three of us go back to the flat, and as I put my key in the lock, my heart does a huge flipflop and I turn to Viv in alarm, feeling the color drain from my face. "I locked the door, didn't I? I could have sworn I locked the door."

Mark pushes me gently aside and takes my key. "You two stay here. Let me just check everything's okay." He pushes open the door and goes inside, as Viv and I huddle together, terrified I've been burgled. The door slams shut and a couple of minutes later Mark opens the door, frowning.

"I think you'd better come in," he says, and as we follow him into the living room my heart thumps so hard against my chest I think I may very well be sick. I know what to expect. Overturned chairs; emptied-out drawers; all my belongings strewn all over the floor. Oh shit. My grandmother's pearls. I kept meaning to hide them, but they were in the drawer of my bedside table. An inventory of my things flashes through my mind, and I pray they didn't find the earrings Viv gave me for my twenty-first birthday. Not that they're diamonds or anything, but the sentimental value is enormous.

Oh shit. I'm not sure I can handle this.

We walk into the living room and I stop with a gasp. Sitting on the sofa, with her head in her hands, looking absolutely terrible, is Fay. The owner of the flat. Who isn't supposed to be here for another six months.

"I thought you were in Greece?" I hear myself saying. "I know this might sound like a stupid question, but what on earth are you doing here?"

19

It wasn't such a stupid question. It transpired that Fay had fallen head over heels in love with a hunky blond Australian she met on Paros. His name was Stu. He was an "internet entrepreneur" (at which point even Mark raised his eyebrows), and Fay decided that she was going to spend the rest of her life with him.

They did Paros, then decided to go to Santorini, where they'd heard of an Australian bar manager who was looking for a replacement. Everything was idyllic, she sobbed (for by this time the waterworks were starting), and they'd sit and watch the sunrise every morning, talking about their future.

They had a great team of young people working at the bar, and soon it became the place on the island. They worked hard and they played harder, and even though Fay knew they weren't going to manage this bar on this little Greek island forever, she thought she'd found her true love, and she'd go anywhere, do anything, for him.

Fay had decided to go back to Sydney after the summer. She would live with Stu and find a job out there. Waitressing. Nannying. Anything, just so she could stay there with him. Until she walked in and caught him in bed with Paola, one of the great team of young people.

That was on Wednesday afternoon.

"I'm so sorry," she sobs, wiping her streaming nose and eyes with a crunched-up tissue. "I know I should have let you know but all I could think of was that I wanted to come home."

"I understand," I say soothingly. "But what are you going to do? Where are you going to live?"

"What do you mean?" She looks at me, uncomprehendingly, her tears already starting to dry up.

"You weren't thinking of moving straight back in here, were you?" I see that's exactly what she meant. "You can't just kick me out, Fay. I'm really sorry about your failed holiday romance"—she flinches but I ignore it—"but we agreed that I would stay here a year, and so far it's only six and a half months. Quite frankly," I continue, "I haven't got anywhere else to go."

"Well, neither have I," she says, standing up and crossing her arms, staking her territory. "And it's my bloody flat. Show me your lease, then. Show me where you signed on the dotted line and said you were taking out a lease for one year."

We didn't sign anything. We just liked each other . . . then . . . and took it on trust.

"I can't believe you're behaving like this. Can't you see I'm pregnant, for God's sake?" The hormones are once again threatening to hit, and I can feel a hot sting behind my eyes that means tears aren't far behind.

"And I can't believe you're behaving like this. Pregnancy has nothing to do with it. You're acting appallingly. It's my flat. And I'm the one who's been through hell and back."

"Okay," Mark says, taking control. "We don't seem to be getting anywhere, and we all need a bit of time to think about this. Why don't we sleep on it and discuss it in the morning?"

"Fine," says Fay, turning to go into the bedroom.

"And where do you think you're bloody going?" I step sharply toward her, and block her way. Ha! At times like this a spectacularly large stomach definitely has its advantages.

Mark looks shocked. "Maeve!"

"Yes." Fay tries to stare me down but I stand my ground. "Maeve!"

"Where am I supposed to sleep?" I look at Viv for some moral support and she nods.

"I think Maeve has a point."

"Why don't you come and stay at mine?" Mark says, looking first at me, then at Viv. "Both of you."

"No way," I say, shaking my head. "There's no way I'm leaving all my stuff in the flat with her here. How do I know I won't come back tomorrow and find everything destroyed?"

"Oh, for God's sake." Fay rolls her eyes to the ceiling but I'm not budging. "In that case," she states, "I feel exactly the same way and I'm not going anywhere either."

"Can we just behave like adults here, please?" Mark says, completely aghast at our immaturity, but I don't care. I'm not moving.

"I am an adult," I say petulantly. "She's the one who's behaving irresponsibly."

"Right. How about this, then? Fay can wait in the bedroom and we'll stay in the living room and talk about what we're going to do, and that way neither of you is in danger of having their belongings trashed by the other." I know Mark thinks we're ridiculous, but I'm six months pregnant. How dare she just come back and throw me out onto the street?

I say this to Mark when Fay disappears into the bedroom and slams the door, and he says that while he agrees with me, he also understands why Fay has behaved the way she has, and that when you have a broken heart the only place you want to be is home, and this is her home.

"But you still think she's wrong?"

"Yes," he says, after a long silence even though I know he probably doesn't agree and he's only saying it to make me happy, but I don't very much care. "Yes, I still think she's wrong. The point, however, is that you have to find somewhere else to live."

"Why?" My lower lip sticks out petulantly. "Why should I be the one who has to leave?"

"Because it's her flat, and because even though you can sit here and try to fight it out, you're not going to win. Maeve," he says more gently, "my grandpa always used to tell me to pick my battles wisely. You can't fight them just for the sake of fighting them. It's too much hard work, and this is one that isn't worth fighting."

"I agree," Viv says. I'd forgotten she was even here.

"So where am I supposed to go?" Now the tears really do

start to roll, and both Viv and Mark crouch down, rubbing my back and trying to comfort me. "I'm six months pregnant," I start to sob, "and this is my home and now I have to find a rental agent and it will take weeks and I just can't deal with this right now. I can't fucking deal with this!" I shout to get it off my chest, and then I cry a bit, not really caring that Viv and Mark are shooting one another worried looks over my head.

"Maeve," Mark says eventually. "I have five spare bedrooms, none of which is being used for anything other than to gather dust. It's ridiculous that we're not living together anyway, especially with all that room, and with the baby coming. I wanted to ask you before, but I didn't want you to get the wrong idea, and I didn't know how you'd react."

My tears start drying up.

"Maeve," he continues, "as far as I'm concerned Fay turning up like this is incredibly fortuitous. You know my house almost as well as I do, and I know you're comfortable there." He has a point. "It just makes sense for you to move in. What do you think?"

Of course it makes sense. It makes perfect sense. Except that I'd be giving up my independence. My freedom. Maybe Mark would expect me to start cooking for him, or scrubbing his bathtub out. It's already complicated, this situation. I'm pregnant by the man who's become my best friend, and if I were a different person I'd probably have fallen in love with him, but I'm not, and I haven't. But maybe that's what he'll expect if I move in with him? Maybe he'll come sneaking in to the spare room at night, and anyway, did he mean what he said about the spare room? He didn't exactly press the point and this probably isn't a good idea but then again I do love his house and I do feel at home there. Actually, I probably feel more at home there than here, but that really isn't the point. . . .

Christ. I'm exhausting myself.

"Look," Mark says. "Even if it's only temporarily. Even if we just pack up your stuff and you spend a couple of weeks at my place while you look for something else. How does that sound?"

That sounds perfect.

"Okay," I say. I look at Viv, who is grinning like a Cheshire Cat. "This doesn't mean anything," I hiss, as Mark disappears into the kitchen to look for bin bags to put my stuff in. "We're just friends."

"I know," Viv whispers back. "But you have to admit he's pretty damn lovely."

Well, yes. But tell me something else I didn't know.

"What might we do during first-stage labor?"

Mark and I have the best position in the room. Four other couples are sitting uncomfortably—everything's uncomfortable at seven months pregnant—on cushions around the edges of a bare living room, and Mark and I bagged the beanbags next to Trish, the antenatal teacher, which means we're the first in line for tea and biscuits during the break. (Once upon a time these things would not have mattered to me in the slightest. Is it desperately sad that a fig roll has now become the highlight of my evening? On second thought, don't answer that.)

Mark nudges me and signals for me to lean over so he can whisper in my ear. "Didn't she ask this last week?" I nod and shrug. I do seem to remember that she talked about first-stage labor last week, but who knows, maybe we'll find out something fantastically interesting this week that she withheld before.

"Deep breathing?" From one of the other mums-to-be.

"Yes, that's a good idea!" Trish nods enthusiastically.

"Go for a walk?"

"Another good idea!"

"A hot drink?"

"Ooh yes! Definitely a hot drink! Good one!" Trish smiles encouragingly.

"Watch television?"

"Yes. We might well watch television."

"Read a book?"

"Absolutely! Good idea!"

"Um, excuse me?" I lean forward and Trish looks to me for my suggestion of the day, but I'm rather confused. "Are you asking what might we do during first-stage labor to alleviate the pain or distract ourselves, or are you just asking what might we do?"

"Just what might we do," she says happily, at which point Mark snorts, indicating an impending fit of giggles, and I sit back in amazement. It's like asking what might we do on a Sunday morning. Quite frankly the list could go on forever. As this one does. In fact, it manages to take up the rest of the class.

The antenatal class is not quite what I expected. Not that I had huge expectations, but I certainly thought I'd learn what my choices were, be able to make decisions based on those choices, know what to expect. Thus far I've learned nothing I hadn't already picked up from books. Oh, and I've learned that, should I decide to have an epidural, or — God forbid — a cesarean, I am a very bad person indeed and will be sent straight to hell.

"There have been cases," Trish said last week, in an ominous, hushed voice, "of the epidural going" — her voice dropped to a whisper — "wrong." A sharp intake of breath from the other couples, as Trish looked at each of us in turn, making sure she had our full attention for the horror story she was doubtless about to impart. "I know of a woman who had an epidural, and it" — pause for dramatic effect — "went up."

"What do you mean?" someone said.

"I mean that she had no feeling from the waist up, but felt everything from the waist down."

Everybody gasped in horror, except for me. I rolled my eyes at Mark, and wondered whether I could seriously endure another few weeks of pretending I too was going for a natural birth with only humming and breathing to take away the pain, with possibly a tiny touch of gas and air if it got really bad.

Little do they know I've been considering an elective cesarean. Little are they ever going to know if I want to get out of here alive.

My main reason for coming was to meet other couples who were living locally and also having children at the same time. Although I was being very snobby. I tried desperately to get into the Hampstead class because I was a bit worried about the classes in Dartmouth Park, but the National Childbirth Trust wasn't having any of it.

"I know the computer says it's Gospel Oak," I said on the phone, in my most imperious voice (which, incidentally, makes the Queen sound like an extra in *EastEnders*), "but actually we live just off Hampstead High Street." It was worth a shot, but meanwhile I'm sitting in the living room of a large house in Dartmouth Park. And the people are fine. The other couples seem very sweet. But not my cup of tea. Not that it matters, as I'll be going straight back to work as soon as baby is born.

My idea of hell? Sitting around a table in a local coffee shop with four other women, all of us whipping our boobs out to soothe our screaming infants, sharing our birth stories and talking babies, because really we've got nothing else in common, but the loneliness is such that this is better than nothing.

I don't think so.

On the other hand I know how important it is to get to know other local mothers to find out about what's going on. I have no clue where baby groups are, or nurseries, or child-minders. I need to build up a support network in the area, and that's why I'm here.

"Only another three weeks until the course is over," I whisper to Mark, who finds the antenatal class as patronizing and ridiculous as I do. "Be nice."

"I'm trying," he whispers back, but when we've all put our shoes back on and said good-bye (every week we have to remove our shoes and line them up neatly in the hallway, and every week I curse myself for not putting on old no-name trainers, and I hide my DKNY trainers under the wooden bench because something tells me designer labels would not go down too well here), he breathes a sigh of relief.

"I don't think I can do it." He shakes his head as we stroll up Mansfield Road on our way home. "I think you may have to do the rest of the course without me."

"Absolutely not." I link my arm through his. "You're going

to keep coming whether you like it or not. Baby told me she wants you there."

He looks at me affectionately. "Baby couldn't possibly have told you she wants you there because first, Baby doesn't yet speak, and second, Baby is a boy."

"You wish," I snort, because although Mark has said he doesn't care, as long as the baby is healthy, I know that he would secretly love a boy. Just as I say that I really don't mind, and I would secretly love a little girl. Not that I'd love a little boy any less, but a little girl would be something special.

"I don't care," he says, smiling, as we turn into our street and Mark reaches for his key.

205 Estelle Road.

I love this house. I love everything about this house. I sit at work counting the minutes until I can leave and race back home, because yes, this is home. Now.

Mark said it would be temporary, and I moved in making a mental note to call the rental agents the following Monday. But somehow I never got around to it.

I love the smell of this house, even though I have no clue what it is. It's not beeswax, or lavender, or anything as romantic as lilies. It's not even something as prosaic as Shake 'n' Vac. Just the house's own smell. The smell of home.

I love puttering in the kitchen with Mark's cookbooks, licking my fingers sensuously as I scrape flour, butter, and sugar into the blender and pretend to be the quintessential Domestic Goddess.

Is this what they call nesting?

I love stopping off at the flower shop on the way back from work and coming home with armfuls of stargazers and creamy white roses, and arranging them as best I can in vases that I dot all over the house.

This must be what they call nesting.

I love sinking into the sofa with my legs up on the coffee table, tapping my Garfield-encased feet to Coldplay in an effort to give baby a headstart in the musical stakes. Mark keeps saying that the experts mèan playing Mozart and Beethoven to your fetus, not Coldplay and Travis, but the last thing I'd want is a nerd, and the baby seems to like it just fine.

I love my bedroom, which is almost as big as Mark's and, thankfully, has a small ensuite bathroom, but most of all I love the room that's going to be the nursery.

We're about to start decorating, now that I'm over seven months. Mark tried to insist we wait until eight, but quite frankly even if the baby decided to come now, we'd have a damn good chance, and I can't wait anymore.

I love the pale pistachio paint we've chosen, and the lemon borders. I love the green gingham curtains we're going to order, and the huge teddy bear rug we saw in the West End last weekend and couldn't resist.

I love this house so much I don't think I ever want to leave. I have thought about it, naturally, but for now this is working. Mark seems to be as comfortable as I am. He loves that I'm so happy here. He loves that I do, on occasion, cook him supper, and it's out of the goodness of my heart. He loves that there are flowers in the house, and feminine smells. I think he even loves being pissed off at me for filling the washing machine with lacy knickers when he was just about to stick his T-shirts in.

"You know what it is?" he said one Friday night, when I'd made an effort and we'd just finished a home-cooked dinner of roast chicken and apricot crumble. "I don't think I ever realized before you moved in how lonely I've been. For years. And I'm not lonely anymore."

I snorted. "How could you have been lonely for years? You lived with Julia for years."

"That's the point. I never thought you could be lonely when you were living with someone, but now I think that there's nothing lonelier than being in an unhappy relationship."

"So I'm your Lady in shining armor, sent to rescue you from years of M & S prepacked meals and holey socks."

"Why, are you willing to darn my socks? Because I do actually have a couple upstairs that need—"

"Fuck off!" I grab the cushion I'm sitting on and whack him over the head.

"If you weren't pregnant I'd whack you back," he says indignantly.

"If I weren't pregnant I wouldn't be here and you'd be having boring old pasta for dinner."

"Are you trying to imply I can't cook?" he says, wounded. "Because you can fuck off too," and with that he pours my mango smoothie all over my head.

"I can't believe you did that." I'm completely aghast, looking at my lap as the orange liquid drips off my hair and into my lap. "I can't believe you did that."

Mark sits back, crosses his arms and waits, grinning. He's waiting for my counterattack, but I'm too stunned to do anything. I'm in shock.

I start to laugh.

"God, you look ridiculous." Mark joins me in the laughter, laughing so hard he doesn't notice me grab a handful of spinach until it's too late and the spinach slides slowly down his nose.

With a combined giggle and scream, I turn and run out of the kitchen, because revenge will be his, and I know it's going to be bigger and better than a mango smoothie. I have a feeling it may have something to do with coffee ice cream, which, although back in the freezer, is still ominously runny due to me having forgotten that it was standing on the kitchen worktop for ages.

I can hear Mark running up the stairs behind me, and I shriek as I fumble my way into the nursery.

"No!" I say sternly, putting up my hand to warn him off. "Enough's enough, Mark. Not in the nursery. We've just decorated."

"You can clean it up later," he sings, advancing toward me slowly with two tubs of open ice cream and a large grin. Shit. I forgot about the other tub. "Revenge is mine."

"No," I shriek, but I'm giggling as he gets closer. "Mark, I'm serious. Think of the baby."

"The baby loves coffee ice cream," Mark says, which of course is what I've been telling him for the last two weeks to explain my sudden craving for a flavor of ice cream that I had, before my pregnancy, abhorred.

I'm backed into a corner and there's nowhere to go. With a final squeal, Mark's got me, and he's loving every minute of smearing ice cream all over my face and hair as I try to wriggle out, to no avail.

In the end I give up. Even as he smears the ice cream on I'm smearing it off and wiping it on him until we're both covered. We're both grinning hugely, when the strangest thing happens.

Mark's face is centimeters from mine, and suddenly I want to kiss him.

I'm looking at his lips, and all I can think about is licking them, feeling his lips on mine, his tongue in my mouth, and the smile wipes itself off my face as I feel myself transported with lust, and Mark must sense it, must feel what's going on because the next thing I know he's not smiling either, and the only noise you can hear is the sound of both of us panting, and he's looking deeply into my eyes.

"I think," I whisper, as I tilt my head slightly and move my head fractionally closer to his, "I'm about to have a Häagen-Dazs moment."

"That's the best idea you've had all week," he whispers back, just as his lips touch mine.

20

"No!" Stella gasps, when I tell her that Mark and I finally got it together. "You're not serious! That's like something out of a film!"

It's the day of my leaving do, and I'm briefing Stella on taking over my job. We've popped up to the canteen to grab some tea. She asks how come I'm looking so pleased with myself, and I nonchalantly tell her it must be all the sex.

She asks with whom, and is practically hugging herself with excitement when I tell her.

"I knew it!" she squeals, when she manages to get over her shock. "I knew you two would get together. I'm so excited! How do you feel?"

How do I feel?

I feel quite unlike I've ever felt before, if

the truth be known. I feel settled; comfortable; happy. I feel excited about the baby, about the future, and I feel relieved and grateful that I'm not doing all of this by myself.

I feel absolutely, one hundred percent feminine. I lie in bed at night as Mark sleeps, stroking my burgeoning belly, knowing that this is exactly what my body was designed for. Knowing that whatever heights I may reach in my career, this is the greatest thing I will ever do.

I watch Mark while he's sleeping. Often. I watch him snuffle into the pillow and I feel huge affection for him, because while I never wanted commitment, never wanted a relationship, now that I—albeit unwittingly—have one, I can see why people seek out their "other halves." I can see what it's all about.

Rather like Mark, I never thought I was lonely. I probably wasn't, but life is so much easier, so much more enjoyable now that I have someone to share it with. I have relaxed with that security, and although I don't for a second believe that Mark is my "other half" (as I have no belief in that concept at all), I do believe that he is enriching my life, and that's all that matters right now.

"I feel great," I say, smiling at Stella. "On top of the world." I look down at my belly. "Except I'm thirty-five weeks and I've had enough. I've bloody had enough."

I bumped into someone I knew last week who said that everyone who thought pregnancy lasted nine months was wrong. In actual fact, she laughed, pregnancy lasts eight months and two years, as the last month is so interminably long.

I remember seeing an interview with Caroline Quentin who, at thirty weeks, spontaneously went into labor and out popped a perfectly healthy baby. If it's good enough for Caroline Quentin, how come it's not good enough for me?

"Do you think tonight's the night?" I've started asking Mark every night as we lie in bed, usually after sex, because my hormones have thankfully started working in welcome ways, and my libido appears to have gone through the roof.

"I don't think so," Mark always sighs.

"Why not?" I plead, standing up to show him how much the baby's dropped. "Look how low it is. I swear the baby's head is engaged." Mark just smiles and goes back to his book.

Even the midwife laughed when I saw her this week. "Wanting it to happen early doesn't mean it will happen early," she said.

"But the baby's definitely dropped?" I asked hopefully.

"Hmm. It's definitely slightly lower than last week."

"But my indigestion's much better and I can breathe more easily again. It must have dropped. Partly engaged? Even a centimeter?"

She smiled. "Don't worry. Your time will come."

I didn't bother telling her that my time, at least as far as I am concerned, is definitely here.

"*I'd* like to say"—Mike Jones raises his glass and shouts above the heads of everyone in the room, eventually climbing on to a chair to be better heard—"a few words about Maeve before she leaves." A general cheer goes around the room, for which I am hugely grateful, because I don't quite believe I deserve a leaving do at all, having worked here for less than a year.

"She did a great job stepping in at the last minute and taking over the reins from her predecessor, but when we said, 'Take over where Julia left off,' we meant professionally." Another cheer from the crowd at large as I groan inwardly, covering it with a benign smile. "When we said step into her shoes, we didn't mean jump her boyfriend and get pregnant." More cheering, louder this time, and I'm wondering quite how politically incorrect Mike is planning to become.

"Sssh, ssssh." He calms the crowd. "Seriously, though, we're all very happy with the job Maeve's done here, and we're even more happy that the rumors about Mark were unfounded after all." I look at Mark, who gives a short, tight smile, Mike Jones never having been his favorite colleague in the first place. I know this speech is killing him.

"We wanted to say good luck with the baby, and hurry back soon before Stella . . . where are you, Stella?" Stella gives a shout and raises a pint glass from the back of the room. "Before Stella gets too comfortable in the pregnancy chair. Oi, Stella?"

"What?" She's grinning and I know that whatever Mike comes out with next, Stella is more than equipped to handle it.

"You're not planning on telling me you're expecting anytime soon, are you?"

"Fuck off, Mike!" she shouts, which gets the loudest cheer of the night.

With the inappropriate speech over, they bring out the presents: a basket containing two Petit Bateau stretchsuits and a yellow gingham matching comb and brush, a sexy pair of red lacy knickers that I doubt I'll ever manage to fit into, and a bottle of Antiseptic Nipple spray from Boots.

Just what I always wanted.

"Are you sure you don't want anything?" Mark shouts from the kitchen, where he's busy preparing dinner. "Tea? Biscuit? Baby?"

"Nothing," I shout back, repositioning the vase in the living room, then standing back to get a second look. "Actually, can I have the baby? Now? Please?" I hear Mark laugh, and move the vase back to the coffee table.

Everything needs to be perfect tonight. Viv and Michael have come up to London for the weekend, and tonight they are coming here for dinner. And I feel ever so slightly sick.

Thankfully they didn't ask to stay here. It's not something I could handle right now. They've booked into a guesthouse up the road, and I can't quite grasp the fact that I'm going to be meeting my mother's serious boyfriend this evening, who also happens to be my father.

"You've become the quintessential Jerry Springer family," quips Mark, unamusingly I think. "All you need now is to discover I'm your brother and we'd be guaranteed a slot on the show."

"Oh ha bloody ha. Because of that, you can now do the cooking."

"It's your family. Why should I do the cooking?"

"Because (a) I'll accept it by way of apology for what you've just said, and (b) you're better at it than I am."

"You only needed to say (b)," Mark laughs, and I smile as I

watch him open cupboard doors, checking for cardamom pods and cumin seeds, knowing how much he loves cooking for other people.

I go upstairs to change, again. So far this afternoon I've tried on five outfits, which is quite a feat considering the only things I'm wearing right now are a pair of black stretchy leggings from Mothercare and three men's sweaters from Marks and Spencer. All those sexy little numbers that were supposed to see me through? The men's shirts? The tight sweaters that were supposed to stretch to accommodate the belly? Forget it. They fitted me perfectly until six months, and then overnight nothing fitted at all.

But I manage to find five variations. Do I wear the black leggings and high heels in a bid to look slimmer, or will I just look horribly eighties? Do I wear the gray sweater with the black leggings or is that dull? Should I squeeze into the brown stretchy trousers from M & S, which, although not maternity, were supposed to have seen me through to the end, and really, what does it matter if they're a bit tight and I can't actually do them up anyway? One of my sweaters will cover that in an instant.

Why does it matter so much what my father thinks? But of course I know why it matters so much. It matters because the little girl in me still wants his approval. It may have been my decision to walk away from him completely ten years ago, but I want him to look at me now and be proud. I want him to think I'm successful, beautiful, everything he would want his daughter to be.

And I'd rather not have him think I'm fat, hence the clothing dilemma, although, as Mark said earlier, at thirty-eight and a half weeks pregnant I think I'm allowed to err on the side of large.

I do feel enormous. I've developed the pregnant woman's waddle, belly pushed out and hand resting in the small of my back for support. I feel like a caricature of myself, even as I do it, but it's the only way I feel balanced.

As for how much weight I've put on, God knows. As do the nurses, midwives, and obstetricians, but thankfully that's as far as it goes. Every week they weigh me, and every week, just before I stand on the scales, I announce loudly, "Don't tell me what I weigh." I figure that since there's nothing I can do about it, there's no point in knowing, because even though pregnancy's the greatest excuse there is, I know that I'll still feel horrific if I've put on more than the twenty-five to twenty-eight pounds the books advise. Also, I'm pretty damn certain I've put on about twice that, but I don't really care.

Oh God. I can't believe that Viv's coming with my father.

"Viv, you look wonderful!" Mark has already opened the front door while I am still struggling to get up off the sofa. "You must be Michael," I hear him say, and my heart starts beating very fast as I step into the hallway.

My father—Michael—stops still and looks at me, and neither of us says anything for a while. I had a speech planned. I was going to be cool but polite. I was going to call him Michael and pretend that he was merely my mother's new boyfriend. If the opportunity arose, I was going to dismiss his pleas to be my father again. I was going to tell him that, thanks to his abandoning us, I had become used to not having a father,

287

and certainly didn't need one now. I would say that while I was willing to accept his relationship with Viv, if he thought we were going to have a father/daughter relationship, then he had another thing coming.

But that was before I saw him.

Standing in the hallway, eyes filling with tears, is a middle-aged man who is so familiar my heart is threatening to break. And it's not Viv's boyfriend, not to me. It's Dad. My dad.

"Dad!" A sob breaks out, and the next thing you know he's opening his arms wide and I'm running into them, clinging onto him, and never wanting to break free of his embrace.

I'm sobbing so hard I don't realize he's crying too, and when we finally break away both Viv and Mark have disappeared into the kitchen, and I'm left with my dad.

"Look at you!" he laughs through the tears, holding me at arm's length. "Look at my little girl."

"I'm hardly your little girl anymore." I gesture to my stomach, and we both smile, but I am his little girl! I'm still his little girl!

"I'm sorry," he whispers, the smile gone now. "All these years have gone by and I've never stopped thinking of you and I wanted to write, or phone but—"

"Sssh. It's okay." I put my arms around him to comfort him, because suddenly it is okay. Suddenly I know that I don't have to carry the past around with me any longer. That it's okay to let it go, to move on, and that the only important thing is that we're together again.

We go into the kitchen to see what the others are doing, and I see that Viv's sitting at the kitchen table, also wiping tears from her eyes. But she's smiling broadly, and I know that in her wildest dreams she didn't expect this to happen.

And, looking at her face, I know exactly what she's thinking, for I have had the same thought myself.

We're a family again.

Dinner is delicious. Mark is funny and charming; Viv is positively blooming in Dad's presence, and Dad is, well. Dad is exactly what I always wanted my dad to be. He's both interesting and interested. He's sharp, and funny, and loving, and warm. He teases me gently about his first grandchild, and makes me feel treasured and safe.

"See what happens?" He turns to Viv. "I leave you alone with her for twenty-two years and she goes and gets herself pregnant. Honestly. I can't trust you for a second." There is warmth and humor in his voice, and Viv is head over heels in love.

But I can see he loves her too. He watches her tenderly as she gets up to help clear the table, and, if I didn't know the history, I would think that they were newlyweds. Except they are too comfortable with one another. So comfortable they look as if they've been together forever. As if there could never have been anyone else.

"Maeve, I have your blessing, don't I?" Viv's scraping leftover Moroccan lamb stew into the bin.

"What? So you are getting married?" I thought I'd dread this. But I'm delighted.

"I didn't mean that." She colors, and I'm sure it's in the

cards soon, and that knowing Viv she will wait for the arrival of their first grandchild, wait for all the excitement to die down before making any announcements of their own. "I just meant, you're happy about this, aren't you? Michael, your father, coming back into our lives. You can see how much he's changed?"

I put the dishcloth down and give Viv a hug. "Viv," I say, "he's exactly what I always hoped my dad would be, and he's exactly what I always hoped you'd find. I'm just still in shock that it's him." And we both laugh as a sharp pain stabs me in the stomach and I gasp.

"What?" Viv holds my arm in alarm. "Maeve? What is it?"

"I don't know. Nothing." I breathe out, the pain gone. "Probably just indigestion. I knew I ate too much."

"You're sure you're okay?"

"I'm fine." I smile at her but I'm worried. Strange pains when you're pregnant are no laughing matter and I potter around the kitchen for a while, making coffee, moving slowly and carefully in case the pain comes back.

Viv looks at me with concern when I come back to the dining room and sit down, but I smile reassuringly and stand up to pour the coffee.

And then I wet myself.

"Shit!" I sit down hard, and immediately blush. And then I think I'm going to start to cry. How can this happen? I'm thirty-three years old, and this may well be the most embarrassing thing that's ever happened to me in my whole life.

"What is it? What's the matter?" All three of them are leaning over me and all I can think of is I want my mum.

Thank God she's here.

"Mum!" I wail at her, and she can tell from my face that I

need to speak to her alone. The others leave and I look at her, mortified.

"I think I've just wet myself," I whisper in shame, and she starts to laugh.

"Love, I think that's your waters breaking." She smiles knowingly, forcing me to stand up so she can check.

"That's definitely your waters," she says, grinning, gesturing to the chair. "Completely clear and odorless. My darling girl, your time has come." And literally, as she says it, I feel something I haven't felt for nine months.

A period pain.

Mark pokes his head round the doorway. "Is everything okay?" Viv grins and I smile back. "Mark, it's time." Although this doesn't feel real at all, it feels as if I'm saying these words and tonight I'll go upstairs and climb into bed next to Mark, and tomorrow will carry on as normal.

"Time for what?" Mark is being obtuse, and Viv laughs.

"The baby's on its way."

And suddenly Mark goes into overdrive. "Oh God. Are you okay? Contractions, when are they coming. Shit, I can't remember, is it eight minutes or five minutes? Don't move, no actually, let's walk around and try some deep breathing," and when he eventually stops to take a breath, I start to laugh.

"Mark, relax! I'm fine. These contractions are nothing, just like vague period pains, but we'd better phone the hospital because didn't Trish warn in the class of the danger of infection?"

"Yes, yes, phone the hospital. I'll phone them."

"Mark." Viv gently takes the phone from him. "I think I'd better phone."

"Everything all right?" Dad walks back in, and Viv tells

him. I'm surprised and delighted to see his ear-to-ear grin. "We're going to be grandparents!" he says, nudging Viv. "Who would have thought it?"

"What are they saying, what are they saying?" Mark's flapping like an old woman, and I'm tempted to tell him to shut the fuck up because it's starting to really irritate me, particularly when he's normally so calm, but I know I have to wait until transition to get away with screaming at him.

"Sssh," Viv's trying to listen to the midwife. "Okay. Okay. So in about an hour? Fine. See you then."

"Well? Well?"

"They said that you ought to come in because of the risk of infection, but not to worry too much, and if you wanted to turn up in about an hour, that would be fine."

"So let me just make this very clear." I'm lying on a hospital bed, attached to a fetal monitor unit that is showing contractions are coming every two minutes. I've had the ghastly internal (I swear, the midwife's fingers were thicker than a bloody salami) and it appears I'm two centimeters dilated and could have hours left to go.

"Go home if you want," she says. "You probably won't be ready until the morning and the best thing you can do is get a decent night's sleep, and you'll sleep far better at home."

"Could I stay here?" I say doubtfully, knowing that after a nine-month wait nothing short of the army could get me out of this hospital bed now that I'm actually here. "What about the risk of infection?"

"Hardly any if you're sensible," she says. "It's up to you, but I'd suggest home."

"I think I'll stay here," I say, explaining to the others, when they come back in, that she'd said it was probably a better idea to stay at hospital.

I look at Mark and Dad. "I want to make it clear that when the time comes for me to push, I don't want anyone in here, except maybe Viv. Okay?"

"What about me?" Mark says, his hurt already apparent.

"Don't know yet," I grumble. "I'll see."

"Nnnnnnnnnnnnrrrrrrrrrhhhhhhhhhhh."
The sweat drips off my forehead as I push as hard as I can, lying back exhausted as the contraction, finally, starts to wane.

And I start to cry. "I can't do this," I sob. "I can't do this."

And I truly don't think I can. I don't think I'm going to get out of this one alive, the pain is so completely overwhelming and horrific. I feel as if my body is about to split open, and, at this moment in time, death seems like a pretty good alternative.

Oh no. Oh fuck. Here it comes again.

"Come on, Maeve, come on, Maeve. Good girl, good girl. You're doing brilliantly. Big big push. Big big push. Just one more push." The midwife is about twelve years old. Fresh-faced, no wedding ring and skinny as you like. There's no way in hell she's ever had a baby and I wonder what the hell she thinks she's doing, rubbing my shoulder, encouraging me when she's clearly got absolutely no idea that I am about to die, that this pain is the most horrific thing imaginable, that I am not giving birth to a baby, but to a sack of large King Edward potatoes.

"Don't touch me," I hiss at her, as the contraction subsides again and Mark leans over to wipe the sweat from my brow.

"You can do it," Mark says, from his position next to the bed, all sense of dignity I might once have had now forgotten as he watches me strain until I'm the color of a freshly boiled lobster. "One more push."

"NNNNNNnnnnnnnnnnnnnnnnnnnnnrrrrrrrrrrrrrrrhhhhhhhhh. FUCK OFF!" I scream, and then I squeeze his hand even tighter. "Viv!" I sob. "Where's Viv? I can't do this."

"Yes, you can." She runs in from the hallway, straight over to the bed, where she brushes the damp hair off my face and strokes my forehead as I try to muster some energy from somewhere. "I'm here now," she soothes.

"I can't." I look at my mum, and there are two of her. I'm so tired I've got double vision, and I know I can't do this anymore. I've changed my mind. I want to go home. I want this pain to go away. I don't want this baby.

The midwife suddenly looks at the fetal monitor machine, and I think I might be imagining it but her eyes seem to widen slightly. A second later an older woman appears in the doorway—the senior midwife—who comes straight over to the bed and starts moving the belt around my stomach up. The belt that's monitoring the baby's heartbeat.

"Come on, Maeve love," she says kindly as she moves the belt up and down, looking at the machine with measured glances. I try to see what she's looking at, but I'm too tired and I just lie back. "Right," she says, placing her hands on my hips as she attempts to gently roll me over. "Baby doesn't like this position so we'll have to roll you onto your side." Like an ele-phant I start rolling, and then another contraction comes.

"NOOOOOOOOOOOOOOooooooooooooooooooooooooooo," I scream, vaguely aware that the room, in what feels like a few seconds, has filled with people: the midwife; the senior midwife; an obstetrician; a pediatrician. It is completely surreal, as if a party is going on around my bed. I hear them whisper that they can't find the baby's heartbeat, and I see the panic in Mark's eyes, but I don't care any more. The obstetrician sits between my legs and I watch him through glazed exhausted eyes as he delicately pulls on a pair of latex gloves, looking exactly as if he's about to perform a major piano concerto at the Wigmore Hall.

He smiles up at me. "Just a little episiotomy," he says. "Won't hurt a bit." I no longer care. I just want this over with. I don't care about scalpels, or stitches. I don't even care if my deepest fears are realized and I end up doing something I once thought would be horribly humiliating like pooing on his hand. I don't care. I don't have a shred of dignity left, and the fact that a strange man is sitting between my naked spreadeagled legs means nothing. Nothing could be worse than the pain of these contractions.

As another contraction hits, I know I really have reached the end of the line. This is the last one. I know I can't do any more than this.

The senior midwife has now replaced the obstetrician

between my legs. "Come on, Maeve, that's it. Good girl. Big big push. Big big push. One more. The baby's coming. I can see the head. Here comes the head.

"Come on, Maeve. Just one more."

"You can do it, Maeve," Mark echoes and I bear down, pushing with all my might, screaming with the agony, knowing that it is now do or die.

"NNNNNNNNNNNNNNNNNRRRRRRHHHHHHHH."

Sam

21

Sam climbs out of her four-wheel-drive (bought especially to navigate the rough terrain of Gospel Oak's finest streets), unclips George from the backseat, and deposits him safely in a bouncy chair on the kitchen floor before going back outside to collect her shopping.

Organic carrots; organic potatoes; organic broccoli; organic cheese; organic chicken. Chris has already started to question how their monthly food bill seems to have tripled, despite having the addition of one tiny five-and-a-half-month-old baby who eats little more than a few tablespoonfuls. Chris doesn't understand the importance, not to mention the expense, of organic food. To be perfectly honest, Sam doesn't really understand the importance of organic food either, but everyone else seems to be doing it and if everybody else's baby is eating organic, then George will too.

Not that eating nonorganic food as a baby appeared to do Sam—or any of her friends for that matter—any harm, but times change, and although Sam resents the amount of money it costs, she's not prepared to take a risk just in case feeding George "normal" food might result in something terrible.

George is, after all, the love of her life. The apple of her eye. Her very reason for living. She didn't feel it at first, didn't get the whole mother/baby bonding thing. She had never been good at newborns, had never felt particularly comfortable with them, but had relaxed when all her friends told her it would be different when she had her own.

It wasn't.

For three months George was a screaming bundle of colicky sleeplessness. If he wasn't sleeping, he was crying. If he wasn't being fed, he was crying. The only time, in fact, he stopped crying was when Sam strapped him to her chest in the BabyBjorn and took off around the neighborhood.

At least, she would think, striding through the Heath up to Kenwood, I am reaping the benefits of exercise.

Except that, unfortunately, she wasn't. Sam had assumed that breast-feeding would be the perfect way of getting her figure back. Had been told by well-meaning friends that they could zip into their pre-pregnancy jeans within six weeks of breast-feeding.

These same well-meaning friends had said how fantastic breast-feeding was, that you could eat as much as you liked and still lose weight.

Sam threw herself into eating with wild abandon. She found she was starving, could quite happily graze all day, and continue throughout most of the night. She would sleepwalk downstairs, George latched firmly onto her breast, open the fridge door on autopilot, and reach in for whatever came first to hand. Slabs of cheese. Mountains of tuna salad. Ninety-eight percent fat-free toffee yogurts were a particular favorite, particularly as Sam chose to ignore that they were 100 percent pure sugar to make up for the lack of taste.

Sam lost a stone and a half immediately after George was born. Within eight weeks of breast-feeding, she had put it on again. Plus a little bit more for good measure. She has taken to wearing shapeless smocks, and has refused to worry about the excess weight. If being an earth mother means she has to look like an earth mother, then so be it.

At least, she tells herself, smiling as she watches George try to hold his toes, George no longer screams as he did. Not during daylight hours, at any rate. The colic disappeared at around three months, and since weaning him onto solids (she knew she was supposed to wait until four months, but George was so advanced, so strong and healthy, and so clearly hungry, she decided to do it at three and a half) he's been sleeping almost through the night. That's if you disregard the wake-ups at two-thirty, three, three-twenty, and so on until six o'clock every morning when Sam decides she's had enough and goes in to get him up.

She took him to the baby clinic for a checkup, wanted to make sure the birthmark at the back of his neck was not, as she occasionally thought in a panic, meningitis. Sat in the waiting room with bags under her eyes and lank, greasy hair, and wondered whether she looked as terrible as all the other mothers in there, all with the same vacant, exhausted appearance.

One woman shook her head wearily at Sam as her baby started to wail again, and soon the entire room struck up as a background chorus. I hadn't understood, Sam thought as she rocked George back and forth, shushing him softly to calm him down, people who harm their babies. I hadn't understood how anyone could possibly do such a thing. But now, in this waiting room, unable to quiet George, exhausted with frazzled nerves, Sam knew. She also knew she would never do such a thing, but she knew how you could be on the edge, and how little it would take to push you over.

She had reached into the huge black bag (ostensibly a "diaper bag," despite being the size and weight of a small suitcase filled with rocks) and drew out one of a selection of fourteen pacifiers that were rattling around in the bottom, to silence George's crying. It worked instantly.

A disapproving look from the weary woman, now calmly unbuttoning her shirt as she prepared to breast-feed.

"Do you find," she said lightly, her tone giving nothing away, "the pacifiers good?"

"They're a life-saver," Sam said defensively.

"I just think it's such a bad habit, really. Aren't you worried he'll grow up to be a thumb-sucker?"

"No, fuck off. It's none of your fucking business," was what Sam wanted to say. She swallowed hard and heard herself say lightly, "Not in the slightest."

"Sometimes I wish I could get Oliver to take one," the

302

woman said, stroking the head of her rather ugly baby, who was now sucking vigorously on her left nipple. "But he's just not interested, and it's probably a good thing." She smiled indulgently at her baby, clearly lying.

"Oh push hard enough and I'm sure you'll manage to force it in," Sam said, and laughed, slightly too hysterically. It shut the woman up.

But the pacifiers were causing something of a problem at night. George slept like an angel from seven in the evening until two-thirty, from which time he screamed every time the pacifier fell out of his mouth. Roughly every twenty minutes.

In the early days Chris and Sam would take turns. And on the weekends Sam would put earplugs in and leave Chris to do the night duty while she tried to catch up on her sleep, although it never actually worked. George's screams were far too loud to be blotted out by a couple of balls of wax (even though she did what the instructions tell you never to do: break one earplug into two, roll both halves up and shove them in as far as they'll go). Sam would lie there, rigid, too exhausted to move, pretending to be asleep.

It became a game. Who could pretend for longest. Sam always lost. Always climbed out of bed hissing at Chris that she was exhausted and it was his fucking turn, and did she have to do absolutely everything around here.

They didn't even fight about it anymore. She didn't have the energy. She just got up, every night, at two-thirty and continued to get up until she'd had enough and she blindly stumbled down to the kitchen to heat the bottle.

"What about sleep-training?" Chris said one night, having

spoken to some colleagues who had children, had been through the same thing. "You take away the pacifier and let them cry it out for timed periods."

They tried it that night. Sam sat cross-legged on her bed and listened to George scream, tears running down her face. Eventually, after one hour and fourteen minutes, she jumped up. "I can't do this," she explained to a bewildered Chris as she picked up a hysterical, red-faced George, and cuddled him until he calmed down.

"That's the worst thing you could have done," Chris said calmly. "Now you've taught him that if he cries long enough Mummy will eventually come and get him."

"Oh fuck off," she said in fury. "He's my baby and he needs me. He's a tiny baby. This whole sleep-training's a farce, it just makes them feel abandoned and scared. Poor baby. Poor Georgy. It's okay. Mummy's here. Mummy's here. Ssshhh. I promise I won't leave you again. Ssssh." She didn't dare admit it, but she'd bought the book and was seriously considering starting again on the weekend.

"Red lentil and cheesy vegetable casserole," she mutters to herself, as she flicks through the children's recipe book, stuffs a pacifier into George's mouth, and starts unpacking the shopping at the same time.

George drops the pacifier and starts to whimper as Sam tears open a packet of organic unsalted rice cakes and hands him one. He gums down on it and she breathes a sigh of relief as she busies herself in the kitchen, preparing to cook up yet another batch of food. Holding the cookbook open with her elbows, Sam leans down to pick up the rice cake George has just dropped. Five-second rule. It was on the floor less than five seconds, so she shoves it back in his mouth and just sighs when he drops it again.

"Are you not hungry, darling? Georgy? Rice cake? Mmmm. Yum yum yum. Look. Mummy loves rice cakes." Sam nibbles on it, then takes a bite. "No?" George is now looking past her shoulder at the lights of the digital clock on the microwave. "Oh well. Mummy will just have to have it," and Sam shrugs as the rice cake disappears in a single mouthful.

"Mummy's making red lentil casserole with cheese. How delicious. Can you think of anything more delicious? Red's a color, isn't it?" Sam babbles as she opens the larder and pulls out ingredients. "Red's the color of the post-box. It's a hot color, isn't it?"

George could not be less interested. Even Sam isn't particularly interested, but she read somewhere that the most intelligent children were ones whose parents had spoken to them constantly, even from birth, whose parents had explained everything to them.

Sam is determined to be the best mother of anyone she knows. She's never been competitive before, has never really known the cut and thrust of the design world, having always had the creativity and ability to shine naturally, but now, as a new mother, she is determined to do everything right.

Already she believes that George is super-baby. My son the genius, she jokingly refers to him, although listen closely to her laughter and you'll hear it's false. Georgenius, she coos, as she rocks him back and forth at night, reading him *Where's Spot?* (Against her better judgment. She really wanted to start him off on Rudyard Kipling, but *Where's Spot?* and *Charlie the Chicken* appealed to George in a way that *Kim* just didn't.)

"I think he might be quite advanced," she says, trying to blush with false modesty but failing miserably. "He's definitely going to be walking any second. Look." And all eyes turn to George, sprawling on his stomach, lifting his head, and looking around happily, but certainly nowhere near the point of standing, let alone walking.

"Did I walk young too?" she asked her mother on one of the rare occasions when she popped in to see her first grandchild.

"Darling, I don't remember." Her mother looked at Sam as if she were mad. "It was years ago. I do remember you looking ever so sweet with your little pigtails, though," and she smiled at the memory as she reached for a baby wipe and dabbed a small smear of vomit from her silk shirt with a frown.

"How can you not remember?" Sam tried to hide the disappointment, knowing that she'll never forget these years, never forget George's daily progression, but her mother's tone became irritated as she explained, again, how she had to work in the family business, had no choice, was merely following orders. Sam dropped the subject.

"It's not that I mind about me," she said to Julia that night, ignoring the fact that these late-night long-distance phone calls were going to send Chris up the wall. "But I mind for George. I'm used to her being a crap mother, but she's supposed to fall in love with her grandson, isn't she?"

Julia sighed. "I do think it's bloody odd that she's not around and not helping, and I completely feel for you. But,

Sam. This is your mother. Your mother who is far more concerned with her charity lunches and bloody bridge. You're the one who always says how selfish she is. Maybe you were wrong in expecting her to finally change."

"But he's so gorgeous." Sam blinked the tears away from her eyes as she leaned back on the sofa and turned her head to examine one of the many photographs of George now littering every available bit of space in the living room. "How can she not want to spend time with him?"

"I don't know. I know that if I were in London I'd be there every day, and he's not even my relative."

"Godson's the next best thing."

"Don't I know it. I just wish I was around a bit more, being godmotherish. As it stands, all I'll end up doing is sending him presents from New York."

"You know I didn't ask you to be godmother just because I thought you'd buy him expensive presents?"

"I should bloody hope not. Anyway, you wouldn't have asked if that was the case. Not on what London Daytime Television was paying me."

They both laughed.

"But seriously, Sam, I know you asked me for the right reasons. I know I'm expected to give George moral guidance, and be the person who looks after him if . . . well, heaven forbid . . ."

"Yes, I know. That's exactly why I asked you. But I also want George to be able to come to you when he's older, to ask anything of you."

"And I want to retain the ability to say no," Julia laughed.

"But Sam, can I just say one more thing about your mother . . . Your mother is your mother, she's not going to change. It's the only certainty in life and you have to stop expecting things from her."

"I know. I know. It's just that it still bloody hurts. All these years I thought I'd buried all the pain of her not being around, not being interested, not knowing how to mother, for Chrissakes, and now I've had George, all those feelings of resentment and anger feel just as raw as they did ten years ago."

"Maybe you should think about seeing someone."

"God!" Sam started to laugh. "How long have you been in New York exactly? A few weeks and you're already buying into all that therapy rubbish?"

"I don't actually think it's rubbish," Julia said defensively. "I wish I'd been to see someone when I was with Mark. Would have given me the impetus to leave years before."

"How is Mark?" Sam's tone was tentative. "Have you heard anything?"

"Nope. Have you seen him?"

"Amazingly, no." Amazing only because Mark lives just a few streets away, but Sam had always known that however much she loved Mark—and she truly did—when he and Julia split up she would have to make a choice, and her loyalties lay with Julia.

There was a long pause before Julia spoke. "The baby is apparently due any day now."

"Are you okay with . . . everything?" Of course they've talked about Maeve. Sam and Bella both listened for hours as Julia poured out the tears. It took a week. A week of crying and pain, and then Julia professed to be over it. She said the tears were a result of shock, and the pain was for the life she had once thought she wanted, but by the end of the week she had closure. At least that's what she said.

Bella and Sam didn't believe her at first. Couldn't believe that Julia, Julia who had winced in pain at the sight of cooing babies, who could spend hours in Mothercare dreaming of chubby fingers and curling toes, Julia who was convinced the reason for her inability to get pregnant was Mark, could move on so quickly. So easily. So relatively painlessly.

But it seems that Julia had moved on. She still found it hard to accept that there might be something wrong with her after all, but with every day she knew she'd made the right choice. She was exactly where she needed to be, doing exactly what she needed to do.

"The amazing thing," Julia said after a pause, "is that I think I'm genuinely fine. I wouldn't go as far as to say I'm happy for him, but if you'd have told me this time last year Mark would be having a baby with the woman who replaced me at work . . ." They both snorted with laughter at the ludicrousness of the situation before Julia continued, "I would have either smacked you or screamed with rage. But I'm fine. I'm actually . . . oh God. Am I going to say this? I'm actually relieved it's not me."

"So children really aren't on your agenda, then?"

"Not yet. I'm having such a blast here. Working like a madwoman, out every night. I wake up each morning with the most astonishing surge of energy. Sam, my feet barely touch the ground in New York, and I love every bloody minute of it. I can't think of anything I want less right now than having a fat stomach, a boring husband, every evening spent in front of the telly, and a screaming baby keeping me up all night."

Sam absentmindedly stroked her own fat stomach and sighed. "Oh shit," Julia said. "I'm sorry. I didn't mean that. It's just the whole domestic thing. I thought I wanted it so badly, the whole thing. Husband. Baby. Nice house. And I just don't. I feel like I was dead during all that time with Mark. Not that it's his fault. It was us. We were just so wrong for one another, and I look back at that person and know she wasn't me, just a vague shadow. This is the life I need to lead now, and if things change in the future, I'll deal with them when I get there."

Sam wanted to ask if Julia had come to terms with the possibility that she might not be able to have children, but she couldn't. Not yet. And she knows Julia. Knows she will, rather like the ostrich, have buried the fear deep, deep enough for her not to have to face it.

"And the delectable Jack?"

"We still see one another, but really as friends."

"Friends who occasionally have sex, by any chance?"

Julia giggled. "And what, pray tell, other sort of friend is there?"

"You mean, when they're handsome and funny and think you're the best thing since sliced bread?"

"Exactly. I didn't mean you," she snorted.

"I should bloody hope not. But you and Jack. Definitely not an item?"

"Definitely not. I'm not ready for that, but he's a fantastic friend."

"And the sex?"

"Why, fantastic!" Julia laughed. "As if you really needed to ask."

Sam shakes some organic spinach leaves into a bowl and hesitates over the cheese grater. It's definitely clean, but definitely not sterile. Can she be bothered? She hesitates, wonders whether anything terrible would happen, but knows she could never forgive herself if something did. With a sigh she puts the kettle on to boil—again—and dunks the cheese grater in a bowl of boiling water for ten minutes to sterilize it.

"This has become the house of fucking water," she said in fury last night, as Chris walked in, dumping his coat in the hall. She had lifted the lid of the sterilizer and dumped it quickly in the sink, but not before it had left a trail of steaming puddles all over the kitchen worktops. This added to the fact that for the past five months she had refused to heat bottles in the microwave, and had heated them in a pan of boiling water, meant that her surfaces were indeed rather liquid. "All I do," she said in exasperation, wiping the puddles away for the sixteenth time that day, "is mop up fucking water."

"My day was lovely, darling, thank you." Chris chose to ignore her comments. "I'm very tired, and I've had back-to-back meetings with potential stockists all afternoon, but what a pleasure it is to come home to my beautiful wife, and a delicious home-cooked meal." He leaned forward to kiss her, which she ignored, feeling the rage already building up. Deep breaths, she told herself, chopping celery into smaller and smaller pieces. But the rage was too strong.

"You can make fucking jokes," she said viciously, "but you

haven't been stuck in all day with a screaming baby. You have absolutely no idea what it's like for me. You have no idea how hard I've been working and I've got no help and then you breeze in here and expect me to be in a good mood when I'm completely fucking exhausted and I'm fed up with it. I'm fed up."

"And what do you think I do all day? You act as if I'm leaving the house every morning to go to a party. You're not the only one who's suffering, Sam, you're not the only one who's run off their feet." Chris thought he understood what Sam was going through, but, really, there was only so much a man could take. And what about him, for heaven's sake? He'd had a nightmare day. He was run off his feet, trying to finish three tables and a sideboard, and he came home only to be completely ignored or screamed at by this wife that he barely recognized anymore.

But it was different for Chris. He couldn't understand why, for three months, Sam had been unable to get dressed. This wasn't because she didn't want to, or because she was too exhausted, but because George screamed solidly. All day. The only time he would be quiet was if he was walked up and down the stairs in Sam's arms, or pushed around the Heath in a pram. And heaven forbid she should stop walking to try to grab a coffee.

Sam was trying to look after George, to keep the house clean, to do the ironing, to cook children's meals for George and grown-up meals for Chris, and to retain some sanity at the same time.

But the worst thing of all was the loneliness. She couldn't

remember being independent. Or vivacious. Or fun-loving. She could barely remember ever leaving the house.

"At least you get away from it!" Sam screamed. "At least you get out of this fucking house. I'm trapped here all day, and I haven't got a minute to myself, and then you come home and crack jokes about home-cooked meals. How do you think that makes me feel?"

"Like a takeaway pizza?" Chris said hopefully. Contritely.

There was a long pause as Sam felt the anger start to diffuse. She would give in. This time.

"Make sure there's extra pepperoni," she grumbled, as she dragged her feet up the stairs to run a bath.

22

"*I was in labor for* forty-six hours." A ruddy-cheeked woman bounces her smiling, chubby daughter up and down on her knee as Sam tries to look interested. "And eventually I ended up having an emergency cesarean. They were going to use a ventouse, or forceps, but thank goodness they bypassed it and went straight for the knife." She chuckled as she reached for another slice of carrot cake, and Sam knew it was going to be her turn soon.

"How was your birth?" All eyes turn to Sam, who wonders whether it would be possible to grab George from his position under the Baby Gym, sandwiched between two babies who look as bewildered as he, and run out.

She gazes into the expectant faces of the mothers sitting around a stranger's living room, and smiles. "Absolutely fine." She's never met these women before, for God's sake. Her birth is nothing to do with them, and, quite apart from anything else, repeating it day in day out bores her rigid. And it's not even as if George is a week old, when she might have quite enjoyed talking about the horror of giving birth. He's six months. Why the hell are they still asking her? What, in fact, is she doing here, in this room with these women she doesn't know, pretending that they all have something in common, just because they have babies the same age?

"Were you at UCH?" one of the women asks, and Sam nods, before jumping up—excellent timing—to rescue George from the grip of one of the babies next to him.

"Tell me we can leave," she whispers into George's ear, disguising it with a kiss and a cuddle, but George shows no sign of having heard. With a resigned sigh she puts him down and reenters the mothers' circle.

The mother and baby group is a last resort. Sam thought she was prepared for motherhood. She thought she'd be happy strolling around the streets with her OshKosh B'Gosh–clad child, smiling benevolently at all she passed. The perfect mother with the perfect child.

She envisaged picnics on the Heath. Had dreamed of throwing her baby up in the air while he/she giggled uncontrollably and gazed at her with adoration. Sure, she had expected exhaustion and sleep deprivation, and she knew she wouldn't have any more time for herself (although she couldn't have imagined quite what that actually felt like), but nothing had prepared her for the loneliness and the boredom.

Her friends either have much older children, and are busy ferrying them back and forth from nursery school to play dates, or no children at all.

"You'll meet people, no problem," her friends with children had said. "Join the mother and baby group. Or baby massage classes. There's always loads going on."

Thus far, she'd avoided all of them.

She'd seen them in the tea shop in South End Green. Gaggles of mothers, surrounded by prams and associated debris, all looking exhausted but fulfilled. Or in Hampstead, more glamorous groups of women, making the effort to wear makeup, their Touche Eclat doing a brave job of covering up the shadows under their eyes.

And she'd passed them on the Heath. Groups of women gathering outside the One O'Clock Club, all of them smiling indulgently at Sam as she trudged past with her secondhand pram.

She had avoided them because she was terrified of being a mother. While she realized that motherhood was the fulfillment of a lifelong dream, and while she accepted she was thrilled to leave her job once she became pregnant, the thought of being a full-time mother, or worse, of anyone looking at her and thinking she was a full-time mother, filled her with dread. And confusion. She never thought she'd feel this way.

She'd seen it happen to other people. Once sane, intelligent, interesting women with careers and opinions and strong viewpoints dissolved into shadows of their former selves the minute they had a baby. They didn't have time to read the papers, and even if they managed to catch the news once a week they didn't have the energy to form an opinion on the story of the moment. Their short-term memories seemed to completely disappear. Their talk consisted solely of topics related to babies, children, child care, and the hell of finding a decent mother's helper.

"You're being so judgmental," Chris had said when she tried to explain her fears. "How do you know these women are 'mindless mothers,' as you say so disdainfully? How do you know they're not just like you? They could be incredibly bright, they could have careers too. You're not superior to them, you know."

"I know." Sam was immediately defensive. Indignant. Ashamed. Because she knew Chris was right. That was exactly how she felt.

But five months of talking to herself all day was enough. At least, she had thought wryly, as she blabbered away one morning to a disinterested George about paint colors and whether she should go with Old White or Barley White, George will be getting the benefit of having everything explained to him. At this rate he won't just be Georgenius, he'll be Einstein the bloody second. (Even if his particular area of expertise will be vegetable purees and paint colors.)

She knew something had to change when she was pushing George along the road, and spied a woman pushing a buggy farther up the road. Quickening her step until she was almost jogging, Sam eventually managed to pull up alongside her. She looked nice. Her baby looked around the same age as George, and she definitely didn't have that exhausted look in her eyes. Her buggy was a snazzy three-wheel-drive, and her trainers were Adidas. She looked like someone who could be a new friend.

"Hi," Sam said with a smile and a raise of her eyebrows as if to say, "God, what a nightmare. Babies. Buggies. Screaming. Managing to stay young and trendy, despite being a mother. You and I are in the same boat, surely have so much in common, why don't we walk together, and then perhaps a cappuccino afterward . . . here's my number, call anytime you like. Really, day or night."

"Hi." The woman smiled back cautiously, slightly coldly.

Sam continued unfazed. "Great buggy," she ventured, slightly out of breath, having exerted herself more in the last two minutes than she'd done in the last fifteen months. "We were thinking about one of those. How do you find it?"

"Very light," the woman said, as Sam relaxed and they fell into step, side by side. "And easy. I love it."

"And she's gorgeous," Sam cooed, peering over at the little girl snuggled into a sheepskin to protect against the cold November air. "How old is she?"

"Five months." A pause. "Yours?"

"Almost six months. It goes so fast. I can't believe it."

"Mmmm."

"I'm Sam, by the way. This is George."

"I'm Emma. And that's Chloe."

"Are you going to the Heath? We could walk together. If you are. I mean, if you'd like."

Emma shook her head. "We're actually going up to South End Green. I have to get some shopping. Sorry, but nice to meet you." She smiled as she maneuvered the buggy around the corner, and Sam stood for a while, fighting the urge to run after her, to say that she too needed things from the shop. That she would join them, but of course that would be desperate, and Sam couldn't appear desperate.

"It was nice to meet you too," Sam found herself shouting, as Emma and Chloe disappeared from view. "Perhaps I'll see you again?" This last was said as a question, and Emma turned around with a smile, shrugged, and nodded, and then left. Sam stood there as a hot flush crept up her face. She recognized that smile. That was the smile she gave when frumpy full-time mothers tried to befriend her. It was a smile that said: Don't think about being my friend because I am not one of you. I am better than you. You are a full-time mother and I have so much more going on in my life than just my child. You're bored and lonely and desperate, and I am none of those things (even if I am).

Sam turned her head and examined herself slowly in the window of the wine shop. Black stretchy leggings that were once a size 10 but had almost certainly been stretched, if not into oblivion, then into what Sam dreaded might have been a size 14. Flat black boots that were the only comfortable things she had to walk in, although admittedly they weren't exactly making a fashion statement. Pushing George closer to the window, she looked at her face and frowned.

And she knew then why Emma had granted a small, tight smile before running away. Sam looked exactly like the desperate women she herself avoided. Oh God. Had it really come to that?

This isn't really me, she wanted to shout. Look! Let me show you photos of what I really look like, what I used to look like. But now, the desperate reflection in the shop window really was Sam, and that was when all resistance to the mother and baby groups finally broke down.

Sam re-enters the mothers' circle and sips her coffee. This is her first meeting, although the other mothers have met twice before, and a couple of them were in hospital together or know one another from prenatal classes.

She feels like something of an outsider, not helped by the fact they have decided to meet at someone's house every week, and Sam can't help feeling uncomfortable sitting on the sofa of a woman she's never met before, tucking into carrot cake that one of these women — amazingly — has found the time to make.

There are four other women there. Natalie with her daughter, Olivia; Emily and her son, James; Sarah and daughter Laura; and Penny with Lizzy.

"Thank God there's another boy." Emily leans over to Sam and laughs. "I felt completely outnumbered last week."

"It is extraordinary, isn't it," says Sarah, in whose house they are all sitting, "how many people have had girls recently? You two are the only people who seem to have boys."

Everyone murmurs in agreement.

"Lucky for the boys, though," Natalie says. "I'd better teach Olivia about the birds and the bees early."

"Would that be before or after the ABCs?" Penny says, smiling.

"My daughter's a genius," Natalie puffs proudly, a twinkle in her eye. "ABCs? She'll be writing her first novel within the year."

"Thank God," Sam laughs. "I thought I was the only one with a genius child."

"Oh no." Natalie shakes her head vigorously. "All of us have genius children." The other mothers agree, laughing. "In fact, this isn't just any old mother and baby group. This is a mother and baby group especially for genius children. I mean honestly. Look at my daughter. See the way her tongue's lolling attractively at the side of her mouth? That's actually sign language. We've been learning it together and what she's actually saying is, Mum, I'm bored and why are you forcing me to lie on a play mat when intellectually I am so superior to this."

"At least I know I'm in the right place," Sam says.

"Speaking of the birds and the bees—" Sarah ventures.

"Yeuch!" Natalie says forcefully, as Sam decides she definitely likes her. "Do we have to?"

"I just wondered whether you'd all done it yet."

"Sex?" Emily laughs. "Are you nuts?"

"You don't mean it still hurts?" Sam's horrified. Admittedly sex has been the very last thing on her mind, but she and Chris have managed to have it a couple of times, and even though the first time was rather strange, it certainly wasn't painful.

"No! I meant why, for God's sake. Who'd want to?"

"I've got to say I agree," Penny chips in. "I'm running out of excuses but the truth is I'm just completely exhausted. And I hardly feel sexy with saggy boobs and a fat stomach. God. Sex is just the last thing I can think of. The only thing I want to do when I climb into bed at night is sleep."

"I, thank God, haven't had sex once," Natalie says. "I've been telling Martin my stitches are painful. Bless."

Sarah frowns at Natalie. "Stitches? I thought you said you had an emergency cesarean?"

"Your point?"

They all start laughing.

But it's true, Sam thinks sadly, even as she's laughing. She and Chris had an amazing sex life, not that you'd know it now. Everyone told her that it all changed when you got married, but it never had for them. Up until George was born they had still managed to have sex at least three times a week. She can count the number of times since on the fingers of one hand.

The first time she laid eyes on Chris she was at a party, six years ago. She knew most of the people there and, despite being on the husband hunt at the time, thought it wasn't going to be a party at which she'd pull. Julia was supposed to have come with her, but had dropped out at the last minute thanks to a stinking cold, and Sam hooked up with a couple of other friends just so she wouldn't have to walk in on her own.

She'd had a great evening. Had downed cocktails like they were going out of fashion, had flirted innocently with inappropriate men, and had danced the night away.

Toward the end of the evening she found herself in the kitchen. Sitting on the kitchen counter, legs swinging against the washing machine, she was laughing at the efforts of Tony — not her type at all — to chat her up, when something made her turn her head.

The front door was opening and in walked someone who made Sam's heart, literally, stop. The smile left her face as she leaned forward to see better. There was nothing special about him. Average height. Average looks. Nice smile. Typical male brown leather jacket. But put it all together and Sam knew, beyond a shadow of a doubt, that this man was going to change her life.

"I'm going to have him," she thought, except she unfortunately thought it out loud, leaving a bewildered Tony standing in the kitchen by himself as she jumped off the counter and went to meet her destiny.

"I'm Sam." She held out her hand as Chris looked at her and a smile spread across his face. He had been in the process of taking off his jacket but he stopped to shake her hand. And didn't let go.

"Chris."

"So shall we go, Chris?"

He never bothered taking his coat off.

They went to a hotel in Swiss Cottage, unable to think of anywhere else other than a hotel that would be open so late. Sat in a huge plush sofa and talked about everything. The more they talked, the more Sam knew.

He dropped her home and she skipped in without even a kiss goodnight. But still she knew.

The next night he phoned her at six. She had, by this time, caught Julia's cold. She was lying in bed, a box of tissues on one side, the television remote control on the other, and a mug of lukewarm Lemsip on her bedside table.

"What are you doing?" he asked. "I'm jealous," he said, after she had told him. "I wish I was there too but I have to take care of some unfinished business."

"Are you going to tell me what this unfinished business is?" she teased.

"Yes. I've been seeing someone. And now I'm not going to see her anymore. But I don't think it's fair to tell her over the phone, so I'm going to have dinner with her tonight so I can tell her."

"Okay," Sam said happily, not once doubting him, and not wanting to know anything more about this mysterious girl. She didn't matter, not now.

At eleven-fifteen Chris called again. "What are you doing?"

"What do you think I'm doing?" she laughed. "I'm still lying in bed."

"Sounds wonderful," he said again. "I'll be over in fifteen minutes."

He was. And he never left.

Sex was always amazing between them. Sam felt completely sated when she was with Chris, even after six years. It was an extraordinary physical union that they clung to, no matter what else had happened during their day. It never felt dull, or became a routine. The sensations were always as strong as they had been, even now, and it had become their way of ending the day.

Even if they argued, they still came together before going to sleep. Now, post-George, the very thought of sex was exhausting, which was perhaps one of the reasons things hadn't been going so well. Sex was never just sex for Sam and Chris: It was about closeness; intimacy; trust; and neither had felt quite the same since their sex life took a downturn.

Sam felt increasingly estranged from Chris. She thought he had no concept of what her life was like, how trapped she thought herself to be, how difficult it was to retain the Sam of old when she was knee-deep in diapers. Chris felt much the same thing, for different reasons. Each time one of them made a false move, the grudges deepened, and for the first time in their married life, they weren't rediscovering their love for one another at the end of the day.

Sam still looked at his body appreciatively, as he wandered round the bedroom with nothing on late at night, but it was usually through eyes half closed with sleep as she sank under the duvet and mumbled a goodnight.

She could appreciate his body, his physical presence, just as long as it didn't encroach upon hers. Not now, not when all she dreamed of was a decent, uninterrupted night's sleep. Not even when she was craving closeness with another adult, fighting off the urge to merge with total strangers in the street. Not even that was enough to restore her sunken libido.

Sam shakes her head sadly and brings herself back into the present. Back into this living room, with its chocolate-brown velvet sofas and animal-print cushions, against which five women are lolling while their babies lie quietly on assorted play mats on the floor.

"God, I can't wait to get back to work," Natalie says. "Isn't that ridiculous? I couldn't wait to leave to have a baby, and now I'm desperate to get my head around something other than HiPP organic bloody food jars."

"Tell me about it," Penny laughs. "So are you going back?"

Natalie shrugs. "I've got six months' maternity leave."

"Six months!" A chorus of disbelief strikes up around the room.

"Not all of it paid," she laughs. "But two weeks, and I'm

back. You know, I really thought I'd be fantastic at this. I've waited to be a mother all my bloody life, and the truth is I wasn't planning on going back at all, but I feel like my brain has stopped. God, I adore Olivia, wouldn't change her for the world, but I can't do this full-time mother bit. I'm just not cut out for it. Penny, I think you're completely fantastic but I couldn't do what you do."

"You mean stay at home and look after Lizzy? Natalie, I couldn't do what you do either. It's not that I don't miss work. I really do, but I've found it easier to give it up because my mother was never around when I was growing up, and I don't want Lizzy to have the same thing. I totally understand women needing to feel recognized as an individual rather than as a mother, but I've had that individual recognition, and now I'm choosing to be recognized as a mother. It's enough. I was always scared that it wouldn't be, but it is."

Sam looks at Penny admiringly. Penny has just said exactly what she feels. Or perhaps, exactly what she wants to feel, because although she too wants to provide for George what was missing in her own childhood, she now suspects she needs the recognition too. But she's hoping that will go away.

"I have to admit, I feel guilty as hell that it isn't enough," Natalie says, before laughing. "But not so guilty that I could stay at home with her all day. I mean, she's gorgeous, but the highlight of my week is now going to a mother and baby group. How sad is that? Anything just to have normal grown-up company."

"Except even then you end up talking about babies," Emily laughs.

"Well, yes," Natalie has to concede. "But at least it's conversation."

"What did you do, Penny?" Sam's curious.

"I worked for a bank."

Sam pictures Penny in a high street branch of Barclay's. She looks the type. Maybe she was even manager, for despite the leftover maternity leggings and voluminous gray sweater, she might have aimed for more.

"Which bank?"

She mentions an American investment bank. "I was head of Mergers and Acquisitions there."

Sam almost has heart failure.

Natalie, it transpires, is the marketing director of a huge pharmaceutical company. Sarah started her own internet fashion site that's so successful Sam regularly reads about it in the financial pages. Emily is a nursery-school teacher.

"I know," Natalie laughs, seeing Sam's expression. "We're a bit of a mixed bunch, aren't we?"

"You can say that again," Sam says, almost overwhelmed with shame for judging these people, for assuming there was no more to them than their children, and for finding fault with that. "You can definitely say that again."

23

Chris comes home at ten to seven, twenty minutes after Sam has put George to bed. He's late, having stopped to get more ice-cube trays for Sam. She's in the middle of a cooking frenzy, whipping up great batches of organic food for George, freezing it in ice-cube trays as soon as it's cooked.

It's a Friday night, and it's been a tough week. Before George, or BG as he has come to think of it, he would long for the weekends.

BG, Friday nights meant hitting the pub with the men who shared his workshop, fellow craftsmen and artists. He'd stay for a couple of drinks, then meet Sam for dinner. In their younger days they'd hit the West End, try out different busy, buzzy restaurants each week, occasionally following that with a club, but the last couple of years they'd tended to stick with local restaurants.

Friday nights meant a pizza, or a curry, or Chinese takeout. They'd have a long meal, unwind over a bottle of wine, flirt suggestively in the knowledge that Friday night was a sure thing, and that however late a night they had, however much energy they exerted, the best part of Saturday morning would be spent fast asleep.

BG, they'd go out for dinner a lot. Nowhere expensive, but good, local restaurants. They'd go to cafés in Highgate, or local Italian restaurants in Hampstead. Or Sam would cook. Chris would come home and the delicious smells of Sam's experimenting would hit him as he opened the front door.

There was nothing better than finding Sam in the kitchen. It made him feel loved, cherished, and truly that he'd come home, for his mother was also a cook, and her currency of love had always been food.

And he loved the fact that he considered them to be one of the happiest couples of anyone they knew. Not perfect, never perfect, but he still looked at Sam and saw the girl who'd bounded up to him at the party six years ago; the girl with the sparkling eyes and confident smile; the girl he knew, within one week, he was going to marry.

Sam was his best friend, and, even better than that, she was the best lay he'd ever had. And he was married to her! Christ. Surely life couldn't get better than that.

But that, he thinks ruefully as he puts the key in the door, was BG. Now he finds he's married to a shouting, tearful, angry witch. All his time at home is spent treading on eggshells; he's careful not to put a foot wrong, to send her off on a screaming fit, and he's more and more relieved to get out of the house for work.

The only bright spot in his home life is George. Georgenius, he thinks with a smile. That gorgeous chubby smiling bundle. Flesh of his flesh. The most perfect creation he's ever laid eyes on. Chris walks into the room and George's eyes light up.

There is no greater feeling in the world than when Chris sits on the sofa on a Sunday afternoon, George asleep on his chest, a warm soft bundle of pure love.

In their rare moments of intimacy, Chris and Sam sit in bed together and grin at one another. "Can you believe how gorgeous he is?" Sam squeals, clasping her hands together in a bid to contain the emotion. "I know. He's just amazing." Chris shakes his head, unable to believe they created such a perfect child. "Amazing," she echoes, and they look at one another, their eyes brimming over with love for George.

Sometimes they look at one another across the cot, standing on either side, gazing down at George, arms and legs sprawled to all four corners, fast asleep. "Do you think other people love their children as much as we love George?" Sam will whisper, sure that no one in the whole world could love their son as much as she loves hers. "I'm not sure," Chris will whisper back. "But I doubt it."

George is perfect. But his relationship with Sam has become anything but. Chris isn't sure what's going wrong, but he knows that something definitely is. He feels neglected. Abandoned. Unwanted. He knows he shouldn't be feeling these things, that George, after all, is a priority, but nevertheless he cannot stop them. There are occasions when all it will take is a kind word, a loving look, an affectionate kiss, but instead he is faced with anger. With exasperation. With indifference.

Chris is trying his best. He has offered to get up with George, and occasionally Sam has let him, but he doesn't seem to have the same knack, and Sam invariably appears in the doorway, looking pissed off, and takes George out of his arms. If it weren't for the fact that George immediately quieted down in his mother's arms, Chris would be furious.

Apart from quieting his son, there are other things Chris is, apparently, hopeless at. He can't make a bottle in the right way (too little powder or too much); heat the bottle to the right temperature (it's either boiling or too cold); change a diaper properly (doesn't do it up tightly enough); feed him in the right way ("For God's sake, Chris, you need to be quicker than that or he'll start screaming") or give him a bath ("And what planet are you living on?").

And so he doesn't offer anymore, which prompts Sam to shout that she's the only one doing anything in this bloody house. It's a no-win situation.

For once, the house smells delicious. It smells like the old days. He knows that smell, the smell of onions gently sautéing in butter. His heart lifts as he considers this unexpected surprise. Could tonight be the night when he gets the old Sam back? Will she have made a delicious dinner for him? Could they restore some of the magic they seem to have lost?

He walks into the kitchen to find Sam standing at the sink, washing up.

331

"Hi, darling." He kisses the back of her neck. "George in bed?"

"You know he goes to bed at quarter to seven. Where else do you think he'd be?"

Chris decides to ignore the curt tone. He's fed up with arguing. Tonight he just wants to enjoy the evening. "Is he asleep? Can I go in and say goodnight?"

"No. Sorry. Once he's in bed you know what he's like. If he sees you he'll start screaming again when you leave. You can get him up in the morning, though."

"Yeah. I will. Is your mother coming over tomorrow?"

"Yup," Sam says, nodding. "She said she'd take him out for the day."

"You mean, and leave us together? Just the two of us? Freedom?"

"I know." Sam grins, and for a minute they have a glimpse of the old Sam and Chris, of how well they can actually get on. "Isn't it fantastic? What are we going to do?"

"I know what I'd like to do." Chris grins, putting his arms around her waist and pulling her close, nuzzling into her neck.

"Oh, Chris." She pushes him away in exasperation.

"What do you mean, 'Oh, Chris'? It's been ages."

Sam wants to argue that they had sex last week, but she knows Chris will say that for them, that's ages, and she can't be bothered to have a fight. "Okay," she says, her heart not in it, although she figures she can always manufacture a headache or a period tomorrow morning. "Apart from that, what are we going to do?"

Chris lets her go and walks out to the hallway to hang up his coat. "What did we use to do on a Saturday BG?"

"Jesus. I can't remember! Did we actually have a life BG?"

"I'm not sure, but I know there are photos around here that prove we did."

"So what did we do? Seriously."

"Shopping?"

"Sometimes," she agrees, remembering their occasional sojourns to Portobello, meandering down the road looking at antiques they couldn't possibly afford, stopping for a cappuccino and a couple of pastries on Golborne Road on the way home. Although it really wasn't that often. Not more than four times a year, come to think of it.

"Walks on the Heath?" Chris offers.

"Nope. That's definitely post–George. We used to talk about going for walks on the Heath a lot, but I'm not sure we ever actually bothered."

"Well, Saturday mornings were never an option really. We always had a lie-in after a Friday night."

"True." And then Sam remembers. She remembers waking up late-morning and snuggling into Chris, covering his back with kisses to wake him. She remembers him rolling over and drawing her close with an arm heavy with sleep. They'd lie for a while like that, and then slowly Chris would open his eyes, pull her closer for a kiss.

They would have lovely, languorous sex. And afterward Chris would have a shower, she would jump in the bath, and they would drive up to All Bar One in Highgate for lunch. Puttering around the village, they'd usually find things to buy in the afternoon: books; furniture; food. Often Julia and Mark would be with them, and however badly Julia and Mark might have been getting on, the four of them always worked. They'd all known one another for so long they were like family. Anything could be said, no censoring was permitted.

With a pang Sam realizes how much she misses Julia. When Julia phoned to say she was staying in New York, all those months ago, Julia was so full of excitement and vigor, so like the Julia that Sam used to know, hadn't seen for so many years, Sam couldn't admit how upset she was, how hard her life would be without Julia.

But even she could never have envisaged quite how much her life would change with George.

"Tell you what." Chris comes back in the kitchen and reaches for the paper. "I'll give George breakfast, you can sleep in, and when your mother's collected George I'll come back to bed for some more sleep." He grins. "Or something, and then we'll play the rest of the day by ear."

"God," sighs Sam. "A lie-in. Are you sure?" I'm not getting up, she decides. I'm not going to come down to the kitchen to make sure Chris is doing it properly. To make sure George is getting enough to eat. Bugger that. I'm going to sleep, and if George decides to be fussy with his food tomorrow morning then that's Chris's problem. Not mine.

"You need to sleep, love." The prospect of sex tomorrow morning, plus a day spent on their own, has lifted Chris's spirits. He suddenly feels both loving and loved.

"What is that smell, anyway? What are you making for dinner?"

"Oh that? That's a fish pie."

"Mmmm. God, I haven't had that for years. It reminds me of my childhood. Have you got peas too?"

Sam makes a worried face. "Chris, it's not for you, it's for George. I mean, you can have it if you like, but it's pureed."

Chris's heart, on a cloud but a few seconds before, starts to sink. "Oh. So what are we having?"

"Umm." Sam thinks hard. "There's spinach and potato bake, or cauliflower cheese, or chicken casserole."

"And are they all pureed?"

Sam shrugs apologetically. "There's always a takeaway curry."

"Again?"

"I could eat curry every night of the week," Sam states defensively, which isn't quite true, but given that this will be the third night this week they've ordered it, it might as well be. "Did you get the ice-cube trays?" Sam unclips the Magimix and gets ready to scoop as Chris goes to the hallway and brings in a plastic bag.

"Will six be enough?"

"Should be. Thanks, darling." And she blows him a kiss as she starts to drop the fish-pie puree, teaspoonful by teaspoonful, into the trays.

Sam wakes to the sound of George screaming. Somewhere she had read that a baby who wakes up smiling is a secure baby, and although there is no reason whatsoever for George to be insecure, she cannot avoid this nagging doubt when he wakes up crying, which he so often does.

Just hungry, she tells herself, rolling over as she hears Chris sigh and climb out of bed.

"Turn the monitor off," she hisses as he's about to close the bedroom door, knowing that she'll never be able to get back to sleep if she hears George cry for much longer.

She reaches for the earplugs and jams them in, thankful for the instant peace, for although Chris has taken the monitor, the walls of this small terraced house are thin, and George's faint cries are still audible.

Lying in bed, she can already feel her body start to wake up. I will not, she wills herself. I will go back to sleep. Every bone in her body is exhausted, and she tries thinking about beaches, soothing turquoise water, hot white sand and gently rocking hammocks, but each time she does she finds herself, within a few seconds, thinking about George.

She lies there, gradually waking with each thought. I hope he's eating enough, she thinks. Did I tell Chris he can have one of the baby yogurts in the fridge? What if he's being picky and Chris thinks he's had enough, when I know he hasn't and you just have to persevere?

At twenty-eight minutes past seven she realizes there's absolutely no point in staying in bed. Now fully awake, there isn't a hope in hell of her going back to sleep. She climbs out of bed, puts on her dressing gown and curses the irony of the impossibility of getting up during the week, and the ease with which she manages it now.

Chris looks up, surprised. And guarded. He knows she's checking up on him. He and George have been having a great time. George stopped screaming the minute the bottle was plugged into his mouth, and apart from making a mountain of banana muesli (Chris poured in far too much milk, and had to keep adding more of the powder to thicken it, ending up with a bowl of banana muesli that would have happily served six starving babies), everything's been great.

George has just finished his banana muesli, and is starting on a baby yogurt Chris found in the fridge.

"I thought you were going back to sleep." Chris turns around, defensively, enjoying this time with George because he, after all, never gets to spend time with George on his own. He's been telling George all about his work, and about the things they're going to do together when George is a bit older. He's told George about the stresses and strains of running your own cabinet-making business, and he's warned George about following in his footsteps, even though he admitted he'd be very proud.

"George and I were having a man-to-man talk," he explains to Sam, who is relieved to see that both her boys are fine, but is, nevertheless, wide awake. She kisses George all over his face and squeezes his fat little feet. "I love those toes," she tells him, clenching her teeth together to stop herself from biting them, so delicious is her son. "I love those toes," she growls again as George smiles with delight.

Sam fills the kettle with fresh water, flicks it on, and puts a couple of slices of toast under the grill. "I couldn't bloody sleep, and the minute I decided I was going to stay awake I was starving. Do you want some toast?"

"No. I'm fine. What time is your mum coming?"

"She said nine." Sam butters the toast and sits down at the table. "Can you believe this bloody weather?" The rain drums hard against the window.

"November in London. What a pleasure." His tone may be derisive, but he is used to spending every November, every winter, in England. His business may be getting busier, but he cannot see it stretching to exotic holidays for a very long time to come.

"I've just been lying in bed thinking of beaches. That's what I could do with now. Some sun. A proper holiday. It's been years."

"We went to Torquay in the spring," Chris says defensively. "Hardly years ago."

"No," she concedes vaguely. "It just feels like years ago. Do you think we'll ever have a proper holiday again?"

"Not unless we can leave George with your mother or bring someone along to help."

"Well the first is definitely out of the question. You know my mother, she'd have heart failure if she thought she'd have to have George overnight, let alone for the duration of a whole holiday."

"Yeah, I know. I can't believe she's taking George for the day," Chris agrees. "Do you think she realizes that she'll actually have to feed him? You'd better demonstrate how a bottle is warmed up, just in case she breaks a nail in the process and sues you."

"Oh, come on." Sam gets defensive, for while it's perfectly reasonable for her to criticize her mother as being the mother from hell, it's not acceptable for Chris to do the same. Chris ought to just support Sam by agreeing with her when she's in mother-hating mode, and keeping quiet the rest of the time. "My mother's not that bad."

Chris decides to keep quiet.

"Anyway," Sam moves on, "when you said bring someone along to help, what did you mean?"

"I meant like a nanny or something. Au pair."

"But we talked about this before George was born. I don't want to have help. I want to do this by myself. I can understand women handing their children over to be brought up by someone else if they have to work, but as long as I'm at home I need to be there for him, and I don't want anyone else involved."

"I know, I know." Chris is tired of this argument, still unable to understand her resistance. "The first five years are the formative ones," he parrots. "And your mother wasn't around and you're not going to do the same to your child. It's just that I thought you might have changed your mind now you've had him."

"What? Suddenly decide I can't be bothered to bring up my own child and hire a nanny?"

"No, I didn't mean that. I thought maybe you'd consider having some help, maybe someone who can look after him a couple of days a week, just to give you a break. You could go out for lunch with friends. Have a massage. Go shopping. Whatever you want. Simply get away from it all for a while, recharge your batteries, make yourself feel like a human being again. You're the one always accusing me of being able to get away from it. You always say you're the one who feels trapped, but it doesn't have to be like that, Sam. You don't have to spend every minute of every day with George."

Chris takes a deep breath and continues. "And before you say anything, most of the women you know have their mothers around to help them. I'm not about to start criticizing your mother, but she's not exactly the most maternal of women, and although you've tried to hide it I know how devastated you are by her lack of interest. The fact is she's too caught up in her own life, and too selfish, to be of any real help with George. So you can't compare yourself to other women because you haven't got any help at all.

"All I'm saying is that you don't have to feel guilty about not doing everything yourself. George isn't going to suffer, and he isn't going to grow up like you and resent his mother for being completely disinterested in his life, because you're not."

He speaks slowly, impressing the point. "You are not your mother, Sam. You never have been. If you had been anything like her I would never have fallen in love with you in the first place." This manages to raise a small smile on Sam's face. "The point is, it's okay to admit you can't do it all yourself. It's okay to show some vulnerability and ask for help. And Sam, you need some time off. For you, for me and for us. For our marriage."

Chris tails off, shocked at the amount he's just said, more shocked at the calmness with which he managed to deliver it. Sam too is shocked, and if she's honest, the thought of handing George over for a couple of days a week sounds like bliss. In fact Sam has never been more tempted by anything in her life.

But she has made a commitment to George. And, more importantly, she has made a commitment to herself. She is going to be the best mother in the whole wide world. And the one thing she is absolutely sure of is that the best mother in the whole wide world would never farm her children out.

Not even for two days a week.

24

"*I bought the most divine* sleepsuit for my darling grandson." Patricia glides through the door, leaving a trail of Opium in her wake. "Where is my little angel?"

Sam smiles as she hands George over to her mother, who covers his face with tiny little kisses that make him laugh. This is a side of her mother she hasn't seen, and it fills her with warmth, and hope, when she sees it now. Perhaps they are wrong. Perhaps being a bad mother does not necessarily mean you will be a bad grandmother. Perhaps Patricia will come through after all.

"So what are you planning to do today?" Sam smiles, running her fingers through her hair as she turns, sensing her mother's disapproving looks, for her mother is of the old school: the school that believes you should always look your best, just in case.

"Actually, Sam, I don't think I can have him for the day." Sam's face falls, and Chris catches her eyes with an "I told you so" look.

"But you said you would take him out for the day."

"I know, darling, but I'm so incredibly busy, and things have changed now. Of course I'll take him for an hour or so this morning, but there's a bridge game this afternoon and someone dropped out, and I said I'd make up the four. Don't give me that look, Sam, I have a life too."

Sam grinds her teeth. "And your life is so much more important than your grandson, isn't it?"

"Don't start. I'm helping out as much as I can. Your father and I can't be expected to stop everything for you, no matter how much we love our grandson."

"Love him? You barely even know him." Sam realizes there's no point in saying these things, but she's had enough, and even if her venting doesn't achieve anything, vent she must.

"What are you talking about, Sam? I have to tell you I really don't need this. I had a million things to do this morning and I'm not doing any of them because I'm spending time with George, and all you can do is try to make me feel guilty. I'm sorry that I'm not the kind of person who wants to be with their grandchild twenty-four hours a day, and I'm sorry that I have a life too, but that's just the person I am and you'll have to accept it."

Chris leaves the room, shaking his head in disgust. He

learned long ago not to get involved, but the sheer selfishness of Sam's mother never fails to horrify him. His parents live in Newcastle, in the same house he grew up in, and they try to come down to London a couple of times a month to see him. He knows that were it not for the distance between London and Newcastle, his parents would come around every day. They would offer to baby-sit every night, anything to spend time with their beloved grandson. He always knew Patricia and Henry were selfish, but he never realized quite how selfish. And anyway, everyone they had spoken to BG said that it would be different when the baby was born.

"You should never underestimate how wonderful it is to be a grandparent," said one grandparent of six years' experience. "It's a different kind of love to when you have your own children. Quite, quite overwhelming. I think perhaps because it is love without responsibility, you are free to just give everything of yourself, to love with total abandon. Wait and see, Sam's parents will fall in love just like the rest of us once the baby's born."

How wrong she was.

Not that he is particularly surprised, but Sam has been devastated. Devastated because she too believed that Patricia would be different. She had put up with the self-centeredness all her life, had fought for her mother's unconditional love, and had only given it up as a hopeless cause when she met and married Chris. She was starting a family of her own, she decided, and this was the family that mattered.

Sam thought she had dealt with it by slowly removing herself from her mother's life. Where once she telephoned regularly, dropped in to see her parents, sought her mother's advice on daily dilemmas, she had managed to reduce this, before George was born, to perhaps once every couple of weeks.

But George has brought all her own parenting issues to the fore. She had dealt with the pain herself, but now she was dealing with the pain all over again, only this time it was worse because it was her own child. While Sam could live with her mother not wanting to be around her, she couldn't live with her mother not wanting to be around her child.

Chris treads carefully around the subject of her parents, with the eggshells on which he steps seeming ever more fragile. He tries not to say anything, to quietly support, for if he were to say what he truly felt, the floodgates would open and the full force of his own anger and disgust would surely alienate him and Sam still further.

The best thing he can do is leave the room.

"Fine," Sam says. "I haven't got the energy to argue with you anymore. I'm exhausted, I've been up all night for weeks and weeks, and I thought that today I'd be able to go back to bed and catch up on some sleep, but if you have bridge"—she spits the word out with disgust—"then I'll have to understand. What time will you bring him back?"

Patricia, oblivious of her daughter, looks at her watch. "Eleven? I could maybe manage eleven-thirty if that's better. I thought I could take him for a walk."

"Fine," Sam mutters. "I'm going upstairs to have a bath. See you later." And up she goes, trying to contain the tears that are already welling up, knowing that the one thing she will not do, will never ever do, is cry in front of her mother, show her mother how much she cares.

There is only one plus, as far as Sam is concerned. An hour, hour and a half maximum, when you have to have a bath, sterilize bottles, wash up Tommee Tippee bowls and try to look vaguely human, means there's definitely no time for sex. Not a hope in hell.

"You're not serious. You and Chris are having problems?" Julia can't keep the shock out of her voice.

"Oh God. I shouldn't have said anything," Sam moans into the phone.

"Sam, I'm your best friend, for God's sake. If you can't tell me, who can you tell?"

"I didn't mean that, I meant that saying it out loud makes it . . . I don't know. It makes it . . . real." She exhales deeply, partly frightened, partly relieved.

Last night they were watching television, for a change. They still haven't found a baby-sitter, and, given Patricia's reluctance to baby-sit or have anything much to do with George, they are lucky if they manage to go out once a month. If Chris's parents are down they'll baby-sit, otherwise each night follows the same routine: dinner at eight, TV until nine, Sam going to bed at ten past nine, swearing to Chris she won't go straight to sleep, that she'll wait for him to come up to bed, then promptly falling asleep as soon as her head hits the pillow.

But last night there was actually something watchable on the box. A two-part drama portraying the breakdown of a marriage. Sam found it both compelling and disturbing. She watched it with pounding heart, barely daring to breathe. Sitting on the sofa, curled up with the sort of body language that any old amateur could see meant Keep Away, she stole furtive glances at Chris every few minutes, wondering if he knew, if he could see how close to the mark this program was, but he didn't look at her.

Sam watched the actress on screen grow more and more unhappy. Her husband didn't understand her, they had drifted apart, had nothing in common, and the longer she watched the more she knew. This was her story. She hadn't slept much the night before. She climbed the stairs to bed feeling sick, knowing that her marriage was over.

"Are you okay?" Chris asked, standing in the doorway and looking at her with concern.

"Hmm? Yes. Fine." She avoided his gaze, and ducked under his arm to go to the bathroom. "Just tired."

She ran a bath and climbed gratefully into the hot bubbles, staring at the cracked tile above the hot tap, wondering why she felt so detached.

My marriage is over, she kept thinking. Why don't I care more? Sighing, she held her nose and sank her head under the warm water, welcoming the muffled silence, wishing it could go on forever.

She reemerged, ran some more hot water to drown the sound of the television Chris had switched on in the bedroom, and replayed some of their married life together. She remembered how it had been in the beginning, but surely even then there were warning signs, and with sudden and shocking clarity she knew that she had married the wrong man.

Not ambitious enough, her mother had said. A cabinet-maker? "Samantha, that's someone we pay for a sideboard, not marry," she had said in horror, when Sam announced she had met the man she knew she was going to marry.

Sam had been devastated, and desperate to prove her mother wrong, she now decided. Even though, she finally realized, lying in the bathtub, her mother had proved to be right.

The truth is, Chris should have been in the pages of the interior style magazines. He should have been charging thousands and thousands for his walnut dressers and cherry tables, selling them to the Chelsea set as fast as he could make them. Chris Martin should have been the first name on the lips of every interior designer worth his salt.

But where was Chris Martin? He was, she thought with sadness, exactly where he was six years ago when she met him. In the same Wandsworth workshop, with the same struggling furniture-makers, making the same cupboards and dressers and sideboards.

Sam had no doubt his work was beautiful. She had no doubt he was talented. But beauty and talent were nothing without ambition, and although Chris had upped his prices slightly every year, the fact was, his business only just managed to keep their heads above water.

This wasn't supposed to happen, she thought, submerging again to rinse the shampoo. She was supposed to have fallen in love with the man, not fallen in love with his potential.

But of course, lying in the bath, almost entirely submerged in misery and unhappiness and depression, Sam decided that this was exactly what she'd done. That when she got married at

Chelsea Register Office, she took him for better or worse, but was pretty damn certain it would get better: All he needed was a good woman behind him. All he needed was Sam.

Perhaps, she thought, her own career provided the mitigating circumstances for his. Sam was, after all, at the forefront of the graphic design world, her designs in almost every household in the country, her salary more than enough for the three of them.

It had never seemed that important when she was working. She had always assumed that at some point Chris would fulfill his potential, and even if it took longer than she had thought, it wouldn't really matter because they had everything they could possibly need. The only time it would be a problem would be if they had a family, but even then they would find a way to cope.

And she had thought they had.

Sam and Chris had sat down when she first discovered she was pregnant, and had looked at their finances. They had looked at how much money they could afford to put away each month, and had decided that although it would be difficult, if Sam decided not to go back to work full time (as she had already decided), they could just about manage, provided she found some freelance work.

Sam had spoken to some design consultancies, and had been assured of plenty of work when she decided to start again. They had in truth all been desperate for her to work for them, and all are waiting for Sam to contact them when she decides she is ready.

If she decides she is ready.

The truth is Sam has never felt less ready for anything in her life.

She had said this to Julia already this evening, before the conversation moved on to Chris; before Sam admitted her marriage was over. She had told Julia of her fears, of how ridiculous she felt, expecting Chris to provide when she had always been such a staunch feminist, but had shrugged and said she never expected motherhood to be so wonderful, had never expected not to want to go back to work.

Although perhaps Sam is scared of going back to work. Perhaps there is more to this than merely motherhood. If anyone can see this, Julia can, Julia who knows Sam better than anyone, Julia who is shocked to hear Sam's fears about her marriage.

"You don't think," Julia says tentatively, and somewhat wisely, given that she is not a mother herself (although she has read every book ever published on babies), "you might be suffering slight postpartum depression?"

"Don't be ridiculous. What on earth makes you say that?"

Julia thinks how different Sam is now, how the light seems to have gone out in her life. She thinks about the anxiety that seems to afflict Sam constantly about George: She reluctantly admitted to Julia that every time she walks down the stairs with George she imagines the horror of tripping and dropping him; that when she walks down the street she's convinced a car will hit them; that she no longer reads the newspapers, because every story about a baby being harmed feels like George is being harmed, and she found herself sobbing for hours about these children that were, and were not, George.

And Julia knows how isolated Sam is, how desperate she is for company, yet how difficult she finds it to leave her house. She knows all of this, yet she does not know how to say this without risking their friendship, because Sam is in no fit state to hear it.

"I just think you don't seem like yourself right now, you seem a bit down. I thought maybe you could go and see someone."

"Absolutely not," Sam snorts, exactly as Julia knew she would. "I've got a gorgeous baby and I'm absolutely fine. The only problem I've got is Chris, and although I'm not planning on walking just this instant, I can't see this marriage lasting out the year."

"Are you really that unhappy?" Julia's voice is filled with sadness.

"Julia, you have absolutely no idea. I never thought I could be this lonely or this miserable with another person. The only thing that keeps me going is that there's always divorce." She gives a resigned sigh. "That it is just a question of picking the right moment."

And then there is a silence. Julia does not know what else to say.

25

No one knows about failing to realize your potential better than Chris. Sam may think that he's quite happy puttering along, laboring over walnut-inlaid console tables that take weeks to make, and selling them for, effectively, peanuts, but Chris knows exactly what he's doing.

Chris knows about the big time. He knows about pricing yourself into a higher market, about lucrative deals with some of the larger stores, about taking on a team and producing greater numbers in less time.

Over the years he's watched most of his contemporaries do exactly that. One of them quit cabinetmaking to manufacture solid beech tables—sleek, modern, functional with just the tiniest hint of farmhouse nostalgia—that are as ugly as sin as far as Chris is concerned, but are currently to be found in every branch of Habitat up and down the country. If Chris weren't such a furniture snob, Sam would have snapped up one of those tables in the January sale last year.

Chris always knew he had the talent. He pays more attention to detail than almost all of his contemporaries, his furniture is more beautiful than all of theirs put together, yet he is still the least successful. And, up until very recently, that was the way he liked it.

Because Chris knows the price to pay for success. He knows that arriving at the workshop at nine in the morning and leaving at six-thirty at the very latest are not exactly practical when you're aiming to hit the big time. He knows that you can forget all about Saturday mornings in bed with your beautiful wife when you're aiming to hit the big time.

When you're aiming to hit the big time, the big time must be the only thing that matters. The big time becomes your wife, your mother, and your child, with very little room for anything else.

He's seen it happen to countless people. They start off like him, loving every minute of their hard work, grieving when a piece of furniture is sold, taking a day or so to get over the feeling of losing a limb. But when fame and fortune beckon, there is no room for passion. There is no time for lovingly stroking smooth burnished mahogany legs. There is no place for the true craft of making furniture you love.

And there is no room for family.

Chris loves his family. He loves his mother, his father, his two brothers (he's the middle child without the desperate need to be noticed, to be loved, that so often afflicts middle children), and most of all he loves Sam and George.

But even before George came along Chris made a decision to put Sam first. He made a decision to have breakfast with her every day, and to be home by seven every night.

He made a decision to keep his workload down so he could still take pleasure in following his passion, and not spend all his spare time worrying about how he was going to fulfill orders.

Chris sighs as he picks up some cotton wadding, carefully dropping just two small drops of linseed oil on the outside, before moving it smoothly, sensually, in a figure of eight on the lid of a large cherry chest. Up and down. Around and around, French polishing until the rich, glowing beauty of the wood emerges. He loves this work.

But he loves spending time with his family more.

Although now he's not so sure. Gradually he's been accepting more orders, pushing himself to the very limits of his capabilities. Gradually he's found he's had to work longer and longer hours in order to meet the demand for his furniture. Gradually he's coming round to the idea of a spread in *World of Interiors*. Hell. Other people would kill for an opportunity like that.

And gradually he's starting to realize that there's no place like home. Not when home has become an arena for fighting. For shouting. For raised voices. When he feels as if, as he has already told Sam, he is constantly walking on eggshells in his own house. When he seems to be able to say or do nothing right, and when everything he does say or do elicits a frosty stare from his wife or an exasperated sigh.

He tries to be a good husband, a good father, but increasingly of late he is beginning to see that he is neither of those things. He cannot be a good husband or Sam would not treat him with such contempt, and surely he cannot be a good father or she would not step in and remove George at every opportunity.

He had thought, for a while, that this was normal. That this happened to all new parents once they had brought the baby home. He had excused it on the grounds of hormones. Ironic only because everyone had said how lucky he was that Sam had had such a lovely pregnancy, had been so happy, and blooming, and in love with life.

He had thought perhaps that he was paying for that now, but still he had known it would pass.

"For God's sake, Chris. The diaper's much too loose," Sam would say witheringly as she elbowed him out of the way and stepped up to the changing table to redo, amid much sighing, his handiwork.

"For God's sake, Chris, the water's much too hot." Sam would elbow him out of the way in the kitchen, plunging the bottle into the freezer amid much sighing.

He had mutely moved out of the way, leaving the room after assuming he was more of a hindrance than a help, and then, a few minutes later, while reading the papers in the living room, would be subjected to Sam shouting that he never did anything to help.

And it was getting worse.

Not the shouting. That, if anything, had subsided somewhat, but the atmosphere in the house was thick with acrimony and resentment. The more time Chris spent at home these days, the worse he felt.

Most of the time he lived his life under a cloud of sadness. He looked at Sam and couldn't understand what had happened to her. To them. He looked at George, at this wonderful, miraculous creature, and knew that their shared delight in his presence, in every move he made, should have been drawing them closer together, not pushing them further apart.

The only place he can still breathe freely, still relax, is in his workshop, and as for the bonuses of his newfound workaholism—the magazine interest, the increased orders, the nonstop phone calls—quite frankly that's something he could well do without.

"Hello, love." Chris manages to fill his voice with warmth as Jill Marsh, an old and favorite client, smiles encouragingly across the desk at him. "We've all been invited to Jill and Dan's for tea next Sunday. Lily's only a few months older than George, and Jill thought the babies could play and we could see the dining table in its proper home."

Sam has never met Jill Marsh, has only heard about her from Chris. She knows they are roughly the same age, but that Jill lives very happily off her husband's income (something big in journalism). She knows that Jill dabbles in interior design when she feels guilty about not working, and lives in Highgate in a Gothic house that has been regularly featured in *Homes and Gardens.*

She also knows that Chris and Jill have always been

friends. Jill likes to tell people that she discovered Chris, a statement ruined only by the fact that Chris is nowhere near where he could be had he not sacrificed his career for his family. But Jill has been more influential than most of his other clients put together, and he has Jill to thank for many of the more recent commissions.

Jill has always wanted to meet Sam. Sam has always wanted to meet Jill, but somehow something always got in the way, and when their pregnancies overlapped, Chris had passed messages between the two of them, offering advice and anecdotes.

Once they had even spoken on the phone, and Sam had known that she would like Jill, that they had the potential to be friends. It was just before Sam was due, and Jill had laughed and said there was no point putting anything in the diary for months, but that Sam should call when they were up to socializing and they would get together.

Seven and a half months on and Sam still isn't ready for socializing, but Chris is. Anything to inject some normality back into their relationship, to recapture something of their life of old.

Chris is only just starting to realize the effects of their baby-imposed isolation. He is only just starting to realize how destructive it is to spend every single night of the week watching television, then going to bed. How soul-destroying to spend every evening with a partner who doesn't appear to like you very much.

Chris misses having a social life. He misses being able to pop out to the cinema at a moment's notice. And while he wouldn't change George for the world, he knows that something has to change, and the only thing he can think of right now is to try to force Sam out into the real world.

The more she isolates herself, the more withdrawn and sullen she becomes, and the only moments of brightness are when she is reminded of her old life: when Julia phones and he hears Sam's laughter pierce the air and roll down the stairs, unnaturally sharp and bright now that he so rarely hears it. When she forgets to hate him, and decides, for those brief pockets of time, that Chris is still the man she married, the man she loves.

And today Jill walked into his office, Jill who doesn't seem to have changed at all, who is the mother of fourteen-month-old Lily, who is as warm, and funny, and as charming as she has always been.

She is a breath of fresh air.

"Okay." Sam accepts the invitation when she is unable to think of a suitable excuse. She is reluctant not because she no longer wishes to meet Jill, but because she feels so inadequate. Seven and a half months on, pregnancy is beginning to sound like rather a lame excuse for the excess twenty pounds. Half her hair has disappeared down the drain, much to her shock and disgust, but she has refused to get it cut, hanging on to her long curls as a memento of the girl she was before George, the girl she plans to be again.

She puts the phone down wondering whether it is possible to lose ten to fifteen pounds in just over a week, and whether she is likely to squeeze into a size 12 at Warehouse (very generously cut, don't you know), or whether she could breathe new life into her maternity leggings that are starting to wear dangerously thin on the inner thighs.

Chris puts the phone down and tells Jill the good news. She claps her hands together, excited.

"I'm dying to meet Sam. I can't believe we've been hearing about one another for all these years, and now you're all finally coming over. And I'm going to meet that delicious little George. Tell me, do you love him more than anything?"

Chris's eyes light up for the first time that day as he thinks about George, and it is only then that Jill really notices the difference, notices how flat he is the rest of the time.

"Are you okay, Chris?"

"Sure." They have a professional relationship, potentially the beginnings of a real friendship, but there's no way he knows Jill well enough to confide in her. Until now perhaps. "Tell me something," he says, unable to stop himself, looking at her with interest, because Jill's daughter is only six months older than George, and yet she looks fantastic, looks exactly as she always has done, only better. Softer. "How do you manage to look so fantastic when you have a baby, how do you manage to cope so well, to still be exactly the same person you were before?"

"Why?" Jill asks gently. Flattered, but concerned. Chris just shrugs and smiles. "The first few months were impossible," she says slowly, trying to judge from Chris's expression what tone of voice to use, what to say to make him feel better. His interest is piqued, and she continues in what she hopes is the right vein, because it is not something she admits to everyone. "I was exhausted. Depressed. Lonely. Resentful."

"How did you pull yourself out of it?" Chris interrupts, wanting to hear all the answers now, wanting an instant panacea to his own unhappiness, his own depression, loneliness, and resentment.

Jill shrugs. "I couldn't even pinpoint when it actually happened. I think slowly, after about eight or nine months, things just started to get better. I found that I wasn't so tired, I wasn't so angry, and because I felt more human I started to go out and make the effort again. It helped that Lily started sleeping around then, but also I reached a point where I couldn't do it all by myself. I got part-time help, and for two and a half days a week I was given my life back. I adore Lily. She is the most wonderful thing in my life, but I needed something for me."

"That's what I've been trying to tell Sam," Chris says sadly.

"She's going through the same thing?"

"Exactly the same thing. She's not the same person I married but she's got this thing about being the perfect mother, and won't have help. Not that we can afford it anyway," he snorts.

"Well, all that could change if that magazine feature comes off."

"I know, but it's more than that. She's just changed so much. She never smiles anymore, never seems happy. Were you like that? Does that change?"

"I wouldn't say I was unhappy, but adjusting to being a mother definitely took months. I wish I could tell you that one day something happened that proved to be the turning point, but actually there was nothing as definitive or dramatic as that. I just woke up one morning and felt light. I felt as if I'd been in a bit of a fog, and suddenly it was gone, and I had energy again, and joy, and every day since then has been getting better and better."

Chris sighs. "I wish that would happen to Sam."

"Does she have friends in a similar situation?" Jill asks gently.

"No. That's part of the problem. She's at home all day with George, and when she's not at home she's on the Heath, but wherever she is she's pretty much by herself. She's got this problem with mother and baby groups—"

"I have to say I understand that!" laughs Jill.

"But meanwhile she doesn't see anyone. Both her best friends now live in New York, and I know she is so lonely, so desperate for friends with babies of a similar age, but won't do anything to find them."

"Maybe she can't." Jill shrugs. "Maybe she's slightly depressed and she needs to come out the other side. It will pass, though. I promise you it will pass."

"Will it?"

"Yes. And even if it doesn't, you're all coming to us next Sunday, and I know that Sam and I will get on, and we'll be friends."

"Can I just ask one more thing?" Chris says, giving her a grateful smile. "Did it affect Dan? That fog you mentioned. Did it ever seriously affect your marriage?"

Jill pauses, unsure at this point what Chris wants to hear, but she has to tell the truth, and he'll be relieved, surely, to hear it. "No. I would say it was a definite rocky patch, but at no point did I ever think about walking out." She smiles reassuringly, expecting Chris to be relieved. Surely she had said exactly what he needed to hear.

"And what about Dan?" Chris says, anxiety still etched upon his face. "Did he?"

"Are you sure I look okay?" Sam whispers again to Chris as they stand on the doorstep of Jill and Dan's house. She pulls her black tunic cardigan (Marks & Sparks—thank God for those tunics that hide a multitude of sins) down over her bottom and tries to pull it together at the front to no avail, so she wraps her blanket coat tightly around to disguise her weight.

Chris hoists George onto his hip as the front door opens, and a little girl stands there looking expectantly up at them. Behind her Dan smiles as he moves her gently out of the way and beckons them in.

"Chris, lovely to see you!" They have met a few times before. "This is Lily. You must be Sam. And the handsome George. Come in, come in. Welcome." Sam extends a hand, but Dan leans down and kisses her on the cheek, putting an arm around her shoulders to guide her down the hallway.

And Sam feels something unexpected as he rests his hand on her shoulder. Something she hasn't felt for a very long time. A flush on her cheeks and a stirring in her loins that is immediately exciting. Ridiculous, she tells herself. A man who is reasonably attractive is attentive and kind, and resting his arm on my shoulder in what can only be a warm, hostlike manner, and I'm on my way to my first orgasm of the year.

"Sam!" Jill appears from the kitchen and embraces Sam warmly. Sam returns the embrace with gusto, for while she wants to hate Jill, wants to hate her for being slim, and happy, and glamorous, for having a beautiful home and a sexy husband, she finds she can't.

"It is so, so lovely to meet you. Did you find it okay? Come in and sit down while I put the kettle on. Did you notice your husband's handiwork in the hallway?" Jill bubbles away as Sam tries to keep up.

"And in here. Look. Isn't he clever? Aren't you lucky?

Now I have to tell you, for someone with a seven and a half?" Sam nods. "Seven-and-a-half-month-old baby, you're looking gorgeous. How on earth do you do it?"

From anyone else, Sam might have questioned this statement. Would almost certainly have assumed it was sarcastic, but Jill has been there, and Jill knows what she needs to hear when she is still feeling fat and exhausted, and there is nothing but sincerity in her voice, and even as she speaks she sees Sam slowly unfurl.

"You are joking!" Sam laughs, but her smile is genuine. "I'm huge. Look! Enormous!"

"You're not," Jill says. "You're gorgeous."

"What about you? Lily's fourteen months and you look like you've just stepped off a catwalk."

"*I knew* I'd like you, Sam!" Jill gives Sam's arm a squeeze and goes off to the kitchen to get tea ready.

"What shall I do with George?" Chris puts George on the floor, where he sits rather like a small chubby beanbag, slumped forward examining the pattern on the Persian rug. He falls on to one side and rolls over, moving his face closer to the pattern before slowly lowering his open mouth to try to eat a particularly appetizing red swirl.

"Oh George," Sam says, scooping him up and covering him with kisses, "you cheeky little monkey," and Chris smiles as he watches them. He can see that Jill has instantly put Sam at ease, and seeing her like this reminds him of the good times.

"Chris!" Jill calls from the kitchen. "Come and see the table. It's in here."

Sam perches on the edge of the sofa as Dan walks back into the room. She pulls in her stomach, then lets it out, thinking how ridiculous she is being. She is a married woman, not to mention a mother, not to mention overweight.

She pulls her stomach in again.

Dan collapses next to her on the sofa, putting his feet on the coffee table, and she is instantly very aware of his proximity. His right leg is casually brushing her ample thigh, but he hasn't seemed to notice.

It is all she can think of.

"Lily is the light of my life," he sighs, stretching lazily and resting one arm along the back of the sofa, "but what I wouldn't give to have a holiday right now."

"God, tell me about it," Sam says, in a voice that sounds, even to her, self-conscious. Go away, she is thinking. I cannot cope with such a dangerously attractive man so close to me who is making me think unsafe thoughts. Don't go, she is thinking. Stay to remind me of this feeling, to remind me that it is still possible, that I am not too old and boring to feel passion.

"Okay." Dan smiles, taking her words literally as she turns to look at him. "Right now I would like to be lying on a hammock strung between a couple of palm trees on a deserted island in the Caribbean."

"Glass of rum punch brought out to you by a besuited waiter?" Sam smiles, enjoying skipping small talk, enjoying the false intimacy this line of conversation is creating.

"Good idea!" he laughs. "What about you?"

"White sand. Turquoise water. Hot, hot, hot. I would be in a bikini, having lost all my pregnancy weight finally"—she didn't mean to say that, but she needed him to know she didn't always look like this—"and I would be lying in the surf to cool down."

"If that's pregnancy weight you should keep it," Dan says, and even though she knows he's just being nice, a part of her hopes it's more, hopes he might be flirting with her. "It suits you."

She flushes.

"And what are you two up to?" Jill walks into the living room, carrying a tray of tea, biscuits, and cakes, none of which, Sam suddenly decides, she will be eating.

"Nothing much." Dan stretches again as Sam tries to will the heat out of her cheeks. "Just sharing fantasies. You wouldn't be interested."

Chris raises an eyebrow. He doesn't say anything at all.

26

Chris is delighted. The morose Sam of these past few months has been transformed in the last few days. It started when they went to Jill and Dan's for tea, where Sam seemed to bask in Jill's warmth, as Chris knew she would.

The four of them had hit it off, had said they would get together again very soon, and Dan had then suggested supper and a movie one night. He said he had some tickets to a sneak preview of *Castaway* with Tom Hanks. Chris had looked at Sam, expecting her to do as she always did, and decline on the basis that she wouldn't trust a baby-sitter to look after George, but to his surprise she nodded enthusiastically.

During the journey home it was as if someone had brought Sam back to life. She was bubbly, talkative, and actually laughed. Spontaneously. Three times! Chris felt all his anger melt away as he looked at her with affection, and after they'd got home, bathed George, and put him to bed, Sam, for the first time since George, initiated sex.

And not only that, she was an animal. She couldn't get enough. Chris had always taken the lead, but suddenly Sam was growling with lust and contorting her body into positions he'd never even heard of.

It was fucking amazing.

Little did Chris know that while Sam was kissing his lips, she was thinking of Dan. While moaning with pleasure as she licked his left nipple, she was imagining Dan. While trailing a tongue down his stomach, she was dreaming of Dan.

She closed her eyes and let lust wash over her body, vaguely conscious of not calling out Dan's name, but picturing him with every moan, every shiver of lust, experiencing a passion she didn't think existed for her anymore. Afterward, when Chris had gone to sleep and Sam was lying in bed, eyes wide open, staring at the ceiling, she indulged in an elaborate fantasy about Dan falling head over heels in love with her, leaving Jill, and Lily. She, Dan, and George would live happily ever after. Who knows, maybe even Jill and Chris would get together. . . . Stranger things had happened.

She ran over every possibility, thought through every outcome, while Chris tossed and turned next to her, and when she eventually went to sleep at two o'clock in the morning she had a smile on her face.

The next few days are filled with thoughts of Dan. In an odd sort of way her newfound crush has enabled her to be nicer to Chris. She accepts now that she married the wrong man. It's not his fault, it just isn't meant to be, and with that knowledge she is able to treat him with kindness, with courtesy, because he, after all, doesn't know that she is just biding her time.

Surely Dan feels the same way. She spends hours thinking about that afternoon, going over every glance, every laugh, every movement. Remember how he kissed her hello? Surely that's far too intimate a gesture, one he reserves for women he finds overwhelmingly gorgeous. Surely it was just her.

Remember how he came to sit next to her, brushing his thigh against hers? A sign if ever there was one. Remember how he told her the weight suited her? Weight! Suited her! He liked her like this! Definitely flirting. She hugs herself and smiles, a warm glow enveloping her body. He was definitely flirting and he definitely feels the same way.

A part of her half expects him to phone, is disappointed when the phone rings and it's someone else. Each time the bell breaks into the silence she jumps. Each time she picks it up she hesitates before pouting into the receiver, ensuring her voice sounds sensual and provocative.

"Hello," she purrs as the phone rings this morning, praying it's Dan, praying he's been thinking about her as much as she's been thinking about him.

"Hello. It's me. What's the matter?" It's Chris.

"Nothing's the matter. Why?"

"You sound peculiar. You didn't sound like you."

"And who else could I possibly sound like?"

"To be honest you sounded a bit like the rabbit in the Caramac ad."

A smile spreads itself upon her face. That is exactly the effect she had intended. "Did I?" Her voice is innocence itself. "How flattering. I must try and make my voice sound like that more often."

"Hmmm. Sounds very interesting." Chris smiles, thinking of his gorgeous sexy wife in bed the other night. "Could produce unexpectedly nice results."

"Is everything okay?" Her voice is back to normal. Sam has no wish to encourage Chris's lustful thoughts mid morning.

"Yup. I've just spoken to Jill. The *Castaway* tickets are for six-fifteen on Sunday night, which means we can go for supper afterward. Jill suggested Montana."

"Great!" The enthusiasm is back in Sam's voice as she starts to plan, already, what to wear. "Sounds lovely."

"And you definitely think your mum's not going to pull one of her numbers and claim to be busy on the night?"

"No. I made her swear. She's definitely going to baby-sit, but we have to be back by eleven."

"Eleven?" Chris lets out a long whistle. "Christ. That's a bit late, isn't it?"

Sam allows herself a smile. "Eight o'clock seems to be bloody late in our household at the moment."

"I'm glad you said that and not me."

"Why? You're usually the one who says it. What's the difference?"

"The difference is that when I say it you start having a go at me about how I don't understand how tired you are."

"Well, you don't," Sam bristles, but Chris refuses to be drawn.

"Sam, we don't have to have an argument now."

She huffs and puffs to herself for a bit, but hard as it is to back down from a really good fight, she concedes on this one. After all, she has more important things to think about.

Like what do you wear when you're going to be seeing the man who could turn out to be the love of your life?

Black trousers. (Still left over from maternity but they'll do.)

Burgundy crushed-velvet tunic top, but surprisingly flattering and low-cut to show off a sumptuous cleavage. (New purchase.)

Black high-heeled boots to add a few much needed inches. (New purchase.)

The other things you do before seeing the man who could turn out to be the love of your life?

You make an appointment at the hairdresser's, and finally say a tearful good-bye to your long blond curls that worked so well when you were in your twenties and your hair was thick and lustrous, but has become stringy and greasy now that you have had a baby, and is beginning to have a distinct whiff of mutton dressed as lamb.

You wheel your baby son off to the gym and park him in the creche while you pay a disgusting amount of money for a year's membership (you could pay monthly by direct debit and stop the direct debits when you—inevitably—stop going after six weeks, but you figure that if you pay it all in one go you'll feel so guilty you'll go every day for the rest of your life).

You make an appointment at the beauty salon in the gym. You decide to have your legs waxed, your mustache electrolyzed, and a full Clarins makeover while you're at it. A flash of guilt hits you when the beautician smiles and says your husband is in for a treat, and for a moment you're tempted to tell her everything—isn't it so much easier to confide in a stranger, and isn't there something so comforting about a woman in a white coat—but you manage to keep quiet about the love of your life.

You drive down to Sainsbury's in Camden Town and stock up with Weight Watchers for Heinz ready-made meals, Go Ahead chocolate caramel bars, 98 percent fat-free caramel rice cakes, and Too Good to Be True slices of cheese. By the time you hit checkout you realize that Go Ahead did not mean eating three individually wrapped cake bars while pushing your trolley around the aisles, so reluctantly you put back the cheese and the rice cakes, and go back to the fruit section, where you virtuously replace the goodies with grapefruit and apples.

You walk along Hampstead High Street in a state, cursing designers who are cutting so much smaller these days. (There's no way you're bigger than a size 12. No way. Those bloody designers are just trying to encourage skinny people to shop there.) Eventually you console yourself with the perfect pair of high-heeled boots (Nine West), made even better by the gorgeous top in Monsoon that has your name written all over it, and turns out to be a perfect fit.

You ring your best friend, who has turned into a party animal and is currently painting New York red, and leave desperate messages on her machine, begging her to call you because you have to tell someone or you might just possibly burst.

When your best friend doesn't call, you drag your old telephone book from out of the drawer and flick through looking for someone, anyone, to call to share your good fortune. But then you realize how inappropriate it would be to phone someone you haven't spoken to for months to blurt out the tale of your desperately unhappy marriage, and the reason for your newfound happiness.

So you pile your child into his buggy (yet again), and push the buggy up Mansfield Road toward the Green, and you park it just inside the doorway of a café (you would sit outside but a gloomy, wet early December is not the most conducive for an outdoor cappuccino, no matter how hot the cup), and you sit your son in a high chair and give him a bottle of juice and a reduced-sugar rusk to keep him quiet, and you daydream.

"Excuse me? Is anyone sitting here?" Sam's reverie is interrupted by a tall woman with a BabyBjorn strapped to her stomach, a tiny newborn baby barely visible but quiet, presumably fast asleep.

Sam gives her a smile and nods, although she isn't entirely sure she wants her space invaded. Not today. Yet isn't this what she's been hoping for these past few months? Hasn't she been longing for a local friend with a baby? Someone who looks very much like this woman? Why did it have to happen today when she is busy thinking about other things, happy to sit here alone, lost in her thoughts of Dan?

"I am deeply envious." The woman sits with a smile as she deftly unclips the BabyBjorn and shrugs a pale lemon snowsuit off a still-sleeping infant. She gestures at George, who's happily gumming down on the rusk, babbling away to himself, looking around the room at all the faces. "We're still at the screaming-all-night phase and I'm longing to get her out of this bloody BabyBjorn and into a high chair."

Sam smiles, warming to the woman, clearly remembering those days with George. "It's not all fun and games. He's about to start crawling and I won't be able to leave him for a second."

The waitress comes over. "I'll have a cappuccino," the woman says. The waitress looks at Sam questioningly, and Sam orders another one, settling in for a while, curious to find out a bit more about this woman.

"You look sort of familiar," Sam says. "Are you local?"

"Yup. Estelle Road. You?"

"Oak Village."

"God, that's so lovely. I'm completely in love with those chocolate-box houses. Are they as gorgeous on the inside as they look?"

"Gorgeous," Sam laughs. "But size isn't one of their bonuses."

"Ah yes. I can see that. Our house is one of those boring old Victorian terraces, but it's huge on the inside. God, doesn't that sound awful? Actually it was my boyfriend's house before, so I'm allowed to still be slightly awed by the size of it. I probably look familiar to you just by being local. Christ, the only thing that keeps me sane right now is getting out of the house and going for a four-hour walk. Anything to shut this little angel up for a while."

Sam laughs at her honesty. "I don't know. I've got a feeling

I've seen you somewhere else, but maybe it is just local. So how old is your little angel . . . a little girl, I take it?"

"Yup. This is Poppy. She's seven weeks. Yours?"

"George. Nearly eight months."

"University College Hospital?"

"Of course. Yours?"

"Yup. We were going to go up the road but then heard they'd had a few staffing problems."

"I heard the same thing," Sam murmurs in agreement. "Someone I know had a cesarean and no one even came to look at her for about twenty-four hours. Her boyfriend ended up changing her sheets and bringing her food from home. Can you imagine?"

"I heard that as well!" The woman starts to laugh. "A friend of a friend. I think her name was Eleanor."

"Nope," Sam says, grinning. "This one was called Janine." The woman laughs. "Do you think it's become one of those apocryphal stories?"

"I don't know, but don't urban myths usually involve something horribly embarrassing like passing out after you've weed in your boyfriend's parents' bathroom sink?"

"Oh God! I remember that one! My favorite was always the girl who pooed onto the conservatory roof when her boyfriend's parents were eating lunch."

They both laugh. "It really happened!" Sam insists with mock-seriousness.

"Oh really? Was it . . . you?" and they both laugh again.

"Isn't it weird how they always seem to involve a boyfriend's parents?" the woman said. "Who the hell thinks of these things anyway?"

"Who the hell knows?"

"Who the hell cares?" and they both smile at one another, somehow each knowing that this is more than just coincidence, that they were somehow fated to meet this afternoon, and that this will be the start of an important friendship.

They may not know very much about one another—they don't even know one another's names—but already Sam can see she might have found her NBF—New Best Friend—and she may not be quite the same as Julia (who Sam still misses on a daily basis), but she's a pretty close match.

"I'm Sam," Sam says, knowing that she no longer has desperation etched on her forehead, knowing that this woman won't be scared off by premature offerings of friendship.

"It's nice to meet you, Sam." The woman extends her hand and Sam shakes it firmly. "I'm Maeve."

"*I could* not believe it," she squeals to Chris when he comes home. "I mean, what was I supposed to have said?" Just because Chris was not her soulmate, and she'd buggered up her marriage slightly by marrying the wrong man, did not mean that they couldn't be friends, and Sam was itching to gossip with someone.

The only people other than Chris in whom she could confide were Julia and Bella, and Julia, obviously, wasn't exactly an option at this point. She would have been a wonderful option had Sam hated Maeve, and had she been able to phone Julia and tell her she'd met the ghastly Maeve and listen to what a bitch she is, and my God she's so ugly, she's positively evil, but of course she couldn't say any of that.

She could have told Bella, but Bella and Julia are now practically joined at the hip, and the problem with threesomes is that, no matter how good everyone's intentions, one invariably ends up being left out, and unfortunately, thanks to geography, that someone appears to be Sam. She's not about to go confiding in Bella when there's a very strong chance Bella will blurt everything out to Julia. Secrets, have, in any case, never been Bella's strong point.

"Did you tell her you knew who she was?"

"Oh God," Sam groaned. "It was just awful. I wanted to tell her because she was so nice, but I just sort of went a bit white and speechless, and when she wanted to know what was the matter I told her I just had a hot flush."

"What did she say?"

"She asked if I was pregnant again."

"And what did you say?"

"I said unlikely unless it was the Immaculate Conception."

Chris takes Sam's hand and looks into her eyes with his most seductive smile. "There was the other night, so that's not strictly true. And we can always have a repeat performance now if you'd like."

"Don't be silly." She shakes his hand off as if he were a naughty child. "The point is that I feel terrible. What am I going to say to Julia?"

"Why do you have to say anything to Julia?" Chris's voice is harder now, he was hurt by her rebuff, her constant rejection of him.

"Julia's my best friend."

"But this is just some woman you met at a coffee shop," he says irritably. "I don't understand why you're in such a state about it. What is the big deal?"

Sam sighs. "The big deal, Chris, is that I liked her. I thought we could be friends."

"You still can be."

"But what do I tell Julia?"

"Why tell Julia anything?"

"Because she's my best friend."

Chris can no longer hide the exasperation in his voice. "What are you so scared of? For God's sake, Sam! You've been banging on for months about how lonely you are and how boring it is looking after a baby all day and how much you miss Julia because now you haven't got a best friend and you never realized before how much you need a best friend, and now you finally meet someone who could potentially be a new friend, and you're not going to pursue it because you're frightened of what your old best friend might say? How old are you? Six?"

"And maybe, just maybe," he continues, fed up with containing his frustration, "you're happy being on your own. Maybe you've been bored and lonely because it's easier to feel sorry for yourself when your life is dull, and it's easy to make other people feel sorry for you. Far easier than making the effort to get up, go out and meet people."

"You bastard," she hisses. "You have absolutely no idea what my life is like. You have no idea because you get to leave every day. You're not the one who's expected to do all the housework, and look after George, and cook, and have a life at the same time. How dare you accuse me of being a . . . a victim"—she spits the word out—"when you haven't stood in my shoes. How dare you." She's so angry she's almost in tears. Angry and humiliated. Because of course she knows he's right.

"Victim," Chris ponders, just before he walks out to go and read the papers in the other room, to try to calm down, to pretend that his marriage is so much better than it is. "Interesting choice of word. And more interesting that you said it yourself. It certainly gives you something to think about." He walks out the door just as an Emma Bridgewater mug comes flying toward his head, crashing into the doorframe with a huge bang and an explosion of blue and white china.

"Mmm, clever," he says calmly, no expression in his eyes as he looks directly at Sam, who's now standing in the kitchen weeping, unable to believe what she has just done. "And that's going to make both of us feel so much better." With sarcasm dripping from his voice, he closes the door.

Sam doesn't say anything to Chris that night. She goes upstairs, runs a bath, and thinks about how lucky she is to have found Dan, how unbearable this would be had she not met her destiny.

When she was eleven years old, lonely, misunderstood, preparing to enter the dark years from twelve to eighteen, she invented an imaginary friend. She knew it was ridiculous for someone her age. This was, after all, the stuff of five-year-olds, but somehow it soothed her to think that there was someone out there who really loved her, who would reassure her even as her parents shouted at her and told her she was not enough.

Her imaginary friend—Jed was his name—was the love she had always waited for. He was a cross between Sting and

Adam Ant. He wore drainpipe jeans and DMs, had short spiky hair, and hated her parents almost as much as she did.

She felt completely safe and utterly protected when Jed was around. She wove elaborate fantasies, so vivid that sometimes she thought they were real, involving Jed's love for her, and her love for Jed.

Lying in the bath, locked in an unhappy marriage, only able to cope by switching off, it never occurs to her that twenty-two years later she's doing exactly the same thing.

Although, she would snort indignantly, how could it possibly be the same when Dan is real? Dan's not an imaginary friend. He's the man she was supposed to have met six years ago, the man she was supposed to have married. Look at the way he made her feel just by touching her thigh with his. Look at the way he's occupying her every waking thought.

This has to be the real thing.

27

As the week progresses ever closer to Sunday night, the more Sam dwells on the notion that she and Chris would have been far better off as friends.

That was always the problem with their relationship, Sam now realizes. Despite having had amazing sex in the past (although it's becoming increasingly hard to remember that now), the reason why she knew so quickly Chris was the man she was going to marry—or at least the reason why she thought she knew—was because she felt so comfortable with him.

She had felt, from the first, that she could say anything to Chris. She could tell him her deepest darkest secrets and he would understand. She remembers back to the first night they met, going to the hotel and talking for hours, and she remembers how much they had both talked, how there was suddenly so much to say neither could get the words out quickly enough.

The truth is, she sees now, by the end of that first evening, Chris had felt like someone she had known her entire life. And nothing had changed in that respect. Sure, they were going through a bad patch and weren't getting on as well as they used to, didn't seem to understand one another as they once had, but basically they were still friends, and it's only now, now that she's had a taste of passion, that she understands what she gave up.

She gave up excitement.

She gave up the evenings of sitting in waiting for the phone to ring, which, while horrific most of the time, gave rise to addictive euphoric highs on the rare occasions when the man of the moment would actually ring.

She gave up the challenge.

And Chris was never a challenge. Chris was just your typical boy-next-door. Pleasant-looking, easygoing, GSOH, or, good sense of humor, as they say in the personal ads. He never had the qualities that Dan has. He wasn't sexy and seductive, dark and dangerous. She thinks about Dan and shivers.

Feeling as if you've known someone your entire life isn't a reason to marry them, she thinks ruefully. She should have known. She should have listened to Bella, who said she'd only settle down when she met the knight in shining armor who would sweep her off her feet.

Look at Bella now, she thinks. She may be still single at thirty-four, but isn't she having a great life? She's at different bars and parties every night. Chatting up dark and dangerous men, men like Dan, and having wild sex in strange bedrooms.

Even Julia's now doing much the same thing. Why had she set-tled for boring married life? When had she bought into the sub-urban horror of marriage and domesticity?

She would, if she could, change everything in her life. Ex-cept for George. George who only has to look at her to melt her heart. Giving George a huge smile, she picks him up for a cud-dle, only to have him yowl in anger at being removed from his current favorite toy—the Hoover nozzle. She squeezes him for a few seconds before putting him back on the floor, where he gratefully falls on the hose.

And that, she knows, is why she hasn't done anything yet. George.

That's why she hasn't been able to sit down with Chris and talk about wanting a separation, wanting to have some space.

As convinced as she is that she has married the wrong man, Sam cannot just walk away, not when Chris adores George as much as she, not when Chris gets him up in the morning on the weekends, and sings the "I Love You" song from Barney before taking him downstairs and giving him breakfast. Not when Chris's eyes light up when Sam regales him with something George has done during the day.

How could she take George away from Chris? And how would it affect George, to come from a divorced home? She doesn't want him to be ferried back and forth, doesn't want him to spend half his summer with her and half with Chris. She wants George to have the best possible upbringing she can give him, and that means being with Mummy and Daddy. Together.

That's why she can't say anything. Not yet. Even though she knows that a child is not a reason to stay together. That having parents who stay together in a household of bitterness and resentment is surely worse than living in two separate households that are filled with love and laughter.

George is not a reason to stay together, but she can't bring herself to do anything about it yet. Once upon a time she used to say, "This too shall pass" when she felt unhappy, or depressed, or without hope, but it's been eight months now and it hasn't passed yet. A part of her is still optimistic, a part of her still thinks that maybe it will all be okay, but of course that was before Dan reawakened those feelings in her.

If she's honest, those feelings had been stirred by Mr. Brennan, her obstetrician, but that was only a ridiculous crush, almost an obligatory crush if your obstetrician happens to be, well, male, really. She never fantasized about Mr. Brennan, not long, drawn-out, elaborate fantasies that were always firmly based in reality, and that therefore could possibly come true. Her fantasies about Mr. Brennan were nothing like her fantasies about Dan.

Sam is aware that had she not met Dan she could well have spent the rest of her life with Chris. After all, she couldn't have missed what she didn't know. She would have bumbled along quite happily, maybe even having more children, and would never know the meaning of true passion.

But now that she's met Dan, there's only one thing of which she's absolutely certain: It's just a matter of time.

"You're looking very nice for the cinema." Chris's surprise was obvious when Sam walked down the stairs.

Patricia popped her head around the doorway from the kitchen where she was giving George his bottle, and raised her eyebrows with a smile. "Darling, is that makeup? How lovely to see you looking human again." Sam snarled at her, then tottered down the hallway to get her bag.

"Mum, he should go down no later than seven. No later, okay? Don't keep him up to play with him or he'll get overtired and all hell will break loose."

"Darling, I have done this before, you know. Don't worry. Just go and have a nice time."

"Okay, but if he wakes up, he shouldn't wake up, he normally sleeps through doesn't he?" She looks at Chris for confirmation. "But if he does you can give him some milk, there's a bottle in the fridge. Actually, just give him some water. Oh God. Milk or water. I don't want him to be sick, but I think he's going through a growth spurt and seems to be very hungry at the moment. Maybe you should give him some more milk now—"

"Just go," Patricia tutted. "He will be fine. I will be fine. I'm a mother too, so stop worrying. I didn't exactly do a bad job with you, did I?"

"Debatable, really," Chris muttered under his breath as Patricia shot him a look.

"Okay, we're going," Sam said, swooping down to cover George with kisses. "Good-bye, monkey, Mummy loves you, be a good boy. Sleep tight."

"Come on," Chris murmured, looking at his watch. "We're going to be late."

And now, sitting in the darkened cinema, Sam is acutely conscious, once again, of Dan's thigh resting gently against hers.

She had felt sick about seeing him again, had been terrified that she would turn into a sixteen-year-old girl and be unable to look him in the eye, and had walked over to greet them feeling horribly self-conscious.

Jill had given her a kiss and a warm squeeze, and she had turned to Dan expecting the same, but he had put his arms around her and given her a huge hug, and said "Hello, gorgeous" in her ear. She could have stayed there all night. He was so big, and tall, and strong, and wrapped in his arms she felt like a tiny little girl in the arms of her savior. Reluctantly she had pulled away and turned quickly to Jill, aware that she might be suspecting something, and wanting to put her mind to rest, not wanting her to know. Not yet.

"Are we late?" Sam had said with a smile, hoping that she was conveying the fact they had rushed, hence her breathlessness.

"Not at all. We were early." Jill linked her arm through hers as she led the way into the foyer. "It's lovely to see you."

Dan had done the popcorn run. Sam loves popcorn, but had declined, not wanting him to think she was greedy, and when Dan returned with three large tubs for Jill, Chris, and himself, he had whispered conspiratorially that she could share his, and she felt honored and special, basking in the spotlight of his attention.

She walked down the narrow corridor first, not knowing who was immediately behind her, but praying it was Dan. Please God, she had prayed. If this is meant to be, if Dan and I are destined to be together, please let him sit next to me. Please give me a sign that he feels the same way.

She squeezed past various legs to reach her seat, and felt a surge of joy when she turned to find Dan immediately behind her. Thank you, God, she had said. Now I know.

She sits pretending to be mesmerized by Tom Hanks's performance in the film, unable to think of anything except Dan's thigh brushing hers, unable to do anything other than time her forays into his popcorn bucket to coincide with his so their hands meet and they turn to one another and smile an apology into one another's eyes. Except those glances, those intimate smiles say so much more than an apology. She is almost holding her breath, waiting for him to do something, to show her how he feels. Each time she reaches for the popcorn, she expects him to gently stroke her hand, even rub a finger, and when he doesn't she knows that he is just as insecure as her.

She considers doing it to him, but knows this is too early, and even though she is absolutely sure of his attraction to her—why else would he have hugged her so warmly—she is not sure that he has thought it through in quite the same way. It's not that she has any doubt of his feelings, it's just that she suspects he isn't in precisely the same place, not yet.

It is only a matter of time.

"Wasn't that the most extraordinary film you've ever seen?" Jill is breathless, excited, cannot wait to talk about the film.

"It was an incredible piece of cinema," Chris agrees. "So realistic, it reminded me of *Titanic*. The realism and the hugeness. What did you think, Sam?"

"I thought"—she rolls her eyes—"it was the most boring film I've ever seen. Maybe if it had lasted an hour and a half I would have enjoyed it more, because there were moments that really worked for me, but three hours? Please. It was all I could do to stay awake."

"I couldn't agree more," laughs Dan. "The slowest film I think I've ever had the misfortune to see."

"Well, you two obviously have no taste," Jill says, smiling, as Sam feels a glow of warmth at her and Dan being referred to as "you two."

They drive separately to the restaurant, Sam and Chris in silence as Sam looks out the window with a smile on her face and thinks about Dan. Chris glances at her from time to time, wondering if she's okay, wondering why she seems so distracted, but she is definitely happier tonight, and he doesn't want to risk her wrath by putting a foot wrong.

They sit down and order a Chablis for Jill and Chris, and a Bordeaux for Dan and Sam, who is more and more excited at finding she has so much in common with Dan, so much more, it would seem, than Jill appears to have.

"Thank God we've found you!" Jill says when Sam expresses her preference for red. "Dan always moans if he has to drink white and we either get a bottle of each and leave half, which is such a bloody waste, or we have nasty house wine by the glass."

"I don't even remember the last time we went out," Sam says, sending a covert message to Dan, letting him know that their marriage is not as good as it may appear, "let alone the last time we drank wine."

"And whose fault is that?" The words and the expression are innocent, but Chris is fed up with being blamed for everything. Luckily Sam's good humor is such she does not rise to the bait.

"It's probably my fault. I've been so tired since George that I'm terrified a glass of wine will just knock me out completely."

"Careful, then," Dan says, smiling, moving her glass away. "We don't want you falling asleep at the table."

"Don't be silly!" Sam laughs, hitting him playfully. "I've got loads of energy tonight, no chance of me falling asleep."

"Good," Jill says. "Because we're all going to enjoy this evening, particularly if you hardly go out. It took me months to trust Lily with anyone, and when I decided that actually I now felt that we had to start having a life again and not everyone who turned up for an interview would potentially harm my child, we couldn't find anyone. Have you got a regular baby-sitter?"

"We have Sam's mother," Chris interjects, "who's about as irregular as you can get. Tonight is probably the, what? Third? Fourth time she's baby-sat?"

"My mother is in fact the anti-mother," Sam says ruefully. "Everyone told us she'd be different as a grandmother and would completely fall in love with her grandchild, but eight months on and we're still waiting for that to happen."

"Dan's mother sounds exactly the same," Jill says. "It's such a bloody cliché, but all she's interested in is her bloody tennis."

"With my mother it's bridge." Sam shrugs in recognition.

Jill continues. "She probably sees Lily once every couple of weeks, and then she'll ring up and make all these ridiculous inferences that I'm a bad daughter-in-law and the only reason she doesn't spend time with Lily is because I'm so busy and she doesn't want to interrupt." Her voice rises as she becomes agitated talking about it.

"Come on, Jill. Calm down." Dan sees she's getting herself worked up into a state.

"I'm sorry, but I just get so angry. Bloody mothers-in-law. Nothing that I ever seem to do makes her happy. I suppose one of these days I'll just have to accept it."

"You know it's nothing to do with you," Dan says. "She's simply an unhappy woman and that's the way it is. She's never going to change."

"That's exactly what I keep trying to tell Sam," Chris says. "But Sam keeps trying to please her, or hoping that one morning she's going to wake up and suddenly be this wonderful warm, gray-hair-in-a-bun grandmother type, and it's never going to happen."

"Must be a female thing. I know I try to change everyone, or at least hope they're going to change."

"Maybe you're just a control freak," Chris laughs.

"Ah yes." Dan gives a knowing look. "Funny you should say that."

"What's that play called?" Sam laughs. *I Love You, You're Perfect, Now Change.* That's what we do, isn't it?"

"That's just what you two do," Chris says. "I don't think everyone does that."

"Nah, mate." Dan shakes his head. "All women do do that. They pretend to be sweet and innocent when you meet them, then they turn into these madwomen once you've married them."

"Charming," Jill laughs. "Remind me to leave you at home

the next time we go out for dinner." She raises an eyebrow. "They always says you should look at someone's friends before you marry them, that you can always tell a person by the company they keep, and I'm sure you can tell a lot about a man by his mother. Maybe I should have thought a bit harder back then."

Dan starts to look pissed off, and Jill backs down. "Sorry, sorry. I didn't mean it, my darling, I was just winding you up." She kisses him on the cheek and he visibly unclenches, while Sam feels like she's about to cry at this display of familiarity.

"I'm just going to the loo," she says, standing up from the table and almost running to the loo. She stands in front of the mirror for what feels like an age, looking at herself, her mind completely blank, and then the thoughts come flooding in.

What are you thinking of? He's a happily married man. Why didn't he push her away when she tried to kiss him? But she is his wife, for God's sake. It doesn't mean he's not thinking about you. It doesn't mean he didn't want you to kiss him. Look how much you have in common. Think about his thigh touching yours. Think how he maneuvered it so he was sitting next to you in the cinema. Yes. He definitely feels the same way about you too.

She walks back to the table calmly, a smile on her face, her serenity restored.

If I don't see any red cars for the next twenty seconds, Dan loves me.

If I avoid all the cracks in the pavement up to the next roadside, Dan and I are meant to be together.

If George sleeps for at least one and a half hours, Dan is sitting there thinking about me too.

This is beginning to get ridiculous.

For the last three days all Sam has thought about is Dan. She wakes up in the morning to George's crying, picks him up and puts him in his high chair in a daze, thinking about Dan.

She dreamily spoons Weetabix into his mouth, and all over his face, thinking about Dan.

She pushes George up and down the hills on the Heath, all the while fantasizing about her future with Dan.

Sam is more certain now than she was before. She saw the way he smiled at her, the way he focused on her so intensely when she was talking. Jill and Chris had ended up talking animatedly about interiors with Jill giving Chris some ideas about marketing and PR, and Sam had ended up, as she knew she would, with Dan.

Dan had stared deep into her eyes and softly—out of the others' earshot—asked her question after question about herself. He had asked her about her childhood, her mother, her tearaway teenage years. He had asked about her work, her aims, her fears. And most of all he had asked about Chris. About how they had met, what she had thought, whether she had made the right choice.

His questions had been far more intimate than you might expect from someone whom you had met just twice. And the way in which he asked them, the way he concentrated on Sam until everything else in the room disappeared, had flattered, excited, and exhausted her. Particularly the questions about her marriage.

She felt he was trying to find out everything about her, to see into her very soul. And why would he be doing that unless he too knew that she was the love of his life? But she had to play it carefully. She couldn't tell him her marriage was in ruins, not while Chris was there, and not yet, but she could infer through short sentences, resigned shrugs, an unwillingness to answer.

She couldn't blame Chris, couldn't say a bad word against him, couldn't, above all, show herself in a bad light, but what she wanted to do most was pose those very same questions to Dan, take her cue from him. If he had said his marriage was over, she would have agreed and said the same thing. If he had said he loved Jill but was no longer in love with her, she would have said she felt the same way. If he had said he was thinking of leaving her, Sam would have said she was thinking of doing exactly the same thing.

But every time she tried to ask him a question, he'd come out with another, and it was only as they were about to go home that she realized she knew as little about him at the end of the evening as she did at the beginning.

And he knew practically everything about her.

That had to be, she thinks, smiling, throwing Huggies into her shopping trolley as George gurgles happily in the baby seat, because he loves me. She looks up and knows that he definitely loves her if she reaches the end of the aisle before the old woman in the red raincoat who's shuffling her way to the bottom. She's about to break into a speedwalk when she sees how ridiculous she's being.

He loves her.

She doesn't have to play these games anymore.

28

"Hi. Sam?" George is sitting in his high chair attempting to lean forward as Sam tries to maneuver the tray on to give him lunch.

"Hang on, hang on," she cries as she drops the phone briefly to adjust the shoulder straps. "Come on, Chicken. Be a good boy and eat Mummy's delicious homemade fishcakes. Yum yum. Mmmm. Delicious." She spoons it into his mouth at the same time as she picks up the receiver.

"I'm so sorry," she says into the mouthpiece, speed-spooning more crumbled-up fishcake into George's mouth, which is open and waiting like a tiny little black bird's. "Hello?"

"So are your fishcakes delicious, then?"

"They're going down a treat," she says,

trying to place the voice, which is so familiar. "Who is it that wants to know?"

"I can't believe you don't know when we only spoke yesterday."

Yesterday? Yesterday was Sunday. She tries to think whether she spoke to anyone yesterday, but no. Her mind is blank.

"Yesterday?"

"Sam! It's Dan."

She drops the spoon, which luckily makes no noise whatsoever, being, as it is, made of orange and turquoise rubber, and George lets out a wail of disapproval, anxious for the next mouthful.

"Dan, how are you?" She thinks of using her Caramac bunny voice, but too late. It would sound ridiculous now, and she curses herself for being so unprepared, for Dan having to listen to her being, well, mumsy, rather than a voluptuous sex siren. But then again, he called her. Her wishes finally came true and he called.

"I'm extremely well. Is this a bad time to call?"

As if there could ever possibly be a bad time for Dan to call.

"Not at all."

"Look, I really hope you don't find this presumptuous, but it's Jill's birthday next Friday and one of the ideas I thought of for a present was a painting, or drawing, of our house because she loves it, and even though I know you're a graphic designer, I thought you might know someone who does this sort of thing."

"I could do it." The words are out before she even has a chance to think about them.

"You could?" Relief and joy in his voice. She knew it! Sam knew it was just an excuse to see her again! "I wanted to ask you but I was sure you'd say no. God, Sam. That's fantastic. It's incredibly short notice, though, her birthday's in two weeks. Could you do it by then?"

"No problem. The only thing I've been doing recently is looking after George."

"Come, come. Now I know you're lying. What about making those delicious homemade fishcakes? They must have kept you busy."

She laughs. "Ah yes. I'd forgotten about those. See how exciting my life is? Looking after babies and cooking."

"Jill only pretends to cook. She has four recipes that she does to perfection, and that's it. All I can say is your husband must be a very lucky man."

Sam blossoms with pride. "Flattery will get you everywhere."

"Now that," he laughs, "is something you definitely shouldn't be saying to a man like me."

A warm flush appears on her face. This is serious flirtation. This is something in which she hasn't indulged for years. Not since long before Chris. And more to the point, she's flirting with Dan! Or rather, he's flirting with her.

Which is not the same thing at all.

She tries to think of something equally flirtatious, or witty, or leading, but finds herself at a loss for words. This is all happening far more quickly than she had expected, and although she's delirious with joy, she's also unprepared, and changes tack to bring the conversation back on to a more comfortable level for her.

"So what should I do about the house? Do you have any photographs I can work from?"

"I've got some from earlier in the year. How about I drop them round to you later today? Are you in?"

Oh God. Her hair needs washing. The house needs tidying. She needs to do a shop. George needs a walk.

"I'm here all afternoon. Later would be better for me."

"How about four? I could come for tea."

Sam cannot wipe the smile from her face. "Four sounds lovely. If you're sure." Insecurity threatens to strike.

"Sure I'm sure. I'll bring the pictures as long as you provide the homemade crumpets."

"Oh ha ha. You'll be lucky if you get a couple of stale Farley's Rusks."

"Don't worry about it. That's pretty much what I get at home. See you later." And he's gone.

Her doorbell rings at 1:45 P.M. Bugger. She's in the bath, face pack on, deep conditioner soaking into her split ends, while George sleeps soundly in his room. She clambers out of the bath, grabs a towel and runs downstairs, dripping water on to the mat as she opens the door.

To find Maeve standing on the doorstep with Poppy.

"Ah." Maeve smiles regretfully. "Clearly not the best time to come over, then?"

Any other time and Sam would be over the moon, but not today. Not when George could wake up at any given moment and she's using this time while he's asleep to get ready.

And she knows Dan was only joking about the homemade

crumpets, but she does want to show him how it is possible to be sexy, gorgeous, a wonderful mother, and a fabulous wife as well. She is planning on whipping up a quick banana bread after she's thoroughly spring-cleaned the house.

"Oh God," Sam moans. "I'd so love to ask you in but I've got a meeting this afternoon and I've got to get ready before George wakes up. Are you okay, though?"

"We're great," Maeve smiles. "Poppy's delicious and I'm bored, and we were passing so I thought I'd pop in, but don't worry. Another time." She turns to leave.

"No. Wait." Sam does a quick mental calculation. If Dan comes at four, they'd exchange photos immediately, and then chat, and then . . . oh Christ. What if something happens? No, she decides instantly. The most that will happen today is a kiss, and even as she thinks about a potential kiss, her loins turn to liquid. I will not sleep with him, not in this house, and not yet, she tells herself firmly. Just a kiss. And five o'clock is George's teatime and six o'clock is George's bathtime so whatever happens he will have left by then but that still doesn't leave me time to see Maeve.

But should I even be seeing Maeve, she wonders. Maeve doesn't know about the Julia connection, but she's so nice! She could be my new best friend! Oh God. What shall I do?

"What are you doing tomorrow morning?"

"Same as usual," Maeve says. "Wandering the streets, accosting any nice-looking mother who could be my friend. Why?"

Sam laughs. "Come over tomorrow for a coffee. Nine-thirty?"

Maeve makes a face. "My little angel has a nap until

around ten. Bugger. It's so awkward having to fit everything around naptime."

"Don't worry. How about ten-thirty?"

"Perfect. See you then."

BY 3:34 P.M. Sam is ready. The house is gleaming, every surface polished to perfection, a bowl of roses on the kitchen table.

She is wearing new jeans and a long blue sweater to cover the pregnancy padding around her hips and thighs that is finally starting to disappear now that her newfound crush has shrunk her appetite to almost nothing.

Her makeup is subtle and discreet, and only visible if you look very, very closely.

A vanilla-scented candle has been burning on the radiator shelf in the hallway, the kitchen smells deliciously of banana bread, and the living-room table has been polished with lavender beeswax furniture polish.

Sam has used every trick of the trade—bar putting cinnamon sticks in the oven, and even that was considered—to make her home welcoming, to reinvent herself as the perfect picture of domesticity.

If an estate agent tried to sell the house this afternoon, there would probably be a bidding war.

She rocks quietly back and forth in the glider rocker in George's room, watching him bang a musical toy, barely even registering the—usually intensely irritating—toy's recorded voice with an American twang: Puppy. Kitten. Hello, Baby.

At 3:55 P.M. the phone rings. It's Dan.

"I'm so sorry," he says, not sounding particularly apologetic, but sounding very rushed. "Something's come up and I've got to go out on a job. I'm out for the rest of the day so I'll drop them through the letterbox this evening on my way back, is that okay?"

"Of course," she says brightly, successfully covering the disappointment, the instant desolation she feels. "Absolutely fine. Don't worry about a thing."

She puts the phone down and wills back the tears. This is ridiculous. This is not because he doesn't love her, it is something beyond his control. He'll call tomorrow. He'll find another excuse, because Sam does, after all, recognize that it is just an excuse. He didn't have to come over at all, she muses, starting to brighten slightly. He could have sent the photos in the post, or dropped them in one evening when Chris is here. He invited himself for tea to spend time with me. This was unavoidable, she tells herself, gazing at George. He'll think of something else.

She has to find something else to think about as well. He is taking up space, rent-free, in her head, and despite enjoying his presence there most of the time, she is also finding it exhausting. She decides that this afternoon she will have a break from him, from thoughts of him.

She calls Maeve.

"What a lovely surprise. I was bored stupid today." Maeve pushes the buggy into the hallway and lifts Poppy out, walking down to the kitchen with the confidence all new mothers share when they are in the presence of their own. They treat one another's houses as their own, open cupboard doors and help themselves to bibs, and bottles, and baby wipes. They adopt a familiarity in the homes of strangers in a way that never fails to shock their husbands on the rare occasions those husbands are around to witness.

"So rude!" their husbands have been known to hiss, when new mothers attempt to bring their entire families, husbands included, together for tea on Sundays. "Can you believe she just opened all our cupboards? Couldn't she have asked? Didn't anyone ever teach her manners?"

And new mothers will shrug, for they understand in a way they know their husbands never will.

So Maeve enters Sam's kitchen, followed by Sam, exclaims with pleasure on seeing a reclining chair still shoved in the corner, and expertly straps Poppy in the chair, dangling a toy bar (on the floor next to the chair) above to keep her quiet and amused.

"Can I get you anything?" Sam says, putting the kettle on. "Does Poppy need anything? I've got masses of formula. George was so allergic I had to try every brand on the market, so whatever you want, I've got."

Maeve raises an eyebrow. "Aptamil?"

"Got it."

"Soya milk?"

"Got it."

"Ah ha. How about . . . Nanny?"

"Of course I've got Nanny. Goat's milk formula was the only thing my poor little lactose-intolerant baby would drink."

Maeve makes a face. "How do you know he's lactose intolerant?"

"He'd come out in this terrible eczema with everything else."

"Okay," she says, shrugging.

"Why?"

"I don't understand why none of our generation was lactose intolerant, and suddenly every other child today is either lactose intolerant or allergic or something."

Sam misses Maeve's point, Maeve firmly believing that lactose intolerance is merely the result of a neurotic mother. "I think they must use far more additives now," Sam says. "God knows I wish they wouldn't, I'd love to be able to give George normal formula."

"It's like all that bloody organic stuff," Maeve continues, now on a roll. "We never had organic food, did we? And what harm has it done us? None. I can't see what on earth is the point in spending three times as much on organic food."

"Oh God," groans Sam. "You know what? I bloody agree with you, but look," and she opens her fridge door and beckons Maeve over to have a look. Organic milk. Organic cheese. Organic bread. Organic vegetables. "Isn't that ridiculous? I think exactly the same thing, but I've done it because everyone else does it."

"I'm sorry, I'm sorry." Maeve can feel herself creasing up with embarrassment. She had no idea Sam would be one of those women, Sam looked so . . . normal. "I shouldn't have said anything. Me and my big mouth."

"You should have said something, because you're right. So what do you want to drink?" Sam opens the cupboard door, and turns back for an answer when none is forthcoming.

Maeve is standing in front of the freezer, the door wide open, looking confused and slightly shocked.

"Sam, I know this might be a stupid question, but why do you have three billion ice-cube trays stacked in your freezer?"

Sam starts to laugh. "Not for ice. I read a brilliant article that said you had to freeze the food you make for the babies in ice-cube trays. It's amazing. Every time I cook I just empty out two or three. It's so easy."

"But Sam," Maeve says, trying very hard not to smile, but she can't quite help it, "you're supposed to turn them out into freezer bags when they're frozen, not keep buying more ice-cube trays."

"You're joking." Sam is mortified as she looks at the trays and trays of frozen baby food, stacked up until there isn't a millimeter of extra space. "No one told me that."

"Oh God. I'm sorry," Maeve starts to laugh. "I'm only laughing because I would have done exactly the same thing but I've seen someone do it. You must have spent thousands on those bloody ice trays."

Sam grins, starting to see the ridiculousness of what she's done. "Not thousands. Hundreds maybe. God, I'm stupid. I can't believe I didn't think of that."

"So I'm not the only one whose brain has shrunk to nothing since giving birth?"

"Clearly not. I just thought I'd hidden it reasonably well. So. Drink. What'll you have?" She walks back to the cupboard. "Chamomile? Apple and rosehip? Peppermint?" She looks at Maeve's aghast face and starts to laugh. "Joke," she says, having almost forgotten about Dan. "Tea or coffee?"

"I would say tea but I don't trust you and I need some caffeine so you'd better make it coffee. Strong. Two spoonfuls and milky."

"Two spoonfuls? Are you sure?"

"Yup. Catching up on the last months when I wasn't allowed to drink any. So . . ." Maeve looks around the kitchen. "This is just as gorgeous as I suspected, but far more to the point, I thought you said you didn't have any help."

"I don't."

"You have to be joking. I feel slightly ill. How in the hell do you manage to keep this place looking so perfect by yourself? Nobody does that." She peers at Sam closely. "Are you some kind of Stepford Wife or something?"

"Trust me," Sam laughs. "The furthest thing. I was having this meeting . . ." She realizes she can withhold the truth but can't lie completely, not to a new friend. "This friend of ours has secretly asked me to draw a picture of his house for his wife's birthday, and I was so ashamed of this house looking like a bomb's hit it that I had a massive blitz this afternoon. If it makes you feel any better, I swear this house never ever looks like this."

"Okay. That makes me feel a bit better. So you draw, then?"

"I was a graphic designer."

"And now?"

"Now I'm a mother who was supposed to have gone back to her job after three months but I'd been unhappy with the company for years, and I just couldn't face it. So now I'm a full-time mother who isn't earning anything, who needs to find some kind of work to keep her sane, but who in the meantime resents her husband for not being able to provide for her in the way she'd like. I'm a mother who will probably have to think of something pretty damn sharpish."

"No beating around the bush with you, then," Maeve laughs. "If it's any consolation, I understand."

"Are you going back to work?"

"I'm supposed to. And before Poppy I thought I would definitely go back, I thought I'd stagnate if I wasn't in the work environment, but I don't know whether I can leave her now. That bloody three-month deadline's looming, and I can't believe I'm going to say this, but the truth is I find being a mother strangely fulfilling." She sighs. "I spent years building up my career, and just as I was getting somewhere I got pregnant. I thought Poppy would be a temporary blip, but I simply don't miss the adrenaline of work, and I really think I'm happy at home, with Poppy.

"I worked in television," Maeve adds, as an afterthought.

"I know." Their eyes meet, and Sam realizes she must now confess. "Oh God. Please swear to me you won't run away if I tell you how I know."

"I swear to God I'll take at least ten minutes to run away, given that I have to get Poppy's snowsuit back on and get her strapped into the buggy again." She's joking, but curious. How could Sam possibly know she worked in television?

Sam groans. She likes Maeve so much. Feels so comfortable with her. Knows that they have the potential to be such good friends. She also knows Maeve may very well cut her off before they've even started.

"You know your boyfriend?"

"Mark. Yes. Extremely well."

"You know his ex-girlfriend?"

"Julia. Yes. Not so well." Her voice is slowing down with recognition.

"Julia's my, um. How shall I say this . . ." Sam is pained. ". . . She's my best friend."

"Ah." Maeve sits back in her chair. "Does that mean that you have a huge problem with me and you hate me madly and in fact the only reason you invited me over is so you can pinch a hair out of my head while I'm not looking and make a voodoo doll once I've gone?"

Sam laughs, despite herself. "I thought maybe you'd have a huge problem with me," she says. "Because I do still talk to Julia. A lot. And I just don't want things to be awkward."

Maeve thinks for a while before speaking. "As I understand it, Julia and Mark were incredibly unhappy for many years, and both of them mistakenly thought a baby would heal their relationship?"

Sam nods.

"And now that Julia is living in New York she is in fact having a high old time, out with different men every night, hitting the hot spots and making *Sex and the City* look like *The Waltons.*"

Sam nods.

"And while I know it must have been difficult for her when she first heard about Mark and me, and Poppy"—Sam is about to nod but she quickly restrains herself, not wanting to be disloyal to Julia—"I would imagine that she probably doesn't feel very much about it now. Unless of course I'm barking up the wrong tree entirely."

"No. I'd say you'd just about summed it up."

"So are you planning on phoning Julia and telling her everything about me?"

"Well, no. I wasn't actually. I don't know what I'm going to tell Julia about you."

Maeve reaches forward and places a hand on Sam's, her voice suddenly filled with rich, deep sincerity. "So why don't we just see each other for a while and see how it goes?"

Sam smiles, relief flooding through her. "But this isn't a relationship?" she says warningly.

"Definitely not." Maeve smiles. "We're just seeing each other. No one has to know. Oh, and one other thing. No PDAs."

"PDAs?"

"Public Displays of Affection."

"That, my friend," Sam says, extending a hand and shaking Maeve's firmly through their shared smiles, "is a deal."

An hour later they're still at the kitchen table when the doorbell rings. Sam jumps up and goes to the door, to find Dan standing on the doorstep.

As her heart jumps into her mouth, Dan grins his sexy grin, apologizes, and explains he went on a job to interview an American rock star who's in town performing, but the rock star had an unfortunate experience with one of the tabloid journalists scheduled just before him, and subsequently put a stop to all other interviews.

"Who were you doing it for?" Sam is so impressed she can hardly breathe.

405

"*Telegraph.* I just spoke to the editor. I'm going to do a piece on celebrity tantrums instead. Ironic, naturally."

"Naturally."

"When the stories fall through, the freelance hack gets to play. So here I am."

"To play?" She can't help herself, and even as she stands in the front door, one hand on her hip in a suggestive pose, one eyebrow raised, she remembers that Maeve is in the kitchen, and instantly wishes she'd go, wishes Maeve were anywhere else but here.

"What's that delicious smell?" Dan doesn't rise to the bait, and Sam is surprised, disappointed, but then she remembers how she hadn't risen to the bait in their phone conversation earlier, and she knows he is just getting back at her.

She forgives him.

"Homemade banana bread." She smiles as she steps back to let him in. "I've got a friend here. Come in and meet her."

Maeve eyes Dan up and down with caution. She knows men like this. Has slept with men like this many, many times. He is flirtatious and dangerous, and she is (much to Sam's relief) cool as she says hello, and quiet as she sits at the table and watches how Sam changes when this man's around.

He is, she reflects, as he stretches long legs out in front of him and leans back in his chair while Sam fusses around him, a man who is comfortable in his skin. Too comfortable, perhaps. He expects everyone to love him, and Maeve has never been good at loving men like that. Sleeping with them, yes. Loving them, no.

But he is, without question, dangerously attractive.

And Sam has, without question, fallen hook, line, and sinker.

No wonder she had made such an effort with the house, had baked banana bread.

It was all for Dan.

Dan finishes his banana bread, lavishes praise on Sam, who almost melts into his arms, and turns on Maeve, firing charming, disarming questions at her. Asking her who she is, where she lives, what she does, how old is Poppy, what kind of birth.

At this point Maeve, who is uncomfortable enough in this situation anyway, notices that Sam too is dismayed by Dan's attention to her. I will not get involved in this game, she thinks, standing up to leave.

She shakes Dan's hand with a forced smile, and gives Sam a hug. She knows Sam is in dangerous territory with this one. She knows Sam is blinded by his attractiveness, cannot see how harmful he could be, how she could be risking everything for a fling with this man.

But, more than that, she can see he doesn't feel the same way about Sam. Sam is in love, and he is not. He is loving the attention, loving encouraging Sam, but for him it's all a game, and the most he'll commit to is a sordid little affair.

Does Maeve know Sam well enough to tell her? And if she does, what on earth is she going to say?

29

"You know what this sounds like?" Julia has heard Sam's voice like this before. Not for many years, but she knows Sam better than anyone, remembers how Sam always fell for the unobtainable. Julia was there when the latest love of her life turned out to be the greatest shit of her life. "This sounds like Paolo all over again."

Paolo had been Sam's gym instructor. Everyone in the class had drooled over the six-foot Italian, who had loved every second of it, but none had fallen quite so heavily or seriously as Sam.

Sam turned up at every class, made sure she was in the front, had soon progressed to clear favorite. Paolo would tell the others to watch Sam, would nod his approval at her, wink and smile, and have whispered conversations after the class.

Sam was a woman obsessed. A woman possessed.

The only benefit, she had later joked, was that she'd never been so thin in her life.

All her time was spent at the gym. Soon she was suggesting coffees, then drinks after the class. Sam was astonished Paolo said yes, but Julia kept warning her to be careful, that he was a man who needed women to fancy him, who would encourage Sam to feed his own ego, but who wasn't really interested.

One night she ended up seducing him. The sex was terrible. Neither particularly interested. Paolo dressed and left immediately afterward, and she lay in bed relieved he was no longer there, and wondering where it had all gone so horribly wrong.

She couldn't see it immediately, but in time she realized Julia was right. He was a natural flirt, a man addicted to women's attention, who would take it as far as he could to ensure those women still fancied him, disregarding any emotions that might arise along the way.

It didn't surprise her when she later discovered he had a long-term girlfriend and two children.

It does surprise her, however, to hear his name right now, on the phone with Julia, when she has finally cracked and told Julia everything. She knew Julia would disapprove, knew she wouldn't fully understand, but she wasn't expecting this.

"Paolo? He's nothing like Paolo! How can you say that when you haven't even met him?"

"You've just told me that Dan is, to all intents and purposes, happily married—"

"I didn't say happily," Sam interrupts fiercely.

"No, but he's still with his wife and he seems to get on with her—he is, after all, commissioning you to do a picture for her birthday so it's unlikely they're heading for the divorce courts next week."

"So? It doesn't mean they're happy."

"No, but they're together. Anyway, he's married, happily or unhappily, and yet he's sending you clear signals that he wants to get involved with you. He's flirting with you in front of his wife and your husband. I'm really sorry to say this, Sam, but I just don't believe decent people do that sort of thing."

Sam snorts in disbelief. "Decent people? You're being ridiculous. What if I'm right? What if he knows he married the wrong person, just like me, and he can't help it when I'm around?"

"Sam," Julia says gently, "if that were the case, if he really did think he'd married the wrong person and was trapped by a child, he still wouldn't make those leading comments to you, encourage you the way he's doing. The whole thing smacks of Paolo. It smacks of a deeply insecure man who's married and reasonably happy, but is either constantly having affairs because he's addicted to sex and tries to justify it by saying he loves his wife and child and the affairs are just satisfying a physical urge, or a deeply insecure man who's never going to cheat on his wife but likes to know that he still could if he chose, and encourages any woman who shows him the slightest bit of attention.

"Either way I can't see how this is going to result in a happy outcome. If you really want to know what I think, it's that you've got another Paolo-league crush, and he has no intention of doing anything about it other than bask in your adoration."

"I knew I shouldn't have told you," Sam says belligerently. "I knew you wouldn't understand."

"I'll tell you what I don't understand, Sam. I don't understand how you can even think that Chris is the wrong man for you when you've been together six years and he's wonderful to you, and you love him, despite what you're saying now. The only reason you're feeling so unfulfilled is because, I think, you've been suffering from some kind of postpartum depression, and you're miserable and looking for something, or someone, to blame, and Chris is closest to you so Chris gets the blame."

Sam considers putting the phone down, slamming it in anger, but then decides she has a few choice words of her own for Julia, and tries to interrupt instead.

"I haven't finished," Julia says. "If you walk out on Chris now, you're going to regret it for the rest of your life. I thought you were getting better. I thought these last few weeks you'd sounded more like the old Sam, had got some of your energy back, and I thought you were pulling yourself out of it, and now I realize it's just because of some dodgy bloke. Sam, you're married now. You have a child.

"When are you going to take responsibility for your life?"

Sam doesn't even wait for the dramatic pause. She slams down the phone and bursts into tears.

Chris phones five minutes later.

"What's the matter?"

"Nothing," she sniffs, unable to tell him the truth. "I'm just feeling a bit hormonal."

Chris doesn't need to ask anything further, well versed in sudden outbreaks of tears due to hormones. "Poor love. Can I bring you home anything?"

"No. I'll be fine."

"Listen, Jill just phoned saying we should all get together, and I thought maybe, given the baby-sitter situation, we should have them over for dinner. Say thank you for them having us for tea. What do you think?"

"Yes," Sam says immediately. "Great idea. It's her birthday next Friday, so what about next Sunday? Nothing fancy," she says, already planning a gourmet feast with which to impress Dan still further. "Just a casual supper."

"Great! I'll ring her back and suggest it. You know, it's so nice to hear the old Sam again. I'm so happy that you want to go out again, that we're starting to see people."

"Only Jill and Dan."

"But it's a start. And I really think this Maeve is good for you. I'm only beginning to realize how hard it must have been for you with Julia going away. You've been a different person since you met her."

"Have I?" She laughs inwardly at the irony, for of course it is Dan that is making the difference, but how convenient that Maeve has entered her life at roughly the same time.

"Yes. Actually, that's an idea. What about inviting Maeve and Mark too? I know Mark would get on with Jill and Dan, but obviously I don't know Maeve. Do you think it would work? Or," he hesitates, "would it be too weird for you, seeing Maeve and Mark together as a couple?"

"I think that's a brilliant idea! Maeve was here the other day when Dan popped in and they seemed to get on." She knows that's not exactly the truth, and that Maeve didn't seem to take to Dan all that well, but surely that will be diffused when all six of them are together.

Maybe before her phone call with Julia today she would have felt awkward about seeing Maeve and Mark together, would have felt it was something of a betrayal to Julia, but not now.

Now she's covering up the hurt with bravado, and deciding that Maeve is going to replace Julia in every possible way.

Thank God it's Sunday.

Monday, Tuesday, and Wednesday morning she finished the painting of Dan and Jill's house. Wednesday afternoon she joined Maeve at the One O'Clock Club on the Heath, then spent the rest of the day sitting on the floor of Maeve's living room while Poppy and George respectively lay and crawled about.

Sam thought she was going to feel strange, walking into Julia's house, knowing that Julia no longer lived there, but, after the initial shock, she could see that Maeve was far more comfortable in the house than Julia had ever been. Maeve had filled each room with books, and paintings, and flowers, had turned the bare bones of a house into a proper home.

The house had come alive since Maeve had moved in, and for the first time Sam understood what Julia had meant when she said she had never felt comfortable there, had always felt overwhelmed by the size. The house was imposing, but Maeve had made it feel cozy, had made it hers.

The strangeness that Sam had expected to feel lasted about

five minutes. Five minutes of walking through the rooms, silently reminiscing about the good old days, wondering why it felt so very long ago.

She had invited them for Sunday evening, had said that she knew Maeve hadn't taken to Dan but that Jill was lovely and anyway, she'd like Maeve to meet them both properly, she was sure she'd change her mind about Dan.

Plus she wanted Maeve to meet Chris. Then surely Maeve would see why Sam was so sure their marriage wasn't working. And if Maeve is to be her new best friend, she needs to support Sam unequivocally when the shit hits the fan.

Maeve had been delighted and had phoned Mark at work on the spot. He insisted on talking to Sam, who had almost cried at the familiarity and warmth in his voice, had put the receiver down softly feeling safe and loved.

Jill had phoned to ask if she needed anything, if Sam wanted her to make pudding, or a starter, and had then offered bread-and-butter pudding, laughing as she confirmed what Dan had said: It was the only pudding she could make but she did it fantastically.

Sam felt momentarily saddened after Jill phoned. Were she not planning on stealing her husband, she would almost certainly have been Jill's friend. Sam is warm toward Jill, but not too warm. Responsive without being gushing. Sam has to keep her distance or she knows she'll never be able to run off with her husband.

NOW, tonight, there are fifteen minutes to go before everyone starts to arrive. The salmon is marinating on the worktop, the vegetables are sliced and diced in preparation, the olive ciabatta sits waiting to be warmed up in the oven.

Chris carefully stacks the bottles of wine in the fridge, and checks his stock of mixers. Tonic? Check. Soda? Check. Orange juice? Check. Lemonade? Check. He's looking forward to this, had forgotten how much he enjoyed socializing, how often Sam and he had done this BG.

He smiles in appreciation as Sam walks into the kitchen. Ghost has done her proud tonight, a dark green beaded top hiding her rapidly shrinking hips, a floor-length bias-cut skirt swishing sexily as she moves.

"You look lovely." He kisses her on the cheek, turns to embrace her, and she smiles as she moves away, out of his reach, pretending to check the salmon marinade. She has not bought the outfit for Chris's benefit, naturally, but it's nevertheless important that he approves; makes her feel even sexier than when she had first checked herself in the mirror this evening.

The doorbell rings and Chris walks out to answer it, followed by Sam, her heart already pounding in anticipation, her breathing already shallow with nerves.

Jill makes a face, starts apologizing as soon as the door opens.

"We didn't know what to do," she says, bread-and-butter pudding in hand as she gestures to a sleepy pajama-clad Lily, arms wrapped around her daddy's neck as she struggles to stay awake. "The bloody baby-sitter phoned just as she was supposed to turn up, saying she had a headache and couldn't make it. We didn't know what to do, so we brought the travel cot. We'll have to put her down here. I'm so, so sorry."

"Don't worry about that." Sam gestures them in. "But will she be okay to go home again?"

"Unlikely." Jill makes a face. "But what can we do? It's always a bit of a nightmare when her routine's broken, but hopefully she'll sleep in the car on the way home and we'll be able to lift her straight out and into bed. I'm so sorry about this. Where can we put her?"

Jill, Dan, and Sam tiptoe quietly upstairs, and unfold the travel cot outside George's room.

"I won't put her in George's room," Jill whispers. "I don't want to wake him, but it's nice and dark out here."

"What about the monitor?"

"Don't worry. We don't use one anymore. We'll hear her."

"Okay, but let me open George's door a fraction, just in case."

"Really, you don't have to."

"I'd feel better about it." Sam quietly pushes George's door ajar.

Jill stays to put Lily down. Dan follows Sam down the darkened stairway, putting his hand on her shoulder halfway down. They both stop, a wave of nausea washing over her as she knows this is it. The moment she's been waiting for. The answer to her dreams.

She turns as if in a dream, everything happening in slow motion. Dan's head moves slowly to hers, and she stays still, eyes closing, head tilting slightly to one side. A soft kiss lands just at the side of her mouth. Her head still tilted, she waits for more, only opening her eyes when she feels the shadow of his head move away.

"I just wanted to say thank you," he whispers. "For the picture. It's beautiful."

"Oh. Thank you." Her voice is a whisper, and she waits for more, for a continuation of the kiss.

"No, really. I mean it. You're incredibly talented."

"Flattery," she says, a smile playing on her lips, "will get you everywhere."

"I bet you say that to all the boys," he teases softly.

And here it is. The invitation. The one she can't resist. Not anymore.

"No," she whispers, looking deeply into his eyes. "Only you."

"Is everything okay?" Jill whispers behind them, coming down the stairs, even her whisper managing to be cheerful. Sam is furious and embarrassed in equal measure. What if she heard? What if she saw? No. Impossible. She would not be so cheerful in the face of an adulterous husband.

"Fine, darling," Dan says. "I was just telling Sam how incredibly talented she is."

Jill's hand flies to her mouth. "I can't believe I didn't say anything. Sam! I love it, I love it, I love it! You're amazing! It's the best birthday present I've ever had and I can't believe you painted it! Thank you!" She flings her arms around Sam, who reluctantly pats her back lightly, waiting for her to disengage.

"You can see it was a hit," Dan says, smiling, and Sam smiles back at him over Jill's shoulder as the doorbell rings again, forcing them all to disengage and go downstairs.

"God, it's good to see you." Sam smiles up at Mark and rubs his back with affection. "We've missed you."

Mark shrugs, a twinkle in his eye. "So? You didn't call . . . you didn't write . . . what was I supposed to think?"

"I do feel guilty," she says, realizing with a start that she does.

"Don't," he admonishes gently. "I know how it is when relationships end. I know you're not supposed to take sides, but it's difficult not to. And besides, you were always Julia's best friend. You had to take her side even if"—he nudges her playfully—"I was the one you wanted to stay friends with."

"Come inside," she says, linking her arm through his. "Come and meet our friends," and they follow Maeve and Chris into the living room.

The women lead the small talk. Jill's baby-sitter nightmare leads to further stories of child-care horrors, and the men listen with amusement, punctuating the stories only with the sounds of Pringles and peanuts being munched, and glasses being refilled.

And then the men switch places, group together to find common ground, start with the match of the day, move to the horrors of having wives obsessed with babies, gradually reveal their softer sides as they compare notes and eulogize the joys of fatherhood.

Maeve and Jill are instantly at ease. Sam does her best to relax and join in, but all the while she is sitting chatting with

418

them she is aware of Dan directly opposite her. She isn't consciously trying to catch his eye, but she keeps pretending to glance at Chris, her eyes sweeping over Dan on the return journey, hoping to catch his, to swap a secret smile.

The corner of her mouth still burns where he kissed it. She tries to focus on Jill and Maeve, pretending to concentrate, to listen to their experiences at Gymboree, but all the while she is going over their kiss, wondering what would have happened had Jill not interrupted, wondering how far they would have gone on that darkened stairway had they not nearly been caught.

"Darling? Shall we sit down?" Chris is blossoming in his role as benevolent host, and leads the way to the dining table, assigning seats to their guests.

If Dan loves me, he'll smile at me before he sits down.

"Mark, why don't you sit on the left of Jill, and Dan, you sit on the right next to Sam."

Dan looks at Sam and smiles.

Thank you, God. I promise I'll go to church soon.

The evening is a great success. Maeve is still unsure of Dan, is not unaware of Sam's eyes following him around the room, of Sam's attention being focused almost exclusively on Dan.

Maeve drops her napkin at one point, convinced she will see Dan's hand fondling Sam's leg under the table, but a quick crawl in their direction proves her wrong.

She's surprised. More so having met Chris. Sam's flirtation with Dan, her desire to take it further was so obvious, Maeve had assumed there had to be something intrinsically wrong with her husband. He would surely have had to be arrogant. Dislikable. Charmless.

She had not expected Chris, had not expected the quintessential boy-next-door, and does not miss his constant glances at Sam, glances filled with love, hope, and confusion.

She can see he so clearly still loves his wife, is so clearly hurt by her lack of interest in him, despite not having cottoned on to her deepening crush on Dan. Maeve tests the waters, tries to find out what he knows, whether he suspects. She waits until Jill is deep in conversation with Mark, and Sam deep in adoration with Dan, before turning to Chris.

"So Jill and Dan. How long have you known them?"

"Jill I've known for ages through work. But we've only become friendly as a couple very recently."

"Hmmm. Jill's lovely."

"Isn't she? I'm glad you've hit it off."

"And Dan. Tell me about him."

"Lovely guy," he says, his face a picture of innocence. "The pair of them are salt of the earth."

She doesn't push it any further.

"Who's for pudding? Jill's made bread-and-butter pudding," Chris says gratefully when the salmon has been finished and the conversation has drifted to a natural halt.

The table murmurs its approval, and Maeve gathers some plates, following Sam into the kitchen.

"Do you mind if we just dash upstairs and check on Lily?" Jill pops her head round the door.

"Of course!" Sam forces a smile as Jill and Dan disappear upstairs.

Mark and Chris clear away the last of the plates and follow the girls into the kitchen.

"It's good to see you, mate," Chris says. "I've missed you. I've got some old port I've been saving for a special occasion, and I think tonight may just be the night. It's a Fonseca 1987. What do you think?"

"I think tonight is definitely the night," Mark says. "Down in your wine cellar, is it?" They both laugh at the old standing joke between them. Chris has always referred to his dingy damp basement with a rickety old Habitat wine rack in one corner as his wine cellar. Mark's professional wine cellar, housing hundreds of rare and important wines, is referred to between them as the crappy wine rack.

"Are you coming?" Chris opens the door and starts walking down.

"Be there in a sec." Mark takes his plates over to the sink and leans over to plant a kiss on Maeve's neck.

Sam sees the kiss and smiles. She never saw Mark and Julia like this. Never saw displays of affection between them, and it is reassuring, life-affirming, to see that two people can be this happy, this loving.

This is what she will have with Dan. This is what her future holds.

"You're terrible." A tinny voice drifts across the kitchen and all three of them jump, laughing as they see the monitor perched on a shelf. Sam moves over to turn it off. After all, it's hardly fair to eavesdrop.

She is not even halfway there when Jill's voice continues. "That poor Sam has got the hugest crush on you and you're encouraging it, you naughty thing."

All three of them freeze in horror.

"I know." Dan's voice emerges, laughter and pity intertwined. "The poor cow's having multiple orgasms whenever she looks at me."

"Oh, don't be mean. I think it's rather sweet."

"Only because of what she looks like. If she were five foot nine and gorgeous you wouldn't think it so sweet." They both laugh softly as Sam prepares to throw up. She wants to switch it off, to pretend this isn't happening, but she can't move.

"True. But be nice. And do stop leading her on. I know it's your favorite game, but those puppy-dog looks are getting too much even for me."

"I know, it is rather pathetic, isn't it? You're just jealous," Dan says softly. "Come here."

The sound of them kissing jerks Sam out of her inertia, and she flicks the monitor off, turning to catch the shocked expression on Maeve's and Mark's faces.

"Excuse me," she whispers, as she turns to flee from the room. "I think I'm going to be sick."

30

The one saving grace was that Chris didn't hear.

At least, that was what Sam told herself. Repeatedly.

The rest of the evening was, unsurprisingly, something of a disaster. Jill and Dan came back downstairs to find everyone, bar Chris, pale and shaky. Sam couldn't even look at them, and within a few minutes had retired to bed, claiming to have a sudden migraine, where she lay curled in the fetal position, shame and humiliation engulfing her to the point where she was unable to do anything except moan.

Jill realized very quickly what had happened. She had walked into the kitchen to ask Maeve if Sam was okay and spied the monitor, still switched off, on the window shelf. She visibly paled as she turned to Maeve and asked in a thin voice, "The monitor . . . ?" She had intended to say more, but Maeve's steely gaze stopped her.

"Yes," Maeve said, "the monitor." She stared her down, and Jill quietly turned and whispered something to Dan. A few minutes later they said good-bye to Maeve and Mark, unable to look them in the eye, collected a very tired and unhappy Lily, and left.

The only one who didn't have a clue about what was going on was Chris.

"What's happened?" he said, immediately after Jill and Dan left. "Did I do something wrong? Or was it you, Mark? Did you piss them off? Scare them away?" He had fallen into the easy banter he and Mark once shared, but his grin elicited nothing from Mark, just a shrug and a shake of the head.

Mark and Maeve left shortly afterward.

Chris cleared up in silence, taking a cup of tea and three Nurofen Plus up to Sam when he had finished. He hesitated outside their bedroom door, listening to her moaning, then padded in and sat next to her on the bed.

"How do you feel?" he said, stroking her back. "Is it really that bad?"

"It's terrible," she groaned.

And burst into tears.

Chris rubbed her back gently, his hand moving in slow rhythmic circles until her sobs reduced to uneven hiccups.

She was so filled with shame she could hardly bear to look at him.

As for Chris, he was aware that something had happened. He might have been thick-skinned, but he was not thick. He had, despite what everyone thought, noticed the way Sam shone when Dan was around, and was aware that she had been harboring a secret teenage crush. But he believed in his marriage, believed in Sam, and knew it would pass.

He also knew that something must have happened. He could guess, but he didn't want to go down that route, didn't want to think about what might have taken place. It was enough to see that that night would almost certainly mark the end of her crush. That it, whatever it was, had passed. Abruptly and definitively.

It was over.

And that was the only thing that mattered to Chris.

Sam doesn't sleep much that night. For a change. Instead of lying there fantasizing about Dan, she hears his voice, his patronizing tone, over and over. Trying to push it out of her head, she forces herself to focus on other things, but his voice keeps slipping in.

The poor cow's having multiple orgasms whenever she looks at me.

Oh God. Oh God. Sam cringes, physically, at the humiliation, at how wrong she'd been, how stupid for ever thinking it was anything more than Dan leading her on.

And, worse, he'd seen her for who she really was. She thought she'd been sexy, and curvaceous, and gorgeous, and he thought she was ridiculous.

The poor cow.

He'd seen the person she was terrified others would see: the fat, suburban wife. A laughingstock. She knew what he was thinking: She was a joke, a nothing, an object of ridicule.

Pathetic.

This is, she thinks, the worst night of my life. I will never be able to live this down. I will never be able to see Maeve and Mark again. I will never get over this.

At 4:34 A.M. Chris starts snoring gently. Sam sits up in bed and watches him, watches his body moving gently as he snores, his back softly rising and falling, and she waits for the hatred to come.

She had lain awake these past few months, waiting for him to snore. Had waited for him to justify her irritation, her rage. Had lain in bed hissing at him to shut up and hating him for not being the man she was supposed to have married.

Tonight she waits for those feelings to rise up through her throat, like bile, and is astonished to find none there. It's Chris, she thinks, tears welling up in her eyes. Look at his body; that back I know so well I could map out every mole with my eyes closed. Look at that hair, that thick shaggy hair I would recognize in a sea of a million people. The familiarity of him, the safeness of the man she knows almost as well as she knows herself, is suddenly overwhelming, and she finds her throat closing with emotion.

Oh my God, she thinks, shaking her head in amazement. What was I thinking? What have I done?

"Chris?" she whispers, reaching out to touch him.

"Sorry," Chris mumbles, rolling onto his side, so used to being prodded and hissed at in the early hours of the morning that he now does this automatically.

Sam smiles even as the tears start rolling down her cheek, and spoons in behind him, tucking her knees in tightly behind his legs, wrapping her arm around his chest.

"Mmm," Chris murmurs, drifting out of sleep just for a second.

"I love you," she whispers, smiling, as the horrors of the evening gradually start to leave the room. She clutches him tighter, holding onto him, knowing that he truly is her rock, will always look after her, will always rescue her.

My husband, she thinks, burying her nose in his hair and inhaling deeply, thanking God he didn't hear, didn't know.

Father of my child.

The man I love.

Maeve turns up three days later. She's waited what she considers to be an appropriate time, given that Sam hasn't returned her calls, and she wants to make sure she sees Sam before Christmas.

"I was going to ring first," she says, unzipping Poppy's snowsuit, "but I figured you'd probably think of an excuse for me not to come over and I was worried about, well . . . you know. How you'd be . . ." Maeve looks uncomfortable, but Sam laughs as she holds the door open.

"I'm fine," she says. "Coffee?"

Maeve follows her down the hallway, concerned about the act Sam is putting on. After all, Maeve was there that night. She heard. She can only imagine the humiliation Sam must be feeling.

Sam busies herself with the coffee while Maeve transfers Poppy to the bouncer, only turning to look at Sam when Poppy is strapped in and quiet. "Sam? Are you okay? Really? I mean, I heard the other night too. It was horrific, and I would be mortified if it happened to me, and I don't mind, you know, I understand, I'm just worried about you."

Sam sits down at the table with two mugs of coffee and a wry grin. "I can't even think about it," she admits, "because every time I do I feel absolutely sick."

"I've got to tell you I think the guy's a total fuckwit. I always did, you know. That time we met here I thought he was an arse, and you could see he was totally leading you on—"

"Stop!" Sam puts her hand up, because the one thing she can't cope with hearing again is how Dan led poor pathetic Sam on.

"I didn't mean that," Maeve says earnestly. "I meant, he fancied you! He so obviously fancied you."

"He didn't," Sam sighs, reaching over and squeezing Maeve's arm. "I know he didn't, and it's okay, you don't have to say it to make me feel better. I think the worst thing is I feel so completely stupid. I've spent these last few weeks obsessing about him, thinking that I was married to the wrong man and that Dan would give me my happy ever after, and it was just a stupid teenage crush that I took way too far, and . . ." She looks at Maeve with a pleading expression in her eyes. "And I'm married, for fuck's sake. I'm not supposed to be having crushes. What the fuck is that all about?"

"How the fuck do I know?" Maeve shrugs, and they both laugh.

"I thought about it for hours that night," Sam says wearily. "And you know, when I got married to Chris, I thought I'd never ever look at another man again. And I didn't. For six years I haven't been the slightest bit interested. But I suppose I felt so fat and unattractive, and dull, and Dan seemed to be interested in me, and the fact that anyone could be interested in me went straight to my head, and I blew it up out of all proportion."

"Plus," Maeve adds gently, "being married, or, as in my case, having a live-in partner, doesn't mean you stop fancying people."

"Really? You mean you fancy people too? Even though you've got Mark?"

"Not all the time, but I've certainly entertained the odd fantasy. It's about choice, though, isn't it? Weighing up what I've got and what I stand to lose. I never thought I'd choose a partner and a child over wild sex and wicked men, but now that I've got Mark and Poppy, I wouldn't let anything jeopardize that."

Sam nods thoughtfully. "You're right. I only realized it that night. It took Dan to make me really appreciate what I have. You're so right. I should have left it as a fantasy instead of blowing it up into a potential reality."

"You couldn't help it. He led you on. You were feeling shitty about yourself and he preyed on that."

"He did, didn't he?"

"Yeah. The fucker really did."

Sam sighs. "I've been so stupid."

"So what about Chris, then? Now's probably not the best time to say this but I thought he was lovely."

"He is lovely." Sam smiles. "I think I'd forgotten how lovely he is until about four-thirty Monday morning. Oh God." She makes a face. "I think Julia was right."

"Right about what?"

"She said a while ago that she thought maybe I was suffering from postpartum depression, and even though I don't think I've had it badly, I swear to God I've felt as if I've been living in a fog for the last few months. I hated my life, I hated my marriage, I hated Chris. The only thing I didn't hate was George, he was the only good and perfect thing, but I was convinced my marriage was over, that everything would be fine if I wasn't with Chris."

"And that's changed now?"

"I feel as if I've turned a corner. That huge humiliation"— she shudders again at the memory—"well. It made me question everything. I suppose it's exactly as you just described, but in my case it wasn't weighing up what I stood to lose, it was reassessing and realizing how thankful and grateful I should be."

"You managed to switch the hatred off overnight?" Maeve is slightly incredulous but curious nonetheless. Sam does appear to have a glow that Maeve has never seen before.

"I know. It sounds crazy. But it's as if it's all gone. All that resentment. That anger toward Chris. It wasn't about Chris, it was about me, and I'm not even sure it was about me. Actually I think it was probably chemical. And maybe it hasn't gone away, maybe this is just a temporary reprieve, but it feels so good to love Chris again, to wake up in the morning and feel happy, positive."

"I never realized," Maeve says. "I wish you'd told me."

"I didn't tell anyone. I didn't know. It went on for so long it felt normal. I forgot that life could be different."

Maeve grins. "So if truth be told, you have to thank Dan for patching up your marriage and restoring you to sanity. If I were you I'd send him a card. Hell, why not flowers?"

"Fuck off," Sam laughs.

"Fuck off yourself," Maeve shoots back, placing her hands over Poppy's ears. "And do you mind not swearing in front of the children?"

Chris has got his wife back. His life back. He comes home now to find a smiling Sam, the Sam he always loved. She's attentive, affectionate, glowing, and this time he knows it's not because of anyone outside their marriage.

Unless of course you count Maeve. Maeve, who has filled Julia's shoes in more ways than she knows.

Sam was determined not to phone Julia, her pride too strong, her self-righteousness too marked. One week went by. Then two. Then suddenly it had been nearly two months and Sam was desperate. She missed her. She had Maeve, but Julia knew everything about her, Julia had shared her history, her past. It just wasn't the same. She had tried to phone, had picked up and started to dial many times, but pride always stopped her from making the connection, from making amends.

One evening she sat and looked through old photos, photos of her and Julia, photos stretching back over the years, and, swallowing her pride, she picked up the phone and rang.

"I've behaved appallingly," she said contritely. "You were right and I was wrong, and you have to forgive me because I miss you and I don't want to lose you."

"I miss you too," Julia said, and they both smiled through their tears. "Anyway," Julia continued, "I know what an old battleaxe you are but you always see sense in the end."

They talked for a long time. Sam told her about Chris, about emerging from the tunnel into the light, and Julia did not sound the least bit surprised.

"Okay, okay," mumbled Sam. "I know you were right about that one too, but that's enough about me, what's going on with you? How's your wild and wicked love life?"

"Actually," Julia said sheepishly, "not too wild and wicked."

Sam gasped. "You haven't met someone, have you?"

"Not someone. Jack. It's on again."

"Oh," Sam said dully. "For how long this time?"

"No, no. It's different this time. We're seeing one another exclusively."

"Oh God, you sound so American. I take it that's his expression?"

"Of course," Julia laughed. "But it's . . . nice."

"Nice is good. We like nice."

"Yes. Funnily enough, we do," Julia said dreamily.

"Okay," Sam took a deep breath. "Seeing as you're in such a good space, there's something I have to tell you, too."

"What?" Julia asked sharply, anxiously.

"You know Maeve?"

"As in, redhead Maeve? Mark's girlfriend? Mother of Mark's child?"

"Yup."

"What about her?"

"I'm kind of friendlyish with her."

"And?"

"And I just felt uncomfortable about it. I wanted to let you know."

"Oh for heaven's sake. I thought you were going to tell me something terrible. Why would you feel uncomfortable about it? I met her once, ages ago, and she's lovely. I can totally see why you'd be friends with her."

Sam breathes a sigh of relief. "I just didn't want you to feel usurped or anything."

"Usurped? Just how friendly are you? I hope she's not your New Best Friend?"

"Don't be ridiculous," Sam says, figuring she's said enough for one day. "She's just someone I meet for the occasional coffee. That's all."

"Well, that's okay, then."

It's not necessary to tell Julia the whole truth. Unnecessary to tell her that Maeve has, in fact, become Sam's confidante, soulmate, sister. That Maeve has, unbeknown to her, helped drag Sam out of her well of self-pity.

The four of them—Maeve, Poppy, Sam, and George—

have become inseparable. They have braved One O'Clock Clubs, Gymboree, Tumble Tots, and Baby Gyms, and have started to find other women just like them.

For Maeve's birthday Sam took a secret snap of Poppy, and presented Maeve with a delicate and beautiful drawing of her little girl, beautifully encased in a simple wooden frame Sam had hand-painted with tiny butterflies and bows.

Maeve had shown it to everyone, and Sam had started doing them for other people, initially for fun, for something to do while George was asleep, but Maeve had berated her for not being more businesslike, and had sat Sam down and worked out a price.

Fifty-five pounds!

Sam had gasped at the expense. No one would ever pay that, she had said, but she was wrong, and the commissions were coming in thick and fast.

"I told you you'd never have to go back to an office again," Maeve said, when Sam moaned that she was swamped with pictures of babies. But Sam was loving it, and was making money, and was able to work from the kitchen table while George crawled around at her feet.

"*Happy* birthday, darling." Chris kisses Sam on the lips as Maeve and Mark cheer.

"Happy birthday!" they echo, clinking champagne glasses and leaning over the table to kiss Sam on the cheek. They have dressed up and gone out. Properly out. Not local pizza and pasta, but the Belvedere in Holland Park. A restaurant for special occasions. A restaurant in which to feel special.

And indeed they do feel special. Sam in her knee-length chiffon skirt and camisole top, a pair of perfect diamond studs in her ear—a birthday present from Chris—and Maeve in a tight, tailored dark pink suit, her red hair drawn back in a glamorous chignon.

Sam sips her champagne and smiles. "Thirty-four. A whole year since my last birthday. Feels more like ten."

"I'm not surprised. Look at what's happened in that year," Chris says.

"Georgenius!" Sam and Chris say at the same time, their voices filled with love and affection.

"Amazing." Sam shakes her head. "Amazing how your life can change so much in a year."

"Just think," Chris says. "This time last year you were—what—eight months pregnant? The size of a small whale—"

"Fuck off." She hits him, only able to smile because she has now lost all her pregnancy weight and, much to her delight (but not Chris's), has even smaller breasts than when she started.

"Okay, okay. The size of a small dolphin?"

"Better." She grins.

"The size of a small dolphin, swigging Gaviscon like it was champagne . . ."

"Touché." She raises her glass.

". . . with no idea whether the baby was going to be a boy or girl."

"Life Before George." She shakes her head in disbelief. "I can't believe we ever had a life before George. What a year."

"I know the feeling." Maeve smiles as Mark puts his arm round her and kisses her on the temple. "Life Before Children. A distant dream."

"But I wouldn't change it for the world. Wouldn't change my life for anything."

"Not even Chris?" Mark says, with a grin.

"Especially not Chris." She smiles, turning and planting a huge kiss on his lips as he grins. "I love you," she whispers in his ear, pulling away.

"I love you too," he whispers back.

"Bugger." Sam reaches down and rummages in her bag as her mobile phone rings and other diners look at her disapprovingly. She has to keep it on, she wants to explain, because she has a baby at home, and needs to be contactable at all times in case of emergencies, but of course she can't tell the restaurant, and of course she can't find the phone.

"Shit." She tips the bag upside down and empties the contents onto the floor, reaching down and flipping open the mobile, too quickly to see whether her home number flashes up.

"Hello?" She holds her breath for a second, praying it's not the baby-sitter, praying nothing's wrong.

"Happy birthday to you, Happy birthday to you, Happy birthday dear Sa-am, Happy birthday to you. I'm so sorry I didn't call you earlier," Julia trills. "I was out shooting all morning. How are you? Have I disturbed you? Are you in some desperately swish restaurant about to be lynched for having a mobile switched on?"

"No," Sam laughs. "Well, yes. Ish. Hang on a sec, I'll go outside." She scrapes back her chair, shrugs an apology to the table, and walks quickly outside.

It's a beautiful spring night. Only April but it's warm, and the tulips and daffodils are out in the park, summer almost there.

"Can you believe it?" Julia laughs down the phone. "Can you believe how much has happened since last year?"

"I know. We were just talking about it."

"I'm so sorry I'm not there with you, and I have got you a present that I meant to post last week but I didn't so I'm posting it this afternoon, but there's something else, another kind of present. Well, not actually a present but something I have to ask you." Uncharacteristically, Julia sounds nervous.

"I can't promise I'll say yes, but you can ask anything you want."

"Okay." Julia takes a deep breath. "Will you be god-mother?"

"What?"

"Will you be godmother?" she says again, the bubbles of excitement rising up in her voice.

"You mean . . . you're not . . . are you saying . . . ?" Sam doesn't want to say it, because surely she's misunderstanding, surely it's not possible.

"I am! I'm pregnant! Can you believe it!"

"Jack?"

"Of course Jack!"

"But how?"

"I have absolutely no idea. I thought I'd picked up some terrible stomach bug because I kept throwing up, and eventually I went to see the doctor and when he said he thought I might be pregnant I told him that was ridiculous, not to mention impossible."

"I don't understand."

"Neither do I, and neither does the doctor. Apparently, though, this often happens. The stress of wanting to conceive can stop conception happening, and he says he's seen loads of women like me, who conceive as soon as they stop thinking about it."

"So how many weeks?"

"Six. I'm not supposed to tell anyone until twelve, but if I can't tell my best friend, who can I tell?"

"Oh my God!" Sam starts to shriek. "This is the best birthday present I've ever had in my life."

"So will you?" Julia laughs.

"Will I what?"

"Will you be godmother?"

"Of course I'll be godmother!" she shouts as the tears come. "I'll be the best godmother the world has ever seen!"

Read on for a sneak peek at
To Have and To Hold, by Jane Green,
available from Broadway Books
in May 2004.

1

24 December 1996

Alice takes a deep breath as she opens the closet door and pulls out her dress. She lays it carefully on the bed, gathering her shoes, her veil, her stockings and garter, draping them gently next to the dress, amazed that in just a few hours' time she will be wearing all of this. In just a few hours' time she will be Joe's bride.

"Here comes the bride," she sings to herself, taking small, gliding steps down her hallway into the kitchen, smiling despite the butterflies, putting on the kettle to make herself another cup of coffee. She thinks she needs the coffee to stay awake, so badly did she sleep last night, but the adrenaline is already pumping, and she's waiting for Emily—her maid of honor—to arrive, someone with whom she can share the excitement.

Walking back into the bedroom, she stands for a while gazing at the dress. While not exactly what she would have chosen, she can't deny its beauty, how elegant it is, how impossibly stylish.

Alice had always thought she would have a country wedding. She dreamed, even as a little girl, of a small stone church; of walking through a white wooden gate in a soft, feminine puff of a dress, fresh flowers in her hair and a bouquet of hand-picked wild daisies in her hand. The groom had been unimportant: her fantasy had ended at the church door, but she knows the groom—even in her fantasies—would never have been as handsome, or as successful, as Joe.

At university, when she and Emily sat up late into the night discussing their knights in shining armor, Alice said she thought her ideal man would probably be an artist, or a craftsman, or a gardener. She had laughed as she said it, laughed at the unlikeliness of any lasting relationship, let alone marriage, given that her longest relationship at that time had been three weeks.

And before meeting Joe, her longest relationship had been three months. Not a good record, she had groaned to Emily when they were both planning on growing old together. "Means nothing," Emily had reassured. "Once you find him you'll be married for life. Me? I'll probably get divorced after six months." Alice had laughed, but even as she laughed she was thinking she wished she could be more like Emily, Emily who didn't want to settle down, who was quite happy flirting and flitting from one boy to the next, who claimed to have been born with a fatal allergy to commitment.

So a country wedding with a group of smiling toddlers (she had hoped that by the time she got married, *if* she ever got married, someone somewhere would have been able to provide the smiling toddlers) throwing down a blanket of rose petals and giggling as they walked up the aisle behind her.

She had envisaged a sea of straw hats and floral dresses, the sun beating down on her bare arms as she emerged from the church hand in hand with her other half.

When Joe proposed, she had told him about her dream wedding, and he had smiled at her indulgently and said it was a lovely fantasy, but they couldn't possibly get married in the country when both of them lived in London, and anyway, didn't she agree that winter weddings were so much *smarter*? She didn't agree, but felt she had to, because after all, Joe was paying for it. Alice's parents didn't have a penny, and Joe was determined to have a wedding that he judged fitting for the head of the healthcare business in Mergers & Acquisitions at Godfrey Hamilton Saltz.

They would have a lovely old Bentley to drive them to the church (bye-bye, shire horses and lovely old carriage), she would wear a simple but elegant gown (so long, cream puff of a dress), and a friend of his who was a jeweler would almost definitely lend her a stunning diamond tiara for her hair (see you later, fresh flowers).

So Alice went through the motions of planning her wedding. Every evening she would tell Joe of her decisions, and every morning she would have to phone florists, dressmakers, photographers to inform them that actually, she'd discussed it with her fiancé and the plans would be changing. Would they mind terribly, she would say, if instead of pretty mauve hydrangeas and tulips, they had dark red roses and berries, and not the dress she had designed with a tulle skirt to rival anyone in *Swan Lake*, but a sleek, simple sheath of a dress with long bell sleeves and a matching coat (Joe had flicked through some bridal magazines and showed Alice what would suit her), and so sorry, but actually they didn't want informal fun pictures as they had discussed, but formal family groupings that would take place during the reception.

Alice drains her coffee and steals a quick glance in the hall mirror to confirm what she already knows: deep bags under her eyes proving that last-minute nerves are not just an old wives' tale. Alice has spent the night tossing and turning, fear rising up in a wave of nausea, common sense trying to push it back down again. After all, isn't she the luckiest girl in the world? What woman would not want to marry Joe? Joe with his winning smile and easy charm. His broad shoulders and playful humor. Joe who could quite feasibly have married anyone he wanted, and he chose Alice. *Alice!*

Men like Joe did not usually look at women like Alice, or if they did, it was one quick, curious glance followed by instant dismissal, for the Alices of this world held nothing for men like Joe. The only child of adoring parents, he had been brought up to believe he was God (his mother's fault), to believe that every woman would fall in love with him (his mother's fault), and to believe that a woman's role in life was to do whatever Joe wanted (naturally, his mother again).

Even now, on her wedding day, Alice feels like she has to keep pinching herself. Thirty years old and used to unrequited crushes on men who never seemed to notice her, Alice didn't seriously think she'd ever find her other half. She might have had her dream wedding in mind, but in truth she was secretly convinced she would grow old with her cats, a kimono-clad spinster who would surround herself with eccentric people and end up living vicariously through her younger, prettier friends.

Alice has always thought of herself as rather plain. Everyone who knows Alice has always thought of her as rather plain. She was the shy, mousy girl in the playground who was always last to be picked for teams, and even then she knew she was only ever picked because it was a choice between her or Tracy Balcombe, and Tracy Balcombe had flat feet and B.O.

Alice was left until last because no one ever seemed to notice her. At age fourteen she had become known as Wallpaper, a name that would be said with a snigger, although frankly it never bothered her. She quite liked the fact that she faded into the background, that she could watch her classmates and think her thoughts without anyone ever bothering her.

It only started to bother her when she discovered boys. Up until then Alice had been quite happy with her horses. Her sketchpads were covered with badly drawn pictures of horse heads, mostly of her favorite, Betsy, complete with hearts saying "Alice loves Betsy," and "Betsy 4 Alice," and her daydreams consisted largely of Betsy and Alice steaming ahead to victory in local gymkhanas.

But one morning the girls of Lower IV awoke to discover hormones raging through their developing bodies, and Alice found herself dreaming of Betsy less and less, and more of faded jeans and a cute smile that belonged to a boy named Joe at the boys' school round the corner.

They were on the same bus route, and Alice would stand in the newsagent's for what felt like hours, pretending to flick through magazines, waiting for Joe to arrive. She would stand behind him, staring at the back of his head, willing him to notice her, and although, once or twice, he clearly felt her gaze and turned to meet her eyes, there was not a flicker of interest and he turned away to laugh with a friend.

It was to become a familiar pattern. Throughout her twenties Alice fell head over heels for men who didn't notice her. Strong, handsome, confident men. Men who walked through life with an assurance that Alice coveted, that Alice hoped would somehow rub off on her if she got close enough, which she never managed to do.

Until she met Joe again.

She had known Joe for years. He had been a friend of Ty's—her older brother—at school, one of the boys on whom she had had a huge, and painful, crush. She remembered watching him chat up the prettiest girl in her school at a local disco, watched him laugh and smile with her, his face moving closer and closer as he leaned in for a kiss, before taking her hand and leading her out the door.

Rumor had it that he had gone back to her house, kissed her good night, then an hour later shinned up the drainpipe and stolen her virginity. It was the stuff of which legends were made, and Joe was, even then, a legend. At fourteen years old he was going out with a twenty-year-old Danish au pair girl who lived round the corner. According to the boys in the class she was a cross between Farrah Fawcett and Jerry Hall.

Joe was responsible for a thousand broken teenage hearts, and Alice and Emily would sit for hours and talk about how much they hated him, each of them secretly longing for him to notice them.

And then one day the doorbell rang, and Alice ran to answer it, nearly fainting when she discovered Joe standing on the doorstep. Her fifteen-year-old heart threatened to give way as a hot flush crept up her cheeks, staining them scarlet.

Joe had raised an eyebrow, amused. Not his type at all, but

he liked to see the effect he had on women. It reassured him, made him feel secure, and what harm would it do to encourage her a little, it was only a bit of fun.

"Hello, Ty's sister," he smiled, his voice low and flirtatious. "You look lovely. Are you going somewhere nice?" It amused him to see her blush further, and still more to see she had quite literally lost the power of speech. Alice managed to mumble something and stumbled away when Ty appeared.

"Hey, Joe," he said, grabbing his coat. "Hope you're not chatting up my sister," and they both laughed at how ridiculous that would be, as they disappeared up the path.

But Alice had been spun into a fervor. She had called Emily immediately, and Emily had come round to analyze, inspect, and dissect every word. They had locked themselves in Alice's bedroom, each slumped on a beanbag, squealing with excitement as they went over and over the one sentence he had uttered, trying to understand what it meant.

"Say it again," Emily pleaded. "Tell me again what he sounded like when he said, 'You look lovely.' "

They formulated a plan of action. Worked out exactly what Alice would say to Joe when she next saw him, what tone of voice she would use, what she would wear when he took her out, because clearly, he was interested, and whether she would let him go to base one or base two on the first date.

Joe never noticed Alice again.

Fourteen years later Alice had a thriving catering business. She had finally managed to get over Joe and pass six O and two A levels, had gone to catering college, and from there to a yearlong cooking course. At twenty-nine years old she had an occasional staff of three who helped her prepare and serve gourmet dinners for women too busy, or too lazy, to cook.

Alice tended to stay in the background at these dinner parties. She loved cooking the meals beforehand, but stayed in the kitchen making sure nothing got burned while the other girls served canapés and cocktails. Occasionally, should the host or hostess demand, she would come in to receive praise, reluctantly but graciously, smoothing back the loose curls that had escaped her ponytail as she handed out business cards.

She had a small flat with a large kitchen in Kensal Rise, her two cats, Molly and Paolo, and a tiny social life thanks in part to the success of her business and in part to her natural shyness.

Her last relationship—the three-monther—had been with an actor called Steve, but three months of massaging the chip on his shoulder had taken its toll, and she was grateful when one of his auditions actually came to fruition and he took off to Manchester to do rep for three months. They promised to stay in touch, she would come up to visit, but she knew it was just a formality.

So there she was, in the kitchen of her dreams, in the basement of a large house in Primrose Hill. The kitchen was almost back to its pristine state, the plates stacked neatly in the dishwasher, the crystal goblets already draining next to the sink, and her casserole dishes cleaned and waiting in the boot of the car.

The guests were drinking espresso, with homemade petits fours, and Alice said good-bye to the two girls helping her out, knowing that the only thing left to do would be to wash up the coffee cups, and she could manage that perfectly well by herself.

"Oh, you must meet Alice." She heard the hostess banging down the stairs in her high heels. "She's an absolute angel, and the food's fantastic. Also"—her voice dropped an octave or two—"not at all expensive compared to some of the others."

Bugger, thought Alice. Time to put my prices up. She grabbed a cloth to appear busy and practiced smiling, a bright sparkly smile that would invite more business, quickly polishing the granite worktops as she heard the footsteps come into the room.

"Hello, Alice," said a voice that she would have known anywhere.

"Hello, Joe," she said, the smile replaced with a deep scarlet flush.

Joe walks up to greet his ushers, who all crowd round him in a conspiratorial huddle.

"Well?"

"Did you do it?"

"Was she worth it?"

"Could you resist?"

"Bloody better have been worth it, the amount we paid."

"Didn't know whether you'd have the energy."

"So come on then, Joe, what was she like? Did you succumb?"

Joe smiles beatifically and raises a hand to quiet the masses. "Boys," he says, as they wait with bated breath. "It's my wedding day. Show some respect."

"Seriously." Adrian, his best man, puts an arm around Joe's shoulders and leads him away from the boys. "She cost a fortune, and I just want to know if you got your money's worth."

"You mean *your* money's worth?" Joe grins.

"Well, yes. So did you?"

"Don't you mean, did I actually fuck her?"

"No," Adrian shakes his head. "I've known you since you were eleven years old. Of course you fucked her. So did you get our money's worth?"

Joe had sworn his womanizing days were behind him, had vowed he would be faithful, causing much mirth among his friends. The evening before, on his stag night, they had organized a high-class call girl to be waiting in a limo. It was a test, they had said, a test to see whether he really would be faithful.

"I *will* pass," he had said assuredly when they told him of their plan, and several saketinis later made his way out to the limo, fully intending to tell the call girl thanks, but no thanks. He was greeted by a mane of the exact shade of honey-blond hair that he loved, legs that went on forever, and a Wonderbra that was truly wonderful to behold.

"Oh, shit," he groaned, climbing into the car. "I suppose a final fling wouldn't hurt."

It was a marathon, extraordinary, incredible night. He had woken up this morning at the Sanderson Hotel feeling guilty as hell and then felt a hand start to slowly stroke his thigh, and, oh, what difference would a morning screw make? After all, she'd clearly been paid for the night. And it's only sex.

And Alice will never know.

"So did you get our money's worth?" Adrian persists.

"She was a six-foot Russian blonde with a figure that would make Lara Croft jealous and a mouth that never slept. What do *you* think?"

Adrian doubles over and groans in envy. "Fuck," he spits

through his teeth. "I knew it. So was it the best night of your life?"

"Adrian! Please!" Joe looks shocked. "Tonight will be the best night of my life."

"But it was a close second?" Adrian grins.

"Very, very close. And as a final fling Svetlana couldn't have been more perfect."

"Svetlana?" Adrian snorts with laughter. "Was that her real name?"

"Do you know," Joe says nonchalantly, turning to head back to the church, "I don't actually care."

Joe had never thought he was going to get married. Had been quite happy living the quintessential bachelor lifestyle, but by his early thirties he'd started to think it might be quite nice to have some permanence, someone to come home to, to look after him.

The problem was that the girls he went out with were about as far away from wife material as you could possibly get. Yes, they looked great. Tall stunning blondes, the occasional brunette or redhead, they were all polished to perfection, but were so cold, so brittle, Joe sometimes thought that if he bent them the wrong way they might snap.

They were women who were waiting for a rich husband to provide them with a lifestyle their beauty had led them to believe they could expect. They had no careers, avoided the news as if they could catch something nasty from it, couldn't cook, didn't clean, had never ironed a thing in their lives ("Darling, if God had meant us to iron he wouldn't have invented dry cleaners"), and had a deep-rooted fear of marrying a man who couldn't afford a "woman that does."

They expected certain things of Joe—dinners at the Ivy and Hakkasan, nights out at Atticus and Home House, the odd treat from Harvey Nicks—and in return they gave him unlimited performance sex, little pressure (these girls knew that the best way to hook their fish was to let the line run as long as possible), and the guaranteed envy of every man he knew. It was only once they started expecting commitment that Joe would turn around and tell them in the nicest way possible that they'd had a wonderful time together, but that he knew it wasn't meant to be, and on he would go to his next conquest.

He knew he didn't want to marry a woman who wanted him only for his bonus (although his looks and personality weren't exactly negligible), and he knew he wasn't going to find the woman he would marry in the trendy bars, restaurants, and clubs he frequented, but there was something about glossy, streaky blond hair, a leg clad in Wolford stockings, breasts pushed up in La Perla that he just couldn't resist.

And then he met Alice. Alice who turned scarlet when he said her name, who remembered him from school, even when he had no recollection of ever meeting her. Alice who had loose mousy curls and didn't wear a scrap of makeup. Who wore cheap black leggings and baggy shapeless sweaters to disguise her curves. He wouldn't normally have looked twice at a girl like Alice, but he was amused by the way she blushed every time he looked at her, and there was something very sweet about her, and sweetness was not a character trait he was used to in women.

She was sweet, and she was grateful, which in turn made Joe feel generous and kind, rather like a benefactor. She didn't expect anything of him other than his company, and when he gave her what she wanted she seemed in a state of permanent disbelief that he would be with a girl like her.

Plus, he realized very quickly that Alice had a huge amount of potential. She was a lovely girl, she could cook fantastically, she'd definitely look after him, and it wouldn't take much to make her look a whole hell of a lot better. With a diet, a decent hairdresser, and a new wardrobe, she'd be a whole new woman by the time he'd finished with her.

K